NOT YOUR AVERAGE LOVE SPELL

What Reviewers Say About
Barbara Ann Wright's Work

The Tattered Lands

"Wright's postapocalyptic romance is a fast-paced journey through devastation. ...Plenty of action, surprises, and magic will keep readers turning the pages."—*Publishers Weekly*

House of Fate

"...fast, fun...entertaining... *House of Fate* delivers on adventure." —*Tor.com*

Coils

"...Greek myths, gods and monsters and a trip to the Underworld. Sign me up... This one springs straight into action...a good start, great Greek myth action and a late blooming romance that flowers in the end..." —*Dear Author*

"A unique take on the Greek gods and the afterlife make this a memorable book. The story is fun with just the right amount of camp. Medusa is a hot, if unexpected, love interest... A truly unexpected ending has us hoping for more stories from this world."—*RT Book Reviews*

"The gods and monsters of ancient Greek mythology are living, breathing entities, something Cressida didn't expect and is amazed as well as terrified to discover. ...Cressida soon realizes being in the underworld is no different than being among the living. The heart still feels and love can bloom, even in the world of Myth. ...The characters are well developed and their wit will elicit more than a few chuckles. A joy to read."—*Lunar Rainbow Reviewz*

Paladins of the Storm Lord

"This was a truly enjoyable read... I would definitely pick up the next book. ...The mad dash at the end kept me riveted. I would definitely recommend this book for anyone who has a love of sci-fi... An intricate... novel one that can be appreciated at many levels, adventurous sci fi or one that is politically motivated with a very astute look at present day human behavior. ...There are many levels to this extraordinary and well written book...overall a fascinating and intriguing book."—*Inked Rainbow Reads*

"I loved this... The world that the Paladins inhabited was fascinating... didn't want to put this down until I knew what happened. I'll be looking for more of Barbara Ann Wright's books."—*Lesbian Romance Reviews*

"*Paladins of the Storm Lord* by Barbara Ann Wright was like an orchestra with all of its pieces creating a symphony. I really truly loved it. I love the intricacy and wide variety of character types...I just loved practically every character!... Of course my fellow adventure lovers should read Paladins of the Storm Lord!"—*The Lesbian Review*

Thrall: Beyond Gold and Glory

"Once more Barbara has outdone herself in her penmanship. I cannot sing enough praises. A little *Vikings*, a dash of *The Witcher*, peppered with *The Game of Thrones*, and a pinch of *Lord of The Rings*. Mesmerizing... I was ecstatic to read this book. It did not disappoint. Barbara pours life into her characters with sarcasm, wit and surreal imagery, they leap from the page and stand before you in all their glory. I am left satisfied and starving for more, the clashing of swords, whistling of arrows still ringing in my ears."—*Lunar Rainbow Reviewz*

"In their adventures, the women must wrestle with issues of freedom, loyalty, and justice. The characters were likable, the issues complex, and the battles were exciting. I really enjoyed this book and I highly recommend it."—*All Our Worlds: Diverse Fantastic Fiction*

"This was the first Barbara Ann Wright novel I've read, and I doubt it will be the last. Her dialogue was concise and natural, and she built a fantastical world that I easily imagined from one scene to the next. Lovers of Vikings, monsters and magic won't be disappointed by this one."—*Curve Magazine*

The Pyradisté Adventures

"…a healthy dose of a very creative, yet believable, world into which the reader will step to find enjoyment and heart-thumping action. It's a fiendishly delightful tale."—*Lambda Literary*

"Barbara Ann Wright is a master when it comes to crafting a solid and entertaining fantasy novel. …The world of lesbian literature has a small handful of high-quality fantasy authors, and Barbara Ann Wright is well on her way to joining the likes of Jane Fletcher, Cate Culpepper, and Andi Marquette. …Lovers of the fantasy and futuristic genre will likely adore this novel, and adventurous romance fans should find plenty to sink their teeth into."—*The Rainbow Reader*

"*The Pyramid Waltz* has had me smiling for three days. …I also haven't actually read…a world that is entirely unfazed by homosexuality or female power before. I think I love it. I'm just delighted this book exists. …If you enjoyed The Pyramid Waltz, For Want of a Fiend is the perfect next step…you'd be embarking on a joyous, funny, sweet and madcap ride around very dark things lovingly told, with characters who will stay with you for months after."—*The Lesbrary*

"This book will keep you turning the page to find out the answers. …Fans of the fantasy genre will really enjoy this installment of the story. We can't wait for the next book."—*Curve Magazine*

"There is only one other time in my life I have uncontrollably shouted out in cheer while reading a book. [*A Kingdom Lost*] made the second… Over the course of these three books all the characters have blossomed and developed so eloquently… I simply just thought this whole novel was brilliant."—*The Lesbian Review*

Visit us at www.boldstrokesbooks.com

By the Author

The Pyradisté Adventures

The Pyramid Waltz

For Want of a Fiend

A Kingdom Lost

The Fiend Queen

Thrall: Beyond Gold and Glory

The Godfall Novels

Paladins of the Storm Lord

Widows of the Sun-Moon

Children of the Healer

Inheritors of Chaos

Coils

House of Fate

The Tattered Lands

Not Your Average Love Spell

NOT YOUR AVERAGE LOVE SPELL

by

Barbara Ann Wright

2019

CREDITS

EDITOR: CINDY CRESAP
PRODUCTION DESIGN: SUSAN RAMUNDO
COVER DESIGN BY SHERI (HINDSIGHTGRAPHICS@GMAIL.COM)

Acknowledgments

Thanks to Cindy for being an awesome editor and mentor. I owe you and Ruth a Coke.

Thanks to my writing group members: Angela, Deb, Erin, Matt, Natsu, Sarah, and Trakena. You're family.

A continuing thank you to Bold Strokes Books and all its authors. Woo.

Thanks to all the readers. I hope you have a laugh.

I love you, Mom. You were right about everything.

Dedication

For Natsu. You're a unicorn.

CHAPTER ONE

Surrounded, a situation not easy to contemplate and even harder to be in, but Sydney grinned at her opponents as she kneeled on the deck of the pirate ship. The captain smirked, creating more lines in his sun-browned, leathery face. Sydney sucked the cut on her lip and waited, trying to breathe shallowly, but the smell of the unwashed crew surrounding her was giving her a headache.

Or maybe that was the punch to her jaw.

"Knight of the Flame, eh?" the captain said as he held her captured blade. The golden sun inlaid in the hilt winked in the bright morning light. "Thought you lot were supposed to be smart." He glanced toward Sydney's sloop, now tied up alongside the pirate ship with its crew just as subdued as she was. "But you're easy pickings like all the rest."

Sydney's smile widened. "Where's the witch?"

His smug look faltered. Maybe he expected her to beg for her life instead of asking questions. "How did you know..." He chuckled. "That's none of your concern any longer. Now, anything of *importance* to say before we throw you overboard, Madam Knight?"

"I'm a major, actually. And yes." She leaned forward as if sharing a secret. When the pirate followed suit, she said softly, "Where's the witch?"

He made a disgusted noise and stood back, gesturing to his crew. "Toss her and her crew over."

Ah well, if he wouldn't spill his plans like a good villain...

Sydney bent forward and put her palms on the deck, fingers spreading over the worn and pitted wood.

"Begging?" The pirate guffawed. "I'd have never—"

Sydney wrenched one leg beneath her and sprang up. The pirate staggered back with a strangled cry for aid. He swung at her with her own blade, but she was inside his reach too quickly. She crashed into him, sending them both to the deck.

His head *thunked* hollowly against the wood. "Get her. Get—"

Sydney knocked his hand against the deck, sending her blade clattering away, then pressed her forearm over his throat.

"Submit," she said. "You are surrounded."

The sounds of combat rang out behind her, but she didn't bother to look. It would be over swiftly.

"Crew is subdued, Major," a voice behind her called.

The pirate captain sputtered. Sydney grinned as he gawped like a fish in hand. She stood, hauling him along with her and relieving him of his own sword. Holding him by the neck of his filthy coat, she let him see his ship.

Her ship, now.

His crew moaned or coughed from where they lay on the deck, all alive from what she could see and ready for capture, trial, and then, most likely, the gallows. Her undercover squad, still disguised as fellow pirates, moved among them, tossing weapons overboard and trussing the pirates hand and foot.

Senior Recruit Juzail handed Sydney her blade, and she slid it home in the scabbard across her back. Juzail somehow kept a smug expression from his light brown face after he took possession of the pirate captain, but his dark eyes twinkled.

The pirate captain sputtered before managing, "I…" He swallowed. "How?" He gaped at Juzail. "You're…a knight?"

"Not yet," Sydney said. "All recruits. Otherwise, they wouldn't have been able to infiltrate your crew." She tapped twice over her heart with three fingers, the knight's salute. "Knights of the Flame can't lie." Hands on hips, she took a deep breath of the salty air. "Now, where's the witch?"

The pirate swallowed so hard, his patchy beard seemed to bob along his neck. "Not aboard."

"I *know* that." She sighed. "You're going to have to do better, Captain…"

"Smythe," Juzail said.

"Bastards," Smythe muttered.

"Look," Sydney said, putting a hand on his shoulder and trying not to wince at the grime. "You're bested, man. You had to be suspicious when a sloop with one knight and a handful of sailors tried to take this lumbering hulk. Even when I was on my knees, you had to know something wasn't right. You're not a stupid person." She kept her voice friendly, almost drawling as if they were out for a relaxing spot of lunch. "If you tell me where the witch is, I will inform the magistrate when we return to Kingston, and he will tell the court that you cooperated, and maybe you can avoid the fate of most of your crew." All true, but she doubted it would work.

He trembled, and she thought it was fear until a sound sputtered from his lips, a high-pitched, nervous bray, and she realized he was laughing. "They call her the Hawk. Know why?"

She smiled, encouraging him now that he was in the mood to talk.

"Because she swoops down on her enemies before they ever know she's there."

Sydney glanced at the cloudless blue sky. "No one's swooping in to save you now."

He only laughed harder. "You don't know what you're doing, none of you knights. You think you're saving the world by getting rid of magic?"

"Where's his cabin?" Sydney asked. When Juzail pointed in the right direction, she said, "Bring him." Maybe while she was searching his possessions, he'd give something away.

The cabin was a small affair with a narrow bed, a small desk, and a large trunk, with barely enough room to move between the three. Sydney started with the desk, keeping an eye on Smythe in the doorway. She riffled through maps and set aside a logbook for later. Her discoveries didn't make Smythe blink, and Sydney's irritation grew. His words had already grated her nerves; if she found nothing, she was going to be dashed upset.

But finding one of the few witches still practicing magic in the kingdom of Arnvild was worth any little upset of hers.

When she lifted the lid of the trunk, Smythe licked his lips. Ah, progress at last. Beneath a heap of dirty clothes, she found a small velvet bag. "What have we here?" she asked as she tipped a palm-sized crystal ball into her hand.

His gaze flicked between the ball and her face.

"This is how you speak to her?" Sydney asked. "Or is she going to swoop out of this and aid you?"

"If it was possible, I would," a low voice said.

Sydney bit back a cry and stared at the weighty orb. The inside swirled as if filled with smoke, and she caught hints of a pale face, dark hair, and eyes that seemed to glow like green fire. "There you are," Sydney said, just managing to keep her voice from shaking.

"Where you'll never find me," the husky voice said. "And I'll remain free from your tyranny."

Sydney scoffed. "Rather righteous talk from someone who allies herself with pirates."

"Needs must. Whatever witches have become is due to the Knights of the Flame. Ironic, seeing as how you use magic when it suits you."

Sydney gripped the ball so hard, her hand ached. She bared her teeth, hoping the witch could see her clearly. "Heartfire is born of valor and purity. It is the strength that lies in every human spirit and not the filthy magic witches use to perform nasty spells like animating the dead."

The smoke winked away along with the image. From the doorway, Smythe snickered.

Rage built in Sydney's chest, tapping into the very power she'd just laid claim to, heartfire, the energy knights were taught to harness. She channeled it through her hand, setting blue flame licking among her fingers, though it could never hurt her. The globe glowed with dim light before cracks spread along it like spider legs, and it burst into hundreds of pieces.

Sydney threw the shards into a corner. "Chain him up aboard the sloop."

"Yes, Major." Juzail dragged Smythe away, still chuckling, and Sydney followed, happy to be out in the light again, away from the cabin's foul air and the taint of magic.

Her crew of recruits divided themselves between the pirate ship and the sloop, both flying the colors of Arnvild as well as the knights' flame. When they were under way, Sydney pressed Smythe a little more; she wanted to know what the witch looked like and what Smythe had seen behind her in the crystal ball, but he claimed to have seen the same shadowy figure she had.

"She's abandoned you," Sydney cried. They sat on the deck of the sloop, and the wind was at their backs, making it feel as if the ship flew over the water. Sitting easy, Smythe seemed to roll with the waves. Sydney envied him. She didn't often get seasick, but the choppy water that day made for some ugly stirrings in her stomach, feeding her anger.

She swallowed and told herself again that this man had been duped. His stubborn refusal to believe in the evil of magic proved he was more than just a hired sword. He believed in the witches' cause to bring magic back to Arnvild, and that made him a misguided fool who might still be saved.

Sydney moved closer to Smythe's side. "Witches use magic to disturb *the dead.* I have seen it with my own eyes. When the knights attempted to arrest the witch of Elion, he sent a platoon of shambling dead to murder us."

Smythe frowned and didn't look at her. "They can do more than that. The Hawk helped someone I love."

Sydney nodded in sympathy. "They can do good when they want to, but when one goes bad…"

He grimaced. "The Witch Wars were a long time ago."

"Not long enough," Sydney said as she shook her head. "We have learned from the stories. Witches wield too much power for any one person to possess, and not everyone may learn." She put a hand to her chest. "Whereas anyone may join the ranks of the knights and learn the secrets of heartfire, and none of us can wreak as much havoc as a witch might."

He continued to look away. "She's a good person."

Sydney's heart went out to him, truly. No doubt the witch had only helped Smythe's loved one because she needed him, but it would be hard for him to forget such a deed even if he knew the witch had done it to obligate him.

"And now she's leaving you and your crew to hang for piracy," Sydney said.

He nodded glumly, and she thought he might be coming to his senses. But his face was stony as he met her gaze. "Aye, we are thieves and murderers but not betrayers."

With a sigh, Sydney stood. "Well, I suppose I must admire you for that." And she did, somewhat, but she was also angry and tired, and her roiling stomach wasn't helping either emotion. She walked away and found a quiet spot on the deck, out of the way of the busy sailors, and watched the horizon, trying to quiet her insides.

She'd been on this witch's trail for months now. She'd heard the name of the Hawk before, but it only made her roll her eyes. Witches always had delusions of grandeur, and it was just like one to pick a stylish nickname. She should have been called the Mouse or some other animal that was quick, mildly cunning, and good at avoiding the rat catcher.

Sydney banged a fist on the ship's rail. No, what the witch should have done was leave Arnvild for good once she'd gone into hiding. She should have contented herself with haunting some other land rather than trying to force magic on a kingdom that was done with it.

She should have kept her cursed spells to herself.

With one blink, Sydney could recall the stench of rotting flesh from the witch of Elion's soldiers. They'd shambled as if too far in their cups, but their cloudy eyes had been fixed on Sydney and her fellows. They'd reached out with skeletal hands, the skin sloughing off in great strips. The worst part had been the lack of voices. The shamblers made no sound as they tottered forward; they did not scream when stabbed or bludgeoned. They did not stop until they were naught but a pile of bloodless pieces on the ground, and then they twitched, silent but for the rasp their small movements made among the dirt and leaves.

"Major Blakely?"

Sydney gasped, her eyes flying open. Her heart pounded, and her mouth filled with bile, but at least it was from the memories and not anything the sea had done to her. With a deep breath, she returned to the present and turned to regard Williamson, captain of the sloop.

Williamson's pale brows were drawn down in worry, and her ice-blue gaze roved over Sydney's face. "Are you all right?"

"Of course," Sydney said, forcing a smile.

"You were gripping the rail so hard your hands were white. If you've any seasickness, I have a remedy in my cabin." Her cheeks went a little pink. "Or...perhaps a distraction?" She licked her lips, and the pinkness spread to her ears, a nice contrast to her dark uniform. "A...a draught, that is. Though there are ways to keep you occupied instead, if you prefer." Now her eyes went wide. "Books and such. I didn't mean...me, though I could keep you company." The blush had reached her neck. "By *conversation*." She nearly yelled the last words, then bit her lip as if trying to keep any other speech inside.

Sydney smiled. She was used to women becoming tongue-tied around her, even sloop captains. An old girlfriend had called it her aura of charisma, but Sydney didn't know about that. She thought the reaction was adorable, and she'd never been able to resist it. She looked over the captain, who was probably in her early thirties, just a little older than Sydney, and her crisp uniform spoke of a tidy mind. She was petite but quite capable of bellowing her crew into line, and she kept her pale blond hair in a long braid down her back. She shifted under Sydney's appraisal, but her eyes lit up as if asking a question.

"I would like to sample this remedy of yours," Sydney said with a grin. "And you can call me Sydney."

"Adele," the captain said with a returning smile and a renewed blush. "We put the pirate you were questioning down with the others. To clear the deck, if that's all right."

"Perfectly. It's my mission, but it's your ship."

Adele giggled, then seemed appalled at herself. She pressed a hand to her mouth, then cleared her throat. Sydney wondered how long she'd been nursing a crush. They'd been traveling together for weeks, but Adele had barely spoken to her. Maybe it was only now that the mission was over that she felt she could approach Sydney in a non-professional manner.

It made her all the more adorable.

"Let me give you a tour," Adele said with a wink.

Sydney followed her and kept herself from pointing out the fact that she already knew the ship well. If Adele didn't want to say, "Let's go have sex," that was her prerogative, but Sydney would have found such artlessness refreshing. Too many people felt inhibited from saying what was on their minds. In the end, Sydney supposed it didn't matter. This encounter would be like so many others, fleeting. Women loved her, enjoyed her company, and she enjoyed theirs, but they always seemed to want her more as a story than a longtime companion. Even those she called girlfriend were relationships that had spanned months, not years.

The ship rocked slightly, pulling Sydney out of another reverie. Adele turned toward her crew, eyes wide with alarm, telling Sydney that this rocking wasn't a normal movement on the waves. When the motion came again, more forceful this time, Sydney staggered, and several sailors did the same, one falling from a mast to get tangled in the rigging.

"What in the name of the seven bells was that?" Adele bellowed, marching toward the center of the deck. "Someone get Nelson down from there." She moved among the sailors, barking questions, but no one seemed to know what had happened. Sydney rushed to the side and looked over, but they raced along as before, unbothered by any sea monsters or freak stretches of coral in the middle of the deep.

She heard one of the sailors call that they should check the bilge.

The prisoners were down there.

Sydney rushed for the hatch. If the rocking motion meant they were taking on water, the prisoners would be the first to drown. She had to get them up on the deck, sickened by the idea of them screaming and dying while chained. True, most of them were headed for the gallows, but some could be innocent, and they needed a trial before being condemned. A few sailors ran after her as she raced through the crew's section and down another trapdoor into the very bottom of the sloop.

She stopped, the darkness surrounding her along with an eerie quiet. No sounds of rushing water, no clanking of chains or coughs or murmurs. Maybe the witch had exacted vengeance and turned the pirates into lifeless monsters that somehow still walked, and they were even now rising and making their soundless way toward her in the dark.

A sailor behind her lit a lamp, and she breathed a sigh of relief when she saw no shambling horde. Then her mouth fell open as she realized the reason for the silence.

The bilge was empty.

She took the lamp and held it high, but there was nowhere to hide. The sailors spread out and searched the ship to no avail. The larger ship that had belonged to the pirates also stood empty of prisoners. None of them could have made it overboard without first climbing to the decks and being seen.

They'd disappeared.

Sydney returned to the bilge and stared at where the pirates had been shackled to one another. She'd begun to wonder if she and the crew had hallucinated the pirates from the beginning, when something small glimmered from the floor, half hidden in shadow. She kneeled and reached for it, pulling forth a long feather. Dark brown, it had lines of tan and white, and she didn't need a birding guide to know it: the tail feather of a hawk.

Chapter Two

Camille decided that the Knights of the Flame were clearly enamored with two things, gilt and overcompensating.

Okay, maybe that was one thing.

Their entire headquarters was covered in gold leaf and pompousness. The outside had been impressive enough, with columns and banners and statues of famous knights. The marble foyer with its carved, gilded ceiling had carried a certain majesty.

But this room. *Wow.*

A huge, round table dominated a large meeting room. The furniture bore enough intricate carving to give a duster nightmares. Ditto for the carved chairs with their plush, velvet cushions embroidered with sparkling thread. Rich red and gold banners hung from a high ceiling that shone with so much gold leaf, the light coming through the stained-glass windows turned the room into its own sun.

Camille couldn't shake the feeling that she'd walked into a dragon's den. Sure, it was beautiful with all the hoarded gold and gems, but at the heart of it lurked a dragon. The knights might have been everything beautiful, but they were still dangerous.

And now they wanted to know the fastest way to move a large amount of people and goods the length of the kingdom of Arnvild. They hadn't explained *why* they needed to do such a thing. It was probably some scheme to make their vast wealth even vaster.

So, they'd sent for a master researcher from the Grand Library to research solutions to their problem, and Camille had been "volunteered" because of her knowledge about ancient beasts, mythical creatures, and "everything weird."

Weird like magic, which the knights would no doubt need to achieve their purpose. Magic, which they loathed. And hunted people for practicing.

Camille leaned back in her chair and fought not to frown as Supreme Commander Sir Robert, head of the Order of the Flame, reiterated his problem for the third time. The man was as in love with the sound of his own voice as he was with the waxed mustache he kept smoothing.

"How many troops?" she asked, interrupting. "Because you'll need—"

"A thousand," Sir Robert said with a smile. "And the necessary supplies, mounts, and equipment."

"And you want them to arrive when?"

"No more than two days after they are ready for travel. We must move quickly before—" One of the other knights cleared her throat. Sir Robert smiled languidly. "We must move quickly."

Now the knights stared. Camille fought the urge to squirm. It seemed she'd be left to wonder why an army needed to cover a four-week distance in two days. To surprise someone? It didn't matter. Her childhood love of pixies and unicorns wouldn't help.

"Well," Camille said slowly. "You'll need ma—"

"If you've no more questions," Sir Robert said as he rose, prompting her to follow suit.

Camille opened her mouth to ask if she was either dreaming or part of a terrible joke. It was all she could do not to storm out. Someone who decried magic and hunted its practitioners didn't deserve help, but she'd get fired if she said so.

"We'll assign a knight to you," Sir Robert said, "for any other questions you may have about weights or measurements, that sort of thing."

Camille put her hands on her hips, about to protest that she did not need some great armored oaf lumbering behind her, when one of the knights lingering on the edge of the room caught her eye and smiled.

Camille's protests blew away in the face of bright blue eyes and blond hair that acted as a halo around a perfect tanned face with a delicate, pointed chin. The knight wore a tabard with a golden sunburst over a shirt of light mail and a tunic, but Camille could tell by the way she moved that she had the lean muscles of a panther. Her stride was powerful yet sensuous, and when she extended a calloused hand and said, "Sydney Blakely, at your service," Camille could only babble.

"Yes, uh, good, um, thank you." She took the hand and was rewarded by a killer smile that outshone the thread of gold on Sydney's tabard. "I'm...Camille. I..." Shit, what did she do for a living? "I'm... library. Yes, I work for the library." Mortification clogged her throat but helped clear her brain. Or was that from all the blood rushing to her cheeks? "Master researcher," she blurted. "That's...me. I've...had a lot of school."

She wanted to die. Why hadn't she learned how to do that at will? She'd never had this much trouble around women before. Even beautiful ones.

Sydney's brows raised. "Lucky for us, then." She glanced down.

Camille followed her gaze to see her hand still shaking Sydney's as if it had a mind of its own. She snatched her hand back and tried to laugh off her nerves, but the sound came out somewhere between a shout and a donkey's bray.

And it had a snort at the end. Death couldn't come soon enough.

Camille turned and headed for the exit, wanting to run, but Sydney followed, and Camille nearly stumbled. Should they walk together, or was the knight more of an escort, or—

Sydney caught up quickly, her long legs stretching under tight trousers. "I've always wanted to see the library."

"Why?" Camille cleared her throat, trying to keep from snapping, but embarrassment always made her touchy. "I mean, are you not from Kingston?"

"Sheffordshire. I only came to Kingston to join the knights, and then there wasn't time for much except training." She smiled again, and Camille forced herself not to stare at those shapely lips.

This was a knight, she told herself. She didn't like knights because of their swagger and small-mindedness and chirpy attitudes in the face of their own shortcomings. They thought every problem could be settled with a sword or a pretty speech, and Camille had no time for them. And it wasn't as if Sydney was *that* sexy. If Camille wanted a partner, she had plenty of options. Maybe she'd stop by and see Anastasia in the records room. She was always up for a—

They stepped outside, and Sydney ran a hand through her chin-length hair, making it glint in the light. She turned her face upward as if to welcome the sun, stretching her long neck and exposing adorable, bite-worthy ears.

"Lunch?" Camille asked, more than a little breathless.

Sydney's returning smile had a hint of lasciviousness that made Camille's core tighten like a purse string. "Absolutely."

❖

Sydney would have never guessed that her afternoon would go quite as this one had. She'd neither dreaded nor looked forward to serving as liaison to a master researcher. After her adventure at sea, her failure to track down the Hawk, and her loss of her prisoners, she was looking forward to doing nothing but answering questions about her order's needs or expounding upon the strides they made to transform the world into something better. And she'd heard that the library was beautiful inside. Anyone who worked there would surely be excited at the possibility of expanding her knowledge.

And maybe this assignment would keep her mind off the catastrophe she'd made of her mission. Sir Robert had agreed that she couldn't have done anything more to keep her prisoners. Magic was too unpredictable, and the Hawk was clearly more powerful than they'd anticipated.

All the more reason why she had to be caught.

Sir Robert had seemed thoughtful when Sydney told him how the witch had whisked the pirates away. Maybe he'd thought it sounded like a fine solution to his current troop-moving problem. Then he'd sighed, and she knew he'd come back to his senses. Magic was never the answer. It was too much power for anyone to wield.

When Sydney had first seen Camille, she'd begun to enjoy her new assignment even more. Shorter than Sydney by a head, Camille had a curvy, hourglass shape, and her dark blue dress clung to her hips and breasts. The hem fluttered when she walked, as if beckoning Sydney to follow. Her dark, tightly curled hair stretched across her shoulders, though she kept the sides pulled back from her dark, expressive face. Her eyes sparkled with intelligence, and Sydney could have gotten lost in their rich brown color.

Sydney had discarded her best pickup lines in the face of such beauty; no words were good enough, though she would have loved to get to know her better. When Camille stuttered and ducked her head, clearly embarrassed, Sydney wanted to sweep her off her feet and kiss her senseless, just as when every other woman became tongue-tied around her. When Camille asked her to lunch, Sydney knew by the glint in her eye that she had more than food in mind.

Ah, well, so much for conversation. Sydney knew she'd enjoy the encounter very much, but she'd been hoping Camille would at least want to talk first. Instead, Camille had led her through the library's foyer, her shoes clicking swiftly over the marble floor. She'd thrown off a few comments about the history of the place or the number of books, but when Sydney started toward the acres of shelves and volumes, Camille tugged at her sleeve.

"There's...something else I'd like to show you." The slight catch in her voice was still there, but Camille's gaze said she knew what she was about, and she wasn't embarrassed anymore. It was as close as any woman had come to saying what she really wanted from Sydney in a long time.

Camille had stepped close to her and breathed deep, and Sydney's insides had ignited with need. "If this isn't all right," Camille whispered, "you have only to say."

It might have been foolish to respond with, "Anything you wish is all right with me," but Sydney said it anyway. Her training sergeant would have said she was setting herself up to be ambushed and kidnapped, but Camille only smiled and led her to a small doorway off the side of the foyer. It was a quick trip down a flight of stone stairs and into the dimness of the library basement.

Camille rose on her tiptoes and touched her lips to Sydney's, and the rest was a blur of kissing and caressing, pausing only long enough to get rid of Sydney's mail, but they kept the rest of their clothing on as they tumbled onto a group of rolled-up tapestries that were probably priceless. Camille's full lips latched skillfully on to Sydney's, and their tongues meshed as if they'd been kissing for years.

Sydney caressed every inch of Camille that she could reach, taking joy in the soft moans and purrs. When Sydney left off kissing Camille's mouth in order to attend to her flawless neck, Camille took a shuddering breath and said, "We have to stop."

Sydney paused and drew back, pulling her hand back from where she'd been creeping up Camille's skirt. "Too fast?'

Camille chuckled, and her warm breath tickled Sydney's neck. "Yes. And before you point it out, I know I started this."

Sydney grinned and pulled away farther so she could see Camille's face in the light from the dingy basement window. "I would never complain about that round of kissing, even were it all I had for the rest of my life."

Camille blinked before her own smile came out. "There's the smoothness I'd expect from a knight."

"Happy to oblige." And she was. As much as she'd enjoyed kissing Camille, the fact that Camille wanted to slow things down, perhaps to have an actual conversation, tickled Sydney from her head to her toes.

But when they were both on their feet, an awkward silence descended. Sydney hefted her mail on one arm and took Camille's hand with the other. "Would you like to have lunch now? I'm not that bad at conversation."

Camille laughed, and a bit of the tense bubble burst. "Yes, please." She led Sydney out a back door and around a corner of the street to where food vendors hawked their wares by a large fountain in the middle of the square. The library rose behind them in four, statue-adorned stories, topped with a copper dome long gone to green; an impressive building.

Sydney couldn't wait to see the rest of the inside. Maybe since they'd been assigned to each other, this relationship would last a bit, whether it included more kissing or not.

They bought meat pies and sat on the lip of the fountain. At midday, quite a few people strolled the square, eating, talking, or breathing the fresh air and avoiding the pigeons who pecked for food amongst the cobblestones.

"I feel…guilty," Camille said as she turned her lunch in her hands. "The knights didn't assign you to me so I could maul you in the basement."

Sydney shrugged, not certain how she felt about someone being guilty for being with her. "I quite enjoyed the mauling, and my superiors never have to know."

Camille quirked an eyebrow. "I thought that Knights of the Flame always told the truth."

"Only when we speak." Sydney winked before taking a bite, careful not to let the grease run down her chin.

"Good to know." After chewing a bite, Camille said, "What Sir Robert wants is impossible without magic."

Sydney coughed, certain she'd heard wrong. "Surely, you remember who you're talking to."

"I know what your people think of magic, of witches." She held her pie in her lap as if she'd lost her appetite, and her voice turned hard. "And I don't need to do a moment's research to know he can't move his troops so quickly without magical aid."

Sydney's mind reeled, and she wondered just what Camille was playing at. "I know it's *possible* with magic, but surely there are stories about other means—"

"No."

"Examples from history?"

"About magic."

"Anecdotes?" Sydney tried, her stomach shrinking.

Camille's smile was only a little sympathetic. "I'm sure some people could tell a story or two, but if they don't include magic, they're lying."

"Magic is evil," Sydney said flatly.

Camille stood, put her pie on the ground, and pushed it into a flock of pigeons with her foot. They tore into it like wolves. "One thing I can tell you from years of research is that, throughout history, many people thought of various practices as evil until they needed those same practices."

Sydney didn't know what to say. No one had ever disagreed with the tenets of her order so flatly. Camille's gaze was hard, unwavering. There was nothing against the law about having such opinions, but...

Sydney sighed and looked at the ground, her own appetite waning as she thought again of Elion and the shambling dead. "Allow magic in one circumstance, and you will find reasons to use it in others, and then the Witch Wars will happen all over again."

Camille sighed and brushed Sydney's shoulder, a slight amount of sympathy coming through her anger, as if she couldn't stand to see someone upset, even someone she vehemently disagreed with. "I'm sorry I kissed you before I told you all that. I understand if you want to go home."

Sydney's heart warmed. At least Camille didn't insist she leave. "I'm not sorry. And I suppose I should be grateful for your honesty, but…" No doubt even a master researcher made mistakes from time to time. In all these tales Camille referenced, someone had to find a way to achieve the seemingly impossible without relying on the same power that disturbed the rest of the dead. "Would you show me the stories you're talking about?"

"Where magic accomplished great deeds? Of course." Her smile bloomed anew, and she glanced wistfully at where her lunch had disappeared.

Sydney stood and offered Camille a bite of pie as they returned to the library. Sydney let herself enjoy the afternoon again. Camille was beautiful and clearly intelligent and only a little misguided. Sydney could bring her around as she never could have brought the pirate captain; they'd find a non-magical solution, and one more person would be brought into the light.

And maybe one of Camille's history books would have a clue about where witches chose to hide when they went to ground, and Sydney could get back on the trail of the Hawk.

❖

Camille set yet another book in front of Sydney, delighting in the fact that someone wanted to learn. This entire day had been full of surprises.

And not just because of the kissing. Camille hadn't spent time frantically snogging in the basement since she'd been a teenager, but there was something irresistible about Sydney. It was more than just good looks. She radiated…something. Honesty or dedication, maybe. Camille could tell from their brief talk by the fountain that Sydney truly believed magic to be evil, and she seemed saddened by some memory or maybe by the lessons she'd learned at the chapterhouse. Camille had expected haughty anger; Sydney's face had shown genuine pain. With that, Camille doubted Sydney would change her mind quickly, but no one could maintain the stubborn idea that magic was wholly evil after being presented with so much evidence to the contrary.

"Um," Sydney said, and the quiet word seemed to reverberate in the silent library. She gestured to the stack of books Camille had put in front of her. "I don't know if I can get through all this."

Camille was about to say, "It's only eight," but stopped herself. Not everyone read so much that they'd dreamed of becoming a master researcher since the age of ten. "We'll start with this one." She took the first leather-bound book off the stack and opened it on the table's scratched, well-worn surface. The library took pride in its battered furniture and carpets, leaving the inspiring awe to the marble floors of the foyer or the richly painted frescoes and ceilings.

Camille sat beside her and tried to ignore her scent of leather, metal oil, and sandalwood. Kissing time was over; this was work. "Here is the history of the Battle of Bourjon when the Coven of the Moon helped turn the tide in Arnvild's favor."

Sydney leaned forward, frowning, but her eyes didn't scan the page as if reading. Camille kept her temper in check and turned to an illumination of the scene, showing the witches hovering above the battle and throwing handfuls of tiny objects onto the enemy. "These seeds broke open as they landed," Camille said, "creating vines that held the enemy fast."

Sydney sighed. "I'd wager that the Arnvild soldiers who also got tangled in vines didn't praise the witches."

Camille wanted to grind her teeth, but Sydney's words weren't snide, just doubtful, and Camille reminded herself that they had a lot of indoctrination to undo. She opened another book and put it on top of the first.

"All right, let's look at something less gruesome. This tells of a great flood in Perdue, when the sea rose and battered the coastal village. The Spring Coven helped evacuate the trapped and injured." She cleared her throat and read, "'They came from the south and lifted the people up as they cried out for aid. The witches soothed their wounded bodies and carried those encircled by the raging waters.' How about that?"

Sydney frowned harder. "I can only wonder why the witches didn't stop the flood to begin with."

Camille tried to swallow her irritation, but before she could answer, Sydney held up a hand.

"I'm not trying to be difficult," Sydney said. "Such questions are the exact problem with magic. Once it is introduced, it becomes the solution to everything, luring people to become ever more powerful, and then—"

"I know, I know. The Witch Wars. But magic is just a tool, and in the right hands…"

"Show me these 'right hands,'" Sydney said. "I can't think of anyone I'd trust with that much power."

"I *would* show you," Camille said, her temper rising further. "But there *are* no witches left in Arnvild." Not precisely true. She knew of at least one. Not personally, but she knew people who knew people, and so on. She shook her head, determined that Sydney would never know about any of them, not with her stubbornness. "But there are still witches outside this kingdom, and the world hasn't burned down."

After another sigh, Sydney smiled. "I don't wish to fight, Camille. It's just…" She paused as if searching for the right words. "I was taught that magic disrupts the natural order of things, that those who became powerful enough to tinker with the weather actually caused floods like the one in Perdue."

"There's no proof of that," Camille said. "And moving a thousand troops across the kingdom in two days is also against the natural order of things."

Sydney chuckled. "I actually thought that myself." She lifted her hands. "Please, don't tell Sir Robert."

Camille couldn't help smiling back. "Why does he want to move his troops so quickly?"

"Only the highest-ranking knights are allowed to know, and I am a lowly major."

"Goodness. You're practically a page."

Sydney put a hand to her chest as if wounded. "A squire, at least."

Camille laughed, then quieted as a passing patron gave her a dark look. "All right, but if I find a squire who knows more about the history of magic than you, you're back to being a page."

Sydney took her hand and rubbed a calloused thumb over her knuckles. "I enjoy talking with you even if we're arguing."

"Me, too," Camille said, feeling the heat rise in her cheeks again. She forced the feeling down. It wouldn't do any more good than her anger would. "But nothing changes the fact that Sir Robert needs magic to do what he wants."

With a great sigh, Sydney put her hands behind her head and stretched in her seat. "Even if he would ever accept that, there are no witches here."

Camille pressed her lips together to keep from speaking; it was in her nature to correct misinformation, but she couldn't this time. "Let me show you a few more books." She took another book off the pile, determined.

A few became a handful, which turned into a slew, then a torrent. Their lamp burned out of oil at last, and they sat in near darkness with a lone candle. Soon, the sun streaming through the windows died to almost nothing, and the Kingston bells sounded, announcing dusk. Time for the library to close.

Camille had enjoyed arguing with Sydney. Their debates never turned personal, though Camille could have offered a few choice insults about the Knights of the Flame. But Sydney espoused their good works, of which they *had* done quite a few. As she pointed out, there was far less poverty after their social programs and less crime in the face of their patrols. They pitched in to stop every fire and volunteered at every festival.

But some knights weren't as open to discussion as Sydney. Some had called for all *knowledge* of magic and witches to be purged, and that would only happen if Camille was in her grave. "I think that's enough for one day," she said before such thoughts could get the better of her tongue.

Sydney frowned as they stood. "Already?"

Camille's bad thoughts blew away at the question. She smiled. "I've had a good time, too."

"Where do these go?" Sydney asked as she returned the smile and began to gather the books.

"Leave them. We'll never get them put away before closing. I'll do it tomorrow."

"All right. I'll help you."

"Oh? Will you be here tomorrow?" Her chest warmed at the thought.

Sydney's eyes caught a bit of the fading light and sparkled. "Well, I haven't finished my assignment." Before Camille's hopes could fall, Sydney added, "And I don't want to be anywhere else."

Camille felt the warmth in her cheeks, and her heart picked up the pace. She knew she shouldn't ask the question she wanted to ask, not when they were so divided by their beliefs, but she couldn't stop herself from saying, "Dinner?"

A slow smile spread over Sydney's face, and Camille thought she caught a hint of some other emotion in the way her lips twitched, a bit of sadness, perhaps, before Sydney turned away. "I'd love to."

Camille threaded her arm through Sydney's and headed for the exit. If Sydney was at all concerned about the tales of magic she'd learned that day, Camille knew just how to cheer her.

CHAPTER THREE

Sydney sat up slowly, trying not to wake Camille, but luckily, Camille slept like the dead. She snorted softly before rolling over and pulling the sheet higher on her shoulder. Sydney grinned and eased out from the covers. The first bell of the day hadn't sounded, which meant dawn hadn't yet broken. She didn't want to sneak away like a thief, but she needed a change of clothes and a wash before the day started again.

Camille's apartment was small and narrow, only two rooms plus a small water closet. Sydney visited that before collecting her clothes and tiptoeing out of the bedroom and into the sitting room, which held a table and chairs and a small stove. She penned a quick note to Camille explaining her absence and added a lot of compliments bound to make any abandoned lover smile.

Sydney's heart was a little heavy as she dressed and left. She'd enjoyed her day with Camille immensely, and the night had been fantastic, but part of her had hoped they'd postpone the lovemaking for more conversation. Once they were behind closed doors, Camille had practically leaped on her.

Sydney told herself she was being ungracious with her thoughts. Anyone would be lucky to spend a night in Camille's arms, but she couldn't help a bit of wistfulness as she pictured the two of them getting to know each other beyond their opinions on magic.

The thought made her sigh as she hurried through the lightening streets to the chapterhouse and her own room. She'd been hoping to spot an inconsistency in the tales of witches and magic, something that would give her a clue as to how Sir Robert's plan might be carried out through non-magical means, but she'd come up short, dash it all. She kept thinking about the pirates disappearing from the hold. A witch had clearly cracked Sir Robert's problem, but he couldn't very well go to one and ask for help, especially not a witch his knights had hunted as long as the Hawk.

Sydney used her key to access the back chambers of the chapterhouse. Once she'd washed and changed in her room, she walked toward the great hall to see if she could scrounge some breakfast before she had to meet Camille at the library again.

"Major Blakely?"

Sydney turned in the hall and bowed as Sir Robert strode toward her. "Good morning, sir."

He nodded before heading past her into the dining room, and she wondered if he only stopped her so he could get there first, but he made a quick gesture to his side, and she joined him at his right as he sat at the head of the table.

"How goes the research?" he said as the servants laid warm plates and cups of coffee before them. He didn't wait for Sydney's answer before lifting the covers off several dishes, revealing hard-boiled eggs, mutton, and some kind of fish. He began heaping his plate with everything while Sydney asked for toast.

"The research is what we expected, sir," Sydney said. "Magic and little else."

"Hmm." He chewed thoughtfully, staring at nothing. "Bit like your prisoners, eh?"

Sydney bit the inside of her cheek to keep from explaining yet again that she hadn't known witches could do such things as whisk people away. Of course, if she had known, what could she have done? Lashed them to the deck instead of to each other? So the Hawk would have to take the entire ship? Sydney sighed. She was beginning to see a little of Camille's point. The knights needed to learn more about witches, if only to see what was possible.

"The Hawk seems very powerful, sir," she mumbled.

"She could probably move our troops in a twinkling."

Sydney coughed as she sipped her coffee, and stinging droplets spattered her hand. She managed to set her cup down before Sir Robert leaned forward and delivered two great thwacks across her shoulders.

"Better see the sawbones if that cough gets any worse, Major. In the meantime, ask our master researcher about this Hawk, see if she knows where the witch can be found."

Sydney shook her head. "I don't think the master researcher would help us arrest—"

"See if anyone at the library knows how to contact her," Sir Robert said as if he hadn't heard. "Makes sense you know, witches and libraries. Books of spells and books of knowledge and whatnot." He nodded and threw down his napkin. "Bound to be someone there who knows the witch and can contact her."

"But...sir..." Her thoughts whirled as she pictured her conversation with Camille. *I know you think magic isn't evil, but would you mind contacting this witch so I can set a trap for her?*

"We'll get her to move our troops, then we can arrest her." He nodded as if this was a fantastic idea and stroked his mustache before smiling at Sydney. "Set it up, Major. Time is of the essence."

Sydney rushed to stand as he did, bowing as he made his leave, but she was too stunned for words. The head of the Knights of the Flame had just suggested using magic, a witch, and then he strode away as if it was nothing? She remembered something Camille had said about how people only believed something was evil until they needed it.

"Sir," she managed to bellow. "Even if we find her, she won't... the Hawk won't do it, sir, especially not for me."

Sir Robert frowned as if she was speaking some other language. "Don't ask her to do it for you, Major. Tell her the real reason."

She waited a moment. "Which is, sir?"

He blinked before bursting into laughter. "Oh, that's right. I forget which people know what facts, don'tcha know." He chuckled again before seemingly remembering what they were talking about. "Tell her that if she doesn't cooperate, tens of thousands might die when the Kells march from the north."

He turned on his heel and left. Sydney sagged back into her seat, happy that none of the servants or other knights had been in the room to hear that. She didn't know how Sir Robert knew, but if an army of Arnvild's most fearsome enemies was coming, then many people between Kingston and the border *would* die if a large fighting force wasn't there to protect them.

But how could an enemy army move so swiftly that Sir Robert hadn't heard about it until recently? How come refugees weren't already pouring through Kingston's gates, pushed by the sightings of scouts and the wings of rumor?

The same way Sir Robert now hoped to move his own troops. The Kells had a witch.

❖

Camille knew some people would have been irked to wake up and find their lover flown, but she secretly enjoyed it. She'd always hated the awkward small talk that some insisted on in the morning. She enjoyed having a quiet cup of coffee to herself at the small table in her apartment as she watched the light gradually grow outside her window.

The note had been a nice touch. And she was looking forward to spending more time with Sydney, but mornings had a sacredness she was loath to share.

She wondered when exactly she'd get irritated with Sydney's quest for ordinary among the magical. She had other projects to attend to, other clients who'd hired a master researcher through the library. If she took too long with the Knights of the Flame, other researchers would grab those projects and leave her with only the dullest, least interesting ones. She bet none of them would want to research something as interesting as magic. She hadn't even had a query about magical creatures in years, and they were usually pretty popular.

But she was beyond the scope of her job with Sydney now; convincing someone of the veracity of her research wasn't normally part of what she did. She presented the facts as she found them in texts. She could explain what she'd found, could compile facts so they might be more easily understood, but she felt as if she'd already done that for Sydney. There was nothing in recorded history that proved magic was "evil" no matter which definition one used.

A very short report indeed.

As she put away her cup and dressed, Camille let herself grouse a little. She'd never labeled facts and history with loose terms like good and evil. She'd had her own opinions, of course, but no one had ever proposed questions like: What were the crop yields between certain years? What were the reasons behind these numbers, and were they good or evil?

At least the sex was great. It made her feel a little guilty, though; she wasn't paid to do that, either.

When she saw Sydney waiting outside the library, her heart picked up the pace, and her complaints muted under memories of the night before. Camille was so busy looking down the line of Sydney's body that she missed the look of worry on her face until they stood right next to each other.

Camille took Sydney's hand. "What's wrong?"

"I..." Sydney glanced around as if wary of eavesdroppers, even though few people were near the library at this hour. But noise from the nearby square seemed to be putting her off. "Can we..." She looked to the library.

Camille used her key on a side entrance. She couldn't take Sydney to the small set of offices she shared with the other researchers, so she led her to one of the rooms where delicate manuscripts were kept behind a closed and locked door.

"No one will disturb us in here, though we can't touch anything," Camille said, a sentence that seemed made to be misconstrued between two lovers.

Sydney grinned, but the licentious gleam in her eye faded before Camille even had time to correct her. "I had a word with Sir Robert this morning."

Her tale came out in fits and starts, leaving Camille's anger plenty of room to grow. She'd never been proven right so succinctly. "Now that he needs a witch, they're no longer evil." She paced, waiting for Sydney to try to defend her boss's opinion, ready with some choice words, but Sydney merely hung her head, seemingly gutted by Sir Robert's opinions.

Camille corralled her anger and sat again. Sydney's respect for her order had been evident in her voice yesterday. To see the leader of that order walk unashamedly over its ideals had to feel like the keenest of betrayals.

And she was far out on a limb admitting everything, though Camille didn't know what she could do with such information. She could spread rumors, she supposed, but what good would that do? The only people who might care were other knights, and they wouldn't believe her.

But they might believe Sydney, which left her no one to confide in except an outsider. Like Camille. She couldn't turn away someone so in need.

Especially when this revelation might convince her that magic wasn't evil.

"You're allowed to be angry," Camille said. "I would be. I am. Just because Sir Robert is your leader doesn't mean he's always right."

Sydney only hung her head. "I have to do as he says."

Camille stood again. "You don't *have* to do anything, Sydney. Especially not ask someone for their help, wait until they've aided you, then arrest them. I can't believe you'd even consider—"

"The Kells are invading."

Camille stuttered to a halt, her thoughts wrenched from one direction to another. Anger dropped away in the face of dread. She didn't need to reread a single book to know what the Kells were capable of. Even the few Kellish texts the library had essentially said, we're really great, and everyone else deserves to die horribly because they aren't us.

Still, she had to argue. "But...no one's heard from them in decades. After they stormed Arnvild before the Witch Wars, they pushed farther south and..."

Sydney shrugged. "Maybe they killed everyone to the south, and now they've come back around the globe for us."

The last war with the Kells had cost Arnvild dearly, and they'd had witches then. "Oh, shit," Camille said.

"Sir Robert wants the Hawk to move the troops, that's all," Sydney said, a note of hope in her voice.

Camille had to quash that hope before it truly kindled. "Once she's done that, a request for aid against the Kells won't be far behind, I'm sure." She paused, going back over Sydney's words. "Did you say, the Hawk?"

Sydney nodded. "That's the witch I've been after. If the Kellish troops are moving as swiftly as Sir Robert says, they might also have a witch."

"Maybe," Camille whispered. Her belly had gone cold as Sydney kept talking about how witch vs. witch had been a situation that had to be avoided. She kept hearing that name. The Hawk. She'd heard it before. It had been spoken of by other friends who didn't believe that magic was evil.

"How could Sir Robert do this?" Sydney said.

"Because he's a hypocrite," Camille muttered, able to answer that one without any thought.

"But to ask for help and then arrest the Hawk?" Sydney had tears in her eyes as if her whole world was falling apart.

"I haven't even gotten to my anger about that part yet," Camille said as she leaned forward and pulled Sydney's head to her shoulder, both to comfort and to hide her own distress.

"I've never been dishonest about my intentions toward her." Sydney's voice was muffled as she clung to Camille. "I wouldn't be. Sir Robert isn't supposed to be."

"He's probably content with not mentioning that part until it's too late."

"The worst part is, we do need her help."

Camille pulled away. "You're not going along with his scheme?" She held her breath, waiting for an answer.

"To trick her? No. To ask for her help?" She shrugged. "We have to. I'll just have to suffer any consequences for my own disobedience."

Camille didn't know what to say. She was happy Sydney wasn't heartless, but the idea of going along with any of Sir Robert's plan chilled her.

Thoughts of the Kells chilled her more.

Camille sighed and wished for an option besides Sir Robert's plan and doing nothing. There had to be a way to aid Arnvild and thwart Sir Robert at the same time. It was time to speak with her friends who knew people who knew the Hawk. "Let me see what I can find out."

Sydney looked at her with gratitude, and Camille took the hand she offered and pressed it warmly. She didn't feel as warm inside.

"I'll need a few hours," Camille said.

Sydney nodded and sniffled as she stood, managing to be both sexy and vulnerable, a heartbreaking combination. "I'll leave you to it. Don't want to get in the way." She smiled sheepishly. "But if you need someone to fetch or carry or fight, I'll be at the chapterhouse."

Camille only managed a wan smile. After Sydney left, Camille sank into a chair and tried to calm her worry for her kingdom and her anger at Sir Robert. Even if Sydney refused to trick the Hawk—and Camille would have been disgusted if she hadn't—that didn't mean the other knights would be so conscientious.

And now Camille had to take Sydney's secrets and go behind her back. She had to find a way to contact the Hawk, both to seek her help and to warn her. As much as she wanted to, she couldn't trust Sydney to tell the Hawk everything. They just didn't know each other well enough.

And if the betrayal of Sydney's confidence cost their relationship?

Camille sighed. So be it.

❖

Rowena the Hawk bent over the crystal ball and gently placed her hands on it. She barely breathed as she focused on the delicate magic of imbuing the rock with a sending spell that would allow it to communicate with the other orbs she had scattered around Arnvild.

"Bloody, buggery heartfire," she mumbled as the magic flowed from her into the crystal. She'd known the heartfire magic of the knights was powerful, but she'd never expected a jolt to flow through *two* crystal balls with enough power to destroy them both. She should have severed the connection to the pirate's crystal when she'd shut off the picture, but she'd hoped to get some good eavesdropping in.

"But no," she mumbled, deepening her voice to a mocking tone. "We have to destroy all the super bad magics."

"Concentration is key," Ember said from somewhere behind her.

"I know." Rowena kept her voice low but couldn't help the growl. The unseen magic that passed from her fluttered, and she felt it dance over her skin like cobwebs before she redirected it again.

"Think of all the reagents you'll have wasted if you lose focus," Ember said. "It's what you always say."

Reagents and hours of work. Stupid knights. At least Rowena had managed to whisk the pirate crew away and leave her calling card in their place. She grinned, wishing she could have seen the knight's stupid face when her captives had disappeared.

That glee improved her focus greatly, and she finally sat back from her finished crystal ball with a satisfied smirk. Using such delicate magic always left her feeling as if she needed a nap, and this was no exception. She leaned back in her chair and rested her head on Ember's knee.

From her seat on the desk, Ember tilted her head down, and Rowena's eyes were drawn to the scar that cut across her face. It had faded to a slim white line in the years since Ember's creation, but it still leaped out as it slanted from her right temple, through her eyebrow, across her nose, and down her cheek to her jaw. All the time she spent outside sparring with the husks didn't help. The rest of her face had turned as brown as a bean, but that line would remain white forever.

Still, the bright green eyes smiled along with her full lips. She didn't lament the scar because she'd never been told to. Rowena never mentioned it, even as often as she gazed at it, so Ember didn't think it out of the ordinary. After all, the only other "people" she spent time with—the husks—were covered in scars, and they didn't seem to mind.

Not that they *could* have minded.

"What did you do with the pirates?" Rowena asked.

"Loaded with provisions and sent on their way after they told me some stories." She grinned. "They were very entertaining."

Rowena sat up and laughed. She tousled Ember's short red hair, leaving it to flop artfully around her face. She always forgot to comb it. "Out the front door? I'm sure they're loving that."

Ember cocked her head, making the numerous earrings on her right ear jingle. "I warned them not to go near the husks if they saw any and about the giant spiders in the lower tunnels that sometimes get out, and that they had to keep to the path down the mountain, or they'd be eaten by the yeti." She cocked her head farther and stared at nothing. "They seemed upset and wanted you to magic them home. When I said that spell required time and energy to prepare, and that you only did it when you rescued them because you prepared it in advance, they yelled at me. They were very angry."

Rowena snorted. "I bet."

"I told them that I thought you'd let them stay until the spell was ready, but I told them what you wanted me to say, that there isn't much room, so they'd have to stay downstairs with the husks, and some of them bite." She shook her head. "They don't bite unless you tell them to, though."

"And I would have. Can't have them thinking me a liar."

The pirates had probably thought she was threatening them, but Ember was simply doing as Rowena had asked. Her body was that of an adult's, but her rapid-fire way of speaking put some in mind of a child, and they either thought she was joking or underestimated her.

And some of the husks *would* bite if instructed.

"So," Rowena said, "they decided to risk the spiders and the yeti?"

"And your traps. They wanted to speak to you, to thank you," Ember said, her brow wrinkling. "Why didn't you want to talk to them?"

Rowena turned away and began sorting through the reagents on the table, putting them away. "I just didn't."

"But why?"

Rowena sighed. She couldn't help but be proud of Ember, her homunculus, her finest creation, but sometimes, Ember was too inquisitive by half.

"They're couriers, hired swords," Rowena said. "Not friends."

"You saved them."

"A good crew is hard to find."

"They believe in you."

"That's enough," Rowena snapped over her shoulder, then felt like a dog for doing so. "I'm sorry, Ember. I just…they're just…not friends." Her stomach tightened in knots as she thought of speaking to a crowd of people, even for a moment, without the distance of the crystal ball.

Ember's arms went around her shoulders. "You don't need to say sorry. Everything you do is all right with me."

Rowena sighed. Ember's inability to really understand her was one of their problems. Ember couldn't be a lot of things. "Go and spar with the husks."

"All right." Her arms went away, but her steps paused by the door. "Maybe you should get some more friends."

Rowena snorted again and didn't bother to reply. Ember was already gone. Oh yes, her mountain hideaway with its traps and beasties and husks was the perfect place for friends. "Please, come to my party," the invitation would read. "Including possible poisoning, maiming, and even death! Oh, and Knights of the Flame will also be looking to hunt us down and find a way to either bar us from our home forever or throw us down a dark hole. Refreshments provided!"

Bringing magic back to Arnvild was worth not having friends. She couldn't let the bloody, buggery knights win. They were fine with their heartfire, magic of pure destruction, but they wanted to eradicate powers like hers, those of creation. And they couldn't get it into their thick, pig-headed skulls that trying to have one without the other would set the entire world out of balance.

Besides, Arnvild was her home, and no set of tight-assed, more-righteous-than-you idiots was going to keep her out of it.

As she finished putting away her reagents, her crystal ball flickered, and the sounds of tinkling bells filled the air. Someone was handling one of the orbs she'd sent to her contacts in Arnvild.

Rowena passed a hand over her own ball and added to its power with her life force. She used just a tad, wanting to see before she was seen. The rat-like face of Abe the clockmaker in Kingston peered back at her, his brows drawn together as if searching for her in the crystalline depths.

"You won't see me unless I want you to, Abe," she said dryly.

He jerked as if she'd appeared in front of him, but she knew he only heard her. "Hawk, is that you?"

Rowena sighed. Every. Time. "One of these days, I'm going to say no just to see what you do."

She'd expected a nervous laugh, his usual response to her sarcasm, but he swallowed. She tried to look around him to see if anyone else was in his shop—perhaps a knight with a sword to his neck—but the fishbowl quality of the ball made searching difficult, and he held it so close to his face. Besides, he didn't offer the signal they'd come up with for hostage situations. If he didn't tip her off, she wouldn't know to rescue him.

Not that she could, at the moment.

But he didn't know that.

She shook her head to clear it. "Is this a social call or…"

"I have some bad news," he said, and she could see the sweat beading on his forehead. "Rather bad news. I've heard from the bookseller, and she heard from a librarian, a master researcher, actually, and—"

Rowena sat forward, heart pounding. "What did you tell them?"

"It's what they told me. The bookseller must have mentioned you to the master researcher at some point."

"Shit." Rowena covered her mouth with one hand. Three contacts burned in less than a month. "Did the bookseller tell the knights, too? Abe, you need to leave your shop, and—"

"You're not listening. We have more to worry about than knights."

"Ha. You're not going to think that for long if they're coming for you."

"It's the Kells," he said, coming even closer to the ball. One brown eye ballooned to fill the entire sphere until she could see the capillaries running through the white and hear his lashes trembling against the crystal. "They're coming to kill us all. We need your help."

Rowena's ears filled with the sound of nothing, and she sat back, all her other worries evaporating. Arnvild's most fearsome enemy on top of everything else? Wasn't that just her luck?

CHAPTER FOUR

Rowena hurried into her workshop, digesting what her informant had said. The Knights of the Flame wanted her help moving troops to defend Arnvild against the Kells.

"Bloody hypocrites," she muttered. Of course they wanted her help now that they found a way for her to be useful, and of course it was a trap, as her informant said. And of course it had to be against the buggery Kells, so Rowena had to help.

She passed the long wooden table that dominated her workroom. It was dotted with reagents and materials like those she'd used to create Ember: clay, plant fibers, minerals, the occasional pig organ, everything she'd needed to make a fully functional human being.

Except for the magic. Giving up that much of her life force had nearly killed her.

But as she felt Ember's movements in the tunnels above, she knew it was worth it. Closer than a sister, closer than a child, even, Ember was part of her. And if the Kells tore through Arnvild, she'd never get to introduce that part of her to her homeland.

Once everything was safe and witches had been accepted again.

That'd be the bloody day.

Rowena passed through the doorway at the back of her workshop and entered her study, stopping to inhale the comforting scents of old leather, ink, and paper. She kicked off her boots before setting foot on the plush carpet. With a gentle pull of her magic, the lanterns hanging from the chandelier flared to life, as did the two on her desk, illuminating the dark wooden surface and the tall shelves that made up the walls of her study.

"Dansk," she said, "bring me any books on the Kells."

Slow footsteps whispered across the carpet as the husk standing by the door shuffled into motion. At first glance, Dansk seemed much as she had been in life, the same dark hair and unblemished pale skin. One only had to look at the blank white eyes and the still chest to see that life had fled the body.

Until Rowena had animated it anew.

Dansk hadn't been her name at birth. The villagers who lived below Rowena's lair never told her the names of their dead. They simply washed them, dressed them in something serviceable like plain tunics and trousers, and gave them to her in a solemn ceremony that she assumed brought them comfort. It was an honor, they'd told her, to give their dead to the witch who tended the sick, drove off bandits, and saved their village from fire.

At least they knew the value of magic.

Even if she had to go to them at the base of the mountain because they were too frightened to come up the mountain to her.

Or maybe that was because they didn't want to see their loved ones...repurposed.

Oh, well. Keeping some distance between them suited her better, anyway.

Dansk couldn't carry on a conversation, but she knew the whereabouts of every book in the library, and she didn't need the use of ladders. She slowly scaled the shelves, her bare feet squeaking gently on the wood. She climbed down with one book tucked under her arm, set it on the desk, then climbed again.

Rowena sank into her plush leather chair and opened the book, a true account of Arnvild's last war with the Kells, written by a soldier who'd escaped the battlefield by hiding under a dead horse. On his return to what was left of civilization, some had called him a coward, but he seemed incredibly sensible to Rowena's eyes.

The two armies had met on the battlefield, the Kells whooping and hollering as they stamped like horses, eager to run into battle. They painted their faces and their armor with red streaks and blotches, as if they were already covered in blood. And maybe they were. Rumors about the Kells included everything from infighting to human sacrifice to cannibalism. No matter what was true, the sight combined with the noise afflicted more than a few soldiers, turning their thoughts and their feet toward home.

The writer referred to some rallying speech from the Arnvild king that made his troops as eager as the Kells, and battle was soon joined. As soon as the two armies were engaged, they found out the real reason for the Kells' noise, to cover the other half of their army as it flanked the Arnvild troops from a forest to the side.

No one had suspected such tactics. Out of all the rumors, none ever said the Kells were clever.

The battle turned into a rout, and the Arnvild king discovered the second surprise of the day. During the battle, the Kells had sent troops to cover the only avenue of retreat, and what remained of the Arnvild forces ran straight into their waiting swords.

The writer spent a long night on the battlefield, half crushed by his own horse. He'd heard the screams as the Kells toyed with dying soldiers. The Kells laughed as they flayed the wounded, howled along with their cries of agony, and those who spoke Arnvild's language mocked them all the while.

One Arnvild soldier had cried for mercy, saying she had a family.

The Kells had laughed and said, "Dreams don't have families. Only the Kells are real. The rest of the world is smoke."

Rowena shuddered. How could one defend against an enemy who didn't even believe they existed? One didn't have to have a conscience in a dream.

Sitting back, Rowena rubbed her temples. Dansk had set two more books on the desk before retreating to her place beside the door. Rowena drummed her fingers on the table. She knew that other books would have similar accounts, but she read them anyway. The few survivors left in the Kells' wake had the same stories. After they'd passed through Arnvild, they'd ventured off to attack other "dreams." Now they'd returned to do it all over again.

"Shit," Rowena said quietly. Witches hadn't been very involved in the Kells' first attack on Arnvild. There had been fighting among the covens at the time, and the Witch Wars were soon to come, slowing down Arnvild's recovery and nearly wiping out anyone left.

Well, that wouldn't happen this time. Rowena could move Sir Robert's bloody troops to the border. And she could do it without being caught by that witless moron. But she wondered if the knights would be enough. Everything about them said arrogance. Sir Robert knew the Kells were dangerous, but he'd probably never cracked a book, might not know that the Kells were clever or that they spared no one, not even knights who practiced courteous warfare with prisoner exchanges and free passage for the wounded. No accounts existed from the small villages the Kells had devoured in their march across Arnvild, but others had written of trying to visit relatives in those same villages and finding naught but scorch marks.

Rowena concentrated on Ember's life force and called to it, summoning her to her side. Ember spent more time with the soldier husks than Rowena did. It was time to find out which could be deployed if necessary. And if Rowena didn't have enough husks, well, there had to be plenty of graveyards between her lair and the border.

❖

Ember heard Rowena's call and was tempted to ignore it. Not because she didn't love Rowena, no. That love ran deep, deeper than her love for her own arms or legs or eyes, all of which she'd give up to help Rowena, the woman who'd given her life.

But Ember was *bored*. Bored in underlined letters as if in a book. She liked reading. Sometimes. She liked helping Rowena and sparring with the husks and talking with the occasional visitor more, but something still tugged at her like an invisible rope.

Boredom.

It was a word that sank into the bones, that sifted through all her memories and found them wanting. That made her feel bad sometimes, like now, when she dragged her feet instead of leaping to Rowena's call. Rowena might want her to learn something new, which would be nice, but it wouldn't make her legs still or show her new colors or give her new feelings because books were so...distant. They had people running across pages and space and time, but none of it was here, now. None of it...sang.

She'd been created in the mountain lair. She'd explored every inch. The spiders were fun. The husks were fun. The workshop was fun. Or they had been fun until Rowena had let Ember see through the crystal ball.

Ships and waves and pirates and things. She'd asked what those things were so many times that Rowena had finally snapped at her to go play, which she had, pretending she was a pirate on a ship on the waves surrounded by things. But pretending had become boring, too. She wanted to see the ship, ride the waves, meet the pirates. Maybe some would let her touch the things. The point was, there were *other places to go.*

But Rowena said they couldn't. Even the village below was out of bounds for Ember. Rowena only went to the base of the mountain to perform the most solemn of ceremonies when someone died, and she feared Ember would ask embarrassing questions, and then Rowena might not be invited back, and then where would the new husks come from?

Ember had said that Rowena could make a list of embarrassing questions, and Ember wouldn't ask them, but Rowena said any questions would be embarrassing at such a time, and she didn't trust Ember to keep still.

Ember sighed. That was true. She couldn't keep still.

But now she knew there were other places that might not be so solemn, pirates who might welcome questions and touches and other explorations. The whole of Arnvild waited. Rowena couldn't go anywhere because she was a witch and knights would arrest her, but Ember wasn't a witch. Rowena said people wouldn't understand someone who was created rather than born, but Ember was certain she could explain well enough.

"How many husks do we currently have?" Rowena asked as Ember crossed the threshold into the study.

"Hello to you, as well," Ember said.

Rowena looked up and blinked, then she sighed. "I see you've decided to be peevish since last we saw each other."

Ember grinned. She'd just learned peevish. It felt right when she was *bored.* "We have thirty husks if you count the two you have in the workshop."

"That's not many," Rowena said, tapping her chin with a pencil. "Even if each one is worth ten live fighters, that's not many."

"Some aren't fighters at all," Ember said, nodding toward Dansk. "You'd have to retrain them." Then she brightened. "Are you going to? Are they going to fight someone? I'm a fighter. I know how. Are they going to see the pirates? I could go."

Rowena gave her a dark look. "You're not going anywhere."

"But I'm practically a husk—"

"You are not." Rowena shouted as she stood. "You are so much more than that. I taught you..." The words faded as Ember laughed.

"I only said it to try to get you to let me go. I shouldn't have. Now you're angry." She frowned. "And I shouldn't laugh if you're angry. I'm sorry." She truly was, but yelling was just so funny. It echoed in her ears.

Rowena took a few deep breaths, and Ember waited for her to catch her calm. "You are too precious, Ember. You're unique."

"But not made of glass." She had proven that once by leaping from a cliff. Rowena had been so angry as she'd put Ember back together, but she'd had to concede that Ember did not shatter. Whatever damage was done to her, Rowena could fix.

"I know." Rowena came around the desk, and her face pinched, and Ember felt her own face pinch, too. Rowena was sad, and that always made Ember sad. "But I can't..."

Ember sighed, still sad for Rowena and sad for herself. It didn't matter what she was made of if Rowena would never let her go. "You should have more friends," she said again. "I'll always be your Ember, but you should have more friends besides me."

"You've been reading too many stories."

"Stories have friends."

"My point exactly."

"Friends who go on adventures."

"And die."

Ember threw her head back and laughed again. "You'd never let me die." The very concept was sillier than anything she'd ever heard, and she opened her arms for Rowena to rush inside. The hug was tight, but that was fine since Ember wasn't made of glass.

"Come on," Rowena said. "You can help me *plan* an adventure. That's the best I can do."

For now, Ember thought, but she used another ability she'd recently learned and kept a secret.

❖

Nothing in Kingston's library pointed to the witch known as the Hawk, and Sydney was tempted toward relief *and* despair. If she never found the witch, she wouldn't have to choose between following orders and doing what she knew was right.

But without the witch's help, the Knights of the Flame would never arrive in time to save the border towns from the Kells.

Camille kept her mind occupied, even as she seemed more than a little distracted herself. They'd been together for three days now, and Camille still hadn't lost interest. If anything, she seemed to become more interested when she discovered that Sydney wouldn't carry out Sir Robert's plan to plead with the Hawk for aid, then betray her once that aid was given. Still, Camille didn't really seem to want to get to *know* Sydney. Maybe she was also seeking to keep her mind off their troubles while they still had the liberty to do so.

Breathless in the library storeroom after one such distracting activity, Sydney fumbled back into her clothes as Camille did the same. "Has Sir Robert been pressing you for progress reports?" Camille asked.

Sydney frowned as she thought of her recent encounters with the supreme commander. He asked what she'd uncovered, but he never appeared fazed by her failure. "He's been calm. Come to think of it, I've never seen him express any other emotion. He takes things in stride." She sighed. "I always wanted to be like him in that way. Most of us do."

"I'm sorry," Camille said, laying her hand on Sydney's shoulder. "I know his plans hurt you."

"Maybe he won't betray the Hawk," Sydney said, hoping it was true. "Maybe he'll make it clear that she'll go to prison or be permanently exiled for her witchcraft, and it will be up to her to choose whether she helps or not."

Camille stared at her flatly. "Oh yes, making her choose between her freedom and the people of her homeland. How chivalrous."

Sydney rubbed her temples, wondering if she'd feel as if she was on the cusp of a headache from now on. "Every time I see him, I want to say something, to ask him why, to protest, but the words just die."

"Take me with you next time," Camille said. "I have more than enough to say for the both of us."

She went on to speak a few choice phrases, but Sydney was barely listening. She knew the reason why she hadn't objected to Sir Robert's plan. She wanted to walk the thin line of obedience and dedication a little while longer. When the Hawk entered the field, Sydney would have to choose a side, but for now, part of her could pretend that her order was all she'd ever thought it was, a beacon of goodness for all the world.

Late at night, another part of her whispered that maybe Sir Robert's plan wasn't such a bad one. The magic used to move the knights would be the last magic cast in Arnvild. After it was done and the Hawk was dealt with, their kingdom would see an end to witches. If magic was going to have one last act, why shouldn't it be a righteous one?

But it was more than the imagined rage on Camille's face that made Sydney turn from such a plan. Some things just felt wrong in the gut, and asking for help while holding a club ready to strike was one of them.

"Do you?" Camille asked, leaning into Sydney's line of sight with a concerned expression.

Sydney blinked before sighing. "I'm sorry, my sweet. I wasn't listening."

A flash of irritation crossed Camille's face before she smiled again. "I understand your preoccupation, but…"

"We have work to do, I know. You hope to find the Hawk so we can warn her what's to come."

Camille's gaze shifted away. "Isn't that what you want, too?"

Sydney kissed her cheek, hoping she didn't feel unappreciated. "Yes. You've been wonderful, darling, and I can't thank you enough for your sympathy and insight." Sydney expected a beaming smile, but Camille turned her head away as if embarrassed.

"It's…nothing, really. You're wonderful, too." She sighed as if tired of hefting the world.

Sydney's heart went out to her. "I'm so sorry. You must be as worn out emotionally as I am, and I've only been thinking of myself. Come, let's take a rest. Separately," she added with a wink, "so we can be assured of…sleep. I'll go to my chapterhouse if you'll find a quiet corner, and we can clear our heads and meet again in a few hours."

Camille nodded hurriedly, still not meeting Sydney's eyes, though Sydney had no idea what Camille should feel bad about. After another kiss on Camille's cheek, Sydney strode away, grateful she had such a selfless companion.

Out of Camille's charming company, though, Sydney's doubts raised their hydra-like heads again. Anger accompanied them this time at Sir Robert, at the Hawk, at the Kells. And only one of those was within reach. As the midday bells rang across the city, Sydney built up a furious stride as she reached the chapterhouse. It seemed the right time to do the brave thing and confront Sir Robert. Maybe that would finally put her heart at ease.

She hailed various companions as she strode through the halls, but more and more of them seemed to be avoiding her eye, giving her a nod but not returning her friendly hellos. When Juzail, one of the recruits she'd commanded on the pirate ship, approached with an excited smile, she beamed, relieved that she hadn't been transformed into a stranger who no one knew.

She'd clearly been thinking of magic too often lately.

"Major." His handsome face was alight, brown eyes sparkling. "Isn't it wonderful news?"

Sydney shrugged. "It must be since you seem so delighted, Juzail, but I confess I don't know which news you're referring to. Did the lovely Delilah consent to step out with you?"

He blinked, his grin slipping. "No, Major, the march. We march tomorrow."

Sydney almost asked where, but of course, she knew. Her time had run out. The knights were going to head for the border without a witch. They couldn't afford to delay any longer. But why had no one told her? "I…" She tried to collect her rampaging thoughts. "I'd better get my gear together."

He nodded eagerly but stopped when Colonel Foster stepped up beside him and touched his arm. "Go about your duties, Recruit."

Juzail stiffened with a look of panic before nodding. "Colonel. Major." He headed off almost at a sprint.

"Excuse me, Colonel," Sydney said as she made to step around. "I've just heard the news, and I—"

"A moment, Major." Foster smoothed her short gray hair and looked decidedly more uncomfortable than Sydney had ever seen, but her blue eyes were resolved as they bored into Sydney's. "You won't need to gather anything. You're excused from this expedition."

The air went cold, and Sydney's ears filled with a tinny sound. She felt her mouth moving, but all that emerged was a sound like, "*Mwuh?*" So many emotions shot through her, they left her hollow, and she felt like Camille's card catalogue as she tried to sort through them and find one to land on.

"I was just coming to find you," Foster said, her tone not unsympathetic but with an edge that brooked no argument. "I'm sorry Recruit Juzail got your hopes up." Her clap on the shoulder nearly toppled Sydney. "Sir Robert's orders. You're to remain here to continue the assignment he gave you."

Sydney fought a torrent of emotions. She wanted to tell Foster the truth but couldn't manage it. She couldn't even have said her name at that moment. It felt as if she was floating around the room, watching herself from the ceiling.

Left behind. Out of the hardest, most difficult battles she'd ever heard of. Left out to search for the witch.

Or was it that? Foster continued with her curious, appraising look, and when Sydney didn't respond, her lip curled slightly. Derision? Sydney wasn't used to such on the faces of her superiors. Even after her failure to catch the Hawk or hold the pirates, the other officers had clapped her back and said things like, "Never mind. You'll get her next time."

But perhaps this was her real punishment, and if the other officers thought Sir Robert had lost faith in her…

That was why he hadn't told Sydney she was staying behind. That was what he wanted people to think so he didn't have to explain that he wanted to use a witch, then betray her. Sydney had become part and parcel of his dirty little secret.

She went even colder. Was it his plan to use the Hawk, trap or kill her, then blame that dishonor on Sydney?

"By the flame," Sydney whispered. She stumbled to the wall and sagged on it.

Foster's sneer grew a little before she said, "Never mind," with a note of false cheer. "You're sure to get in on the next one." She hurried away, no doubt wanting to spare Sydney the further dishonor of weeping in front of a superior officer. Soon, everyone would either be ignoring her, sneering at her, or staring in pity.

She had to talk to Sir Robert.

Sydney began a march through the dormitory on her way to search the practice fields, when she saw a package waiting outside her door.

A pity gift from another knight? With a snarl, she picked it up and carried it into her room before anyone could see it. She tore away the string and brown paper but paused when that left her with a heavy wooden box. "What in the seven bells?"

When she opened the box, the lid fell from her nerveless fingers and thudded to the rug. Inside, nestled in a bed of velvet, was a perfect crystal sphere. She lifted it out and marveled at the weight, at what this could mean, before glancing around, afraid someone would see her through the wall.

Holding a tool of magic.

Sydney nearly jumped out of her boots when the sphere said, "We need to talk."

Camille was overcome with guilt. She hoped all the sex made up for the fact that she was keeping information from Sydney. Not only did she know *how* to contact the Hawk, she'd already done it. Well, by proxy, anyway. All the "research" she and Sydney had been doing for the past three days was just a blind as Camille waited for the Hawk to decide what she wanted to do.

And so, sex. Not that Camille hadn't enjoyed it, but using it as a distraction made her feel even guiltier. She wasn't sure exactly why; she didn't really know Sydney, didn't owe her anything. Still, Sydney had been honest with her about Sir Robert's plans. She could have concealed that information or given her assignment with Camille to another knight. She didn't owe Camille anything, but she'd confessed as soon as she'd found out, and even as Camille admired her honesty, here she was, betraying it.

She hurried from the library. With her thoughts this chaotic, she couldn't rest. To her luck, none of the librarians saw her leaving, so she didn't have to answer any uncomfortable questions. With all the time she'd spent on Sydney, she was never going to get a good research assignment again. But that seemed the least of her problems.

As the bells tolled for midafternoon, Camille turned three corners, nearly jogged through the market in Kingston's grand square, then made another left into an alley and the door to a bookstore.

Camille passed under the large wooden sign and opened the narrow door. She slipped inside sideways, avoiding the stack of books that half blocked the entry. Hetty always took in more strays than she sold, and she'd run out of places to put them long ago. Luckily, her grandfather had bought this store instead of renting it, so Hetty only had to spend her money on food and any other items she might need for survival.

Not that Hetty paid attention to such mundane concerns.

Shelves crowded the shop from floor to ceiling, and books overflowed onto the floor, leaving little trails through the shop that looked like animal footpaths through a forest. "Hetty?" Camille called.

"In the back."

Camille sighed and began picking her way over and around stacks of books. Hetty was always in the back instead of up here trying to make some sense of this paper hoard. Camille feared that someday, she'd find Hetty buried under a leather-bound avalanche.

An old desk stood next to another doorway that led to the kitchen. Camille only knew it was a desk because she'd excavated it one day. Strangers would see a fort made out of books. Camille would have loved it as a child.

She pushed aside the curtain shielding the kitchen. Hetty sat at a table in front of a small, clear area. A teacup and book sat in front of her, and she looked up from reading as Camille came in. Hetty nodded sharply, and her glasses dropped from where they'd perched on her tightly curled gray hair. Her brown eyes seemed enormous behind the thick lenses, and she smiled widely.

"Camille. Twice in one week."

"Have you heard from the witch?"

Hetty put a finger to her lips before rising. She pushed past Camille and looked into the shop. "Not so loud. And don't use the W word."

"No one else is here, Hetty." Camille sat in a chair that only held one book, then stood as the pile on the table hid Hetty from view. "She's taking too long."

"I had to wait to contact the watchmaker so it looked normal, then he had to contact…you-know-who…and we have to wait until—"

"I'm tired of waiting. I'm tired of having to lie to my friend."

Hetty tilted her head and pursed her lips. "Your friend the *knight*."

"Don't start." She fought a jot of guilt.

"Since when are we friends with the knights? They're the reason the you-know-whos were all driven out to begin with."

"I know," Camille said, unable to stop a sigh of exasperation. Hetty had been a friend of Camille's mother and was also a distant cousin; she'd passed on her prejudices as well as a love of books.

"Sydney is different from other knights," Camille said. "She warned us in the first place, giving us time to warn the witch." She held up a hand before Hetty could protest. "I'm sorry. The *you-know-who*."

"Oh, she's *different*." Hetty scoffed.

"I'm not going to argue with you," Camille said. All the guilt and worry and waiting had built up in her until she felt as if she was going to burst. She clenched her fists and repressed the urge to shout. When Hetty rubbed her shoulders, Camille jumped, then relaxed a bit.

"My girl, you are *tense*," Hetty said.

"I should be," Camille said, closing her eyes. "I met a knight who made me question everything I know about the knights, then she told me a secret that *confirmed* everything I know about the knights. Except it makes her different, too. And now I'm keeping a secret from her and intentionally misleading her, and even though I know I shouldn't, I've been reading about battles with the Kells and freaking myself out."

"Nasty stuff."

"And they could destroy us whether the…you-know-who decides to help or not."

"She will," Hetty said. "Abe said she always helps when she's needed."

Camille stepped away so she could look Hetty in the eye. "Even when her own life is on the line?"

Hetty shrugged. "I don't know her, but Abe says she's fearless."

"If I was her, I'd be tempted to drop a few spells on the knights for even planning to betray me."

Hetty smiled. "They wouldn't be much use in fighting the Kells then."

"Well, now you know why I'm not a *you-know-who*."

Before Hetty could respond, a voice from beyond the curtain called, "Shop."

Hetty hurried out, and Camille peered out to see a small boy move nimbly around the piles of books to put a note in Hetty's hand. He waited until she dropped a coin in his palm, then he scampered out.

"You're in luck," Hetty said after she'd lifted up her glasses and read the note. "Abe has news."

Camille pushed the curtain aside so fast she nearly tore it down. "Well?"

Hetty grinned. "The you-know-who is going to contact the knights, one in particular." Her eyebrows shot up. "Your Sydney."

Camille's stomach shrank. She'd been certain the Hawk would contact Sir Robert, not Sydney. "Is she going to tell Sydney that I knew about her the whole time, that I've been lying?" Camille suddenly thought of Sydney feeling betrayed not only by Sir Robert but by Camille as well. Her stomach churned. She couldn't stand the idea of Sydney being beset on all sides by liars. If anyone was going to confess about what Camille knew, it should be her.

Camille pushed past, knocking over several stacks of books. She squeezed out the door, and as soon as her feet hit the pavement, she ran.

CHAPTER FIVE

Sydney dropped to her bed at the sound of the Hawk's voice coming from the crystal ball. Before she could even begin to ask questions, the Hawk said, "So, your leader, the bastion of honor and chivalry, plans to solicit my aid and then betray me. What's he thinking? Exile? Imprisonment? Death?"

Sydney's mouth worked, but no sound came out except a breathy, "How—"

"Exile would be tough," the voice said while the crystal ball whirled with smoke, showing nothing but a human outline and eyes that glowed green. "I'm already living outside Kingston, and there's nothing you can do to keep me out of Arnvild altogether." She snorted a laugh. "Unless you're going to employ a witch to cast a spell on me, but then you'll have to betray them with another witch and then on into infinity. So, it'll either be imprisonment or death."

Sydney took a deep breath. "I don't want to do either."

"Hmm, much as I hate to admit it, that does correspond with what I've heard about you."

"You've heard about me?"

After another of those jaded snorts, the haze in the ball cleared, revealing a woman who seemed much younger than anyone Sydney had pictured. They looked to be about the same age, in their early thirties. The Hawk had very fair skin, and her hair was a fascinating cascade of brown waves that reached past her shoulders with a streak of white at her right temple that was half-hidden by a barrette. Her eyes sparkled like emeralds, but her full lips drew Sydney's eyes. They looked so... kissable.

She'd never thought anything of the Hawk's would look kissable.

"Your Sir Robert has to know I'd be even harder to imprison than I would be to catch," the Hawk said. "He's going to order you to kill me."

Sydney wanted to deny it, but in her heart, she suspected the same thing, and it was against the knights' code to speak a lie. "I think he's going to blame the whole thing on me," she blurted. She shut her mouth hurriedly, wondering why she'd even admit anything to this witch. It couldn't just be the kissable lips. She'd often wondered if her pledge to tell the truth was more than a simple pledge, if it could be a geas of some sort, a spell compelling her, but she'd never tested it. She'd never been a liar, not even as a child. She could remember the one time she'd done it with perfect clarity. She'd been four and had lied about the amount of sweets she'd eaten; she'd been sick for days, both from the candy and the words.

And look what years of telling the truth had gotten her. She now blurted things out to any woman with kissable lips.

The Hawk stared with a considering expression. "That sounds about right. If the whole 'recruit then kill' scenario looks like it was your idea, his hands remain completely unstained."

"But he'd be telling a lie." Sydney stood and clenched the ball, feeling heartfire roaring within her. She calmed it before it could smash this ball like it had the other one.

The Hawk leaned close, eyes burning. "Are you in the chapterhouse?"

"What…yes."

"Are there other people in the chapterhouse?"

"I…yes. Why?"

"Then go against the knightly grain, display some common sense, and keep your bloody voice down." She said the last in a whispery sort of yell.

Sydney tried to duplicate her tone. "We can't lie, so he can't tell everyone this is my idea. There's your common sense."

The Hawk sighed. "You really are a child, aren't you?"

Sydney felt herself flush and breathed through it. Her heartfire was still too ready to burn. "We appear to be nearly the same age, madam."

With the lift of an eyebrow, the Hawk smiled. "Madam? Ah well, it's better than you simply spitting 'witch' at me. There are ways around lying, Major, or haven't you figured that out yet?"

"I have, *witch*. One simply doesn't speak."

"Oh," the Hawk said, voice rising and taking on a mocking air. "Is that what one does? One can also tell half truths and drop hints until those around one draw the conclusions one wants them to." After another sigh, her voice returned to normal. "He's been the leader of your order a long time. He'd find a way."

"But that's..." Sydney lowered her voice. "Completely dishonorable."

"Welcome to knighthood."

Now the heartfire really was burning. Sydney dropped the ball on her bed before flames engulfed her hand. She tried to recall all her training, but the lessons drowned in the crackle echoing through her skull.

The Hawk leaned forward again, peering up from Sydney's blankets. "Ooo. I've rarely gotten to see that in person. For destruction magic, it certainly is pretty."

"What?"

A pointing finger solidified out of the smoke. "Your magic flame."

Sydney's ire turned to confusion, then horror as she registered the Hawk's words. She shook her head, trying to drown out the whole conversation. She couldn't handle the idea that Sir Robert was dishonorable *and* that heartfire could be magic all in the same day. The Hawk didn't seem kissable anymore. She looked cruel, her lips cocked in a mocking smile and her eyes pitiless.

After a few deep breaths, Sydney calmed herself, and the fire dampened inside her. "Will you help the soldiers?"

"Yes," the Hawk said as she sat back. "To stop the Kells. And what will you do when the time comes to kill me?"

"I won't do it."

"Well, I want to believe you," the Hawk said with another sneer. "But I will have measures in place to protect myself. I suppose when the time comes, and you fail to kill me, you can always tell Sir Robert that you tried but couldn't get through my defenses."

"That would be a lie," Sydney said through her teeth.

"Just testing you." She snorted a laugh. "So, what will you do when he confronts you? Tell everyone his odious plan?"

Sydney drew herself up. "I will tell the truth if asked. It will be up to his conscience to decide what he shall do."

The Hawk chuckled, but it seemed sad. "Well, at least you're still the fool I thought you were. Welcome to knighthood, indeed." Before Sydney could retort, the Hawk said, "Tell Sir Robert to gather his troops in an uninhabited circle of land in two days' time. Somewhere clear of trees and as bare of fauna as you can make it. The closer he can get to his target, the better."

Sydney blinked and tried to swallow her ire enough to respond. "Good…that's good. He's already planning on marching because—"

"Don't care. I'll be in touch."

The view in the ball flickered and went out. Sydney blinked at it. Her anger surged, and she had to restrain herself from grabbing the ball and either engulfing it in heartfire or throwing it against the wall.

Camille was ready to throw a punch. She'd never done so before, but how hard could it be? She had her fist ready and was now trying to decide which part of the guard to hit.

"…can't let just anyone roam the chapterhouse," the guard was saying as he blocked the doors. His chin was square like a brick. That was out; Camille didn't want to break her hand.

"And all the knights are deep in preparations for an important mission and don't have time…"

Maybe a swift kick to the knee? Did knights have armored knees under their trousers? She should have paid closer attention to what Sydney wore instead of being so concerned with what was underneath all the clothing.

"I've been a guest of the knights before," Camille tried again, though she barely heard herself. The guard didn't have armored plates on his boots. If she stomped right on his instep… "I'm a master researcher working with Major Sydney Blakely." The guard kept droning, and Camille raised her foot.

"Camille?" Sydney stepped through the door behind the guard. "Thank the flame. I need to speak with you."

Camille froze, standing on one foot. Sydney's expression seemed relieved, maybe a little haggard, but it wasn't the rictus of betrayal Camille had been expecting. Sydney nodded at the guard, whose mouth shut with a snap upon her arrival. Sydney stepped outside, giving

Camille's raised leg a curious glance before she took Camille's elbow and steered her away.

Camille barely kept her balance. "What—"

"The Hawk contacted me," she whispered. She patted a bag slung over her shoulder as if its presence should mean something.

"She...did she?"

"Yes, though how she found out what Sir Robert was planning, I don't know."

And she truly seemed as if she didn't. From the stories Sydney told, she was a good tactician. She could even conceive of deception if her pirate story was accurate, but even with her experience and after Sir Robert's deviousness, she couldn't see that someone close to her might betray her. Camille's stomach turned over, and she was glad she didn't have a mirror handy. She couldn't face herself.

"Maybe Sir Robert decided to give her a sporting chance by warning her," Camille said.

If Sydney caught the sarcastic note, she didn't acknowledge it. Her face lit up as if that was the solution she was hoping for, then it darkened in the next second. "No, sorry, that doesn't make much sense because you see—"

"It was a joke, Sydney. A badly timed one. Where are we going?"

Sydney pulled up short on the side of the busy street. "I'm not certain, now that you ask. My head is spinning." She breathed deeply and put her hands on her hips. She wasn't stupid. She'd figure out what had happened, and Camille should make sure it was sooner rather than later. But when Sydney said they needed to speak in absolute privacy, Camille led her to the library again, to the basement and one of the storage rooms with a door.

"I never thought that a place where everyone can come for knowledge would be home to so many conspiracies," Camille said dully. She waved when Sydney's expression turned apologetic. "Never mind me. Sarcastic jokes are how I deal with stress."

Sydney nodded and opened her bag. When she pulled out a crystal ball, Camille gasped. She'd read about such witches' tools, but she'd never seen one. She took its weight in hand and peered into the depths but saw nothing save a distorted view out the other side. Excitement tingled through her, and she had so many questions about how it worked. When she opened her mouth to speak, Sydney put a finger to her lips. She took the ball, put it back in the bag, and then covered that with several odds and ends lying around the storeroom.

"I don't know how much she can hear without the other person knowing," Sydney said quietly.

"But aren't you just going to tell me what she already told you?"

Sydney's mouth shut, and she frowned at nothing before shaking her head. "The Hawk has agreed to help us. She wants the troops out in the open in two days' time so she can transport them, and she thinks Sir Robert will order me to kill her afterward, then tell everyone that was my plan all along." Her cheeks flushed, and she looked down. "The flame forgive me, I think he might do so, as dishonorable as that seems." She closed her eyes so tightly, the lids wrinkled, then she swallowed.

Camille put her arms around Sydney's shoulders and pulled her close, ready to hold her if she needed to weep. She wanted to admit that she'd been the one who leaked Sir Robert's plan, but she couldn't add to Sydney's misery. And she told herself it wasn't important right then; it was better that the Hawk knew the plan so Sydney wouldn't be forced to carry it out.

And she didn't *want* to tell.

"Don't go," Camille said. "Tell Sir Robert what to do. He'll move his troops and order you to come and carry out his plan, and then you simply don't go."

Sydney drew back. "Break my word?"

"Don't give your word. You said before he never listens. Just let him talk, don't respond, and don't go. Make him do his own dirty work. His plan against the Hawk won't succeed now that she knows about it."

"But that would be…" Sydney sat heavily on a wooden crate. She mumbled a few more words, and Camille caught, "Dereliction of duty."

"Sydney," Camille said, kneeling. "Do you really want to remain a knight and continue to follow Sir Robert after knowing what kind of man he is?"

Sydney's shoulders slumped so far she seemed as if she might fold in on herself.

Camille gave her a moment, then chuckled. "Unless you're going to wrest control from him."

"Yes." Sydney stood so quickly, Camille fell back with an *oof*. Sydney bent and lifted her to her feet as if it was an afterthought. "I know there are others who think as I do. Sir Robert may have lost his way, but that doesn't mean the order is lost."

"I didn't mean—"

Sydney began to pace, stroking her chin. "I can't do it right now. We're about to go to battle, and we'll need unity against the Kells, but after the fight is done? I'll refuse to kill the Hawk, go with my comrades to face the Kells, then stand up against Sir Robert when the day is won." She seemed again the confident, radiant woman Camille had first clapped eyes on in the chapterhouse.

Camille started to object, then thought better. Maybe Sydney could make the knights into a different organization. And after she'd accepted the Hawk's help, maybe she'd be open to the idea that magic couldn't be evil, not if the Knights of the Flame were willing to use it.

Maybe she'd even change the world and save magic.

With a sigh, Camille said, "How can I help?"

As Sydney helped pack crates in the armory, she wanted nothing more than to lose herself in the preparations to march on the Kells, but so far, all the sorting and celebratory drinking had been tainted by the fact that she was also planning an...uprising.

She hated that word. It was more like a cleansing, a restoration to the values she'd learned as an initiate and recruit.

By the flame, she could use all the pretty words she wanted, but nothing would make a rank betrayal of her core values sound any nicer. And no matter what she called it, nothing could be done before the march and the battle. Sir Robert was a good tactician and a better fighter. The order would need him for the fight. But afterward, Sydney would call him out honorably and make him answer for his crimes. He couldn't know that the Hawk was wise to his plan. When she appeared, Sydney would praise her for coming to their call. Anything Sir Robert did against her then would be a betrayal of that call, and the knights would see how far he'd fallen from the path of righteousness. When the battle was over, they'd remember.

Maybe her words would make him rethink his actions, and he would see the error of his ways and continue to lead the order as a paragon of virtue.

Sydney could only hope so.

After packing her gear, she'd begun helping the others. Many of the knights seemed reluctant to speak to her at first. She didn't sense animosity, just general discomfort which probably signaled that they didn't know what to say. One recruit finally admitted that rumors were flying about why Sir Robert had ordered her to stay rather than march. Some assumed she'd fallen out of favor and wanted to distance themselves from her; others thought she might be suffering from some embarrassing affliction and didn't want to force her to speak of it.

Sydney didn't want to ask what *affliction* rumor had diagnosed her with, so she told the truth. Sir Robert had ordered her to continue researching faster travel, and she was to catch up when she succeeded. But now she had succeeded, she added, and was coming along. All true, and if Sir Robert was going to leave her behind, he would have to command her in person.

And he'd had a chance. She'd reported to him after she'd spoken with Camille. He'd been writing on a sheaf of papers the entire time, and she'd had to fight the urge to demand he meet her eyes. She'd barely told him the Hawk's instructions before he'd rung the bell on his desk and said, "Very good, Major." Then his aide had opened the door with a humorless smile that meant, *Get out*, politely but firmly.

Sir Robert hadn't even asked how she'd found the Hawk and spoken to her. She'd left the crystal ball with Camille, but still, he might have inquired.

In the armory, as Sydney loaded another crate with arrows, she paused. Maybe Sir Robert suspected the Hawk of being able to listen in on his office, and he feared giving away his plan. Maybe she *could* listen all through the city of Kingston, and that was how she knew to contact Sydney.

A chilling thought. And a mad one. The Hawk wouldn't have let her pirate crew be taken if she knew of the knights' every plan.

But they'd been rescued.

"Major?" one of the initiates asked, shaking her out of her nerves. "Are you done with that crate?"

With a start, Sydney stepped back. "Yes, sorry. Done," she said with a smile.

"Thinking of the battle ahead?" he asked, a little green, no doubt more than a little scared. "Everyone is."

She clapped him on the shoulder and gave him her most winning, confident smile. "Not to worry, Johansson. Remember your training and stick close to the superior you're assigned to."

He breathed deep and smiled back. "I'm glad you're coming with us, Major."

She'd been hearing such words all day, and they felt good to her heart. She only hoped the faith of her fellow knights would remain when it came time to confront Sir Robert.

If any of them survived. The Kells stood between all of them and the future.

❖

Camille packed her clothing and provisions. She didn't know how far Sir Robert was going to go into the countryside before calling in the Hawk. Would she need something besides clothes and food? "Why am I doing this?" she mumbled. "I've never been camping, and I already hate it." After a sigh, she sat on the edge of her bed. "I don't need to go."

This was Sydney's fault with her hopeful eyes and her fight for a more honorable order and the fact that Sydney was more scared for her fellows than herself. It was hard to ignore someone who wanted to protect people's lives and their futures.

"No reason to let her turn you into a camp follower," Camille said. But with another sigh, she went back to her knapsack. She wasn't a camp follower. She was supposed to be the contact between Sir Robert and the Hawk; that was the tale she and Sydney had decided on, though Sydney hadn't liked the deception.

All the more reason to give it up and not go.

But still, she packed. She had clothing for four days and a jacket in case it got cold and an oilskin in case it rained and some food and water, though she'd mooch off the knights all she could. She grabbed a pot of face cream, a comb, and a wrap for her hair at night. Who knew if they'd have the chance for a bath. She stuffed in some soap just in case and some mint wash for her teeth.

"What else?"

How many books could she fit on top? One. She sighed again. She had to bring her journal. She'd made some notes about the Kells. She'd also recorded everything she'd seen and heard about Sir Robert's quest for magic in case Sydney needed information for her coup.

Sydney had wanted to tell Sir Robert about finding the crystal ball in her room, but Camille had convinced her to leave that part out.

Sydney had frowned hard, but Camille had said, "I'll do all the lying."

"That doesn't make it right." Sydney had stomped back to the chapterhouse but hadn't sent word about a different plan. Camille assumed she could show up at the chapterhouse at dawn, and Sir Robert would believe her story. If Sydney had confessed to him, she would have sent word.

Unless Sir Robert had thrown her in prison.

Camille picked up the crystal ball. She'd asked Sydney how she could help, and lying seemed like an easy way to do so, even if it pissed Sydney off. "How did I get so mixed up in this?" she said.

"You tell me," the ball replied.

Camille yelped and tossed it. It thumped on the carpet. Camille's heart pounded, and she drew her legs up in case the ball decided to grab her.

"Bugger," the ball said. "Could you give us some warning before you do that? For the love of magic, seeing the room spin gives me a headache."

Camille slid from the bed and scooted close. Inside the ball, mist swirled, barely revealing a shadowy, dark-haired form with bright green eyes. Camille started to ask who it was, then reminded herself that she was actually an intelligent person. "Hawk," she said softly. "How long have you been listening to me?"

"Long enough to hear you and your girlfriend planning a coup and then arguing and smooching. After that, I mostly heard rattling and things moving around in bags and such. Are you really a camp follower?"

Camille's questions blew away on a wave of irritation. "I am a master researcher, thank you very much."

"Just teasing, love." The Hawk chuckled. "I guessed your profession already." She held up a hand. "Don't worry. I'll go along with your plan. It doesn't matter to me, and I hate to see a fellow book lover in trouble, even if she does have terrible taste in women."

Camille's ears burned, and she didn't even know where to begin with her rebuttal. For some reason, "She's not my girlfriend," popped out of her mouth.

The Hawk stayed silent just long enough for Camille to want to start babbling explanations, then the Hawk said, "Forgive my assumption. All the kissing sounds threw me off."

"We're...close," Camille said, "but not...that close. Look, I don't have to explain myself to you or anyone."

"Well, I beg pardon. I was just as curious as you are as to why you're going to such trouble for your not-girlfriend whom you kiss because you're so close."

Camille took several deep breaths. Sydney had told her that the Hawk was exasperating. She hadn't expected to encounter it so quickly. "I'd like to point out that you're going to a lot of trouble, too, and you're not even getting one kiss."

The Hawk grinned, a flash of white teeth in the fog. "Too true. I guess we can both say we do what we do for the good of Arnvild."

Camille smiled back. If Sydney overthrew Sir Robert, that *would* be good for Arnvild, after all.

If the order survived the Kells.

"I'm worried about the knights," Camille said. "And everyone else if the Kells break through."

The Hawk nodded. "We're all worried, except for Sir Robert, of course, who only wants help moving his troops and wouldn't deign to ask my help for the fight."

"Maybe he couldn't stretch his warped principles that far," Camille said with a snort.

"Well, he's gonna *have* to warp them because I'm helping whether he likes it or not. Innocent people won't be shielded by his principles, no matter how widely he swings them around."

Camille laughed, liking the conviction in the Hawk's voice as well as her words, never mind the bitterness and sarcasm. "Why did you speak to me just now? Don't get me wrong, I'm happy to run down Sir Robert all day, but now that I know you can listen whenever you like, I'm going to hide this ball. You had to know I'd do that; you could have kept eavesdropping."

The Hawk shifted. "Well...you sounded sad, so I thought..."

Camille blinked, surprised and strangely pleased, but the ball went dark before she could respond. She set it down with a smile, then grabbed a blanket, rolled the ball inside, stuffed that in her pack, then chucked the whole thing under the bed.

❖

Rowena sat back from her crystal ball and frowned. Of all the aggravating people she'd been forced to speak to recently, for some reason, Camille was the worst. The question was, why?

She wasn't annoying like Rowena's Kingston contact, Abe, whose panicky nature irked her. She hated his breathless speech and general aura of doom. And Camille wasn't a hypocrite like Sydney, who continued to limp along under the delusion that the Knights of the Flame could be redeemed. Camille wasn't even irritating like the rescued pirates had been with their endless questions and general…in-person-ness.

No, Camille was aggravating because she was loyal to someone who didn't deserve it and because she cared about people she didn't know and had decided to put her own safety at risk for people who might put her in jail for associating with a witch. And according to Abe and his contact, Hetty, Camille had never been afraid to speak out in favor of witches and try to teach the knights that magic wasn't evil, which sounded like a head-meets-wall exercise Rowena could sympathize with.

So now, because of all those reasons, Rowena had come to admire Camille. *That* was aggravating.

Rowena covered her crystal ball, tired of spying. Camille was much prettier than Rowena expected of a bookworm, which she knew was shallow and clichéd and ironic. Something in Camille's voice had made Rowena think of her as older, but her first good look had revealed that they were probably close in age. Camille's clear, dark skin seemed to shine in the light, and her black hair looked gorgeous in its fall of curly splendor.

Rowena curled a lip. That was positively poetic. More aggravation.

Ember popped her head around the corner. Rowena had felt her proximity but had been too distracted to focus on her.

"What's this feeling?" Ember asked as she touched her chest. "Annoyed is one of them, but there's another."

"It's nothing." Their emotional connection was another aggravation she didn't need at the moment.

"It's more than nothing. Maybe it's anger. At the knights?"

That was another twist of the knife on Camille's part. Why would Camille even bother with Sydney? The knight was attractive, in a pretentious ass sort of way, but really, was that an excuse for so much kissing? Someone as smart and loyal as Camille deserved...

"Is it jealousy?" Ember said. "I remember from when I recovered so quickly after my fall, and you were jealous because it's harder for you to heal, and your knee still hurts during the rain from that accident when you were little."

Rowena felt the heat in her cheeks and fought the urge to snap and rage. "You didn't fall. You jumped."

Ember's arms snaked around her from behind. "Are you still jealous because you can't jump?"

Rowena barked a laugh. "I can, but the result wouldn't be the same." She gave Ember's hands a pat and moved out of the embrace. "I don't want to talk about my feelings. They're...stupid."

"You always say that, but talking is *all I can do*." Boredom rocketed down their connection.

"Ember, don't start."

"You're going to help the knights. I want to help, too."

Rowena took a deep breath and turned to find Ember the picture of petulance, complete with an out-thrust bottom lip. "Sending soldiers off to war is not a remedy for boredom. It's serious business."

"If I fight with them, I'll save some." She blinked prettily.

"And maybe lose your own life."

"I'm faster and stronger and tougher than any regular person."

"But still mortal."

Ember threw her hands in the air and paced along the room, pausing to smack the rough stone walls.

Rowena fought to remain calm under the force of two torrents of aggravation. "You'll get your chance to see the world when—"

"When witches are accepted again? When will that be?" An edge of whining crept into her voice.

"Do you think I'm dragging my bloody feet?" Rowena yelled, boiling over at last. "If we're lucky, my helping repel the Kells' invasion will convince more people to rethink bigotry and realize magic isn't evil. Or maybe it won't. Maybe I'll be hunted for the rest of my life, but that doesn't matter because you're *bored*."

Ember's eyes narrowed. She usually backed down before Rowena's anger, but of course, she'd choose this already frustrating day to find more spine. "You just want to keep me here because without me, you wouldn't have anyone," Ember said, anger bright as a star inside her.

True, but it still hurt. "I want to keep you safe."

"You wouldn't leave even if you could." Her accusing finger pointed as if she could read Rowena's mind as well as her heart. "You'll stay here forever and rot like an untended husk, and you want me to rot, too." With tears streaming down her cheeks, she fled.

"Ember," Rowena shouted, but she heard the exasperation in her voice along with the love, and she knew Ember would sense it and keep running.

Rowena sagged into a chair. Every rain brought a bloody big flood lately.

What *would* she do without Ember? It didn't bear thinking about. Before Ember, Rowena had been a heartbeat away from painting faces on the rocks and talking to them. Ember was supposed to be the perfect solution, someone who would understand her.

Rowena sighed. She should have seen this coming. She'd always been a rebel, too. And maybe she needed someone else. Maybe she should use the crystal balls more for conversation than just for spying or receiving updates from her contacts.

If she could find someone only a little less aggravating.

Ember ran until her chest filled with burning and her eyes settled down. She hated tears for robbing her of sight and making her nose run and her face ache. Why did they always come when they weren't wanted?

Another question, but whom did she have to ask now? Rowena had too much fear and anger these days, and Ember was tired of the way those emotions twisted the gut. Rowena wasn't even excited by new faces and voices and big magic. She never would be. She was never leaving this place.

And that meant Ember couldn't go, either.

As much as Ember burned to see an end to boredom, she couldn't abandon Rowena. Oh, Rowena would be sad, sad, sad, drowning in unwelcome tears. No matter her words, that was a truth. Rowena needed her.

Ember paused in the tunnels and watched a husk shuffle past with a broom, a moving dead thing. She'd never felt so like them.

But they couldn't change. She could. Better than the husks— maybe better than regular humans—she could change in unheard of ways.

She just needed…momentum.

And Rowena might cry and cry, but Ember would tell her they didn't have to part forever, just enough for a little change, then Ember would come back, or Rowena would come out, and the world would be much brighter, and more humans would be alive from Ember's helping, and everything would be a bloody, buggery rose garden, as Rowena said.

But could Ember stand the sadness, even for a little while? Rowena would share it with her, then Ember would be sad herself, and the unwanted tears would flow again and spoil her aim with her sword. More than that, Ember didn't want Rowena's sadness to even exist. She wasn't even sure she wanted happiness if it had to have sadness for a companion.

Well, there had to be a way around sadness, momentum to push past it. What had she said before? Rowena needed a friend, someone to help her through Ember's absence, someone she knew through the crystal ball; perhaps a new face that was pleasing to the eye.

Perhaps the knight or the librarian?

Chapter Six

For Sydney, it had been a *long* two days' march into nowhere. Per the Hawk's instructions, Sir Robert had chosen a vacant location for their departure and stayed away from the many villages surrounding Kingston as they marched.

Sydney hadn't minded camping or the long march. She'd been happy to have Camille along, though they weren't able to spend much time together. Camille had seemed irritated that she couldn't walk at Sydney's side, but as a major, Sydney had to circulate among the troops, making sure all was in order.

As time wore on, Camille had fallen back through the ranks until she was hurrying to keep up. She'd never been on a march, and it was clear that her boots weren't up to the task. The first night, Sydney had helped her treat and wrap her blisters before loaning her a pair of thicker socks.

"We'd better set up your tent before dark," Sydney had said as she laced Camille's boots.

Camille blinked. "I thought I'd stay with you." Her smile had been sweet and hopeful. "We've spent a lot of time wrapped in blankets together but never much time sleeping."

Sydney chuckled, fighting awkwardness. "I'd love to, but on a march, officers are on duty day and night. I might have to rise in darkness if there's cause."

Camille shrugged. "I can fall back asleep after you're gone."

"Um." Sydney felt heat in her cheeks and fought not to stammer. "I'd be the only officer with a...companion. It wouldn't be proper."

Camille's brows lifted. "Everyone would think I'm a camp follower, is that it?"

The heat blazed now. "No."

"Is that what everyone thinks? That I came all the way out here because I can't get enough of your body? Is that what you think?"

Sydney waved a hand to shush her. "I don't. Everyone knows you're here to talk to the witch, but if you stay in my tent..." When Camille's look threatened to melt her on the spot, she spoke faster. "Listen, I need respect right now, and there's already been a little snickering. I have...a reputation." Now her face was close to igniting as she thought of all the women she'd met on her missions, but she never *indulged* until the mission was over.

And the women didn't usually stick around to meet her comrades.

Camille's stare turned cold. "And now I'm just part of that *reputation*, am I? Did you ever think of telling people that it's none of their business?"

"That's not really...the officer to subordinate relationship..." Sydney sighed. "They just need to see me in a certain light."

Camille shook her head. "Playing politics already. You're going to fill Sir Robert's shoes well." She grabbed her bag and began to limp away.

"Where are you going?" Sydney asked, unable to keep the weariness out of her voice.

"Somewhere else."

"Stay with me tonight, and we can find you a tent tomorrow."

"Oh, no. Can't tarnish your reputation." She shuffled on without another word.

In the morning, Sydney discovered that Camille had slept under the wagons. She rode on one the next day and scribbled in a journal, avoiding eye contact. When they made camp at the site Sir Robert would use to transport his troops the next morning, Sydney commandeered a tent for Camille but sent one of the recruits to deliver it. It was the coward's way out, but Sydney hoped that by the time she'd returned from fighting the Kells, Camille would forgive her.

❖

Camille added sleeping under a wagon to the list of things she'd rather never do again. The weather was all right, especially with her oilskin covering her, but every creak, snore, rustle, or chirp had kept her awake all night. Even without the knights, the outdoors was alive with noise.

She wouldn't have been able to sleep anyway, not while feeling so unwanted, needy, and in the way.

She'd hoped to catch a bit of sleep while riding on the wagon the next day, but the driver seemed determined to find every rut in the road, and she was so nauseated by midday that she had to walk, her steps blearing into one afternoon of misery.

When the recruit led her to a tent that evening, she could have kissed him even as she sneered about cowardly Sydney not delivering the news herself. Camille had already written "spending any time with Sydney" on her list of things to never do again. She couldn't be a blight on Sydney's *reputation*.

"Why am I out here?" she mumbled once she was safely inside her tent. "Because Major Sydney Loose-Trousers got me into this whole mess." She leaned her head back. "I shouldn't have come."

Logically, she knew it was Sir Robert's fault, but she lumped him in with Sydney and the Kells under "People to Blame." The thought that she was being unfair flitted through her mind, but she buried it under anger and self-pity about her sore feet. She sighed, wrapped herself in her blanket, and tried to make a pillow out of her pack, but it proved as lumpy as last night. She took out some things since they couldn't roll or blow away indoors and paused when she touched the smooth side of the crystal ball.

She pulled it out, telling herself she simply craved conversation after not speaking all day. And she needed to let the Hawk know the troops had arrived at their destination and would be ready for transport in the morning.

It had nothing to do with a need for sympathy or the desire to complain. It wasn't that the tantalizing features she'd glimpsed in the swirling depths intrigued her or that she appreciated the way the Hawk had reacted to her sadness or any charming embarrassment the Hawk had displayed.

And it wasn't as if she'd been thinking of the Hawk all day, wondering what she looked like in person, wondering what it would be like to get to know her, or occasionally picturing her in Sydney's place during some of their lustful encounters.

Not *all* day.

"Ugh, what is wrong with you?" she asked herself. All the talk of Sydney's reputation led her to thinking of bit of her own. Well, her lack of reputation. She'd slept with her fair share of people, but she didn't share that knowledge often. Well, maybe with Hetty, but no one else. She didn't have many friends. Either Sydney overshared, or her lovers looked to spread stories.

Based on some of the things Sydney had said, women jumped on her all the time. Maybe that was the difference. People expected Camille to be shy—and she did get tongue-tied sometimes—but she usually made the first move in relationships. Maybe it was usually the "jumper" who talked.

Camille didn't see any need to share. She enjoyed her life all on her own; she found so many qualities intriguing in other people, so what was the harm in flirting if it might lead to some wonderful nights?

Because it might also lead her into the wilderness to sleep under a wagon.

She sighed again and reminded herself that she was helping. And she'd met one intriguing woman already on this adventure, even if Sydney was currently pissing her off.

And there was another intriguing woman to get to know, a powerful, mysterious witch who helped those who needed it even when it might cost her life or her freedom.

"Are you there?" Camille asked the ball. When she got no answer, she felt a bit of a fool for talking to an inanimate object but tried again. "Hello? Hawk?"

The ball swirled with mist before a voice said, "I'm here," and the same shrouded form appeared.

Camille smiled. "You sound breathless."

"I was in my workshop and ran to catch you before you gave up."

Camille smiled wider, then reminded herself that the Hawk only wanted to catch her because she'd have news of the knights. She cleared her throat and fought any musings about the wonders a witch's workshop might contain. "We've reached a large open area with no one else around. Sir Robert wants to leave from here."

The Hawk snorted. "I'll bet he's got it all worked out."

"I haven't heard anything about his plans regarding you," Camille said, nearly whispering.

"Don't worry. I'm not going to appear in person."

"Oh." Camille was surprised by how far her stomach sank. She'd been doing too much imagining. "I was looking forward to meeting you."

The Hawk said nothing, and Camille felt the need to babble rising within her. She held it back until the Hawk said, "In between the transport spell and Sir Robert trying to kill me?"

The words were sarcastic, but Camille laughed. "I guess I thought you'd appear, he'd try something, you'd thwart him, they'd vanish, and then…"

"Hugs and air kisses?"

"Something like that."

The Hawk ducked her head, and Camille wondered if she was fighting the urge to blush or maybe chuckling softly. "Speaking of what happens after the knights are gone, how do you plan to get home?"

Camille froze. She hadn't even considered that. "I'll…walk."

"Alone? For two days? Do you even remember the way?"

No, she didn't remember the blasted way. She'd been following everyone else. But surely this many people left tracks. And there was a road. But they'd passed other roads, going in other directions, and not all of them had helpful signposts. She wouldn't even have a wagon to sleep under.

"I didn't think about it," Camille said, dread sitting inside her like a weight.

"Perhaps you should've."

Camille frowned. "I'm not used to all this, thank you very much."

"I only meant—"

"There are some gaps in knowledge that only experience can correct."

"It's all—"

"And I was too busy thinking of the fate of the world." She breathed hard but forced herself to not hyperventilate.

"Finished?" the Hawk asked. When Camille didn't answer, she said, "Good. Just keep the ball with you. I have a map. I can guide you."

That was a small comfort, at least. "And if I get into trouble, you can whisk me away?"

"I want to make you feel better and say yes, but transferring matter—living or not—from one place to another takes a lot of preparation and power. I won't be able to do it again so soon after moving the knights."

The comforting feeling plummeted. "Oh."

"I can look up my closest contacts and ask them to meet you and make sure you're all right."

Camille smiled again. "Thank you. I realize you don't have to go to the trouble, but I'm glad you're willing."

The Hawk chuckled. "Well, a good, sympathetic contact is hard to find."

Yes, a contact. That's all they were to each other, and Camille knew she shouldn't romanticize it. The awkward silence felt warm with hopes dashed.

"Is that all?" the Hawk asked after a moment.

Camille sighed, trying to tell herself that the Hawk was a busy witch. Hadn't she just said that transportation spells took a lot of time and energy? And since they didn't know exactly what Sir Robert planned to do, the Hawk no doubt had other preparations to make.

"Yes," Camille said. "I'm looking forward to seeing what happens tomorrow."

"I'll try to make it entertaining." Still sarcastic, but her words also had a humorous edge.

"And I look forward to speaking to you again and to one day sharing hugs and air kisses," Camille said.

After a braying laugh with a huge snort following, the Hawk cut the contact. Camille laughed, too, delighted by the fact that the Hawk might have retreated because that snort was incredibly embarrassing.

Rowena sat back from the crystal ball even though she'd dismissed the image. She had a strange fear that Camille could still see her even though Rowena was the one with the power.

Where in the world had that snort come from? She'd sounded like a pig in heat. She rubbed her temples. Why did just speaking with Camille put her on edge?

And why did she offer to help Camille get home? That wasn't part of the plan, but worry had leaped into her mind. Then her annoyance at the lack of planning had faded in the face of Camille's anger. Seemed they both felt their lives were somewhat beyond their control at the moment. A familiar feeling and one she couldn't ignore in a…

Friend?

Since when did she care about making friends?

Since Ember had mentioned the buggery concept, of course.

Rowena nearly leaped out of her chair. Now wasn't the time for pondering. As she strode into the workroom, she felt Ember nearby. Ever since their argument, Ember had left her blessedly alone, though Rowena felt a little guilty now.

"Want to help?" she called.

Ember peeked around the door. Her hair was neatly combed, something she did only for important occasions. Rowena felt the anticipation running through her and winced. Ember had been hoping that Rowena would call for her? Guilt piled atop guilt.

"Here, take these feathers and put them at the four compass points," Rowena said.

Ember took the bag of feathers and the compass. Her tongue poked out of her mouth as she concentrated on placing a long feather on the floor's chalk circle, then consulted the compass again and moved the feather ever so slightly.

"Feathers because…" Rowena said.

"Creatures of the wind for movement," Ember said, not taking her eyes off her task.

Rowena beamed proudly. She consulted a book that lay on the table amidst a jumble of ingredients and reagents. It was an old book of spells she'd annotated over the years. The original version of the transport spell called for freshly killed birds at the compass points, but Rowena found that feathers worked just as well, and nothing had to die. Her way required more energy from her and therefore a longer recovery time, but her energy replenished itself. The birds couldn't spontaneously resurrect after a few days.

Not that they appreciated it. She'd had to putty quite a few bird bites in the husks sent to collect discarded feathers from the mountain-dwelling raptors.

"Ungrateful buggers," Rowena muttered as she set candles between the symbols drawn inside the circle.

"Flame for its speed," Ember said. "I don't remember why we need ungrateful buggers." Her grin said she was joking, but it wasn't so long ago that she would have been serious.

"You've come a long way," Rowena said, fighting the desire to get emotional. Too many bloody things were happening. "You could start practicing on your own if you wanted."

Ember shook her head emphatically. "Too much sitting."

Rowena chuckled. Learning how to meditate and harness one's life energy did require too much sitting. That was probably the real reason the knights hated creation magic. Turning one's negative emotions into destruction magic was so much easier.

But it was still magic.

They worked for hours to complete the preparations. Transportation spells were difficult. The fact that she had to move so many living somethings—and have them remain alive—added to the difficulty tenfold.

And if it went wrong, they could all get scattered to the ends of the world or wind up inside it.

No pressure.

Thankfully, she'd cast this spell before, though there were more knights than there'd been pirates, and she wasn't bringing the knights here. One of her contacts near the border had scouted a desolate arrival location.

The spell would be so much easier if she were standing at the sending or receiving end, but she couldn't get in reach of Sir Robert, the bastard. So, she had to add diamond dust to the circle for permanence, and there went the money she'd been saving for a new stove. She needed copious amounts of limestone and red clay, the former being the most common stone found at the starting place close to Kingston, and the latter covering the end point. The rock would help ground the spell and keep the knights from being flung to the four corners, but she'd had to repurpose nearly every husk to gather and grind it up. She tiptoed among the piles of grit as she made her final check.

Now all it needed was her energy. Rowena yawned and stretched. Everything was fresh and should remain intact for a few hours while she—

A chime came from the other room. Someone was handling one of her crystal balls.

"Bugger, bugger, bugger," she said as she stomped in that direction.

"You could ignore it and get some sleep," Ember said.

"Ha. Since when?" She suspected who it would be as she concentrated. Sir Robert was trying to catch her on the hop.

"Hawk? Are you there?" Camille's voice.

"It's not even dawn," Rowena said as she cleared the picture. Camille's face was lit by a candle, which brought out her rounded cheeks and made her dark eyes flicker orange.

Camille yawned, making Rowena copy her. "Sir Robert wants to arrive at the border *before* dawn, so he wants to leave now."

"Of course, he bloody does." Rowena sighed. She'd pulled plenty of all-nighters ending in spellcasting. What was one more? Thwarting Sir Robert's plans to kill her would at least give her sweet dreams later.

"He wants to know when you're getting here," Camille said with a smirk.

Rowena grinned. "Tell him soon, then have everyone who's traveling pack themselves together as tightly as possible, a real squeeze." She smiled wider. "Tell them to get as close as they would if chained below decks on a ship."

Camille laughed, a sweet sound that begged to be heard again. "Okay."

Rowena cut the line, went to the workroom, and sat on the floor at the northern point of the circle. At a light touch on her back, she turned.

Ember laid several pillows behind her. "In case you fall back afterward and just want to sleep." The connection hummed with affection and concern and a hint of Ember's guilt, no doubt from their spat.

Rowena squeezed her hand. "Thank you." She faced the circle again and began her mental exercises, preparing to pull a bugger-load of energy out of herself, not for the bigoted egomaniac and his knights but for the lives they'd hopefully save.

Sydney's heart wanted to pound out of her chest. She'd gone into battle many times and was used to the dry mouth and the sound of her pulse in her ears, but this was different. She was about to participate in *magic*. On *purpose*.

And Sir Robert expected her to clap the Hawk in irons as soon as she finished the spell. He'd even had his aide deliver a set of manacles to Sydney, and though he stood calmly at the head of their mashed-together company, she caught the occasional glance from the corner of his eyes.

The knights behind her shifted uneasily, and she was glad she stood near the outside of the mass. They stood in a large, open field of grass and little else. As instructed, the knights had tried to take up as little space as possible, and they couldn't stay this way for long.

The Hawk was probably waiting at the border, and Sydney was supposed to leap on her right after the knights appeared. The Hawk would resist, and Sir Robert would expect Sydney to kill the person responsible for making sure the knights were able to defend their people. If Camille was right, he'd act mortified and denounce Sydney's actions. He would *lie*, though she didn't know how he'd manage it. Maybe he planned to have Sydney taken prisoner before she had a chance to accuse him. Camille had said he probably wanted to get rid of a too-honorable knight and rid himself of a dangerous witch in one go.

And rob the other knights of a fellow warrior just when they needed all the help they could get.

But what made him think he needed to get rid of Sydney in the first place? Did other officers suspect his dishonor? Had he committed other uncharitable acts? Maybe when his plan failed and she spoke out against him, a chorus of voices would agree.

No doubt the Hawk would be one of them. When Sydney made no move against her, Sir Robert would have to call for her death and reveal himself to be the kind of man who'd use someone and then kill them. Maybe he even hoped she would appear here to cast the spell, and he'd have Sydney attack her then.

Before she helped them? What good would that do?

Sydney swallowed, her throat so dry the movement hurt. Yes, she was more than a little nervous. There were just too many unanswered questions.

Camille stood off to the side of the squashed column, a lantern at her feet. Sydney smiled, sorry about the harsh words between them, about her worry for her reputation, and for having dragged Camille into all this in the first place. She hoped her look conveyed the apology she'd make on her return.

After a moment, Camille returned the smile, and it seemed a little apologetic, too. She was such a good person; she'd sulked the night before, but they were all stressed. When Sydney got home, she'd try harder to be whatever Camille wanted, and maybe Camille could look past the physical side of things and see…

What? Who Sydney really was? Besides a knight planning a coup against the leader she'd pledged her life to. Sydney didn't even want to date herself at the moment.

She gasped as pain built in her temples, and her head throbbed as if she'd jumped in the ocean and sank too quickly. She could no longer hear her fellow knights, the snorting horses, or the creak of the wagons in the back.

The spell? She glanced around the empty field. The Hawk hadn't appeared. Maybe at the back? Sydney pushed through her pain and stood on tiptoe but couldn't see past everyone else. She looked to Sir Robert.

He stared at her, his gaze triumphant.

She tried to speak but couldn't. Sir Robert pulled something from his pocket and tossed it in her direction. Without thinking, she lifted her hands to catch.

Rowena gasped. The spell had been going well, the energy flowing from her seamlessly, though it made her feel as if her lifeblood was leaking. She felt a small tug as if the spell was trying to move her, too, but that was normal. She just had to redirect that pull…

She yelped as the spell resisted, and she moved inches toward the circle, yanked by a powerful force. The circle glowed, the candles flaring. The pages of her books fluttered in an impossible breeze.

"What's happening?" Ember yelled.

A howl built around them, echoing through the cavern, a moan building to a shriek.

"I don't know." Rowena redoubled her efforts, trying to focus the power that now wanted to rush from her and take her body along with it. She felt the knights begin to shift through space, but something was drawing her *with* them. She resisted, holding them in place, but now that the spell had begun, it wanted to finish. Spells in progress couldn't be stopped by the caster. They took on a life of their own, especially the complicated ones. It was up to the witch to hold them to their purpose.

Even when it felt as if they were tearing her in half.

She closed her eyes and fought her rising panic. "Breathe, idiot, breathe," she mumbled. She heard the voice of her old teacher in her ear. "You control the magic, not the other way around. It wants order; it wants to be directed."

But now the magic felt as if it bloody well wanted her dead.

No, not dead, just moved. Last time she'd cast this spell, it hadn't fought so hard. Maybe this was because she wasn't at the departure or arrival end? No, that shouldn't matter when she was using the right materials.

She was still holding the knights, knowing that if she sent them, she'd go with them, but she couldn't hold them forever. She'd eventually appear in their midst, drained and weakened, and then Sir Robert would...

Rowena's eyes snapped open. Sir Robert had to know she wouldn't give up without a fight, even if she was weak. He was an ignorant man, but that didn't mean he was stupid. He'd planned something to make her show herself.

On the other side of the circle, a person-shaped shimmer hovered in midair. Ember gaped at it. Rowena cursed. Someone was coming through, and Ember stood too close to the circle, close enough to be caught in the spell, and as she stared, she seemed confused and almost...happy.

"Ember, get back. Someone's going to appear, and it might be a knight."

How was Sir Robert doing any of this?

The answer came to her in her teacher's voice again, a witchstone.

The bane of all magic, some witchstones drained a witch's power and held them to one spot. Apparently, others could draw a witch to them. The person fighting to appear was no doubt the knight holding the stone, though it wouldn't be cowardly Sir Robert himself. Rowena would either have to go to the knights, or the knights would come to her.

She had to get away from the circle, but as she tried to lean back, her body felt like solid lead. The witchstone pulled her forward, trying to push her into the circle to become part of the spell.

Rowena snarled. She clamped down on the energy leaving her body, wrestling with it to obey her and not the stone. She would not be moved, and she would not let this knight appear. Since she couldn't stop the spell, she would complete it on her terms.

Or she'd die trying.

Rowena cried out as the witchstone fought her, twisting the magic. The spell didn't care how it was being used as long as it was completed. She felt herself slipping.

"Ember," she cried, "they're using a witchstone. If a knight appears, stop them."

Ember chewed her lip. She'd wanted a friend for Rowena, and when she'd seen the silhouette, she'd rejoiced. Here was a friend appearing from thin air.

But now Rowena was in pain. The magic wasn't acting like it was supposed to, and Ember had to do something, but what? She'd planned to jump in the circle and move with the knights, but Rowena was straining away from the circle as it was pulling *her*, and *she* couldn't go. The knights would kill her.

When she cried out for Ember to stop the knight trying to appear, Ember made up her mind. Rowena didn't want a knight as a companion, she still wanted to move the knights, and she didn't want to go with them. So, someone besides a knight had to appear here, the knights had to move, and someone else would have to go in Rowena's place.

Ember grinned. Easy peasy.

She'd have to act fast.

Simple. She'd been born fast.

Ember backed up a few steps to Rowena's side and leaped, shoving Rowena out of the way. She felt the spell pulling at her and gave herself up to it.

Camille shook the crystal ball. "Hawk, what's happening?"

Still no answer. Most of the knights were on their knees, some shrieking, others holding their heads. Even Sir Robert was doubled over in pain, so if this was his doing, he hadn't thought it through.

Sydney stood unfazed at the edge of the press, holding a stone to her chest and gaping at those around her. Like the rest of the knights, she stood engulfed in a shimmery haze that roared like a living thing.

"Sydney," Camille shouted, stepping closer. "Are you all right?"

Sydney looked as mystified as Camille felt. Her lips moved, but Camille couldn't hear her. She stepped closer. "What?"

With a pop like a cork leaving a bottle, a woman appeared in front of the column. Even though Camille had never gotten a good look, this couldn't be the Hawk. Her dusky red hair was too short, and a long scar bisected her face. She looked at Camille, then at Sydney. The knights were growing dimmer now, though they appeared to be in less pain. Sir Robert pointed at the redhead and shouted something.

The redhead darted forward, snatched the stone from Sydney's hand and leaped for Camille. Camille cried out as the redhead grabbed her arm, slapped the stone into her palm, and yanked her toward the knights.

The air lurched. Camille's stomach turned sideways, and the ground fell away from her feet. The light dimmed, and Sydney faded as she called Camille's name.

For a moment, all was darkness.

With a snap, reality came back, but Camille staggered across a stone floor in a room lit by candles. From across a large chalk circle, a woman stared at her with wide green eyes.

"What..." Camille gasped for breath and put a hand to her chest, but she wasn't hurt. The knights and the redhead were gone. Camille dropped the stone and watched it roll into the circle, scattering a pile of dirt. "You're the Hawk."

The Hawk gaped at her before saying, "Ember." Her eyelids fluttered, and she fell back onto a pile of cushions.

Chapter Seven

Sydney turned in one full circle, then another. She stood in a field of purple heather, and craggy hills rose in the distance. The lush forests and fields of long grass near Kingston had disappeared, replaced by land that seemed barren and inhospitable.

And lacking any comrades.

The slim, wiry redhead who'd appeared out of nowhere stood a few paces away. She grinned as if the two of them were on an adventure. "I'm—"

Sydney drew her sword and lunged. "What have you done with Camille?"

The redhead drew a short sword and parried. She didn't lose her smile. "The librarian?"

"Yes." Sydney thrust twice more, but her strikes were easily blocked.

"She's with Rowena."

"Who the dash is Rowena?" She pushed, but the woman's defense was like a brick wall. She hadn't yet returned a strike and seemed to be having a fine old time. Heartfire flickered at Sydney's core, but she kept it banked for now.

"You call her the Hawk."

Sydney stumbled, and her anger tipped over into confusion. "The... What? How?"

The woman blinked slowly. "Do you mean, why is she called the Hawk? I'm not sure. It might have to do with the birds that live on the mountain. Many are hawks, I think, though some are eagles. I'm not certain which is which as they won't let me get close. I've been pecked before, and it's a terrible pain because they don't just bite or make a little hole with their beaks. They rip out a chunk of flesh."

Sydney gawked and tried to make sense of the flood of words. Why were they talking about birds? Her sword tipped toward the ground. "What?"

The redhead rested her sword on her shoulder and looked skyward as if thinking. "Or it might be because she acts quickly, like a swooping bird that's trying to rake with its talons, which isn't fun either, or so I gather. I've seen them cut a husk down to the bone." Her gaze fixed on Sydney again. "What's your name? Rowena usually calls you 'the knight,' or more accurately, 'the bloody, buggery knight,' or sometimes just one or the other, but lots of things are bloody or buggery to Rowena."

Sydney glanced around again, wondering when her comrades would come out of hiding and tell her this was all a prank, and she wasn't standing alone in the wilderness with a madwoman. "I'm..." She knew this one. "Sydney. Major Sydney Blakely."

"I'm Ember. You won't have heard of me because Rowena never mentions me to the people she talks to in her crystal balls, but I live in the mountain with Rowena, and you're probably wondering why I'm here. It's because I was bored, and I wanted an adventure, but I didn't want Rowena to be alone, so I decided she needed some company, and it was either going to be you or the librarian, but I thought she might kill you, so when I knew there was a witchstone involved, and the spell was going wrong, I took Rowena's place and gave the witchstone to the librarian, and here I am." She took a breath. A good thing, too, as her brown skin had begun to pale, and she'd started to list to the side, no doubt from a lack of oxygen.

Sydney felt as if she'd stumbled into a land where nothing made sense. Maybe the spell had scrambled her brain. "The spell..." she muttered. When she'd been standing with the knights, the air around them had grown hazy, and she knew they were being transported. Then Sir Robert had thrown a rock at her, and the rest of the knights had howled in pain. She replayed Ember's words, those she'd managed to catch. "A witchstone?"

Ember huffed. "Can we talk while we walk because I've never been out of the mountain before, and I want to look at everything."

Sydney glanced around again. She didn't see any "everything" to look at. Ember began a sidle away, beckoning for Sydney to follow. Maybe her onslaught of words was designed to confuse her enemies and make them easier to kill, but she could have attacked Sydney a hundred times by now.

"Where are we?" Sydney shouted, anger taking over again.

"Don't you know? You live out here. Well, out here somewhere. You don't live in a mountain, I know that." Ember glanced around. "Well, that's a different mountain over there, a scruffy one, like it hasn't been tidied, and that's a hill." She squinted. "Over there is a bush or a very small tree—"

"I know what the terrain looks like. I have eyes. Where did the Hawk send us? And why did she send you? And where the fuck is Camille?" She breathed hard and told herself to calm down. There was no need to go shouting swears like a degenerate.

Ember's face lit up. "I can tell you're going to be fun. Do you want me to tell the story about the spell again? Maybe while we walk? I don't know the name of the place we are, but if we start walking, we're certain to find something interesting."

"I need to find the knights or Camille or...someone."

"You found me." She flashed her fantastic smile again.

Sydney sheathed her sword and rubbed the bridge of her nose. A headache snaked through her temples and down the back of her neck.

"Are you hurt?" Ember said, her voice soft as if speaking to a wounded animal. "I don't know how to tell since we're not connected like Rowena and me, but I think you're hurt. I have a bandage." She paused and touched her own chest. "Now that I say it, I don't feel her anymore. I must be too far away." She frowned at nothing as if pained by the words.

Sydney was about to snap at her, asking how a bandage could possibly help, but the pain on Ember's face stopped her even if she didn't know what was going on. "No, thank you, I don't need a bandage. I'd like to find the people I was with."

Ember chewed her lip and looked around again. She brightened again as she pointed to a dark smudge on the distant horizon. "That might be the mountain where I live with Rowena. I saw it once in a ball behind one of Rowena's contacts who lives near Arnvild's northern border."

Hope sprang in Sydney's chest. "So, if that's her mountain, we must be near the border, closer to the Kells." And it could be that she'd just discovered the Hawk's location, but she couldn't worry about that now. "Do you know where the other knights went?"

Ember shook her head and put on a sly look. "But we might find them...with walking."

"Why aren't we with them now? We were standing together for the spell."

"Magic stuff," Ember said with a sage nod. "The spell went wrong somehow. Probably because of the witchstone. Maybe they're nearby. Maybe they're back where they were. Maybe...they're walking."

"All right, all right." Sydney took her first calm look at Ember, noting her athletic body, bright eyes, and the scar running across her face that didn't detract from her wide-eyed beauty. "Why do you want me to go anywhere with you? The knights and the Hawk aren't friends."

Ember snorted loudly. "I *know*, but you seem interesting, and you're the only one here. And Rowena doesn't make friends easily, but I think I might if I try. I liked the pirates, and I think some of them liked me, but they didn't talk about their feelings much, and I wondered if that was the way of pirates or if lots of people don't talk about their feelings or..."

Ember chattered on as Sydney fell in step. What in the seven bells was she doing going along with this mystery woman? She should be trying to find Sir Robert, the knights, or Camille. With everything she'd heard, she didn't think the Hawk would actually hurt Camille, but Sydney couldn't just abandon her to possible danger, and who knew what peril the knights had found.

But she didn't see any knights or peril, and that left one direction, the lair of the Hawk.

If Ember was even right.

If they didn't run into the Kells first.

❖

Rowena's head pounded, and her mouth was as dry as sand. She licked her lips, but it felt like kissing parchment. She pushed up on her elbows and blinked at her workroom. She must have passed out after the spell. A good thing Ember had put down the cushions, and she'd covered Rowena with a blanket, too, but—

"Ember," Rowena croaked, her memory coming back in a rush. She struggled upright, her body feeling like stone. She felt for Ember with her magic but couldn't sense their tie. With a force of will, she pressed down the urge to sob as a tide of loneliness rushed through her. Now was not the time to give in to her stupid emotions. First, she would find Ember.

Her stomach rumbled and whined, and she cursed the fact that mammoth spellcasting left her both ravenous and nauseated.

But this one hadn't gone as planned. Someone had used a witchstone, then a knight had almost appeared in her home, and Ember had shoved her out of the way and disappeared.

Rowena stopped as she reached her study. Ember had disappeared. So, where had the blanket come from? The husks weren't capable of such altruism without a command.

A small noise came from the door. Rowena thought through all her spells. Some offensive casting didn't require many reagents, but she was barely on her feet, using the walls to move. She had no more energy to give.

An intruder might not know that.

Still, best to have a backup plan.

She scooped up a tall candlestick and held it upside down behind her back as she shuffled closer to the doorway. She worked her mouth to build up a bit of saliva, then called, "Show yourself or be destroyed."

A head poked around the corner. Rowena would have known those rounded cheeks, dark eyes and skin, and curly black hair anywhere, even though they hadn't seen each other in person. Camille. Rowena tried to keep her shock from showing as Camille's face brightened into a glowing smile.

"Hawk, you're awake. I was so worried." She stepped into the room, arms out as if ready for a hug before she hesitated and cleared her throat, looking down. "I'm Camille, but you already knew that." She chuckled, a sound more embarrassed than amused. "I just said it because we've never formally met, like you said, and..."

Rowena couldn't respond, trying to think how this could have possibly happened. Beautiful women didn't appear in her home every day.

Or any day.

"Um," Camille said, shifting as if desperate to fill in the silence. "Sorry I had to leave you on the floor. I couldn't find anyone to help put you in bed. I got a blanket out of the first bedroom I found. I hope that's all right."

"Fine," Rowena said breathlessly. No other words appeared no matter how desperately she searched for them. Why was it so much easier to speak to someone through the crystal ball than in person? She tried to think of what to say, a hello or a welcome or a what the bollocks are you doing here, but nothing came to mind. Camille's face was honest as well as lovely, and for some reason, that made her harder to talk to.

Rowena heard a muted pop behind her, then a small thump. The candle that had fallen from its upside-down holder rolled past her foot.

Camille gave it a glance. "So, anyway...hello." She shifted awkwardly. "Is your name really Hawk, or—"

Rowena found some words at last, anything to cover her awkwardness. "It's Rowena. Why are you here?"

"I have...no idea." Camille's smile appeared again, but it slipped as if she was nervous. "I was with the knights. They seemed to be disappearing, then they were in a lot of pain, then this redheaded woman appeared, took a rock from Sydney, threw it to me, and the next thing I knew, I was here."

Rowena's confusion gave way to irritation. Oh yes, she hadn't forgotten the bloody witchstone. "The rock, where is it?"

"I left it in there."

Rowena turned back toward her workshop, following the line of Camille's pointing finger. She found the out-of-place stone and lurched toward it, her body screaming at her to sit down and rest or better yet, lie down on a giant sandwich and eat her fill before drifting into exhausted sleep.

She didn't touch the stone but poked it with a pencil. If it was a witchstone, it would remain inert until a spell was cast, but she didn't want to take any chances. There was no way to stop a spell once it had been cast, but a witchstone could disrupt the flow of magic, creating unpredictable results. Some witchstones could also hold the spellcaster in place while the spell was disrupted. But this one had seemed to pull

Rowena toward it and pull itself toward her. It had taken Ember and given her Camille, but how?

"Where are we, anyway?" Camille asked from the door.

"My home in Mt. Plaedies," Rowena mumbled. She put a hand to her forehead. She had no idea where Ember or the knights were. They could be at the northern border where they'd been headed; they could be at the field where they'd started; they could be at the bottom of the buggery ocean.

Ember might be fighting for her life.

And Rowena didn't have enough life force to bring her back, wouldn't have enough for a few days, maybe even longer with how the witchstone-plagued spell had drained her. She rubbed at that ache in her chest again.

Camille was saying something about caves being cold and dark.

Rowena's temper flared. "If you don't like it, leave." She turned a glare in Camille's direction, expecting to see hurt or tears or a hasty retreat.

But Camille had her hands on her hips and her own glare in place. "I was complimenting how you managed to make a cave so welcoming and not cold and dark like I expected, but you clearly weren't listening."

"Oh, excuse me if I'm a bit preoccupied at the moment, trying to figure out what darling Sir Robert did with my...friend." She'd been about to say homunculus, but Camille surely wouldn't know what that was. "And your bloody knight."

"And you'll be able to figure it out by shouting at me?"

Rowena slashed a hand through the air and turned back to the witchstone.

Camille sighed loudly. "All right, let's not get testy. Tell me what I can do to help."

"Are you a witch? No? Then you can't possibly help me figure this bloody mess out."

"No, I'm a master researcher. I figure out bloody messes for a living."

Rowena snorted a laugh. "Not magical ones, I'd wager."

"I'll never know if I don't try."

Rowena turned again, trying her best glower. She drew herself up as tall as she could, turning the complaints in her joints into an all-out bitch fest. "I am the most powerful witch in Arnvild, and I will not be thwarted for long. If you're smart, you'll stay out of my way."

Her stomach chose that moment to make another loud declaration, dispelling her aura of menace like a gale force wind.

Camille smirked. "Why don't I find the kitchen and make some breakfast? If that's okay with the most powerful witch in Arnvild?"

Rowena turned away, cheeks burning. "That's fine, thanks," she muttered. Oh yes, this research was off to a fabulous start.

❖

Ember knew about sex. She'd read about it at first. And Rowena had told her about it while blushing like mad and including lots of swears. Plus, some visitors to the mountain had offered to share their knowledge physically, and that had been very nice indeed.

Sex had been one of the things she'd been looking forward to during her adventure out in the world, and looking at Sydney definitely encouraged sex thoughts in Ember's brain.

Sydney was lean and muscled. She was quick and tall and tan, and though her face had been scowling since they'd met, her features were pleasingly symmetrical, with a strong chin and large, bright blue eyes. Her hair reflected the sun like a jewel.

But more importantly, she knew things, though she seemed reluctant to speak about any of them. She was a puzzle who'd lived her whole life outside of Mt. Plaedies, and that meant she'd had a great many adventures and seen many things and heard different things, and Ember wanted to know each and every one of them.

As they walked, Ember fought the urge to stare, remembering that it was rude, but she never minded anyone staring at her. How else was she supposed to remember what a person looked like if she couldn't *look*?

"Where have you lived?" Ember asked.

Sydney stopped scanning the countryside to blink at her. "What?"

"I lived in the mountain with Rowena, and you lived..." Sydney needed a lot of prompting, but Ember didn't mind. Maybe no one ever asked her questions.

"Why?"

Ember blinked now, mystified. "Why what?"

"Why do you care where I've lived? Why does it matter?"

She might as well have asked why Ember kept breathing or why there was something instead of nothing. "Because…I want to know."

"I gathered that," Sydney said slowly. "*Why* do you want to know?"

"Because I want to know everything about you."

"Again, why?" She seemed genuinely confused and more than a little upset.

She wasn't the only one. No one had ever asked Ember such questions. Rowena put her off at times, claiming that too many questions gave her a headache, but she'd never wanted to know *why* Ember was asking. Ember sighed, missing her connection to Rowena. She'd never considered the fact that distance might weaken it. She'd never noticed until now how much she depended on it to help her understand their conversations. With Sydney, with anyone else, she'd have to explain everything.

Oh, well. It seemed a small price.

"I want to know everything," Ember said slowly. "Everything in the world. The mountain was small. Nice but small, and it only had so much information. Now I'm out here, and I want to know everything, and you're here, and you're fascinating, so I thought I'd start with you."

"I'm fascinating?"

"Quite."

"Huh." Sydney seemed thoughtful. "Well, Ember who appeared out of nowhere and spent her entire life in a mountain, I think you're more fascinating than I am."

Ember grinned, feeling nice. "You can ask me any questions you want, and then I can ask you questions, and we'll be fascinating together."

Sydney still seemed confused, but she had a small smile, and that was a good sign. "I live in the knight's chapterhouse in Kingston. Before that, I lived on a farm with my family in Sheffordshire."

"What's a chapterhouse like? What's Kingston like? What was being on a farm like? How many in your family? What do they look like?"

Sydney put up her hands as if warding off an attack. "Whoa. One at a time." She began descriptions, and they all had words that needed further defining, and it sounded wonderful and magical and otherworldly. With a little prompting, Sydney expounded beyond physical descriptions and into what certain surroundings or events made her feel until Ember could picture herself in those places, surrounded by those people.

"You've never been out of the mountain before?" Sydney asked.

"Well, I've been outside the mountain on the slope but never far. Rowena says I'm not ready, that there's too much I don't understand, and that lack of understanding can get me killed, but I know how to fight, and I know how to run away, so I still don't see what the problem is. And now I'm out here finally, and it's not nearly as bad as Rowena feared."

"Are you Rowena's daughter? Were you born in the mountain?"

Ember cocked her head. "I guess you could say I'm her daughter in that she made me, but since I carry part of her life force, you could say I'm actually part of her, but that all sounds a lot like philosophy, which I've never been very good at. I guess you could say it's also magic, which I've done some of, but I wasn't very good at that, either. I was born there, but I didn't come out of anyone like human babies do, which sounds very messy and painful, and if I'd come out of someone like I am now, I think that someone would have exploded because I've never been smaller than this—"

She noticed that Sydney had stopped some paces back. "You're not...human?" Sydney asked. Her hand wandered to her sword grip again.

"Well, I look human, and I have all the requisite human parts, so I guess you could use philosophy again to say that I'm human even though I've always been this size, and I didn't come out of anyone." She pointed to Sydney's hand. "Do you want to spar some more?"

Sydney froze as if just realizing what her hand had been doing. "I..." She licked her lips. "If you're not human, what are you? There are no more, um, sentient non-humans. They were magical and were destroyed long ago."

"You think I'm magical?" Ember was delighted. She'd read about dragons and fairies and whatnot. She loved those stories and had wept when Rowena told her the creatures were no more. "Magic creatures were all so wonderful and powerful. I guess it's nice you think I'm wonderful, but I don't have any special magical abilities. I can fight well, and I'm a little tougher and faster than other people, regular humans, if you want to think of them that way. Rowena said I'm a homunculus, which is very hard to spell, so I don't use it that often. It's really just a person who's built instead of being born, though both kinds of person started from nothing and became something. It's just that Rowena built me with her hands, where other people are built on the inside of a person...somehow." The books she'd read were unclear on exactly how that worked.

Sydney was frowning hard. Maybe the fact of the matter was that she was "a little slow," as Rowena said. Some of those who'd come to visit the mountain fit that bill. Sydney didn't seem slow, though. She'd been very fast when they'd fought.

Maybe she was just slow on the inside.

"She created you," Sydney said slowly. "How?"

That took a while to explain, though at least Sydney started walking again. By the time Ember was through, Sydney seemed to understand a little, and she'd begun to stare, which was all right because that meant Ember could stare back.

"You obviously think," Sydney said. "Can you feel?"

"I feel a lot. Happy, sad, angry. I think I've done them all."

Sydney touched her wrist softly, a nice touch. "Can you feel that?"

"Yes. I like touches, but pain isn't very much fun. Rowena has patched me up every time I've been broken, and I would describe it as interesting but not fun. She says I'm lucky that I'm tougher than other people because I've done some 'stupid bloody stunts,' but I didn't think they were stupid because she says the quest for knowledge is never in vain, and that's all I wanted. Then she argued that I could just read about broken limbs and such; I didn't actually need to experience them, but I disagreed because I read about how a broken arm felt, but that was nothing to actually knowing how it feels, which is bad."

"We differ there." Sydney had a funny look on her face, somewhere between sad and scared and mystified. "I just need to know it hurts. I don't have to try it."

"That difference between us probably qualifies as philosophy," Ember said, "which I've never been very good at, if you remember."

Sydney barked a laugh. "Me neither, but I've been thinking a lot about it lately, ever since my life stopped being so black and white."

Ember thought about that one. "There are lots of colors. Can you not see them?"

Sydney gave her a flat look. "Not that kind of black and white. Before now, people were either good or evil, just like choices. Now, nothing seems simple." She opened her mouth as if she would say more, then didn't. "I don't want to bore you."

That tickled. Ember laughed until she felt sick. "You can't be boring. Only my home is boring."

"Good to know," Sydney said, and she seemed a bit happier. "I hope we find my comrades soon. Are you certain you don't know where they've gone?"

"Oh yes. I would tell you if I knew."

Sydney's crooked smile stirred Ember's interest even further. "I'd think any compatriot of the Hawk's would know how to keep a secret or tell a lie."

Ember tilted her head. "I know how to keep a secret sometimes, but I like talking much better than silence. I've never seen the point in lying."

This time, Sydney's smile was so bright, Ember was tempted to kiss her just to share in it. "Me neither."

"Once you tell one, you just have to keep going."

"Exactly." She seemed as if she might say more, but a dark look passed over her face as if someone had pulled a curtain that changed her expression. She looked away.

"What's the matter? Are you hurt this time? You were smiling, and you stopped very quickly."

"It's just…" Sydney swallowed. "Forgive me. After some recent troubles, I don't know whom to trust anymore."

"Oh, that's easy. You can trust me. And you can trust Rowena to help the people of Kingston. If she thinks you're trying to hurt people or her or me, she might hurt you, but I doubt she'd kill you, not unless she had to. And she won't hurt Camille; you can trust in that. Even if she gets very annoyed, which I have seen and felt, I doubt Camille can talk as much as I do, so Rowena probably won't get as annoyed with her as she gets with me, so that's all right." She thought for a moment. "I don't know many other people very well, so I can't say whether you can trust them or not."

Sydney's smile was back, a little less glorious and a little more amused, if Ember was reading it right, but she was happy to see it again. "And if we meet someone else, and I'm not sure if we can trust them?"

Ember nodded as she thought about it. "I'll help you. You're probably better with expressions than I am since you live out in the world, but if any people we meet say something, I'll ask them if they're lying, and then you can tell by their expressions, and if they say something else, I'll ask if *that's* a lie, then I'll keep asking them things and remember what they've said before, and if they get something wrong, I'll tell you."

"And you'll do all this just for the experience of the thing? Why do you trust me?"

That one was easy. "Rowena said you're one of the few knights who seems as honorable as she claims, even if you're still a buggery Knight of the Flame. She doesn't speak with just anyone, you know."

Sydney was quiet a moment, her expression thoughtful. That was fine; thinking was good, but talking was so much better. "A week ago, I would have said you could trust any knight," Sydney said, "but now, I'm not so sure. Thank you for trusting me. I won't betray it."

Ember beamed. "Of course not. And even if you decided to attack me, I know I can beat you."

Sydney frowned. "Because of that little outburst?" She pointed behind them toward where they'd started their walk. "I was emotional. That wasn't a proper match."

"I don't know what a proper match is, but I did do better than you."

Sydney's mouth opened and shut a few times. She seemed a bit angry, but Ember wasn't sure why. They had fought, and Ember had been better. She'd blocked all of Sydney's attacks and was certain that if she'd launched her own, they would have landed. To say otherwise would have been a lie. Unless...

"You didn't think it was fair, maybe?" Ember asked. "Even though we both had weapons. You weren't ready? But you were the one who attacked."

Color had risen in Sydney's cheeks. "All right, all right. You could have bested me back there. All I'm saying is that you can't say which of us would win were we to spar again."

"Oh, I see." She put her hand on her sword grip. "We can try again if you're ready now."

Sydney glanced at her weapon as if considering. "Well... No. We have to find the knights. Barring that, we have to find Camille. Unless we run into the Kells, in which case our fighting abilities will both be tested, though not against each other."

"I'd nearly forgotten them," Ember said, excited by the prospect. She'd never fought a real enemy before. She'd fought the soldier husks, and since they couldn't be killed, she could fight to her fullest ability, but to face someone who actually wanted to kill her?

And whom she might have to kill?

That thought did strange things to her stomach. Meeting the Kells seemed much less exciting now.

CHAPTER EIGHT

When Camille brought Rowena some bread and cheese, she was happy to see that Rowena seemed to have settled down a bit. There were few things Camille liked less than being yelled at for something that wasn't her fault, especially when she wasn't completely sure what was going on.

Rowena mumbled a thanks as she read from a book. She was surrounded by bits of herbs and stone. Little jars and dishes littered the surface of the table, and several cabinets with tiny drawers sat along the table and walls. She occasionally tapped a pale finger against her full lips.

"You're welcome." Camille leaned against a table and studied the workroom as she ate an apple. She wondered where Rowena got her supplies since she lived in a cave. Camille hadn't heard the sound of water or felt any discernible humidity. Based on what she'd read, that hinted they were above rather than underground. Maybe a hill or cliff or mountain. But for a woman who could move people across time and space, getting groceries was probably a snap.

Except she'd implied that transporting anything took a lot of effort. She must have had someone to make deliveries. But Camille hadn't seen anyone else around. The redhead? She'd appeared out of nowhere, and Rowena had said something about a person called Ember. She must have been a helper or an assistant. Or a friend.

Or a lover.

Rowena did seem fixated on finding her. Whatever they were to each other, Camille told herself not to be foolish. She had no right to any kind of jealousy. She barely knew Rowena, and she'd been in a relationship with Sydney while she'd been communicating—flirting— with Rowena.

Ugh, stop. She was stranded in a possible cliffside cave with a witch she barely knew. She should not be thinking about flirting or jealousy or any other type of feelings.

Although...her eyes kept coming back to Rowena. Without the haze of the crystal ball, she was as lovely as Camille had imagined. She was pale, as if she hadn't been in the sun in a long time. Her hair was dark brown, fading toward the ends, and the eyes that had blazed so green seemed darker in normal light, closer to hazel than the emerald shining from the crystal ball. Camille wondered if Rowena did that on purpose or if it was some side effect of the spellcasting. In Camille's short absence, Rowena had donned a corset-like bodice over the loose-fitting black dress she wore. Its silvery surface glowed in the candlelight, revealing a leafy pattern and showing off her small waist and lovely curves.

Camille couldn't help a smirk. Rowena was either vain, or she was trying to impress someone.

And Camille was the only person there. Interesting.

Even more surprising, Rowena had pulled part of her hair back; a heavy silver clip covered the white streak Camille had noticed just above her right ear.

Rowena glanced over her shoulder. "You going to help, or are you just going to stand there?"

Camille started, then chuckled. "I can't pass up the chance to show off my skills. Give me a description of what happened."

Rowena spoke quickly, the words clipped as if they'd had all the feeling sucked out of them, but the way she kept touching her chest said that the loss of the redhead, Ember, meant a great deal.

When the story was over, Camille catalogued all the information in her head and pointed over one shoulder. "How is your library laid out? I'll start looking up this witchstone thing."

"Just ask Dansk for whatever you need."

"Who?"

"In the library." Rowena sounded distracted as she bent over her tools again.

So, Rowena did have some helpers. There'd been no one in the library when Camille peeked before, but it had been very early. Maybe Dansk was up by now. Camille went to look again, stopping to ogle the shelves of books and the comfy-looking sofas and chairs. Put in a bed and set up food delivery, and she could live in this room.

No one sat in the chairs or behind the desk. Dansk must not be awake yet. With a sigh, Camille lit a few more candles and lamps, wanting all the light she could get if she was going to start poking through the shelves. She'd need a ladder to reach the higher shelves but didn't spot one in the corners. Maybe there was a storage cupboard—

Camille gasped as she turned. A person had appeared in the shadows near the door, revealed in the stronger light. Camille put a hand to her chest and breathed out slowly. "Dansk? You scared me. I didn't even hear you come in."

The person didn't respond, and Camille's heart calmed enough for her to look closer. The eyes were white as if covered in frost, and the chest didn't move. A statue? If so, it was the most lifelike one Camille had ever seen. She took a step closer, wondering where Rowena had gotten it.

Wondering why she'd dressed it.

It was too perfect.

Camille reached out a trembling hand and touched the still, cold cheek. Waxy and gray, but it was undeniably flesh. Dead flesh. Her stomach dropped.

"Dansk," a voice from the doorway said.

The corpse stepped forward, and Camille backpedaled, hitting the arm of the sofa and tumbling over it onto the cushions. She scrambled back, her heart in her throat as she pressed against the farthest side. Her breath came in gasps as terror clogged her throat, but the corpse had stopped after one step.

"It occurred to me that you might not know how to use a husk," Rowena said quietly. She stepped to the corpse's side. "There's nothing to be afraid of. Dansk is designed purely to help in my study. It wouldn't know how to kill you even if I ordered it to."

The words entered Camille's ears, but few made sense to her brain. Kill, she heard that one right, and she shifted upward over the arm of the sofa and staggered down, backing up until she hit the desk. "D...dead," she said pointing at the corpse.

"Yes," Rowena said slowly.

"That's…a dead body."

"Correct."

"A dead body that's up and moving around."

"Wow, I knew you were good at research, but I had no idea you were this good."

"Fuck you," Camille shouted, unleashing the strongest swear she knew. "I have kept my composure so far, even though I have no idea where I am, and Sydney is who knows where, and you are not nearly as nice as you were in the ball, but that is a *dead body*, and it is *standing* and *walking*, and…" She felt tears coming and clamped down on them, hating that her go-to response to very strong emotions was to weep like some soppy hero in a terrible romance.

Rowena sighed and ducked her head, and Camille vowed to chuck a candelabra at her head if she laughed.

Her face was set, though, as she looked up. "Magic falls into two basic categories," she said, her tone even as if she was used to lecturing. "There is creation magic and destruction magic. Both pull from a witch's internal energy sources, but creation magic pulls from one's life force, and destruction pulls from emotion." She gestured to the corpse. "This is a husk. It once was a person, but the body was donated after death by a nearby village. I imbued it with a bit of life force and used creation magic to make it move. I gave it one task, which it will continue to do until it falls apart, an instance I prevent with occasional maintenance."

Camille leaned back on the desk, her pulse calming in the face of learning even if she still avoided looking at the…husk.

"There are other husks here, all assigned to different tasks. Some defend the mountain, but you're quite safe from them unless you begin a random assault. Which you won't, yes?"

"Yes, I mean…no." She shook her head. "I don't want to hurt anyone."

"Good. Me neither. You have nothing to fear."

Camille swallowed, feeling strong enough to glance at…Dansk. "So…it…she's not…alive?" Like everyone in Kingston, she'd heard the lessons given by hierarchs every solstice eve when the seven bells rang seven times at midnight. They said flesh was a shell, and the true self fled at death to find the meaning of existence.

But to find that shell up and walking around horrified her.

"No, Dansk is no longer alive," Rowena said. "All the life force is gone except the bit I gave her. All she does is find things in the study." She turned. "Dansk, bring me information on witchstones."

When the husk began to move, Camille couldn't contain a little noise of alarm, but she watched in fascination as the husk moved to a shelf, climbed it, and brought down a book. It continued this throughout the room until it had left a pile of books on the table and went back to stand in the corner where she'd first seen it.

Camille wound up near the door again, staying out of the husk's way. "Who was Dansk when she was alive?"

"I have no idea. The villagers tell me nothing about the corpses they bring me. I give them a name so I can order them about."

"It seems so…wrong."

Rowena snorted. "She's a tool like any other."

"She's a person."

"Not anymore." She glared, her voice angry but also tired as if this was an argument she'd had before. "When you don't have living servants because some stupid morons have made most people afraid of witches, this is your only option."

"What about the villagers that give them to you? Couldn't they work as servants?"

"Well, what does it say about them that they're more comfortable giving me their corpses than they are volunteering their labor? Even if they don't fear me or wish me harm, they don't want to get too close."

The loneliness of it nearly chased Camille's affront away, but having dead servants just seemed…icky. "So, this is all you have for company?"

"No, I also have Ember, who I'm going to get back if you would care to start the research you offered." Rowena gestured to the pile of books.

"And who is she? A villager who became comfortable with you?"

"No." She picked up the first book, glanced at the title, and set it aside.

"A relative?"

"No."

"Then who?"

"Why do you care?" Rowena turned, hands on her hips.

"I'm just curious to see who would live here with the dead people besides you." Not quite true. It would have made her feel better if Rowena and Dansk had known each other in life, though she couldn't say why. "Is she another witch?"

Rowena rolled her eyes. "You'd probably just call her a dead person, too, even if she's not."

"She's a husk?" But the memory Camille had of the smiling face and laughing eyes didn't fit with the icy creature in the corner. Even a glimpse had told Camille that.

"She's a homunculus."

Camille searched the catalogue of her mind and found a tantalizing whisper, but she couldn't catch hold of it. "A what?"

Rowena's smile was slightly evil as she waved to the library. "Look it up." She swept from the room, and Camille wondered if she regretted freshening her appearance for her uninvited guest. Camille certainly regretted ever finding anything intriguing about her.

Camille went to the pile of books. She sat behind them and pulled over a stack of blank parchment and a pencil. She opened the first book and began to read until she got an idea of what the book was about, a history of various magical items. She began to skim for witchstones, but the interesting word Rowena had thrown out kept pulling at her.

She licked her lips with a tongue like sandpaper and didn't look up. "Dansk," she said quietly, almost a whisper.

The husk stepped forward, and Camille resisted the urge to clamp her teeth shut. She only looked out of the corner of her eye. "Please…" Camille swallowed and tried again. "Please, bring me a book that defines homunculus."

The husk was away in an instant, but it only took two steps, reached down to pull a book from the lowest shelf, then placed it on the table.

Camille couldn't help shrinking back a bit. "That will be all, thank you," she said in a rush, the words crushed together, and the husk faded back to the corner.

The new book gave the definition as a created person and even had some of the steps that went into the creation, those that took a great deal of life force from the creator and tied the two together emotionally, almost psychically. Only powerful witches attempted it, and only the most powerful succeeded.

The loneliness of it all hit Camille again, making her glance in Dansk's direction. Rowena couldn't find anyone to share her life except the dead, so she'd made Ember. No wonder she was frantic to get Ember back. It was almost enough to excuse her for being such a colossal ass.

Camille was tempted to go to her, say she understood, even apologize since she still found the husks incredibly creepy. But she really didn't care to face Rowena's sarcasm again before she made progress on the witchstones. She bent her mind to that task, copying fact and rumor about witchstones, how they were made, what they were for. Like most topics on magic, many authors disagreed. Rowena had many tomes written by actual witches, a find that made Camille want to steal several. Many of their stories held encounters with witchstones, full of feeling but with very little usable data. Whenever Camille found a tale of a witch countering a witchstone, she wrote furiously, copying the salient points and looking up many of the words she didn't know. After a few hours of research, she was almost at ease ordering Dansk around, and she had a huge pile of books before her.

Camille separated her research into columns, making sure to note where each tidbit was from and starring the items that received more than one mention in different texts. Those were the most likely to be true. She noted that there seemed to be different types of witchstones. All of them disrupted spells, but some held witches in place. According to Rowena, this witchstone tried to drag her through the spell and ended up getting Ember instead. Camille couldn't find any descriptions to match. One stone was rumored to have the power to attach to a witch like a barnacle and prevent them from moving at all. So, there might be unique witchstones that were unlike any other.

She commanded Dansk to search the pile in front of her for mentions of special or unique witchstones, then took the texts from it without flinching. When her back began to ache and her eyes started to blur, she stretched and admitted that having a library corpse was pretty handy. She wouldn't have gotten so far in her research if she'd been climbing about the library as well as researching.

It was still icky, though. Camille hoped Rowena did maintenance on the husk before it started falling apart on the books.

While standing, Camille opened another book, this one with a mention of a unique witchstone, if Dansk was to be believed. Camille skimmed the first twenty pages or so, slowing when she read about the discovery of a fairy hoard.

She barked a surprised laugh as she dropped back into her seat. "A fairy hoard?" She'd read about them before in her fascination with magical creatures. Some scholars debated whether or not fairies had ever existed. They'd supposedly disappeared long ago in the time of unicorns, dragons, boggarts, and imps. The author of this text apparently shared that skepticism by the way they'd written mockingly about the claims of tiny skeletons mixed with a hidden treasure trove. The author speculated that the discoverers had probably found the lockbox of some ancient tribe who'd been killed before they could recover their goods.

Camille clucked her tongue. Even if the author didn't believe in fairies, it wasn't up to them to speculate without facts.

The author did a good job of listing what the hoard did contain even if they called the skeletons "animal bones." The book listed coins, jewels, and a myriad of other rich objects, including what the local witches described as a witchstone, one with very peculiar properties, like the ability to draw forth any witch who cast a spell around it.

Gotcha.

Camille wrote that down, picked up her notes, and headed from the room to find Rowena speaking into her crystal ball. She looked up when Camille entered, said, "Contact me again with any news," then draped a cloth over the ball.

Camille bit back her curiosity and hurried forward. "I found it." She didn't know whether to be flattered or angry by the surprise in Rowena's eyes. "There's mention of a witchstone that pulls witches to it if they cast a spell around it." She showed Rowena her notes. "It was found in a supposed fairy hoard. Maybe Sir Robert had access to that treasure?"

Rowena studied the notes for a moment. "You did all this in a few hours? You've almost written a book on witchstones yourself."

Camille allowed herself a little preen. "Piece of cake."

"This fairy hoard was found almost two hundred years ago. Those who dug it up are all dead by now."

"Sir Robert could be a descendant. Or he could have purchased it somewhere."

"It still disrupted my spell, so we can't have it in here when I cast another large one." Rowena rubbed her chin. "I wonder how far away it has to be." She slapped the small table. "I really don't want to throw it out for someone else to find."

"There was nothing about it disrupting a transportation spell," she said. "I guess the witches who experimented on it didn't try one, so there's no data on where it could have sent Sydney, Ember, or the knights."

"My contact near the border hasn't seen any of them, either. Lucky for us, he also hasn't seen any Kells."

Camille gasped. "I'd forgotten about them. I guess this means we have some time for the knights to get in position?"

"Why would Sir Robert do this?" Rowena stood and paced. "Was he so determined to catch or kill me that he'd put the entire kingdom in jeopardy? Did he think the spell would work, and then he'd catch me with the stone?"

Camille bit her lip and thought about it. "He might not have known anything about witchstones except that they're anti-witch." She sighed. "I can't see him combing through a library, can you? Someone had to have given him the stone and told him enough about it to get him to use it."

"Someone who didn't care whether the knights were there to meet the Kells? Who knows about magical artifacts and isn't keen on witches?" Rowena snorted. "I'd like to meet this person and wring their bloody neck." She tilted her head and seemed thoughtful. "Though I can see Sir Robert as a pawn rather than a mastermind. Maybe it was one of the bloody fairies."

Camille nodded. Sir Robert as a pawn made sense. Though that still left them with a big problem and now three potential enemies: the Kells, Sir Robert, and the so-called mastermind who had yet to show themselves.

And who was possibly a fairy.

No, that was beyond ridiculous.

Later that night, Camille set about making tea. She'd become quite familiar with Rowena's kitchen in a short amount of time. Luckily, it was well stocked. She didn't know who did most of the cooking, Rowena or Ember, and she didn't want to ask. Any mention of Ember sent Rowena to sniping. Her sarcasm was clearly a mask for pain, but that didn't make it any less annoying. Maybe she usually yelled at her husks. They probably did a lot for her and Ember, maybe even the cooking. Camille tried not to gag at the thought of corpses preparing luncheon.

And she wasn't going to let Rowena treat her like a walking corpse.

She brought the cups to the workshop where Rowena sat staring at the covered crystal ball as if willing someone to contact her. It was getting late. Rowena's worry would probably keep her up, but Camille didn't know where she was supposed to sleep. She was just glad her pack had been close enough to get caught in the transport spell. Even if she had to bed down in a quiet corner, she'd have a blanket, a change of clothes, her face cream, and her cap. Small comforts.

Rowena grunted a thank you when Camille set a cup at her side.

"You'll find her," Camille said quietly, breaking her vow not to mention Ember, but she had to do something to ease Rowena's pain.

"You don't know that." She sounded beyond tired, her voice shaking with worry.

"You've succeeded in everything you've planned since I met you."

Rowena snorted a laugh. "That wasn't long ago."

"It's still a one-hundred-percent success rate."

A tiny smile rewarded her. "I may have succeeded with the transport spell, but it didn't go according to plan."

Camille shrugged. "You made a person. You can do anything."

Another barking laugh, but this one had genuine humor behind it. "You make 'em, then they leave you. Way of the world, I guess. I just didn't expect it so bleeding fast." She clenched a fist. "But Ember didn't leave. That bastard Robert stole her from me."

"You'll find her," Camille said again. "With your tenacity, you're bound to succeed."

"I've sent some husks to search for her," Rowena said, smoothing her hair. She disturbed the clip she'd put in earlier, displaying the white streak in her hair for one moment before it became hidden again in her dark locks. "They're exploring in wider and wider circles, but they're not good at complex tasks, and they can't speak to anyone they meet. And if they find Ember, and she doesn't want to come home..." Her voice broke a little on the last word.

Camille was up in a moment. She drew Rowena into her arms. "It's all right."

Rowena sagged against her so briefly, Camille thought she imagined it as Rowena pulled away. "I'm okay." She wiped her eyes furiously and looked everywhere but at Camille. "It's fine, you're fine, everything's…" She took a deep breath.

Camille rubbed her shoulder. "I'll help you. You're not alone."

Rowena's lip trembled before she turned away. "Thank you. Good night." She hurried out of the room without another word.

Camille sighed and wondered if she'd ever seen anyone so self-confident and so awkward at the same time. She gathered her things and went to the library. The couches in there had looked pretty comfortable. Maybe she could throw a blanket over Dansk. She shivered. Who knew creepy could become normal so quickly?

CHAPTER NINE

Sydney's throat was parched. She didn't think she'd ever spoken so much in all her life, especially not to an attractive woman who seemed so interested in her. Women who were interested usually made an attempt at small talk, then winked or leered or broadly hinted that they should find a convenient room or storage cupboard or clump of bushes. After a vigorous round of lovemaking, all that was left to do was say good-bye.

Ember didn't seem to know what a broad hint was. Her stares were openly admiring. From anyone else, they might have even been rude, but there was something about Ember's curiosity. She didn't seem to expect a reaction or think she was owed physical affection. She just wanted to know everything and wanted Sydney to know everything about her, too.

A woman who wanted to know Sydney and not just her body. That was more than refreshing. It was a little…frightening.

Especially since Ember wasn't wholly human.

She shook her head and tried to banish the uneasy feeling, certain Ember would have reacted this same way with anyone. But that was a little depressing. Sydney wanted someone to be interested in *her* *specifically*. All the women she'd dallied with had thought her a little special, at least for her charm.

Or had they? Maybe they would have behaved the same way with anyone they found attractive. Even Camille, who'd seemed so tongue-tied and nervous upon their first meeting, admitted that Sydney wasn't the first woman she'd taken to the basement to be alone. Maybe she'd had plenty of charming women. Sydney would have to get up the courage to ask her.

If they ever saw each other again.

"Are you angry or sad?" Ember asked. "You're frowning, but there's something about your lips that says sad. Rowena gets that look sometimes, and that means she's lonely or possibly bored. Are you bored? You can't be lonely since you're not alone."

Sydney chuckled. "No one could be lonely around you."

Ember beamed. "Thank you. I try to take up room." She stretched her arms out, and Sydney had to agree. Her bubbly personality took up a lot of space. Even for as short a time as Sydney had known her, the flame of affection had kindled. She wasn't going to ask if they could find a convenient clump of bushes, and she was still a little mystified as to why Ember hadn't already asked for anything physical, but Sydney had been enjoying their conversation as much as she'd enjoyed her liaisons.

And as much as she hated to admit it, the "not wholly human" thing kept popping up in her mind.

"You're bored, then," Ember said. "Are you tired of talking about your life? We could talk about something else. You mentioned horses, and I don't know anything about them besides the few things I've read, so you can talk about them."

Before Sydney could respond, Ember rubbed her pierced ear, setting the three dangling ornaments ringing together. Sydney had seen this gesture often enough over the past hours to know it meant she was thinking. "Or we could spar. Rowena sends me to spar with the husks when she's tired of talking. She says, 'Go dump some of that bloody great energy you have,' but I don't ever get rid of all of it. She said that when I was newly formed, I even kicked in my sleep."

Good to know that she did sleep, then. At least one thing would keep her quiet. And thinking about that could keep Sydney's thoughts away from phrases like, "when I was newly formed."

As if summoned by the thought of rest, a great yawn overtook Sydney, and she put her arms above her head and stretched. "How about a break?"

Without waiting for an answer, she plonked down on a hummock that stood slightly larger than the surrounding grass. They'd been walking over a fat lot of nothing for miles, just some rolling scrubland with clumps of heather, grass, and the occasional spindly bush or ditch. Ahead, Sydney could see the start of some proper hills and Ember's mountain beyond. To the right somewhere was the border, and a forest sat in the distance, little more than a green blob. On the Arnvild side, the fat lot of nothing extended as far as she could see; the ocean was somewhere far behind them, but she hadn't caught a glimpse of that, either.

No wonder no one lived out here. Even the animals seemed to have abandoned it. She'd seen one lone bird since she'd been walking, and she suspected it was lost.

Or it had come out here to die.

Ember sat cross-legged on the ground, watching intently as Sydney took off her pack and brought out a canteen and a ration bag. She shared both, and Ember took only as much as Sydney did, watching carefully as if fearful of making a mistake.

Sydney had to smile. "We're going to need to find more food and water. We can't make it all the way to your mountain on what I've brought."

Ember rubbed her ear again. "I didn't think about supplies. I'm sorry." She ducked her head as if heartbroken.

Sydney nearly choked on her water. "Hey, it's all right. It's your first time out in the world, and you managed to bring a weapon and your trousers. I'm impressed."

Ember smiled, then her eyes widened. "Do people often forget those on their first time out in the world? I could see forgetting a weapon, maybe, though I always wear mine in case I want to spar with the husks, but I'd get cold immediately if I wasn't wearing trousers outside, and if I was walking out instead of using a spell, I'd go back for my trousers right away."

Sydney let the talk wash over her. She'd already deduced that these "husks" were some kind of servants for the Hawk, though she'd never heard of anyone called the husks. She bet they got tired of having to practice weapon-craft on command. Maybe they were people born to the sword, always ready to fight. They'd be a handy ally against the Kells.

Sydney looked to the north again and wondered where the Kells were now. Probably somewhere in the green blob of a forest. She should have paid more attention to maps. The blob and the fat lot of nothing had names, as did the mountain, but dashed if she knew them. She didn't even know how big the blob was. It could conceal a host of enemies.

When she saw the flash of color among the heather clumps, she blinked, thinking she'd imagined something moving after wishing for it for so long. It came again, closer, a hint of green that quickly vanished as if someone was trying to stay hidden, but the color of their clothing stood out among the purple and brown.

Sydney stood, peering to get a better look. Ember was at her side in an instant. "That bush just moved. An animal?" Ember asked.

"The only animals I know that come in green are lizards, and I don't think there are any lizards out here," Sydney said.

"Special lizards," Ember said, awed.

Sydney frowned. "Or someone wearing green who is trying to stay out of sight."

If anything, Ember seemed even more excited. "Kells?"

Sydney's heart dropped, but she told herself not to be afraid of stories. The Kells might be fierce warriors, but they were human. They could die.

She stepped on the hummock and caught five separate disturbances, that same flash of green moving through the coarse terrain. They must be belly-crawling, though they were fast for that. "Fight or flee?" She knew which one she'd choose. Captives or corpses could give her information about where they were. But she wanted to give Ember the chance to—

"Fight." Ember drew her short sword and stood in a ready stance. "They'll run when they see how good we are."

Sydney didn't know about that, but she drew her own sword. "Come out," she called. "Speak if you're a friend. If not, stand away or prepare to defend yourselves."

The rustling stopped, and Sydney waited for a word, a rush, or a retreat. When a cloaked figure leaped up as if from the ground itself, she realized they hadn't been crawling but using the ditches to move.

Golden skin glowed from within the depths of the hood. The figure only stood as high as her shoulder, but it thrust with a short, thin blade, and she batted it away by instinct alone.

Sydney cried, "They're fast," hoping Ember took heed. She met the next thrust with a push so she could work her way closer to Ember.

Two opponents had already found her. Sydney fought the urge to gawk as Ember moved as if she was a reed, bending backward to let a swing go over her body, all while blocking the attack of her second opponent. She jerked to the side and straightened quickly enough to launch a counterattack.

By then, Sydney's attacker made another lunge, and another emerged from a ditch to join him. As fast as they were, excitement boiled through Sydney, and she channeled her bloodlust and fear, focusing it until heartfire coiled within her and her left hand was sheathed in blue-white flame.

Her two opponents took a step back, and Sydney heard a shriek from behind her. It didn't sound like Ember's voice, but Sydney maneuvered around anyway, trying to keep all the attackers in sight so no one could stab her in the back. She caught a glimpse of Ember still up and fighting while one of her attackers was on the ground; a fifth had replaced him.

One of Sydney's opponents darted in, wearing the same sort of cloak as the first. She parried his lunge, knocking his blade far to the side, then stepped forward, swinging her hand as if she held another weapon therein. She slapped the attacker's shoulder, and the heartfire leaped to him as if she'd touched a torch to burning pitch. He leaped back and rolled as the fire raced across his clothing.

The other attacker came on, and she thrust her hips back to avoid the lunge, but the blade grated along the armor of her midsection, cutting through her flame-emblazoned tabard and screeching across the chain mail beneath. She felt the sting but couldn't stop to see if the blade had penetrated her armor. She swiped for the hood with her left hand, but the attacker ducked and darted away.

Sydney followed hard with her own series of thrusts, backing the attacker toward the ditch he'd sprung from. When he hit the edge and stumbled, she came in fast, darting under his flailing blade and impaling him in the gut. She put her shoulder behind the thrust, knocking him into the ditch before yanking her blade free.

She turned to see Ember kicking one of her opponents while skewering the second. Before the first could recover from her kick, she launched another attack and nearly lopped his head off. Sydney gaped. Whoever these husks were that she'd sparred with, they had to be very skilled. She clenched her fist, refocused her energy, and the heartfire winked out.

The opponent Sydney had burned was moaning in the grass, smoking and blackened. The others were unmoving. "Are you all right?" Sydney asked Ember.

She nodded, and Sydney was relieved to see she was breathing hard, at least. She wasn't completely inhuman.

Ember pointed to Sydney's ripped tabard. "You?"

Sydney parted the material to look. A few dented rings, but the mail was intact. She shook her head. "A graze. Let's see what we have here." She kneeled beside the burnt one and pulled his hood back.

She peered closely at the blackened face. His skin was golden like she'd thought, creased in pain as his breath rattled. Fine lines ran across his face as if someone had tattooed every inch of him with a pattern of scales.

"No, they *are* scales," Sydney muttered. His features were blunted, his lips so thin as to be almost nonexistent, and his nose barely rose from his face, the nostrils small and teardrop shaped. She didn't know whether he actually had no hair or eyebrows or if the heartfire had burned them away.

His eyes flickered open as she studied him, and she was surprised by how normal they seemed, a rich brown with a hint of gold at the edge of the iris. A capillary had burst in one, flooding the white with red.

Even though he'd attacked her, and his strikes would have meant death, Sydney lifted his head carefully, not wanting to cause undue pain. "Who are you?" she asked softly.

His eyes locked on hers, but he only breathed and winced.

"Why did you attack us?" she tried. She fought the urge to mourn for this poor, misshapen creature. "We wouldn't have harmed you. We were only passing through."

Ember laid a hand on her arm. "He might not understand you. He doesn't look human."

Sydney glared at her. "Of course he's—" She'd been about to say that he must be human. He was just…disfigured. Then she realized who…what…she was speaking to. "Do you know…" She didn't know what to say. Asking if Ember knew any other non-human sentients seemed ridiculous, especially given that she'd never left her home before. "In your studies, did you ever read about someone like them?"

Ember kneeled, her own face pinched. "No. They have skin like a lizard's, but I don't remember any magic creatures who looked like lizards." She shrugged. "Except for dragons, but they were much bigger, with four legs and wings and snouts and long tails."

Sydney sighed before she could continue, not wanting to get drawn into a discussion of dragon characteristics. "Who are you?" she tried again softly. "Do you have people nearby? We'll stay away from them. We didn't mean to cross into your territory."

He smiled at that, showing bloody teeth that were sharper than a human's. "All," he said, nearly a whisper.

Sydney leaned in close. "All? All what?"

His eyes slipped closed. "All ours…" With a last rattle of breath, he stilled.

Sydney laid him down and stood, pondering his words. "All ours?" Did he mean the territory? Everything around them belonged to these creatures, at least in their minds? There couldn't be many of them, or she'd have heard of them, surely. All of Kingston would have been interested in a large group of lizard people claiming the border. "They can't have been here long."

"They made us kill them," Ember said, still kneeling. "I never killed anything that can talk before." She looked at Sydney with tears in her eyes. "I tried to wound them, to show them I was better, but they kept coming, and they made me kill them."

Without thinking, Sydney drew Ember up and in, still rattled by the deaths herself. Ember's arms went about her without hesitation, and her face turned into Sydney's shoulder. Her hair smelled of sage.

"Will there be more?" Ember asked, her voice muffled and heavy with sniffles.

"I don't know," Sydney said, rubbing her back. "I'm sorry I don't have any answers. Maybe if we hurry, we won't meet any more."

Ember leaned back, nodding and rubbing her nose. She wiped Sydney's shoulder. "I got some tears and snot on you. I'm sorry."

Sydney barked a laugh. "This tabard's done for anyway."

"Thank you for holding me," Ember said, her head cocked. "Your body feels very nice."

"Um, thanks." Sydney fought the urge to be shocked. Ember had said it so casually, but her words forced Sydney to think of the way Ember had felt against her, in spite of the fact that Ember wasn't human. They'd fit together well, Ember's breasts pressing in just under Sydney's own. Her sage-scented hair brushed warmly against Sydney's cheek, and the strength in her arms was a comfort.

Ember cocked her head, smiling as if she could read Sydney's mind, but for once, she said nothing.

As they began walking again, Sydney realized it wouldn't be long until sunset. She'd hoped they'd find a village or farm for the night. Since there were lizard people here, this part of the world clearly wasn't as abandoned as those in Kingston seemed to think it was. Four stout walls were infinitely preferable to a night under the stars.

But as dusk crept on, and Sydney only saw more nothing, she chalked it up to just the sort of luck she'd had since this whole adventure started.

"Looks like camping is our only option." Sydney swallowed hard. Walking all day and worrying about what had happened to Camille and the knights had exhausted her. But she still had enough energy to hone in on the fact that they only had one tent and one blanket.

Ember brightened. After the lizard people, she hadn't said much as they'd hurried away from their small battleground, and now, as Sydney set up the tent, Ember rambled on with questions about camping and requests for more stories.

As she pulled out rations for their evening meal, Sydney relayed a few tales, finding Ember very easy to talk to. "Every camping trip I've been on involved military maneuvers, and nothing very interesting happened. Animals tend to stay away from large groups of people, and no outlaws or brigands were stupid enough to raid an armed camp."

"Brigands and outlaws," Ember said. "Are those like pirates?"

"I guess so, but pirates are on the sea. Read about them, have you?"

"Some, but I also talked to the ones Rowena rescued."

Sydney's belly went cold. She kept forgetting that Ember was connected to the Hawk, the witch Sydney had been hunting for over a year, the witch who'd stolen a group of pirates from under Sydney's nose and made a fool out of her.

Ignoring whatever Ember said next, she dug in her pack. "If we don't find a settlement tomorrow, we'll need to do some hunting." The realization made her even angrier. She didn't have a bow and arrow or a spear; even if she did, she'd never been a hunter. When she was little, her family had grown or raised their own food on the farm, and once she'd joined the knights, she'd had foragers to hunt for her if the need arose.

"I know how to do that," Ember said excitedly. "I was always catching things on the mountain when Rowena let me go outside, mostly on the higher peaks, but maybe there are animals living out here like those living up there, and I can trap them or catch them pretty easily."

Sydney didn't respond. Hunting experience was one point in their favor, at least.

"You're scowling," Ember said. "Did I say something wrong? Do you not want to eat the animals?"

"It's fine, you're fine." Sydney sighed. "I was just...thinking about...everything we still have to do, the people we have to find." She took several deep breaths and tried to let the anger go. It wouldn't help a dashed thing at the moment. "I hope Camille and the others are okay."

Ember opened her mouth, then shut it as if she feared that what she had to say was wrong. Sydney didn't know what that was, but she supposed she should be grateful that the Hawk taught Ember some tact. With all the things she'd blurted out so far, the words she held back might be heinous indeed.

"The sun will wake us up early," Sydney said. "We should get to bed."

"Do you cuddle on your right or your left?" Ember said.

Sydney whirled around, but the light had faded so much, she could barely see where Ember sat. The air wasn't more than chilly, so they'd decided not to risk a fire. "What?"

"Rowena likes to sleep on her right side, so if we cuddle together, I'm behind her on my right, too, but I can sleep on either side, so we can fit together and be warmer."

"You...you and the Hawk...sleep together?"

"Sometimes. We did a lot when I was newly made because I would get so cold. Then I'd sleep in front of her, and she'd put her arms around me."

"Oh." Sydney's mouth went dry. "Did you..." She shook her head and went back to arranging the blanket inside the small tent. "It's none of my business."

"Were you going to ask if we have sex?" Ember's voice said from right behind her.

Sydney jumped, nearly knocking the tent over. "No, I mean…" Her heart sped up. Now that she knew how close Ember was, she could feel her heat. "Like I said, it's none of my business."

"Why? I said you could ask me anything. We haven't had sex. It never felt right since we're like the same person. At least in some ways; I always know what she's feeling when I'm close to her. I have had sex with some of the people who've visited, though. Some were better at it than others."

"Okay," Sydney called as she climbed in the tent. "That's all right. I don't need stories, thank you."

The blankets rustled as Ember crawled in beside her. As Sydney removed her chain shirt, she imagined Ember's cocked head and wondering expression.

"If you don't want to hear stories," Ember said slowly, "then I suppose you don't want to tell them?"

"That's right." Sydney didn't know what was wrong with her all of a sudden. She wasn't shy about sex. If Ember wanted to talk about it or even wanted to do it, why would that matter?

The thought felt wrong even as the image of Ember's muscular body curled around Sydney caused heat to course through her. It was the stress, she told herself, and the fact that Ember was not completely human.

That hadn't stopped the brief vision of them together.

No, she was on a mission. She never indulged while on a mission. She'd never even had company in her standard-issue tent until Camille had tried to join her.

It just wasn't done.

Sydney lay down and felt Ember do the same, but there was no cuddling. The blanket barely stretched over both of them, leaving no extra to wrap around and serve as a buffer between their bodies and the tent's rough canvas floor. Sydney tucked one arm under her head and tried to make herself comfortable, tried to ignore the breathing and the very presence of the woman behind her. Maybe her desire to abstain was more than just military discipline. She didn't want Ember this way, not in the middle of a crisis, worried for comrades and loved ones, dirty, and tired. With Ember, she wanted somewhere soft and safe and private. A place they could get to know each other's bodies as they'd gotten to know each other's minds.

Strange, she'd never really thought like that before. It hadn't seemed to matter. But as strange as the thoughts were, they banished Ember's non-humanity from her mind.

❖

Ember lay still in the dark and wondered what she'd done wrong. Sydney clearly didn't like to cuddle, though she'd seemed happy to do so after Ember had wept earlier. But then she'd asked about sex.

Ember would have been happy to oblige, but the topic had seemed to make Sydney withdraw even further. She hadn't reached out or made a suggestion, nothing to signal her consent, and Ember didn't want her to feel forced or obliged or anything like that. The very thought was icky.

She remembered the way Sydney had held her close earlier, the tender firmness of her embrace. Afterward, her tanned cheeks had turned pink, but she hadn't seemed embarrassed like Rowena did sometimes. From the way her hand lingered on Ember's arm, it had looked more like arousal.

So, why did Sydney shy away from cuddling now? Maybe she didn't know that Ember wanted her. She'd spoken a bit of her former bedmates, and by the way Sydney spoke of Camille, Ember guessed they'd had sex, too. Therefore—as Rowena liked to say—Sydney's reluctance couldn't come from a lack of experience.

Camille.

Ember nodded to herself. Maybe Sydney was like a character in a book who didn't want to have more than one bedmate at a time. The thought was intriguing. Rowena had expressed similar tendencies when Ember asked about her sex life. She'd said she wasn't the "love 'em and leave 'em type."

Ember tried to imagine someone so compelling that she only wanted them forever and ever.

She could listen to Sydney talk forever. All her stories were amusing and enlightening and wonderful. There was just so much of her to *know*. And her face was fascinating and open, with expressions almost as loud as words. It had been the closest thing Ember had ever seen to her connection with Rowena. When Sydney held her close, the tender, protective force of the embrace had caused a warmth of jitters in Ember's stomach. The thought of her now, lying so close, moved that warmth even lower, tempting Ember to bring up the subject of sex again, but she knew that wouldn't be right, not after she'd been rebuffed.

Because of Camille.

A different feeling fluttered through her now, something she had a hard time putting a name to. She'd only had glimpses of Camille, both in Rowena's crystal ball and in real life, but the memory made Ember frown, and she felt an intense dislike brewing. The feeling surprised her. She'd never disliked someone she'd never met. She'd hated characters in certain stories, but that was because the glimpses the book provided into their minds had been off-putting. Besides, they weren't real and didn't care if she hated them. She'd disliked a few of the people she'd met, but she hadn't hated any. She'd thought she might have to hurt one of the pirates when he threatened a husk, but the husk had defended itself well, and the pirate had settled down.

So, what was there to hate about Camille?

Ember frowned harder. Maybe she should ask Sydney about her tomorrow. Maybe Sydney would list some traits that made Camille worth her ire, but just the thought of Sydney talking about Camille made the angry feelings deepen, and Ember pledged to ask about anything else.

And she wished Rowena was here to interpret these feelings through their link.

After a sigh, Ember closed her eyes and let her body rest.

At dawn, her eyes opened. She couldn't see anything in the dark tent, but she knew the sun had just lifted over the horizon because she always woke up at dawn. Rowena called it a quirk, something unique about her that couldn't be explained. Ember liked the quirk because with the maximum amount of daylight every day, there was more she could see and do.

Sydney remained still, her breathing deep with the occasional small, rumbly snore. It hadn't bothered Ember. Rowena snored like a rockslide.

Ember eased up and paused. She found the rumbles amusing, another positive trait in Sydney's favor. But she couldn't keep counting the positive things and letting her liking grow, not with Camille on Sydney's mind.

With a sigh, Ember eased out of the tent and into the morning air. She didn't like these conflicting feelings. It felt the same as when there was something she dearly wished to do, but she knew Rowena would be angry. Then she had to do whatever her heart desired while dreading Rowena's disapproval. It tainted the entire experience.

The only answer was to act as if Camille didn't exist because Ember couldn't stop asking Sydney for stories, and she couldn't help being impressed or endeared or whatever else these feelings were. Perhaps Sydney's interest would switch from Camille to Ember. Sydney thought she was magical, after all.

Ember belted on her sword, then drew it to take a few practice swings, limbering up in the morning air and trying to drive all these confusing thoughts away. After she'd woken up her muscles, she stretched her arms before sitting in the scrubby grass to stretch her legs and back. A soft noise came from behind her, something like a sigh, and she turned, expecting to see Sydney emerging into the growing light.

A hood-shrouded, scaly face looked back at her, and she had only a moment before it rushed her.

❖

Sydney awoke with the sounds of her dreams lingering in her ears. The memories were muddy, but she recalled being trapped in a dark cave with no way out and wind shrieking all around her.

When she heard another soft *whoosh* of air, she thought she must still be dreaming, her eyes on the cusp of closing again, but when the sound repeated, her waking mind finally came to life.

Something was moving outside the tent, leaving the foliage whistling in its wake.

She fumbled for her sword, sore muscles protesting after a night spent on the ground. She grabbed her chainmail with the other hand and staggered outside, fumbling to her feet.

In the dim light, she saw Ember standing behind a golden-skinned lizard person, her arm wrapped around its throat. When another of the creatures came at her through the semi-darkness, she leaned on the captive in front of her and launched a kick back at the new attacker, driving it away.

Sydney saw another hazy form come from the bushes. She pitched her chain shirt at the lizard who was already staggering, making it fall backward. She drew her sword and tossed the scabbard to the side before rushing the newcomer. Heartfire sprang to life in her left hand.

The creature ducked back from the glow and drew a mace. Sydney pushed her attack, knocking the mace out of the way and slashing down the creature's arm. It turned and ran.

Sydney gaped, expecting more after the last batch of creatures had fought to the death. She shook off the surprise and turned for Ember, her heartfire flickering as she lost focus on her emotions. In the growing light of dawn, she saw Ember with her slack captive but no other creature.

Sydney scanned the countryside. Those ditch-like crevasses still wound through this area, providing cover. If she could see it from above, she imagined it would look cracked and broken like dry skin.

Or lizard scales.

"What happened?" Sydney asked. "Are you all right?"

Ember nodded. "He thought to take me unaware, but I'm much stronger." She grinned crookedly, and Sydney resisted the urge to hold her close, to make certain she was all right.

"He succeeded in getting the sword from my hand, then I hit him, and when he tried to hit me, I held him so." She gestured at the lizard creature and cocked her head. "Yesterday, they sought to kill us. Today, they want to capture me. Why?"

"I don't know." Sydney scrubbed a hand through her hair before donning her chain shirt. She retrieved her scabbard and belt and put them on, too. "Why didn't you call for help?"

"Because I had him."

"There were more."

"I didn't know there were more until you were already out here."

Sydney rolled her lips together and fought her anger. "Whenever there is danger, you must call me, dash it all!"

Ember continued to stare before she took a deep breath as if with sudden understanding. "Because there might have been some sneaking into the tent to get you, too."

"And so I can help you if you need it."

Ember opened her mouth, but Sydney didn't want to hear more excuses.

"I would say the same to any fellow knight," Sydney said. "I know you can take care of yourself, but the point of comrades is that there is always someone watching your back."

Ember nodded slowly. "I will remember." She stepped closer. "Are you all right? Did one try to attack you in the tent? Did those others hurt you?"

"No, I'm fine."

"You're shaking."

"I'm just...emotional." Bits of her dream were coming back to her. She hadn't been alone in that cave. Camille had been there as well as others, hazy faces she could barely recall, but they'd been people she knew and cared about. And they'd been in trouble, calling for her, and she hadn't been able to find them. Waking up to combat was not the way to finish such a dream.

"You're worried about Camille," Ember said, a strange quality to her voice.

"I'm worried about everyone." She stomped back to the tent. She couldn't consider Camille's plight at the moment. "We need to get moving. That might have been a scouting party. They could return with reinforcements." She took down the tent and rolled it tightly, her fingers fumbling. Her old quartermaster would have been appalled by the sloppy bundle she secured to the bottom of her pack.

She knew why she was so worried, but the anger was new. Anger at herself for not waking up sooner? Anger at Ember for not calling out? At Sir Robert for doing something that made the Hawk's spell go awry? Maybe at the Kells for simply existing. She looked to the north as the sun rose higher. Were they out there now, waiting? Were these lizard creatures stirred up by the Kellish advance?

"What should we do with this one?" Ember stood over the creature she'd choked.

Sydney didn't think it would tell them any more than the other one had, and they didn't have time to linger until it woke up. "Leave it." She donned her pack and started walking.

"You're mad at me?" Ember said.

"I'm angry because I don't know what in the seven bells is going on. I'm angry because these lizard people keep attacking, and I don't know how to make them stop." She sighed and tried to think through her emotions, sort them as she'd been taught to do while learning to use heartfire. The throb in her side and neck made it difficult. "I'm angry because my muscles are killing me, and my left side is frozen because I slept on the bare tent floor."

A warm hand slipped inside hers, and she nearly stopped. Instead, she sighed again, contented. The silent comfort felt nice, an offering and a promise of further help if needed. Sydney gave Ember a squeeze and left their hands clasped together. At least she wasn't alone. Somehow, she knew Ember would help her find Camille or fight lizard people or Kells or Sir Robert. She'd do it for the experience alone, if everything she'd said up until then was any indication. And Sydney sensed she'd help for more reasons than that. They were comrades now, watching each other's backs.

Though she'd never walked hand in hand with any comrade-in-arms before. Maybe it was the bit of non-humanity that made it all right.

Chapter Ten

After a restless night, Rowena sorted through ingredients in her workshop. What Camille had discovered about the witchstone was interesting, but Rowena was still no closer to solving the first of her problems.

Where was Ember?

She could take care of herself, at least most of the time, but there was so much about the outside world that she didn't know. She'd no doubt throw herself into one risky situation after another, and the way she asked questions would offend people. Some wouldn't hesitate to attack, and the smart ones would wait until she was off-guard. Ember knew very little about treachery.

And if someone didn't kill her, her own recklessness might. Rowena couldn't stop seeing her face that time she stepped off the cliff above the entrance to their home. She hadn't been afraid. Her expression had been wondrous as she'd strolled into what could have been her death. Her lack of fear would provide no comfort to those left behind. Up until now, that had only been Rowena.

Who else had she met?

A niggling voice in Rowena's head suggested Ember might have found others to miss her, even in the short time she'd been gone. What if it was someone she could love more than Rowena, someone she'd want to make a new home with? Silly. No one could duplicate their connection, and she'd only been gone one night.

Rowena had wept about it all the same, and it threatened to choke her now. She slammed a box of reagents shut and stalked away from the thought, consulting a spell book. She had everything she needed to bring Ember back. She just needed a location before Ember found trouble…of any kind.

"Looking for something specific?" Camille called from the door. "Can I help?"

"No, thank you," Rowena said archly. She knew she'd been terse since Camille arrived, but she had a lot on her mind, too much to worry about the feelings of someone who'd be leaving soon. No matter how much Camille liked handing out hugs, she had her own life to get back to. "I have everything I need for another transport spell."

"Oh. So, does that mean…I'll be going?"

Rowena straightened. She hadn't thought of Camille's needs, a realization that shamed her, but that only made her even more angry and embarrassed, and for fuck's sake…

"Bloody complications," Rowena muttered.

"Sorry?" Camille cocked her head, waiting, but for what? Her frown seemed a little disappointed.

Wonderful. More feelings. "Transportation spells require a lot of energy," Rowena said. "I have to wait days between such large magics, and I want to be ready when I find Ember."

Camille smiled shyly. "Well, then. I'd love to stay. I want a chance to peruse the library further. I'm learning a lot. And I can help."

Rowena let out a breath, suddenly scared, though she couldn't say why. Probably because she did not need someone else to take care of, someone always so peppy and pretty and eager, who kept getting in the way and filling Rowena's home with the scent of vanilla and apricots or whatever was in the soaps and lotions she used.

Realization came like a thunderclap, lightening Rowena's mind. She didn't have *time* for another person in her life, not when there was so much to do. Yes, time was the problem. Time and nothing else.

But Rowena's cheeks burned, and she didn't know why she should be embarrassed. Camille was the one inviting herself to stay. "You don't need me to transport you. You have two good legs. And you're not doing any good here."

Camille rocked back as if slapped.

"Don't worry," Rowena said, talking faster and faster. "I'll give you supplies, and the husks can walk you down the mountain. The village in the foothills might be able to take you part of the way to Kingston on a cart or something if you give them my name."

Camille had started nodding, but the set of her mouth said she wasn't happy. "Well, just point me in whatever direction home is. Maybe I'll go looking for Sydney and Ember and the knights on my own. With some supplies and some walking corpses, I'll have everything I need."

Her tone dripped sarcasm, and Rowena bristled. Camille had no right to be angry. If anyone deserved to complain, it was Rowena; she'd had her entire life upset in the past few days. "So, why are you still standing here?"

"I'm not." Camille whirled around so quickly, the fabric of her skirt seemed to snap.

Rowena heard her banging around as she gathered her things. She'd know best what she needed from the kitchen and whatnot, so Rowena hurried out of the workroom and down the stairs to where the soldier husks gathered. Most were out looking for Ember, but two of the older ones were left. She directed them to follow Camille and protect her as soon as she came this way to the back exit.

Rowena hesitated. Should she say good-bye? Camille had helped *some*, but she was also angry, *though she had no right to it*. They weren't friends. Rowena didn't owe her anything. They'd shared one embrace during a moment of weakness. It meant nothing, and Rowena didn't want Camille getting too comfortable. Really, she was doing Camille a favor by breaking ties before Camille began to think them friends. It was better this way.

And where in the bloody world was she?

Rowena moved to the bottom of the stairs and listened. No sound. But this was the only exit to the back stairs inside the mountain…

Rowena's breath caught. She'd forgotten the front door, the flashiest and most obvious way into her home. The few visitors she'd gotten headed that way, through the most dangerous path up the mountain while the safe entrance was carefully hidden at the mountain's base. But if Camille had taken the stairs from the kitchen up instead of down…

"No, no, no," Rowena said as she raced upstairs, calling for the husks to keep up with her. "Stupid, stupid."

Her misery doubled when she found the disturbed dust at the front door. Camille had found the latch that opened it without any trouble. Why couldn't she have been stupider?

Rowena hit the latch, and the door began its ponderous rumble open. Daylight hit her like a hammer, and she staggered back, shielding her face. Fresh air streamed in, and her stomach turned over. Her heart pounded as it did every time she had to go outside. She fought the sensation down, ran back for her emergency bag of spell components, then darted into the sunlight before she could think too hard about it, the two elderly husks just behind her.

❖

As she stalked along the path down the mountain, Camille was thankful that her temper hadn't kept her from taking supplies. She'd banged through the kitchen in haste, stuffing food into her backpack, though she had no idea how long it would take her to get to Kingston. She'd have to depend on strangers for part of the journey.

Even strangers had to be kinder than Rowena.

Camille ground her teeth, trying to remember what she'd managed to scrounge before she'd left. Anger and hurt had blinded her, and for all she knew, she'd gotten away with nothing but baking soda, flour, and a few spices. Maybe she could bake a bloody campfire cake.

If that was even possible.

She stopped stomping down the dusty trail that led away from Rowena's door and took a few deep breaths, fighting tears. Rowena wasn't worth tears. Camille had offered to help; Rowena had told her to leave. That was just the way some people were. Camille had thought they'd shared a...*moment*, a few actually, bits of mutual worry and curiosity and maybe even respect, but whatever. Some people were just rude and stupid and vulnerable and beautiful and wanted to sit and rot in their dumb hole in a mountain by themselves, and that was their hard luck.

Camille groaned and leaned against a handy boulder. Maybe she should have waited for the husks to accompany her. Maybe she should have yelled. She could have confronted Rowena about their mutual fears, could have listed the ways they could help each other, but her pride had been screaming at her to leave, and so she'd done so, and now she was probably halfway down the mountain, and Rowena had no doubt forgotten her.

She wished she could summon Sydney with a thought.

A stab of guilt wandered through her. Only thinking of Sydney at the first sign of danger? She deserved to walk home.

With a huge sigh, Camille pushed off the rock and wiped her cheeks. What was done was done. At least the path didn't branch. She only wished it wasn't carved into the mountain instead of running along the surface. The sides of the paths rose like miniature cliffs, so high she couldn't see anything but a small stretch of the path ahead and behind before the curve hid the rest.

Camille started walking again, feet dragging this time. No matter what she should have done or said, she wasn't going back. Rowena said there was a village in the foothills, so Camille would begin her real journey there. She had a bit of money, and if someone was willing to take her to Kingston, she could get more once she arrived. Or maybe, unlike Rowena, someone in the village would be *kind* and offer a discount. If they knew Rowena at all, maybe they'd be sympathetic toward someone who wanted to get away from her.

A rattling sound drew her attention to her right, and a pebble bounced down from above, sending other rocks skittering down the side of the trail.

She glanced up but saw nothing except a bird high in the sky. She wasn't an expert on birds, but she didn't think they dropped rocks on people. Something was moving atop the rock wall.

Camille paused, listening. When no other sound came, she started walking again, faster this time. Her brain began conjuring all the animals that could be slinking along up there, like wildcats, bears, large lizards. There was an island to the north of Arnvild where lizards grew larger than hounds and had acid-laced saliva, and some of the large cats on the plains of Zania had teeth as long as a person's hand.

"Stop it," Camille muttered. This wasn't any island, and it certainly wasn't the plains of Zania. She cursed the fact that being well-read could be a bad thing; she had too many candidates for her imagination to choose from.

Another pebble skittered, and she heard the rasping sound of a footstep on stone. Seeing nothing, she called, "Who's there?" hoping for a stray villager or a husk or Rowena herself, someone to yell at.

No one answered. She started walking backward down the trail, hoping a squirrel or something would appear and make her feel foolish. Foolish was better than dead.

But her mind ignored that thought and recited unwelcome facts. Some bears and big cats would retreat if faced with aggression. Her heart pounded at the very idea, and a ringing noise began in one ear.

Other animals would grow bored if a person played dead. Camille barely contained a humorless bark. She couldn't lie still while an animal sniffed her, nudged her, maybe took a nibble. She shuddered and turned, preparing to run, but the intelligent part of her brain roared from underneath her chattering panic.

No matter what, never run.

Camille took a shuddering breath. To run from a predator was to invite a chase. And she wouldn't be able to outrun anything determined. She began walking backward again, her pace sedate. If something was stalking her, it would eventually grow bored and wander off.

Or attack.

A high-pitched noise came softly from her mouth, something between a tiny shriek and a giggle, the many parts of her vying for control, and none of them was happy. Sweat dribbled into her eyes, and she wiped it with the back of a shaking hand. Her eyeballs throbbed in time with her pulse, making the landscape wobble. She trailed her right hand along the outside wall to keep from running into it, but she stumbled over rocks and shards of shale.

Something dark leaped from one side of the path to the other, a shadowy shape that disappeared over the lip of the wall as quickly as it had appeared.

Camille froze, her breath hitching painfully. She darted to the other side of the trail and searched the top of the wall. "What was it, what was it?" she whispered. She tried to focus on what she'd seen, but the emotional part of her was screaming in her head, and only fear was keeping her from screaming aloud. The primitive part of her brain said if she didn't move, didn't make a sound, the thing stalking her wouldn't know she was here.

"Stupid," she whispered, forcing herself to breathe slower. It knew she was there. "Think."

A leaping shadow. No, there had been things to see even though it moved fast. Fur, dark brown, and with a certain shagginess that didn't put her in mind of a cat.

A bear? No, wrong shape. "Think harder." When the creature had leaped, its forelegs had been extended, but there'd been something about them that bothered her.

They weren't legs.

She remembered the bend of the back legs, the definite knees, and those in front, though extended as if to catch the thing, had the look of hands.

"A...person?" Anger began to seep through the fear. Oh, if this was a person scaring the daylights out of her, she was going to give them a good kicking; she didn't care who they were.

But the fur?

A hermit? "No," she said softly, walking again. Living in the wilderness didn't make someone capable of sprouting fur. Was this some other experiment of Rowena's?

Oh, if that was so, and she survived this, she was definitely marching back up the mountain and giving Rowena a *thorough* kicking, that was for certain.

She picked up speed, debating about whether to make a dash for Rowena's door or continue on her way down. Whatever was stalking her was between her and the relative safety of Rowena's domain. Maybe it would be content to scare Camille down the mountain, out of its territory.

Something peeped over the wall, a flat-featured face sporting fur everywhere but its eyeballs. She couldn't make out any kind of expression before it was gone again.

Her rational brain gave her a flash from childhood of many happy afternoons spent with her favorite book, Miss Elspeth Fogerty's *Myths and Tales of Magical Creatures*. She'd read the words enough to memorize them, but it was the illustrations that kept her coming back, including one of a mountain-dwelling primate that had disappeared into legend.

"A yeti?" she said, louder than she meant to. She clapped a hand over her mouth. An old legend living on a witch's mountain? "How?"

It had to be Rowena's doing. Camille continued creeping. Her rational brain reminded her that even if she'd solved the mystery, she still had a lot to fear. Yetis hadn't been known as the friendliest of creatures, but the facts humanity remembered about them wouldn't fill a teacup. Terrain: mountains. Personality: aggressive. But Miss Fogerty had spiced up her work with a lovely little story about how one expedition had found a hut made of human bones, the yeti's hideaway.

"Stupid Elspeth Fogerty," Camille said. She hadn't taken another step when the furred shape dropped to the path with barely a whisper of sound.

Camille froze, fascinated and terrified and suddenly needing the water closet. The yeti stood upright like a human, but the sheer amount of shaggy, tangled hair made it seem far bulkier than a person could be. The eyes shone like obsidian chips, and the lips parted in a snarl, framing long, sharp canines.

Camille's scream burst out, and she scrambled back. When something leaped on top of the yeti from behind, Camille's scream curdled to a yelp, and she fled down the path, not caring what was happening as long as she no longer had to stare into a collection of killer teeth.

She heard a cry behind her. A yeti might be better than whatever was brave or foolhardy enough to tackle a yeti. Better not to worry, to shut up her brain and run. And thought soon became lost in the air burning in her chest, the stitch growing in her side, and the flashes of red that streaked across her vision. Dimly, she could hear the warnings of her rational brain. Exertion plus elevation did not mix well. Anything could catch her if she passed out.

She made herself slow, casting glances over her shoulder but seeing nothing. She tried to jog *and* watch behind her, resulting in a mad half dance that made her feel as if she was stumbling down the mountain rather than walking. When she heard another sound, she squeaked and picked up the pace again.

When the giant spider leaped in front of her, she almost didn't believe it. As tall as her waist, it skittered toward her, and she backpedaled until she ran into something else.

She screamed as she whirled, trying to keep an eye on both the giant spider and whatever had caught her. This would make an incredible story if she lived to tell it.

Skinny arms covered in paper-like skin thrust her to the side, and she cried out again as she focused on the face of the thing that had shoved her. It had hollow cheeks with that same parchment skin, sunken white eyes, and hair that had fallen out in clumps, some of it taking flaps of skin and exposing swaths of gray skull.

Her rational brain almost gave up, no doubt exhausted from continually pulling her back from the edge of madness. It gave one final cry of, "Husk," and Camille stifled another yelp as the husk moved in front of her, facing down the spider.

Husks. They had to be there to help her. She didn't know whether to laugh or weep. When something else grabbed her arm, she thought another shriek might be in order, but her throat hurt, and those streaks of red in her vision had turned to blobs of black; she could feel unconsciousness calling. She spun again, raising a hand. If fear couldn't keep her awake any longer, maybe anger could.

Rowena ducked under her swing. She cursed and scowled. "Bloody woman, I'm trying to help you."

"What?" Camille turned as the spider made a sharp squeal. The husk grappled with it and had two of its legs in an unarguable grip.

"Come on. Didn't you hear me calling you?" Rowena yelled.

Exhaustion tipped fully into anger, and Camille bared her teeth. "I'm *sorry*. I was too busy with the spider and the yeti and whatever the fuck else you have on this cursed mountain." Her abused throat rebelled and collapsed around the last word, cutting off her voice.

Rowena caught her arm as she staggered. "Here now. It's all right. Come back inside." She glanced past Camille and flinched. "Come on now. It'll be all right."

Camille's anger fled before the soothing tone and the concern in Rowena's eyes. She let herself be led; she wouldn't give in to fear again. Anger could retreat—that was fine—but she still had her pride. Whatever happened, she would...not...cry.

The loss of adrenaline won over pride, and she wrapped an arm around Rowena's waist and wept into her shoulder. She babbled in a voice that kept fading to a whisper, and Rowena stiffened before murmuring comforting nonsense.

Before they went far, Camille straightened. "Yeti?" she managed.

Rowena hesitated before shaking her head, the concerned look still in place; her arm had snaked around Camille's shoulders. "Taken care of."

At the moment, Camille didn't care how. She gave in to her deluge of emotions and didn't curse the tears as they came again. It was enough to be safe and heading away from danger while in the arms of someone powerful.

Her rational brain agreed. She would get answers later, oh yes. And if she didn't like them, there was always kicking.

❖

Rowena tried to ignore her pounding heart. The taste of the air and the feel of the breeze were almost enough to make her forget that Camille was pressed close, sobbing her eyes out.

Was it wrong to feel guilty and fortunate at the same time? It had been a long time since anyone had pressed themselves close to her for an extended period. Except Ember, and she didn't count. Not like this. But why did it have to be in the bloody outdoors?

When she'd first dug this trench, she worried that it had been a waste of time as she could have built a road on the surface of the mountain. But she didn't want visitors seeing how far they'd come or be able to see the dangers she'd planted, so the trench seemed like a good idea. Now, it was a further blessing. She could only see a ribbon of sky above her with white clouds scudding across, but it still seemed desperately open, the clouds too high, the space in between threatening to suck her up.

The world seemed to tilt, and vertigo slashed through her mind, making everything topsy-turvy.

"What's wrong?" Camille asked, her voice deeper and breathier from crying and screaming. "Are you hurt? Did the yeti get you?"

Surprise rallied Rowena for a moment. Trust Camille to know what a yeti was when the rest of the world had probably forgotten. The thought reminded her that the other husk might have had trouble holding the thing back. The yeti could have torn the husk to shreds and be lumbering toward them now.

"There's an escape tunnel," Rowena said through gritted teeth. It had its own dangers, but few compared to the yeti, and if the spiders were up on the surface, maybe they'd abandoned the tunnels below.

She should have checked on her traps and creatures more often.

She headed for a smear of dark gray clay that looked as out of place on this mountain as a pickle in a jar of strawberry jam, though no one had ever spotted it. She freed herself and ran her hands along the base of the wall where the clay had been laid over the rock.

Camille's fingers dug into her shoulder. "Something's coming."

Rowena took her word for it, unable to hear over the tinny sound in her ears, unable to feel much besides the desire to curl up into a ball. Her breath was coming faster. She closed her eyes and focused, searching for the latch that held the tunnel door closed.

"It doesn't sound like a husk," Camille said.

No, husks never sounded like anything, just soft footfalls. Rowena couldn't even listen for that. The thought that she soon might be inside, away from the terrors of a world trying to gobble her up, spurred her to search faster. Camille's fingers dug in painfully, bringing her much needed anger back. She snarled. She'd evaded knights and bounty hunters and angry, misinformed mobs. She was not going to be beaten by the buggery afternoon air.

"Rowena." Camille's voice was something between a whisper and a squeak. The breeze gusted past, making Rowena's stomach plummet even before she processed the rank scent of unwashed fur and musk.

"We have to run," Camille said, and her touch disappeared.

Rowena thrust an arm out blindly, grabbing Camille's dress. She couldn't open her bile-flooded mouth to explain that she'd almost found the latch. She opened her eyes for one brief moment and saw a shadow turning a corner on the trail above.

"Let go, let go," Camille cried. The fabric threatened to slip from Rowena's grasp, but she tightened her grip. If Camille ran away, she'd have to do so without her skirt; luckily, she halted. Rowena caught the edge of her fingernail on the latch, pulling at it with sharp, immediate pain.

The yeti charged as Rowena crowed. Camille screamed harshly with her shattered voice.

Rowena grabbed the latch and yanked. The smear of clay shuddered.

Then stopped.

"No." Rowena straightened and pounded on it. She should have checked. By all that was good and decent, she should have—

Camille slammed into her. "Come on!" She gripped Rowena as if ready to pull her into a run, but the secret door shuddered under the impact, and Rowena fell forward into the dark passage. She heard a breathless cry as Camille staggered after her, then another little shriek.

Camille moved, her knee digging in to Rowena's back, making her cry out. Camille gripped the shoulder of Rowena's dress—including a handful of hair—and yanked her farther into the passage.

Rowena cried out again and tried to twist away. "What do you bloody well think—" She turned enough to see that the way out was still open. The yeti kneeled outside, too big to fit, with one long arm frantically pawing inside. If not for Camille, he would have caught them.

Rowena dug in her bag. She'd memorized all the little pockets years ago. On the inside, third down from the left, she drew out a tiny bottle that held dragonfly wings, popped the cork from the top with her thumb, and blew across it.

A wing lifted, and its surface shimmered briefly as it caught the light. Rowena tapped into her life force, bringing out just a touch for the easiest of spells. The wing contained the essence of precision movement, and Rowena added her life force into that, letting her move a small object that was too far away to touch if she knew precisely where it was. She wasn't likely to forget the lever's location again.

The yeti yelped as the rock wall rumbled and swung toward it. It shuffled away, its roar cut short as the door slammed shut.

After a few minutes of doing nothing but breathing, Rowena dipped into her bag again and pulled out a bit of phosphorescent fungus. Its glow had long since extinguished along with its life, but Rowena threaded part of her life force through it, and the glow sprang up again, picking out the rough-hewn walls of the tunnel.

Walls and ceiling and rocky floor, all spaced so that someone could walk upright but single-file. Rowena let the closeness surround her, comfort her. It was so much safer than the gaping openness outdoors.

"Where is this?" Camille's eyes seemed as big as saucers as she stared at where the tunnel continued into lightlessness.

"It's a secret tunnel that leads to the proper exit and entrance to the mountain."

"The proper exit." Her voice was calm, almost emotionless.

"Yes." Rowena cleared her throat. "I should have mentioned. I just thought that since you'd been looking around… Well, I forgot about the front door, you see. Surely, you've done that? Where I grew up in the country, no one used front doors at all. We always used the back, at our own house or at a friend's or relative's. My mother used to say that only the bloody tax man used the front door, so…"

Camille was still staring at nothing. Too many scares had probably overloaded her system, and she hadn't quite snapped out of it. Rowena went through her spells, searching for something that would help, but although she knew some spells to treat wounds, nothing would aid a person's mind.

"Let me help you," Rowena said as she stood. The light grew as the spell infused the fungus. It would be safe enough to risk the tunnel… and whatever traps remained. "If I remember correctly, it isn't far."

Camille stood before Rowena could lay a hand on her. "I can move on my own. I have two good legs."

"Ah." So, not shock. And Rowena had already seen her in a fierce anger, flashing eyes and snapping words. This had to be something beyond even that. "Camille, I am sorry about not showing you the right door—"

"Is that all you're sorry for?" She looked at Rowena, and her calm seemed to shake a little. She stepped closer. Rowena tried to back up but ran into the wall, pinned in the narrow passage. "Well, that's okay, don't worry about it." She smiled sweetly, like a cat happy to have cornered its prey. "Mistakes happen." She was even closer now; the smell of apricots filled Rowena's nose, and the light jumped around Camille's features as Rowena's hands shook. Camille's full, smiling lips were close enough to taste if she inched just a little farther. "Just look at me. I got pulled out of my life because I wanted to help, and each time I do, I get censured or yelled at or told to walk home as if I'm beyond useless, but do I let it affect me? *No.*"

Rowena licked her lips, more frightened than she'd been of the gaping outdoors. "I'm...sorry."

Camille's glance flicked toward Rowena's mouth. Rowena braced herself for a kiss she hadn't realized she wanted so badly until that moment. She let her eyes slip closed. Only the rush of air told her Camille had backed away, leaving her completely un-kissed.

Camille leaned against the opposite wall some feet away. She had her head cocked, and her smile had changed a little. Still predatory but now also...satisfied.

Rowena straightened her clothes and cleared her throat again. She gestured down the tunnel. "Shall we?"

"After you."

Chapter Eleven

When Sydney saw the smoke in the morning sky, she rejoiced. Finally, a village. She knew this land couldn't be completely devoid of people. It might be a fat lot of nothing, but *someone* would dash well want it. Even in the middle of nowhere where she'd grown up, neighboring villages weren't more than a half hour away. People always spread out over usable land. And the smoke was coming from a large clump of trees that might turn into a jolly good-sized forest.

But as she watched the smoke, she frowned. It seemed rather a lot for one village. A town? Surely not a city, unless the lizard people had made one.

"Fire," Ember said, shading her eyes from the sun. "Should we go around or investigate?"

Her tone said she'd rather investigate than do anything else in the world. Sydney tried not to be too condescending when she replied. "It's a settlement. See how the smoke climbs in individual plumes? That means chimneys." Lots of them, all puffing away on a temperate morning? She told herself not to be a pessimist, but her pulse had picked up, and her head filled with alarm bells.

"Ah," Ember said. "And since we need supplies, we'll be going?" Her eyes practically shone.

Sydney had to laugh, but it curdled quickly. Too much smoke. "Yes, but please remember everything you were taught about asking strangers impertinent questions."

"What if we're about to leave, and we don't care if the villagers throw us out for being impertinent?"

"Then it's fine," Sydney said, grinning. But that smoke kept growing, and she began to think it *was* a larger fire, maybe several close together. Not a wildfire, then. They tended to fill in the spaces between rather quickly.

When the first tendrils of smoke blew over them, Sydney's stomach turned over. The acrid scent carried charred wood but also roasting flesh. She paused, her heart dropping. "They must be…cooking meat," she muttered, tasting bile even though she wanted to believe that the village had picked this day to smoke livestock for the coming winter. But there was another, more sinister smell that came and went.

Burning hair.

"By the flame," she said, losing herself to memory. She'd walked woodenly through a small village south of Kingston, inhaling that hideous smell. They'd burned a witch alive.

And the small village in front of her now wouldn't need so many fires, wouldn't have so many witches to burn, wouldn't smell so much stronger than in her memory.

Sydney ran, ignoring Ember's calls. She recalled the pride in the villagers' eyes when they'd told her they'd caught a witch just as the knights had taught them. But instead of turning her in, they'd taken matters into their own hands. Her blood had chilled at the sight of such rough justice, and now it became ice.

She'd never screamed so loudly at anyone in all her life, but now she could barely breathe.

"No," she whispered, still remembering that shriveled, pitiful corpse. Of all the fates witches deserved, being burned alive wasn't one of them. No one should suffer that. Now, she rounded a copse of trees and stumbled up a small hill, then slid to a halt so quickly that Ember smacked into her, nearly sending her off her feet.

A collection of thatch-roofed houses, little more than huts, sat along a dirt lane, the roofs ablaze. Bloody and blackened forms sprawled in the grass and the dirt. Movement from the left caught her eye, and her hope leaped, but it was only a few pieces of washing waving from a line.

A roof collapsed with a groan of wood. Sydney jumped and shielded her face from the roar of the heat and the billow of smoke that burned her lungs. Ember dragged her back a few steps, coughing, and Sydney joined her, her throat burning as if filled with hot lead.

"What is this?" Ember yelled. "How did this happen? Is everyone dead?"

Sydney couldn't respond, could barely listen, but her mind still worked, and one of Camille's stories leaped to the forefront; Kells killed everyone they met and razed the very ground behind them.

Something moved at the end of the lane, and Sydney squinted. Through the shimmery air, a dark cloak flapped around a short body walking away from the carnage. A taller person strode beside the short one, then both bent over something, unhurrying.

"There," Sydney said through gritted teeth. Anger began to throb within her. Anyone who wasn't gaping or running from this had to have something to do with it. She wanted to run through the flames, but her training cautioned her otherwise, and she dashed around the fire, close to the line of trees. She kept her eyes on the bending figures and saw two more, another cloaked as the lizard people had been and another human with a shaved head, leather armor, and hashmark tattoos running up both arms.

Camille's voice came again. Tattoos were how the Kells numbered their kills. Both humans had them along with several bloody lines, placeholders to be filled in later. They bent over a corpse and laughed as they pawed it.

Looting the dead.

Sydney drew her sword, her fear and disgust lost among the blood and fire. Her head pounded, and rage clouded the edges of her vision.

One of the Kells spotted her charge and scrambled back, calling a warning. It wouldn't help him.

Sydney swung as soon as she was close, catching one of the Kells as he backpedaled. Before he could raise his weapon, she took him across the neck, right across the artery. She pivoted away from the spurt of blood and turned for the next one. Steel rang out behind her as Ember engaged the lizard people.

The last Kell grinned, showing white teeth in a dark beard matted with blood. His sword was shorter than hers, wider, and he swung it with unschooled grace. She dodged, expecting him to take advantage of her distance to find better footing, but he lunged clumsily.

Heartfire bloomed in Sydney's hand, and she swung for these villagers, for the witch who'd met a fiery end. The Kell threw himself to the ground, grabbed her ankle, and yanked.

Sydney cried out as she fell. She swung heartfire wildly. The Kell bashed her hand aside, wincing, and the smell of burnt flesh washed over Sydney anew. He cocked his arm back, sword angled at her chest. She cried out, terror rising past her rage.

A cloaked form crashed into the Kell's side, sending him stumbling. Sydney pushed up, her heartfire guttering in the face of her sudden fear. Ember leaped to her side and lifted the lizard person out of the way. She must have thrown him.

The knights never covered that in training.

Ember faced the Kell. His arm was red, the skin puckered from where he'd touched the heartfire. He brought his sword on guard. Sydney lurched up, seeking to put the Kell on the defensive, but he attacked at every opportunity, even when he had to take a wound for his effort. Between Sydney and Ember, he was soon covered in cuts. They took turns defending while the other attacked. The Kell's style was reckless, almost careless, and his wounds didn't seem to pain him. Sydney knew then how they won so many battles. They didn't care about their own skins.

Ember slashed low, and the Kell thrust his hips back to protect his knees. At the same time, he swung for her head. She dipped lower, and Sydney knocked his attack wide. He switched his focus to her, but Ember stayed low. When the Kell tipped backward with a cry, Sydney knew Ember had used the Kell's previous trick against him.

The Kell hit the ground, his head bouncing off the hard-packed dirt, and his sword fumbling from his hand. Sydney lifted her sword to gut him, but Ember rose in front of her, and Sydney whipped her sword to the side, cursing and stumbling.

Ember raised a leg and bashed the Kell in the face with the sole of her boot. He went limp. Sydney glanced around for more, but they were alone, the others dead. She slid her sword home and breathed hard, the scent of fire and flesh clinging to her nostrils and trickling down her throat, making her gag.

She pointed at the Kell, unable to speak yet, but Ember seemed to understand her question.

"For answers, yes?" Ember said. "Perhaps he will talk more than the lizards."

Sydney nodded. That was sensible, yes, but the bodies in the road still cried out for vengeance.

❖

Ember had never had to take in so much new information at one time. And none of it was nice. Maybe a little exciting, but only because her heart was beating so loudly she could hear it in her ears. It wasn't the good kind of exciting, but the kind she'd rather be done with. And she couldn't share it through her connection with Rowena, had no one to explain it into small, digestible bits she could easily process.

She'd gone through the dead while Sydney tied up the Kell. Sydney didn't seem to want to kill him now as much as she did before. Wisdom had conquered anger, as Rowena said. And maybe he would talk more than their captured lizard person had. Maybe the Kell had known the names of these people; maybe they'd done something to him, and he'd had to kill them. She wanted to believe that, but based on what Sydney said, she feared it wasn't true.

Even if it was, would that make this sight better?

Probably not.

Ember studied face after face, but though the villagers were many things—blood-soaked, terrified, cut down in mid-run—alive wasn't one of them. She found the body of a child inside the trees. It seemed a good place to sit and shed the tears that had gathered behind her eyes. She'd never seen a child before except at a distance, a speck on the landscape from her view on the mountain. This one should have been running and playing, eating, drinking, having fun with friends, or grumbling about chores like a child from a story. She should not have been dead.

Ember understood Sydney's rage, then. As she'd looked for living people, the corpses had seemed almost false, something from a dream or maybe husks waiting for a new purpose, but this one…

Rowena's villagers never gave her children. Maybe this sadness was the reason why.

The grass rustled as Sydney kneeled beside her. "Do you want to bury them?"

Ember wiped her tears with the back of her hand. "Is that what they would have wanted?"

"The hierarchs of Kingston say that flesh is but a shell, that true life lies within, residing in the mind, the seat of reason. When a person dies, they say their true self escapes and finds the meaning of existence, so the body means nothing."

Ember didn't like the sound of that. There were so many better things than reason. "Do you believe that?"

"Not really," Sydney said with a sigh.

Ember smiled and leaned in, receiving an arm around her shoulders.

"Burying them just seems more…respectful than leaving them where they are," Sydney said.

Ember didn't think corpses cared about respect, but if it would make Sydney feel better…

By the time they finished burying the villagers, the day had worn to afternoon, and the Kell was awake. The exertion had dulled Ember's grief and anger, so she was in a better place to question the Kell without putting her fist through his face.

Sydney seemed to feel the same, though Ember could almost feel the coil of heartfire burning within her. As she stood in front of the Kell with her arms crossed, tiny tendrils of flame licked through her fingers.

Ember kneeled beside the Kell and hauled his bound body into a sitting position against a tree. He stared without fear. They'd moved a small way from the village, which had burnt to cinders behind them. The Kell didn't even glance in that direction.

"Why?" Sydney asked through gritted teeth. She jerked her head toward the remains of the village. "Why do that?"

"Because they were in our path," he said, his voice heavily accented.

Ember shuddered, and Sydney's hand glowed white-blue before she took a deep breath. Ember tilted her head at the Kell. "She'll kill you for saying such things. I might kill you."

"You will *wake* me," he said calmly. "This is a dream. You are dreams. You should be thanking me for sleeping, for when I wake, you will cease to be."

Sydney kneeled swiftly. "Don't give me that shit."

He leaned forward as if to meet her rush. "Prove me wrong, little dream."

Ember put her hand on Sydney's arm. She had many questions, and she didn't know how many she could ask before Sydney's anger undid her. "You kill all the people you meet in dreams?"

He shrugged. "What else are dreams for?"

"And your comrade lying dead in the field?"

"Is now awake."

Sydney sneered. "And the lizard people?"

He seemed thoughtful, then shrugged. "Special dreams, created by another dreamer."

"Another Kell?" Ember asked.

He shook his head, smiling as if enjoying himself.

"So…" Ember put her hand on Sydney's arm to stop whatever outburst she might have. She wanted to understand this Kellish philosophy. "The Kells are not the only dreamers?"

"There is also the *Nightmare*," he said, grinning like a madman. "We walk through our dreams, but he controls them, creating, destroying."

Ember held his gaze, getting lost in bright blue. "Who is this Nightmare?"

"The ancient one, the winged one, the eater of flesh and spirit."

Ancient, winged. She didn't know how one ate a spirit, but when she put the first two characteristics with the scaly nature of the lizard people, she had only one answer. "A dragon?"

Sydney scoffed and stood, breaking the spell of the Kell's gaze. He switched his grin to her. "It does not matter what a dream believes. The Nightmare will still come for you, gobble you up." He made a slurping noise.

Ember slapped his knee, bringing his attention back to her. "Did this Nightmare…create the lizard people?"

"He is the father. We help him."

"Of all the ridiculous fucking things I've heard," Sydney yelled. "You're telling me that a *dragon* has been breeding with Kells to create a lizard person army?" She put her arms on her head and walked in a circle. "I never heard such a load of shit in all my life."

The Kell had a satisfied smirk and shrugged again. Since they couldn't prove that they weren't dreams, there was no way to sway him, but they could get as much information as they could.

"Will the Nightmare be angry that you told us this?" Ember asked.

He laughed. "Whether you wake me or he does, it does not matter. I will meet him again in the real world, after he is victorious. You cannot stop him. You are dreams, and he can make of you what he will, do you not see?" He sighed. "Of course not. You are not really alive. I pity you.

I pitied them." He nodded toward the village. "It must be terrible to be a dream. Better to die here than be less than alive."

"Pity this." Sydney drew her sword in one smooth motion and stabbed him through the throat, drawing her blade sideways.

Even as he died, he smiled, his eyes full of wonder, and Ember wondered what it would be like to live completely unafraid.

Sydney breathed as if she'd just run a mile. Ember took her shoulders and gently turned her from the dead Kell. She didn't need to ask if Sydney was all right. Her expression wobbled from angry to horrified to grief-stricken.

"I shouldn't have done that," Sydney said shakily. She bent and dragged the bloody tip of her sword through the grass. "I shouldn't have... I just..."

"It's all right."

"It's not, it's not, I..."

Ember hugged her, offering comfort as Sydney had once offered it to her. Sydney wept into her neck, her cries loud and unabashed. Ember thought to turn her away from the horror of the village, but then she might see the horror of the Kell and her own rage. So, Ember just held her tighter so she wouldn't look at any of it.

❖

Sydney knew she was walking quickly, but she didn't realize she was almost running until she paused, out of breath, and leaned on her knees.

They'd both wanted to get away from the shattered village, but Sydney hadn't realized she'd actually been *fleeing*. Shame washed through her, and not just because she'd run away. She'd cut down that Kell in anger. A bound, unarmed man, and she'd slaughtered him. How was she different from those villagers who'd burned the witch?

She tried to tell herself that her anger didn't come from hatred and prejudice, but it did in a way. She'd been frightened and angry at the Kells before she'd even met one. Now she hated the lot.

And they deserved it, a voice inside her whispered. She wanted to contradict it, to argue that not all Kells could be murderous thugs, but she had no evidence of that. They believed everyone else in the world was fake, so it was okay to kill them. But how had they even come to such a horrid conclusion? Whenever she'd become aware in a dream, she hadn't taken up her sword and killed everyone she saw. Didn't that make the Kells evil?

"Did you believe anything he said?" Ember asked. She wasn't breathing nearly as hard, and she was wearing Sydney's discarded pack, another point in the shame column. Sydney hadn't given their supplies any thought when she'd left.

"The nonsense about dreams or the even more nonsensical stuff about a dragon?"

Ember's mouth twisted to the side. "We have seen dragon people."

Sydney gaped. "You think it might be true?" When Ember shrugged, Sydney bit her temper back. "There are no more dragons and even if there were…" She shook her head. "Dragons were huge. How could they breed with…" She would *not* let herself contemplate such things. "And don't reptiles lay eggs?"

"I never read about dragon breeding." Her head cocked, and she played with her earrings. "But if there was a very tall ladder—"

"Stop right there." Sydney shook her head before any images could take root. Even if she wanted to banish her shame, she wouldn't banish it *that* way.

"Rowena bred spiders in the mountain. And some spell she cast made them very large."

Sydney sneered but turned away so Ember wouldn't see. Ember had been a fine, loyal, sympathetic companion, and Sydney didn't want to openly disparage her…friend…in front of her, but everything kept coming back to magic and the chaos it could bring.

"So, you think some witch might have used magic to…combine a dragon and a person?" Sydney asked, turning back around. She fought a surge of bile. The whole train of thought was so distasteful.

Ember shrugged.

Sydney sighed and rubbed her temples, trying to stave off the headache that had been threatening her for the past hour. "It simply can't be. We can't be facing the Kells, a sinister Sir Robert, an unknown witch, and a fucking dragon." She pulled at her skin so hard, her vision went blurry. After a few deep breaths, she turned to Ember. "I apologize for swearing so heinously."

Ember brightened. "Is one swear more heinous than the other? Rowena uses bloody and buggery nearly constantly. Are there people who find them offensive? Why? How do you know which to use in what situations and with whom?"

Sydney smiled as the chatter washed over her. The world might be full of horror, but it also had curious, steadfast women who made an imprint on the heart, no matter how much of them was human. "I'm glad you weren't hurt."

Ember stopped her theorizing and stared. Her smile began tentatively and grew. "I'm glad you weren't hurt, too. And I'm sorry you were so sad."

"Me, too." Sydney took a step, drawn to her in a way she'd never been before. She caught Ember's hand. "You could have left me when we met, could have gone your own way, had your own adventure. You didn't have to help me try to find…" It seemed wrong to say Camille's name while holding the hand of another woman, but Sydney felt very far from Camille, and they'd never belonged to each other, not like she felt she belonged with Ember.

Still, Ember winced as if sensing that missing name. She began to pull away, but Sydney didn't let go. "Thank you." She pulled Ember closer, taking her other hand, and who or what she was didn't matter. "Thank you."

"It seems impossible that someone wouldn't go with you," Ember said softly. Her gaze trailed from Sydney's eyes to her lips, and though there was heat, there was also softness. She didn't seem to want to devour Sydney in a wave of desire and then discard her. "Everything about you is fascinating."

Sydney grinned. "I was just thinking the same about you."

Ember closed the distance in a single step, pressing their lips together softly, asking a question with her body. Sydney leaned into the kiss, deepening it, letting the feel of Ember's lips, the warmth of her, wash away the horrors of the day. That kiss said more than, "I am here." It said, "I'll be here, no matter what."

Foolish thoughts, perhaps, for someone she'd only known for two days, but they still rang true, and in a time of many lies and faults, that felt like enough. It felt wholly human.

When they parted, their hands still joined, Ember licked her lips, her eyes closed. Sydney put another kiss on her cheek, her chin, her forehead.

Ember sighed. "You kiss like…it means something." Her eyes opened. "Is that a weird thing to say?"

"Weird or not, I love it." Sydney stepped back. Fantastic as the kiss felt and as much as she wanted more, they were still stranded in the middle of nowhere, besieged by enemies, and covered in soot and sweat and blood. She had to believe there would be time for more in a far better place.

A kiss! Ember could hardly believe it had happened. For a moment, even though Sydney had been looking deep into her eyes and holding her hands, Ember thought it might not happen, so she'd bridged that gap herself.

And Sydney had kissed her back. Not even thoughts of Camille could stop her.

After they'd parted, Ember offered to go hunting since Sydney hadn't seemed intent on kissing anymore, at least for the moment. The look on her face said she was still interested, but maybe she was turned off by the grime and everything that had happened that day. It would be nice to have a bath.

Maybe with Sydney.

Once all the trouble was over.

And Camille was miles away.

Ember didn't know why thoughts of Camille still bothered her, even after Sydney had kissed her. She couldn't help wondering what would happen when they were all together, if Sydney would suddenly change interests again, or perhaps she would want them all to be lovers. But Ember had been thinking about the idea of only having one lover, even one love.

Strange that someone she'd only known for a short time could have her contemplating forever.

She shook the thought away and focused on the task at hand. She'd been sitting behind a clump of scraggly bushes, waiting, letting her heart settle and her breath deepen. Rowena had always said that no one could go still like her, that she seemed to fade into the scenery. Ember wished she could see it from the outside.

Soon, her patience was rewarded. A rabbit wandered from a tuft of grass that probably disguised its home. Ember waited, watching until it came close enough, then she leaped, her bent legs working like a spring to bring her up and over before the animal could run. Rowena always said no one was as fast as her, either.

Ember grabbed the rabbit and broke its neck. It was lean, nearly scrawny. She laid it aside and sat to wait again. At least they'd eat tonight. And if Sydney was successful at finding a stream, maybe they could bathe.

Maybe they wouldn't have to wait until all the trouble was over. Either way, Ember smiled.

CHAPTER TWELVE

Safely inside the tunnel, Rowena's confidence came flooding back. How much of her fear had Camille seen? No doubt she'd missed it in her own panic. But why had Camille acted as if she was going to kiss her and then didn't? Maybe Camille expressed her anger by flirting. When she wasn't shouting and raging around other people's homes.

A jot of shame rushed through Rowena. She shouldn't have told Camille to walk home, but she'd been frustrated and angry. She'd never asked for houseguests, especially one so distracting. Even now, she could hear Camille breathing, could practically feel the swish of her skirt. Rowena was trying hard not to smell her, but the scent of apricots had become lodged in her nostrils. She tried to tell herself she found it appealing just because it was better than the dry cavern scents surrounding them, but that wasn't true.

She could get used to having that scent around all the time.

Well, she'd have to deal with it a little longer. Rowena fought to remember the route back into her home. They could rest, then she'd give Camille a task, and maybe she would stay, maybe not. They never had to speak of their argument.

The tunnel widened ahead, and Rowena slowed. The light from her fungus stretched inside to reveal a slight dip in the floor and a selection of tunnels curving on all sides, some made by husks, others made by the weather long in the past.

"What's wrong?" Camille said, her breath tickling the back of Rowena's neck.

She shivered. "I know I set a trap in this room, but I can't remember what it is." She gnawed on her lip. "I don't think there are spiders, but they tend to get everywhere."

Camille made a little mewling sound and coughed. "You...put spiders here?"

"They're *supposed* to stay in the tunnels."

"Oh, right. Because spiders are famous for doing as they're told."

Rowena shushed her but didn't turn, knowing her own raw feelings would respond to anger with anger. "I said, they're *not* here."

"Like they weren't supposed to be up there?" Camille mumbled.

"All right. I should have checked more often." She kneeled by the entrance to the large room. With the light closer, she finally saw a tripwire. "Watch your step," she said showing it to Camille.

Camille followed nearly on top of her as Rowena stepped over. "What does it do?"

"Cave-in, probably."

"You don't know?"

Rowena took a deep breath before she turned. "This was all done a long time ago. And I didn't make a list because I didn't ever want to come here, and it seems I didn't need these traps anyway. I feel foolish already, so do you mind if we just get on with it?"

Camille's scowl eased. "Why the traps? The mountain seems enough of a deterrent—"

"Let's get out of here, and I'll tell you all about it." Not bloody likely, but it shut her up long enough for them to cross the room and go out the other side once Rowena found the right tunnel. Maybe the silence would hold until they got back to safety, or at least until they found the next trap.

At the next junction, Rowena spotted traces of old webbing dangling from the ceiling next to a shaft that tunneled up through the rock. She didn't point it out to Camille. It wasn't fresh, and that left her wondering where all the other spiders had gotten to. Maybe they were all running amok on the surface. Maybe that was why the yeti had been so upset. She hoped they hadn't found their way down to the village. She didn't think that specially augmented spiders were a magical act the villagers would appreciate.

It wasn't long before they reached what looked like a dead end but was another secret door. When they were on the other side, Rowena

NOT YOUR AVERAGE LOVE SPELL

breathed deep. "These are the safe tunnels. Don't worry. I know them like the back of my hand."

"So, no spiders then."

Rowena was about to say, of course not, but if they could get out of the secret tunnels, they could get anywhere. "Nope."

"That sounded very convincing."

Rowena quickened her pace. She was only a few twists, turns, and short staircases from home, and she could hardly wait to be behind closed doors. She'd wash away the fatigue that came from venturing outside. Maybe Camille would be calmer after a bath, too. The thought conjured images best not pondered, but her mind wouldn't banish them easily.

"What in the seven bells?" Camille whispered.

Her grip on Rowena's arm nearly made her jump, and when she looked ahead, she spotted a slew of crumpled bodies on the edge of the light.

Rowena slowed, but she could see they were husks. The tangle of limbs and torsos had been shredded, with dirt and clay spilling out of dead organs in piles of dust. She lifted the light, and spied the landing between this part of the tunnel and the first staircase going up.

"What happened to them?" Camille asked, ever one to ponder out loud.

Rowena could only shake her head and come closer, searching the shadows for enemies, but the space wasn't that large.

"These cuts are jagged," Camille said as she kneeled beside the husks. She reached forward as if she might touch but drew back.

Rowena's anger sparked and grew. These husks were the last batch she'd sent after Ember, and something had been waiting to trash them. The long, harsh wounds dotting their bodies weren't the work of spiders, she hadn't created any creatures with claws, and the yeti was outside.

Swords lay beside the bodies, and Rowena pulled one forth to find it stained dark red. One of the husks had gotten a hit in, at least. A minor comfort. She stood and hurried toward the staircase, desperate to strike at whoever was invading her home.

"Wait," Camille called. "Don't go charging in without a plan."

"I have a plan," Rowena said. "Kill whatever did this." She pulled out a piece of brimstone and wrapped her anger around it. Time for a little destructive magic of her own. The knights might use heartfire to ignite their own hands or what they touched, but if the bastards had bothered to dig a little deeper, they would have learned that they didn't need to get that close.

Thinking of the knights made her even angrier. If this was their work, she would end them. No negotiation; she wouldn't acknowledge their high-handed threats. It would just be fire fighting fire.

They wouldn't stand a—

Something came barreling out of the darkness of the staircase and crashed into her, sending her back into Camille, who screamed as she lost her footing. They both tumbled down the stairs, the light flickering. Rowena landed hard on her back, her head bouncing off Camille's knee. She cried out as her brimstone flew from her outstretched arm.

Something leaped over her in a rush of air.

Rowena rolled over, easing her tight grip on the fungus so she could see. The shadow that had hit her moved on the other side of the pile of husks. It seemed hardly bigger than a cat, but the shadows distorted it. Rowena reached for Camille and hauled her upright. Camille gasped, and Rowena knew she'd seen the shadow. A low hiss emanated from that corner, and a rasping sound echoed around them. Claws on stone.

"Camille, stay back." Rowena dove for her brimstone. She scooped up the stone in one hand, but the shadow leaped into the light.

Golden scales glinted, and claws as long as Rowena's fingers stretched toward her face. The open snout seemed made of teeth, and wings flared around the shoulders. Rowena threw the bit of brimstone, adding her life force to the emotions that had sparked it. It blazed with flame, but the winged horror wrenched upward with a powerful pull of its wings, and the brimstone flew under it into the pile of husks.

The dry, desiccated husks.

"Shit," Rowena cried as the pile became a bonfire, the heat strong enough to drive her back. She heard a screech and turned, thinking of the winged horror flying at her, but it was Camille running toward her and swinging her pack.

The scaled beast entered the light once more, but Camille's wild swing drove it away. It landed between them and the stairs. The air became a smoky blanket, turning Rowena's lungs to heated grit. She coughed and heard Camille doing the same. Her heart began a panicky beat. They needed to get out of here.

Rowena clutched Camille's arm as they stumbled from the room and back the way they'd come. The smoke chased them, filling in all the air. Rowena ducked low and brought Camille with her, leading the way to the exit and the cursed outdoors.

❖

Camille took a few gulps of fresh air and tried to process what she'd seen. Something had attacked them, something Rowena had seemed surprised by. But she'd been surprised her spiders had run amok, too. Maybe this was just another little trap she'd forgotten about.

Anger burned in Camille again, taking her back to how she'd felt when they'd first gotten to safety after the yeti. She wanted Rowena to *beg* her to stay. Maybe she'd walk away now. Maybe she'd keep walking into the sunshine streaming along the ground below the mountain in front of her and—

Rowena wasn't beside her. She turned. The long, downward sloping tunnel had led into a small, scree-filled valley, but Rowena lingered out of the sunshine, standing under a ledge that guarded the secret door to the tunnels. Camille shielded her eyes and stepped back into the shade. Rowena's eyes were closed, and she shivered as if injured.

Camille swore to herself, and her anger vanished. "Are you all right?"

Rowena's chin wobbled as if she was either going to cry or be sick. Camille reached out, but Rowena seemed to sense the movement and drew back, holding herself as the shivering increased. She sank to the ground. When Camille kneeled beside her, the slight sound startled her. She opened her eyes, but the sight of the sun-filled valley seemed to pain her. With a whimper, she closed her eyes tight again and bared her teeth.

"Leave me alone," she spat, her voice strangled.

Impossible to do, given their circumstances. "Rowena."

"Go away. You were going to leave, so leave. What's stopping you?"

If she hadn't looked so pitiful, her words might have garnered the response she clearly wanted, but Camille recognized someone lashing out in fear when she saw it. Maybe that was what their original fight had been about, needing help, looking weak. When Camille's friend Hetty had broken her ankle a few years back, she'd been a bear to those trying to help her, insisting she could do everything herself. After she'd finally allowed Camille to help, she'd apologized. Camille had assured her that, luckily, her friendship was worth trudging through her bullshit.

Would it be so easy with someone she barely knew? Camille sighed. It wasn't as if she could do anything else. She sat beside Rowena, but before any more of *this* bullshit, she said, "I've read about seizures of fear, but I've never seen one. It looks very painful."

"I'm not—"

"Here." Camille shifted until she blocked the light. "It's the outdoors, isn't it?"

"You can't—"

"It's cockroaches for me. I know it doesn't make sense. They can't hurt me; they don't even have teeth, but I had to clear out a few storerooms when I started working for the library, and sometimes, I felt like I was swimming in them." Her bile rose at the thought. "Even now, when I see one, I go silly, screaming and flailing. Of course, after today, I probably won't feel so kindly toward spiders, either, but I've never had a seizure of fear."

Rowena made a dismissive, coughing sound.

"You probably already knew this," Camille said, "but you just have to wait it out. That's what I've read, anyway. I can't imagine what it feels like, but everything I've read says to breathe through it and wait for the world to stop crumbling. If you want me to stop talking…"

Rowena took a deep breath. Her shivering seemed less, maybe because Camille was blocking some of the light and the heat and the smell of outside. "No."

Camille chatted about nothing. Rowena seemed to calm, but her chin still wobbled as if tears were close to the surface. When she leaned forward, Camille put her arms out, certain Rowena was going to pass out, but she merely slumped against Camille's collarbone and took shuddering breaths. Camille held her, thinking of when they'd shared an embrace before. But what kind of abuse was she in for once Rowena recovered?

Well, if she thought she could force Camille to do anything, she could forget it. Fear obviously lived at the heart of Rowena's pain, and Camille wasn't going to let that make decisions for both of them.

When Camille smoothed her hair, Rowena sat back and sniffled, wiping her face. Her hair had come undone from its tie, and the barrette she'd worn in front was skewed, revealing the lock of white near her temple. "Why do you cover that up?" Camille asked. "It's pretty."

Rowena shrugged, not meeting her eyes.

"You don't know that it's pretty, or you don't know why you cover it up?"

"There was a village." Rowena took another deep breath, eyes closed. "I used magic to help them recover some livestock after a flood. Most were grateful, but this one family had once played host to a traveling knight, and unbeknownst to me, the kids had actually listened to the knight's poison. When I was on my way out of town, this boy hit me from behind with some kind of farm implement."

Camille nearly held her breath, her ire rising, though she waited for more.

"When I woke up, my head was pounding and bleeding. The boy, maybe sixteen, had found a couple friends, and they'd bound me hand and foot and were tying sacks of rocks around me."

"To drown you?" Camille gritted her teeth. "Little bastards."

Rowena smiled weakly. "The knight had told them it was a surefire way to kill a witch. I said it was a surefire way to kill anyone. I tried to reason with them; I could see they were afraid. The boy wouldn't listen. Luckily, they'd left my bag strapped around me, so I had my reagents. I think I was more offended right then that they thought I'd be so easy to kill that they didn't even have to disarm me. I got my hands into the bag and cast my way out of the ropes. The friends ran, and the boy faced off with me holding the same thing he'd hit me with." She touched the white lock. "A clump of my hair was still dangling from a jagged metal bit."

Camille took her hand and squeezed. "What did you do?"

"Walked away," Rowena said with another shrug. "Though I did so backward. I don't know what happened to him. I don't care. I learned never to trust anyone again, even someone I've helped."

Camille nodded, tempted to lecture that not all people were bad, but the pain on Rowena's face wouldn't stand for it. "I probably would have done the same."

That got her another smile.

"Was that when you…" Camille gestured at the mountain.

"Stopped going out except for emergencies? Pretty much." She fingered that lock again.

Camille squeezed her hand until Rowena looked her in the eye. "We can't go back in there until the fire's out and we figure out how to deal with that thing, but you don't have to worry. If we meet that kid again, or any angry farmers, I'm going to rip their heads off."

Rowena smiled crookedly. She swallowed, and tears still swam in her eyes. "You'll stay with me?"

Camille took a deep breath with barely a thought for her plan to walk away. "I will."

She convinced Rowena to move away from the base of the mountain, though they stuck to shade when they could, and Rowena seemed careful not to look up. She kept saying the sky would swallow her. Camille didn't bother to contradict her. Rowena no doubt *knew* that the sky wouldn't eat her, but knowing and believing were two different things. Logic often lost to fear.

"Did you get a good look at what attacked us?" Camille asked, trying to distract her as they skirted the mountain, making for the village. Rowena agreed that they couldn't camp at the secret entrance since whatever attacked them might follow. It had gotten in somehow, after all. They didn't know if it could open doors or not.

"Scales," Rowena said, her breath coming harder than the exertion called for, but at least she'd stopped trembling. "Teeth, claws, wings."

"A winged lizard," Camille mused. "Unless you count dragons, there aren't any." She started to laugh, then stopped herself. "You have a yeti, and that's supposed to be a mythical creature, just as a dragon is."

"I did not bring a dragon here."

"How did you bring a yeti?"

Rowena shook her head. "He was here when I arrived. I don't bother him; he doesn't bother me, but he's driven off travelers before. He's usually just curious, rarely shows himself. I don't know what got into him earlier."

Camille shuddered at the memory of the hairy creature blocking her path, the matted fur and hands that seemed all too human. "Maybe he was surprised by a miniature dragon, too."

"There *aren't* any dragons."

"The one that attacked us would beg to differ." Camille took a few deep breaths, getting her own anger in check. She was quickly learning that lashing out was how Rowena dealt with difficulty, and Camille was fine with that for now, when Rowena was under more than average stress.

But once they were safe behind closed doors, if Rowena continued to snipe at her, Camille was going to let her have it.

"Based on what I've read," Camille said, "and I've read a lot about magical creatures, dragons don't normally come that small."

"Even babies?"

"I've never read about dragon babies. In the stories, they just sort of…spring into life, maybe created like your…Ember."

Rowena chuckled. "Homunculus."

"It's not the easiest word to say," Camille grumbled. "Anyway, dragons were always said to be created, not born. In Miss Elspeth Fogerty's *Myths and Tales of Magical Creatures*, dragons gathered to perform dark rituals and create new brethren. Of course, also according to her, they sacrificed humans by the boatload and subsisted almost entirely on babies."

Rowena laughed, and the sound echoed strangely around them. "Good old Miss Fogerty. I'd forgotten about her."

"You've read her?" Camille's heart did a little leap.

"One of my favorites as a kid with all the blood and guts."

Camille grinned so widely, her cheeks hurt a little. There was no better bond than over a good book. "And here I thought you only read for research."

Rowena's face fell. "Being hunted from your homeland will do that to you."

Camille fell silent as she recalled the story of Rowena's attack, the sort of tale that just…lingered, no matter what else happened. And then there was how the knights were after her, how Sydney was after her. Camille hadn't thought of Sydney in a while. Rowena's plight didn't endear Camille to any knights, even though she knew Sydney had been evolving when last they'd spoken. Camille could only hope she was all right so that would continue. Maybe if she wrested control from Sir Robert, they'd no longer hunt witches, and Rowena could live in peace.

Inside a mountain, since she could barely stand being outdoors.

Camille sighed for probably the thousandth time, wondering why she always got involved with such difficult people.

When they reached the beginning of the dangerous trail up the mountain, Rowena paused under some shade. Camille could see the village in the distance, a straight shot down with no twists or trees.

Or shade.

"This is where I meet the villagers when they need me or want to hand over more"—Camille caught her side-eye—"pre-husks."

"Dead bodies."

Rowena sniffed, but Camille held up a hand to stop another lecture on usefulness and the differences between living people and dead ones. Rowena gestured to a blackened spot of earth. "They usually light a bonfire, and Ember notices it pretty quickly. Noticed it, anyway."

"None of that," Camille said before Rowena's chin could droop. "She's alive, and we'll find her." Before Rowena could argue that she couldn't know that, Camille added, "Right. You wait here, and I'll go get some supplies and…things."

"Things? There's confidence I can bloody well count on."

Camille put her hands on her hips. "*Things* for camping. If I don't know what to get, I can always ask. Then you can stay here by the mountain and find us a good spot, and when I get back, we can figure out what to do next." She rubbed her hands together and tried to look more confident than she felt. "Night will fall soon, and if there's anything I know about camping, it's that we'll need a tent." She'd only learned that recently but saw no need to mention it.

Rowena seemed skeptical.

"We can always seek shelter in the village," Camille said. Rowena turned a pale shade of green, and Camille hurried to wave the thought away. "Camping it is. Now, let's see what we've got in the way of payment."

They pooled their money, and Rowena offered a few things to barter. She stressed that Camille should tell the villagers the items were for Rowena the Hawk, but if they were curious about why she needed a tent and supplies, Camille was to look as mysterious as she could.

Camille nodded. If Rowena's aura of mystique was that important to her, so be it. And if some villager wanted greater payment than what she had, Camille could offer a spell or two and lead the villager to where Rowena waited.

Camille only hoped they wouldn't want to trade with dead bodies.

With Rowena's instructions ringing in her ears, Camille strode toward the village, trying out different personas in her mind. She could be the Hawk's strong henchwoman, a fearsome presence not to be trifled with. Or a servant eager to badmouth her job with people of a similar economic station. Perhaps she would play at a devoted worshiper of the witch, tranquil and confident that she was fulfilling her life's purpose.

Or she could simply be herself, a reluctant abductee/houseguest. That didn't add nearly as much mystique, however, especially since the house in question was currently off-limits due to fire and a miniature dragon. At least the fire would probably burn itself out. The dragon...

No one needed to know about that.

Trading turned out to be easier than she thought. Most of the villagers seemed happy to sell or trade for a minimum after they heard Rowena's name. They seemed curious but not overly so, and none seemed as frightened as the farm boy in Rowena's story. Living near a witch had made her almost...everyday. Once the knights had started driving out the witches, slandering them had become a lot easier.

Camille scowled at the thought. Sir Robert and his cronies had a lot to answer for.

With shopping done, Camille headed back up the hill with food, water, blankets, a tent, and other camping utensils. At the last moment, she traded her pot of face cream for an impulse buy, but she knew it would be worth it. The villager she'd traded with seemed excited by a sweet-smelling lotion just for the face; he declared it the fanciest thing he'd ever seen. Camille chuckled at the thought that he'd no doubt get more joy out of it than she ever would.

Rowena waited right where Camille had left her. Her entire body seemed to relax when their eyes met, and Camille wondered if she'd been close to another seizure. When Camille pulled out her impulse buy, a cloak with a full hood to block out the hungry sky, Rowena laughed and threw her arms around Camille's shoulders.

Well worth it, indeed.

CHAPTER THIRTEEN

By the time Rowena and Camille found a campsite and got it ready, the day was nearly done. Rowena breathed a sigh of relief and wished the sun would hurry off. At night, she could pretend the world wasn't so large and could imagine walls just inside the darkness. She rubbed her chest, missing her connection with Ember. She'd never realized that sharing her emotions with another made them so much easier to bear.

Camille hadn't mentioned Rowena's fear again, and she was grateful but also strangely…irked. Part of her knew that was her fear taking over, just a different kind of fear, one that worried about having her trust taken advantage of or her weakness used against her or her troubles belittled.

But Camille wasn't like that. Rowena *knew* that, but she couldn't get her heart to *believe* it. After all, Ember had left her, and they were as close as two people could be.

No, Ember had been pulled away, had sacrificed herself in Rowena's place. That was different.

But she would have left eventually, no matter what. She wanted to travel, make friends, have adventures; she wanted all the things Rowena couldn't give her. Camille might stay with her until the current crisis was over, then she'd leave, too.

"We have an apple and a plum to go with dinner," Camille said, rummaging through their packs. "Which would you like?"

"Doesn't matter."

"You must have a preference." Her tone was light, even after all that had happened.

Rowena pulled her new cloak tighter. "Nope."

"Well, one is tart, and—"

"I said I don't care. How can you be going on about bloody plums and apples at a time like this?"

Camille set the fruit down and turned. Her dark eyes blazed, and her full lips became one thin line. Rowena waited. This was it; she would leave now like she'd done before, and Rowena would be proven right again. Better sooner than later.

"I know you're scared," Camille said, her voice low and dangerous, the rumble of a volcano before an eruption. "But don't take it out on me."

Rowena sneered, ready to tell her that she didn't know what she was talking about, ready to push her away.

And be alone as she was meant to be.

Camille put a hand up. "You're gonna get pissy with me again; I can see it in your eyes. Well, guess what?" She moved closer, and Rowena resisted the urge to lean back. "I'm not leaving."

Was she a bloody mind reader? "That's...I'm not..."

"I will *try* to be patient with you," Camille said. "But if you keep coming for me, I'm going to start hitting back like I should have done the first time you acted like an ass." She crept a little closer, and Rowena resisted the urge to scoot back. "I'm a smart woman, and I've been watching you, and if I wanted, I could take you apart with just a few words."

Rowena swallowed. Camille's voice was angry but also almost... seductive? The tone, combined with how she crept closer, never breaking eye contact, put Rowena in mind of some sleek, predatory animal. Even with all the anger and fear coursing through her, she found Camille alluring.

After a deep breath, Rowena said, "I'm sorry."

Camille relaxed back, smiling, and Rowena almost wished she'd pushed her, wanting to see if Camille would leap on her and attack.

"I just..." Rowena cursed the fact that she didn't know how to finish. It seemed Camille already understood, but she had to say something to fill the silence, and Camille was waiting. "I don't *want* you to leave, but...I feel..." She closed her eyes. It sounded so foolish out loud, but inside, she was still so certain. Sooner or later, everyone would leave.

The warm touch of Camille's hand in her hair made her open her eyes. Camille smoothed near the lock of white at her temple. "This should never have happened," she said softly, her face so close that her features blurred. "Even if it left behind something so beautiful." Her touch trailed down Rowena's cheek to her chin, leaving tingles in its wake. "Your future doesn't have to reflect your past, not if you don't want it to."

Rowena wanted to argue that she knew that, but she couldn't believe it. Hearing Camille say it created a spark within her. Maybe. Maybe.

She leaned in, and Camille didn't pull away, her eyes slipping closed.

A screech sounded from the right, and Rowena leaped to her feet. A shadow came hurtling out of the dusk, wings extended, claws reaching for her face. She threw herself on the ground, tugging Camille with her.

"It's back," Camille shouted, and it did seem like the same creature from before as it landed on a nearby stone, then spun to face them, jaws wide in its reptilian face.

Rowena grinned. They weren't shut up in some cavern with no air now. She dipped into her bag and found the brimstone again, igniting it with a thought and a blaze of emotion.

Another shrieking, inhuman cry came from up the slope on the mountain. Camille grabbed Rowena's hand as the winged lizard flew at them again. Rowena followed where Camille tugged her, but she didn't take her eyes off her target, cocking her arm to throw. When the lizard missed them, she threw the brimstone and wrapped it with her emotion and life force, sending the burning glob into the lizard's side.

Rowena gave it another shot of power, and the fire roared, clinging to the lizard and spreading along the lithe form. It screamed and fell, writhing and shrieking. She turned her attention toward the other cries but saw nothing in the falling darkness. When she heard the roar of the yeti, she knew why.

The lizard things were everywhere.

Camille guided them into the open, and Rowena winced. It would be full dark in moments, but right now, there was too much open sky, too much air. She couldn't keep the cloak tight and her arms free, so she pulled the hood down far and tried to focus anywhere but the openness.

Just above them on the slope, a spider stumbled over the lip of the trail, a lizard thing clinging to its back and tearing out hunks of flesh. Other animal shrieks echoed through the dimness, punctuated by the howls of the yeti.

"What in the seven bells?" Camille said.

Through it all, a human scream drifted on the wind.

Rowena's heart plummeted. "The village."

They ran, Rowena's courage growing as the light continued to fade. Lanterns burned in the village, guiding the way. Rowena could imagine they were all in some massive cavern, the comforting stone rising just outside the circles of light.

The screams grew in number. As Rowena reached the village, a pair of shadows tumbled in the street. Rowena took a jar of needles from her bag and dumped some into her hand. She whistled sharply, and a small shadow broke from the larger, flapping its wings to stay aloft.

Rowena added a dragonfly wing to the needle pile, blew across the lot, then as the dragonfly wing took flight, she wrapped them all in her life force, connecting them. The needles lifted into the air, she added another jolt of force, and they flew as a blur to punch into the lizard's body. It screamed and floundered. Gaping holes dotted its wings, and it fluttered to the ground. Rowena charged and kicked it in the head until it ceased moving.

More people were stumbling into the street amid sounds of breaking glass. The lizard things seemed to be everywhere, but the villagers were fighting back with whatever they had to hand. Camille ran to someone lying in the street and pulled them out of the chaotic mix of running feet and shrieking lizards.

Rowena continued into the fray, flinging needles or fire. There wasn't time for any larger spells that required symbols or circles, and at one point, she had to pick up a broken broom handle and beat one of the creatures away from a group of people trying to take shelter down a cellar door. Camille was shouting, directing villagers to carry out the wounded, and Rowena felt a swell of pride at how coolly she kept her head.

Rowena's foot caught on something, and she pitched forward. She flung her arms out to catch herself and rolled away from an impact that left her head pounding. She almost expected to see the face of that village boy staring down at her with his rake in hand, her hair dangling from the end.

A lizard thing rushed for her face. Rowena put her arms up and tried to kick away, but the teeth sank into the flesh above her elbow. She yelped and then screamed as the creature pulled; she could have sworn someone dipped her arm in acid. She slapped at its head until it let go, and she fought the urge to pant for breath.

Get up and run, her body cried, but she couldn't find purchase on the churned ground, and the thing wouldn't stop coming, snapping and scratching at her legs, nearly tearing through her thick hose.

"Help the witch," someone cried, and a few shouts answered him. Shadows rallied around her, one grabbing her under the arms and pulling her away while the others surrounded the lizard thing and mobbed it under staves and tools and boots.

"You all right?" a villager asked, the face a mere shadow. "Did it get you?" Before she could answer, the speaker touched her arm. She yelped as waves of pain and nausea tore through her body. The villager wrapped a piece of cloth around her elbow and pulled it tight, making the wound sing anew and robbing her of breath.

"Go, go," the villager said. "There aren't many left, and you've done enough. Go. See the healer."

Rowena stumbled away, grateful beyond words that no one clubbed her over the head, that someone saw her value, but she also feared that someone might see a wounded witch as an opportunity. As the villagers passed, though, they touched her shoulders or muttered thanks, and one took her unwounded elbow and sought to help her along, but she shook him off and headed for light and voices.

Inside the largest structure, light spilled into the street, and people hustled back and forth, carrying or helping the wounded inside, then going out to look for more. Rowena had a stray thought about this healer. Many people in the village knew home remedies, but the place wasn't large enough to attract a doctor or anyone whose primary job was to heal.

When she saw Camille directing the wounded and bending over bloody bodies, she almost laughed. Camille *did* sound as if she knew what she was talking about while offering solutions and courses of action. Rowena began to think she must have read every book in creation.

"Rowena," Camille said as their eyes met. She rushed over, reaching for the bloodied bundle of cloth.

"Healer?" Rowena hoped for a calm, sarcastic tone, but her voice shook, and she had a brief memory of snapping teeth.

Camille barked a humorless laugh and led her to an empty chair. From the size of the place, she guessed it was some kind of way station, maybe a tavern, but the furniture was too disheveled to make anything out. Camille unwrapped the cloth and hissed at the sight of blood soaking the sleeve of Rowena's dress. After a grim look, she grabbed the fabric and ripped the sleeve apart.

"Hey," Rowena said. "I could have pushed that up."

Camille didn't respond and kneeled to inspect the wound. "Several puncture marks," she said vaguely. "We need to clean it." She reached for something, Rowena turned her arm, trying to see the marks, but she only caught the glint of a bottle as Camille dumped some kind of clear alcohol over the wound.

Rowena sucked in so hard her throat ached. She wanted to scream, but she bit down on her other fist instead.

"I know, I know, I'm sorry," Camille said. "But it's the best they have." Her eyes flicked to Rowena's. "Here comes one more."

"No, find some water or—" Another slug of liquid fire sloshed over her arm. She kept her teeth closed but let out a garbled cry of pain. She grabbed the bottle out of Camille's grasp and downed some of it, not even tasting, just seeking a balm.

"That's for wounds." Camille grabbed it back and rewrapped Rowena's arm. "Did that creature bite you anywhere else?"

"Some scratches on my legs." She bent to look, but those weren't as bad as she thought. The creature had mostly shredded the end of her skirt and hose. "They'll be fine."

"I'll take you at your word but only because I think you might kill me if I douse you with liquor again."

Rowena brayed a laugh. Camille rose, bottle in hand. When she tilted it back and took a drink, Rowena cried, "That's for wounds," but Camille was already moving away through the crowd.

Rowena knew she should help. She knew a few magical remedies, but magical healing was only temporary. And her arm throbbed. Still, as the number of wounded grew, and Camille seemed overwhelmed, Rowena moved among them, digging in her bag for needle and thread. She had a good deal of anatomical knowledge, but as she began stitching wounds, she hoped no one recalled that all her knowledge came from a homunculus or the dead.

❖

Camille studied the body of the flying lizard and wondered when she'd become an expert on everything. Probably because she was the most well-read person in this village, but that didn't automatically make her an animal doctor or a people doctor or an anything doctor. Still, the villagers had heeded her small amount of medical knowledge, but when Rowena proved better at doctoring than her, they'd shepherded her to this barn where they'd laid one of the creatures. They were waiting outside for answers.

Well, she couldn't disappoint them, even if she didn't know what in the blazes she was doing.

She bent over the body and slid the lantern closer along the scarred worktable. The creature was as long as her leg and had the scaled and pebbled skin of a reptile, but its color was burnished gold. It had wings and talons like the fabled dragons, but the front claws had an opposable thumb and looked too much like human hands. A long neck led to a face dominated by a snout filled with sharp, curved teeth, but there was something about the eyes and the forehead that strayed from reptilian and looked almost human again. When she examined the stomach and chest, she found a patch of smooth golden skin that looked anything but reptilian.

"Urgh. What are you?" Part human, part reptile? Even Miss Fogerty never conceived of something so macabre.

The creature was fascinating from an intellectual standpoint but didn't give any clues about where it had come from or if its fellows had any aim beyond attacking everything they saw. Even the oldest villagers had never seen the like.

A scuffing sound came from the barn doors, heralding Rowena. She must have finally noticed Camille was no longer in the tavern and sought her out. A pleasing thought, even in such dark times.

Or wishful thinking.

"I hardly know what I'm looking at," Camille said. "Reptile characteristics, human-looking bits, and wings that could have belonged to a dragon. They certainly aren't bat or bird wings." When Rowena moved up beside her, gaze locked on the creature, Camille asked, "How are you feeling?"

"Like something bit me on the arm," Rowena said, her voice scratchy. "Thank you for seeing to me."

Camille turned to hide her smile. The sarcasm she expected, but the gratitude was still new. "Welcome." She gestured to the creature. "Any ideas?"

"There are spells to encourage growth in animals," she said. "That's how I created the spiders, but to change an animal so completely?" She shrugged. "If they exist, I don't know them."

"There were mythical creatures who were supposedly well-versed in magic."

"Fairies," Rowena said, "according to literature. Pixies, goblins."

"And dragons."

Rowena sighed. "A dragon survived the purge of its fellow magical creatures and is now making little copies of itself with human components? If Miss Fogerty was alive, she'd be doing a jig."

"It's a theory."

"Which leaves us where?" Rowena asked.

"Asking ourselves if this can be connected to the Kells or the witchstone or Sir Robert."

"Hmm."

They didn't have any evidence that the situations *were* connected, but Camille didn't know for certain that they weren't. Feeling the wideness of the world, of possibilities, she understood a bit of Rowena's fear and took her hand.

Rowena didn't pull away, didn't even glance at her, just turned her hand so their fingers laced. "We don't know how many of those creatures got into the mountain. I don't know if we can drive them all out by ourselves. I don't want to ask the villagers for help. Enough of them have suffered already." She looked at Camille, her expression pained. "If these creatures are connected to everything else, then they were looking for me, possibly us, and I don't want to put these people in any more danger. I have to"—she swallowed visibly—"go find the problem."

Camille felt a rush of affection. She kissed Rowena's cheek, bringing out a pink blush, but Rowena still didn't pull away. "Wherever we're going, I'm with you."

Rowena's smile turned sly. "I didn't ask you to come," she said, tone teasing.

Camille resisted the urge to pinch her and shrugged. "Oh, all right. I'll just stay here." She started to pull away, but Rowena tugged her back in and kissed her soundly.

Sydney had found a stream the night before, but even when relatively clean, she couldn't think about doing more with Ember than holding her tightly. She had a guilty thought about doing what she'd pledged she wouldn't, bringing romance on a mission. It was a boundary she wouldn't cross with Camille, another point of guilt. As she fell quickly to sleep with Ember's warmth in her arms, she hoped Camille was safe and warm and happy and not fixated on Sydney.

The last part was just her own selfishness talking.

In the morning, they began their walk toward the mountain again. The landscape had become more forest since the village, but through gaps in the trees, Sydney was happy to see that Ember's home seemed much closer. In another day or so, they'd arrive. Then Ember could make sure the Hawk was all right, and Sydney would convince her to use her magic to find Camille and the other knights.

Fantastic. She was *so* looking forward to it.

Ember had talked more about the Hawk that morning, certain she could and would help. Sydney had turned away to roll her eyes. Using magic even when she knew it was the root of all their current troubles? She was as bad as Sir Robert.

When the ground dipped into a shallow valley, Sydney spotted dark shapes among a patch of trees where the ground sloped up into a larger hill. Her heart began to pound again. It could be anything, but something about the way they were haphazardly strewn caused her stomach to churn. When she caught more than a few hints of red, she broke into a run anyway, her body protesting after days of walking and fighting and sleeping on the ground. Ember stayed at her side, firing off questions, but they seemed almost directed at the air around them, and she spoke in a worried, rushed tone.

Sydney caught the metallic tang of blood as she pounded up the slope. Ahead, she saw churned earth, crushed bushes, and some low-hanging limbs torn from tree trunks, but the harsh pine scent wasn't enough to cover the smell of a battlefield.

When she saw a knight-issued boot sticking forth from a pile of leaves, she couldn't hold in a moan of pain. She willed herself to run faster, and when she fell in the mud, she used the pain and anger to push off with hands and feet and throw herself at the boot owner's side.

"Sergeant Masterson," she said, rolling the limp body. Masterson's gray eyes stared upward without a spark of life. Her chainmail had been sheared through, and the jade pendant she was so proud of sat in a puddle of blood.

Sydney choked back her grief and pushed up, taking in the rest. She stumbled from body to body, ten in all, scattered among Kells and lizard creatures. Each name bombarded her until she thought she might scream.

Instead, she stood and ripped a nearly severed branch from a tree and beat the ground with it, screaming her rage. She should have been here. She could have helped them.

"Sydney."

She turned to face Ember, who kneeled on the ground, pointing to something. "There are others."

It took a moment for the words to make sense. Ember pointed up the slope. "More knights?" Of course there were. The order had set out with a thousand, and these were only ten.

"The footprints go up, but there's something—"

Sydney ran up the slope, following a path of broken foliage. She'd been blind not to notice it before. Gratitude and hope grew within her. It wasn't too late to save some of her comrades.

❖

Ember had never thought that so few days could have so much crammed into them. Feelings everywhere, one fight after another, more feelings, a kiss, some cuddles, and now even more feelings with another fight soon to follow.

And Sydney was once more lost to emotion. She nearly glowed with heartfire and would pitch herself into danger as soon as it showed itself. Ember almost admired that. She'd done it many times, but her eyes had been open every time. She'd been calm and confident. Stupid, Rowena would say, but Sydney was angry and sad and worried and crying, and she would be even stupider if she got the chance.

Ember had to slow her down.

"I saw another footprint," she called as she ran. "Not from a person."

Sydney didn't even glance at her, but she'd never seemed keen on talking and running.

"It was big. There were probably more unless the thing that made it only has one leg, but I couldn't tell with all the torn-up ground."

Still nothing.

"It was even bigger than the biggest footprint I've ever seen, which was from a bear." She took a breath, ready for Sydney to scoff or tell her she was crazy. Whatever was going on, Sydney didn't want to believe what the Kell had told them. "It looked like a bird's foot or a lizard's. Or a dragon's. I've never seen a dragon print, but I've never seen a dragon before, either. I don't know what else could have feet that big with really long toes like a bird. Unless it was a really, really big bird." She remembered the beaks of the raptors on the mountain and shuddered. "But the Kell mentioned a dragon, not a big bird."

Still nothing.

Ember sighed as she ran. Sydney seemed to get winded so easily. Maybe she'd respond when she got her wind back. But when the sounds of combat echoed from the summit of the hill, Ember knew that wouldn't be the case. Sydney picked up speed even though her breath already came in short, hard bursts through her open mouth. Oh well, if she wanted to throw herself into danger, Ember would just have to make sure she stayed alive.

Above, through the trees, a group of knights stood along the crest of the hill, fighting against a host of Kells with a few cloaked lizard people thrown in. The Kells had pushed them back in places, breaking their line and taking away the advantage of the high ground. The lizard people were faster than any human but didn't seem as skilled as the Kells. As she watched, two went down under the knights' blades.

Sydney rushed the Kells' backs. Her mouth was still open, but her teeth were bared as if she would have uttered a battle cry had she the breath. Something in her seemed to want to warn her enemies before she engaged. Only the unarmed Kell had been different. Rage had Sydney, then, and Ember stayed at her side in case that same rage had her now.

One Kell pitched forward as Sydney sliced him behind the knees. Another turned to confront her, and Ember blocked that blade with her own. These Kells all had the same shaven heads as those before, but this one lacked a beard, had piercing blue eyes and chubby pink cheeks, a face built for laughter. It was laughing now as the Kell tried to kill her.

This one was fast, but Ember was faster. After blocking the attack, she pushed forward, remembering the Kellish aggression and not wanting to give this one a chance. The Kell pressed forward, too, and their blades locked, but Ember twisted the Kell's sword to the side and bent slightly to bring her free arm up and bash the Kell across the nose. The Kell staggered, and Ember flipped her sword up and pushed it through the leather armor and into the heart.

Killing the lizard people had pained her. She'd never taken the life of a human before, but there was something about these Kells, who didn't even acknowledge that others were real and stole their personhood before even meeting them. Ending a life still complicated her feelings, but it was less with the Kells.

And the captured one had said they didn't mind dying anyway. Maybe that made it okay.

Ember whirled and slashed and punched at Sydney's side, guarding her reckless attacks. Sydney still got a slash across the thigh, but Ember stabbed that opponent in the knee before he did further damage. She helped the other knights, too, because Sydney wanted it, and the combat almost seemed like a dance as Ember worked her way faster and faster through the living and dead. Even with the blood and noise, the fear and complicated feelings, there was something majestic in a battlefield.

Soon, all the enemies lay dead, and the knights were thanking her or grabbing her by the wrist and shaking her arm up and down. She tried to listen to their garbled words and asked their names and if they were all right, but they all talked at once, including Sydney, who moved among them like a hummingbird.

"Your thigh," Ember said near Sydney's ear.

Sydney didn't seem to hear, too busy speaking to the fifteen knights who lived and lamenting the comrades they couldn't save.

"Your wound needs a bandage," Ember said loudly. "Blood is trickling down your leg and will fill your boots, and that won't be pleasant."

When Sydney still ignored her, Ember hooked a foot around Sydney's unharmed leg and twisted, forcing Sydney to sit hard on an old, felled tree.

All the chatter stopped. Ember almost laughed. She'd never been one to *stop* the conversation. Rowena would have laughed, too. But when some knights went nervously for their weapons, Ember quickly kneeled and took off her pack.

"All the wounds need tending," Ember said slowly and loudly as she pointed to Sydney's knee. She dug out the meager medical supplies all the knights carried—or so Sydney said—and unrolled the bandages.

The knights muttered and began examining one another as if Ember had cast a spell of reason on them. They'd moved away from the bodies, and the conversation turned into a low, less exuberant drone.

Sydney squeezed Ember's shoulder as Ember dressed her wound, but she didn't seem to have the right words for thanking someone yet. "What happened to you?" she asked the knights.

The whole company stared, then glanced around as if bewildered by where they were, even those who seemed older than the rest.

"Juzail," Sydney said softly, her voice filled with pity. "What happened?"

One of the men turned to her while another knight tended his bloody ear. He swallowed, looked at the ground, then back at Sydney. His whole body seemed stiff as if he had to force himself to look her in the eye. "We were standing with the rest of the order, getting ready for the spell." He gestured to those around him. "All the recruits were standing together. And then my whole body hurt like blazes, and there was this blinding flash. I...must have passed out."

"We all did," someone else said.

Juzail nodded stiffly. "When we came to, we were lying in this scrubby forest." He gestured north. "And there were only twenty of us." He swallowed again, tears in his eyes. Ember frowned. There had been ten dead down below, should have been twenty-five in all, but she waited for the rest.

"We decided to walk south and try to find the others. We found Sir Robert and a few more officers."

Sydney went stiff. Ember burned with questions but held them.

"Not far from where we found them, the Kells attacked with those..." He nodded at the lizard people. "Things. They hit us hard; some of us didn't make it. The Kells captured a few of us and carried them off, including Sir Robert." A few tears leaked down Juzail's cheeks, and he wiped at them hurriedly with the heel of his hand. "I tried to get to him when he went down under their fists, but they had him bound and away so quickly. The enemy pressed on all sides, and we had to run." He gritted his teeth on the last word, but it still came out a strangled sob.

Ember finished with Sydney's leg, and she stood and limped to Juzail's side. "It's all right, Juzail. You survived. I'm proud of you, all of you." She took them all in with her gaze.

Some nodded and seemed invigorated. Some wouldn't meet her eyes. A few stared at nothing as if they hadn't heard a word.

"What do we do now, Major?" one of the excited ones asked.

Sydney put her hands on her hips and spoke without hesitation. "We make camp and do what we can for the wounded. I'll assign some as camp guards, then the rest of us will trail the captives and see what we can find out."

Even those who seemed oblivious brightened a bit now that they had a plan.

Ember frowned. "What about the dragon?"

The company stared, all looking mystified.

"What?" Juzail asked.

"Don't worry about it," Sydney said to him.

Ember started, wondering if Sydney's memory had dulled. "The dragon that the Kell told us about, the one who stood on that battlefield at some point." She gestured down the hill. "The one who made the lizard people."

"Those were…dragons?" Juzail asked, and others fired questions, some casting her concerned looks, others scoffing or looking around as if searching for a joke.

"Settle down," Sydney called.

"You talked to the Kells?" someone asked.

"One we captured," Ember said. "He'd helped burn a village to the ground, and he told us we were dreams, and that Kells were the only people who were real, and that they were being led by someone called Nightmare, who is a dragon, and who made these lizard people with the Kells somehow." She said it too quickly to make a really good story. Under the circumstances, the knights would want the bare facts.

Silence greeted her.

Sydney's cheeks went crimson.

Juzail frowned at Ember. "Who are you again?"

"She's a friend I met along the way," Sydney said quickly. "She's been a great help to me."

"So, you live here?" Juzail asked. "You're not…a Kell?"

The knights stiffened, hands stuttering toward their weapons again.

"I'm Ember. I'm not a Kell. I'm a homun—"

"Human being," Sydney nearly yelled. "Just another human and not a monster like the Kells. She's helping us, and she's a very good fighter, and that's all anyone needs to know. Now, we're going to find that campsite. Shira and Rincelle, you take point, look for even ground, but don't get out of sight of the rest of us. Everyone else, carry packs or the wounded. We'll see to the dead later." She lingered, waving the knights away and saying she'd bring up the rear before she joined Ember. "Why did you say all that?"

Ember tilted her head. "Why wouldn't I say what's true? Don't you want them to know about the dragon?"

"There is no dragon," Sydney said before she lowered her voice. "That was a bunch of Kell nonsense."

Ember tried to see past her own bafflement. She pointed at the battlefield, at the lizard people. "Then what—"

"I don't know, but there's certainly no dragon."

"Certainly isn't something that goes with I don't know."

"Well—"

"If you don't know, you can't be certain."

Sydney put a hand up. "Stop, please."

Ember frowned, wondering at her. Sydney seemed angry, but why? Maybe she was thinking of her dead comrades and didn't want to talk? But she'd seemed happy enough to talk to her soldiers. "Are you mad because of the fight?" She hit on an idea. "Or is it that you don't want to talk about Kells because you hate them right now?" She nodded, understanding that. "I don't like them, either."

Sydney took a breath and closed her eyes. "Just…stop bringing up dragons. And things that fuc—" She cleared her throat. "And things that Kell said."

Ember nodded slowly. She didn't want her soldiers to know about the Kell she'd killed. Ember could understand that, too. She'd been so upset.

But they had to talk about the dragon at some point.

When Sydney marched away, Ember caught up quickly, getting past the dragon to when Sydney had cut her off with the knights. "Why didn't you want me to tell them who I am?"

"Hmm?"

"You stopped me before I could say homunculus."

Red leaped into Sydney's cheeks again. She waved as if shooing the words away. "It would just…raise a lot of questions we don't have time to answer right now. They'd ask you to explain, to tell them where you came from, and you'd tell them about the Hawk." She shook her head. "Big mess of questions."

She wouldn't make eye contact, and the rapid way she spoke said that if she wasn't lying, she was skirting the truth. "You're leaving something out." The anger was still apparent in the set of Sydney's shoulders, but now there was something else. Bashfulness maybe, embarrassment. "You don't want them to know that you know someone who knows a witch?"

Sydney didn't reply, still wouldn't meet her gaze.

"You're afraid they'll be angry at you? Why? I'm not a witch. They shouldn't mind you associating with…" A strange thought wound through her mind. Sydney started being embarrassed when Ember spoke about what she was. Sydney had called her magical, but there had been the look in her eyes before that. Disbelieving.

Maybe even appalled.

Sydney was ashamed of her, ashamed of kissing and cuddling someone who wasn't exactly human.

Ember's insides froze, and her stomach dropped to her toes. She tried to think of what Rowena might say but came up empty. She needed their connection now so Rowena could tell her what to do, what to say, how to feel.

There had been a lot of firsts for her on this adventure, but this was the worst. Worse than thoughts of Camille, worse than killing. It was a feeling akin to guilt but a thousand times harsher.

She'd never even thought to regret who she was before.

Chapter Fourteen

Rowena cursed the fact that it was too onerous to travel at night. One small track led from the village toward the moors to the north and another ran to the high hills and scrubland farther east, but the first ended when it reached the pasture where the villagers kept sheep, and the other petered out even earlier. Here, no one wandered very much.

And trying to keep their footing and direction in the dark would prove difficult in the untamed wilderness. So, that left traveling by the soul-sucking daylight.

As morning dawned, she and Camille retrieved their camping supplies and set out. She kept her hood pulled low, her focus tight and narrow on the ground, her wounded arm only throbbing occasionally. Camille took her arm without a word, guiding her as she would a blind woman, but Rowena could see where to put her feet, at least. She wouldn't be able to see any lizard creatures rushing them, but she could depend on Camille for a warning.

The thought was almost enough to make her stumble. Depending on Camille felt...comfortable. She knew she could depend on Ember for some things, but Ember was a part of her. Camille was...other. And Rowena barely knew her. Circumstance had thrown them together, forcing proximity, forcing them to work together through danger, but in those dangerous instances, Camille had proven reliable and loyal, calm and generous. Rowena cringed, her shoulders twitching, ready for the knife to plunge between them.

She made herself breathe. Worrying about betrayal *and* being outdoors would surely trigger another paroxysm of fear, and she couldn't have that. She told herself it was possible to relax and be vigilant, but even her own brain scoffed at that.

"This is the direction you sent the husks?" Camille asked.

She seized on a different topic to think about, worry about. "The most recent batch went this way, though I don't think we'll catch up."

"Not if they can walk day and night. If they're wandering out here, and someone else finds them…"

Rowena waited for her to finish, but when she didn't, said, "What?"

"Well, if you're not used to them, they're a little…"

"Off-putting?"

"To say the least." Camille squeezed her hand, staving off some of her anger. "I know what you're going to say, Rowena, but most people wouldn't see a walking corpse as a 'tool.'"

"Most people are idiots."

Camille laughed, and Rowena sneaked a peek. Her tone seemed affectionate, not mocking, and she had a glint in her eye. "If I had a drink, I'd toast that. I hope nothing bad has happened to your husks, too."

Rowena sighed, knowing what she was getting at. No matter how useful they were, a group of animated dead wouldn't foster good feelings toward witches. And it would be hard to justify defending the husks against a group of angry villagers; the living would take priority.

Even if she didn't like them as well.

"I wish we could get a better sense of which way to go," Camille said as they reached the end of the northern path and the sheep pasture.

The moors spread out ahead of them in all directions, a bleak, hilly land crisscrossed with animal paths and the occasional clump of trees or jut of limestone. She hadn't been out here except for when she'd arrived, but it hadn't changed from the same bleak shade of gray it had always been. Even the sky seemed duller.

And the openness still seemed ready to swallow her whole.

"At least we'll be able to see anything coming for us," Camille said.

"Don't count on it. This whole area is built on a bed of limestone, and there are caverns that stretch for miles not far under the surface. The village had trouble with a group of sheep thieves not long ago, and they used the caverns to hide."

"Great," Camille said.

Rowena chuckled and set her bag down, happy to have something to focus on besides the outdoors. "I was able to trade for a few more reagents, and I know a little something that might help." She drew a circle in the dirt with her unwounded arm, taking care to mark the four compass points. "It's a spell for locating people. Not specific people," she added before Camille could rejoice. "And it's only good within a mile or so." She added some fingernail clippings and a strand of her hair, surrounding them with ancient symbols for humanity. "There are spells for locating all kinds of different creatures, but this is the only one I have memorized."

Camille bent over the circle, her scent warm and comforting. "You don't know one for a creature that's part dragon and possibly part human?"

"Nope. Maybe the spell would find the possibly human parts of them."

"Not a sentence I thought I'd ever hear."

Rowena had to laugh. It was all a little absurd, and she felt like one of the strangest parts, the tracking witch who was scared of the outdoors.

She sat at the circle's side and focused, sending her life force over the components and merging them together with the circle, igniting the magic and sending it outward. She felt a strong pull north and pointed that way, then another pull nearly due east, not as strong, which meant they were farther away.

When the spell had gone full circle around her, it ended, and she opened her eyes.

Camille stood on tiptoe, looking over the moors. "I found your human to the north. It's a shepherd bringing back a sheep."

"East, then." Rowena shuddered. "Into nothingness."

Camille took her hand, and Rowena huddled into her cloak again, reducing the suffocating outdoors into the ground right in front of her.

It was hard to count time while watching so little, but any desire she had to peek was washed away by the certainty that the sky was waiting for her to look at it so it could swallow her whole. When Camille said, "I see someone," she knew the time had finally come.

After a deep breath, Rowena looked up. They stood at the base of a small hill, the side rolling up before them. Rowena had enjoyed the hills so far; they narrowed her view even more. But this one had a crown of naked rocks at the top, and a small group of people stood among them.

"Knights," Camille said.

Rowena's breath caught, her flaring anger helping drive away her fear. "Do you see…her?"

"Sydney?" Camille asked, her tone slightly teasing. "No." She gasped when Rowena pulled her behind a clump of scraggly bushes. "What are you doing? Aren't we looking for people?"

"If they're knights, and your…friend isn't with them, they'll stab a witch first and wonder who she was later."

"You might be right," Camille said.

Her concerned eyes made Rowena want to lean into her *and* confront the knights to prove she wasn't afraid. Wonderful. Conflicting emotions were just what one needed to cast magic calmly. She growled. "Maybe you should just go with them, and I'll find Ember."

"Don't be an ass," Camille said distractedly while peering upward. "That isn't the whole company, and they look like they're scanning the countryside. Probably looking for the others." She bit her lip. "Do we follow them?"

Rowena glared because she didn't know and because Camille had brushed off her attempt at a fight so handily.

"I *should* go with them," Camille said, face excited.

Rowena's heart plummeted, and she cursed it for ever getting involved in the first place. She wanted to say something withering, but her throat felt too choked.

"Just listen," Camille said, and Rowena knew her face objected even if her mouth wanted to seem indifferent. "I can find out what they've seen and what they know, then I'll sneak away and join you again."

So, she didn't want to *leave*. She only wanted to put herself in a dangerous situation, then return to Rowena. *She didn't want to leave.* Rowena's throat still rebelled but for a different reason. "No." She licked her lips, but all her saliva had dried up. "You won't be able to get away, and they might—"

"They're not going to hurt me," Camille said. "Not once I play the damsel." She stuck her bottom lip out, and her large eyes filled with tears. "I'm out here alone," she said in a breathless little voice.

Rowena shook her head and turned away. Even she wanted to take Camille in her arms at that look. "Then they definitely won't let you slip away. They'll be falling over themselves to protect you."

"Ha. I can do it." She leaned in and kissed Rowena's cheek, her hair brushing against Rowena's neck before she sat back.

Rowena went to make another argument, but Camille was gone, circling around the hill. Rowena hissed for her to come back, but she crept along quickly, then began to climb the hill from a different angle, shouting for help.

"Shit." Rowena ducked again and clenched a fist. She cradled her wounded arm, knowing the knights would do worse if she showed herself. That might put Camille in danger, too. The knights would find out she was a witch and think Camille was her familiar or something.

A little voice tried to say *she* could have played the helpless damsel, too, but she'd rather chew glass.

The knights had turned toward Camille, and a few shouted as they recognized the master researcher who'd helped them. Camille spoke loudly, nearly shouting, and Rowena almost laughed as her words floated down.

"One moment I was standing with all of you in the field, and the next, I'm out here in the wilderness." There were tears in her voice, and Rowena wondered if she should be worried that Camille could lie so well. "Oh, I'm so glad to see you. I've been so alone." She swayed, and the knights leaped to steady her. She leaned on one woman with an axe strapped across her back. "Where is everyone else?"

By their shaking heads, Rowena gathered that they didn't know. When Camille mentioned seeing strange creatures flying overhead that reminded her of tales of dragons, the knights laughed, all of them condescendingly reassuring her that dragons weren't real.

Fantastic. They'd found a group even more ignorant than they were, and now Camille was stuck with them. As they walked down the other side of the hill, Rowena crept around to follow, cursing the knights and all their kind. She couldn't merely watch the ground anymore. She had to sneak from cover to cover. Keeping her eyes fixed on Camille helped, but she bit the inside of her cheek as one knight after another offered Camille an arm or carried her over a bit of bog or lifted her on top of some rocks. Was that the kind of attention she wanted? She'd been with a knight before coming to the mountain; maybe the strong, stupid type was her favorite, and she was just passing the time with Rowena.

But she hadn't seemed happy with her knight. That kind of oaf might be fun for a tumble or two, but for the long term, Camille wanted someone intelligent, right?

As Camille laughed at something the knights said, Rowena rethought that. Intelligent was one thing, but there was also strong and capable. But Rowena had proven herself to be those, too, hadn't she? Maybe Camille had forgotten that.

It wasn't long before a mass of cloaked figures seemed to appear from the earth and attack the knights from all directions. Rowena grinned, hoping some of them might be hurt. But that meant Camille might be hurt, so she dug in her bag and tried to see what she could do.

These attackers weren't the flying creatures she'd seen, but a great deal of short, cloaked figures and some taller people in leather armor. Kells, she guessed, by the shaven heads and the hashmark tattoos down their arms. They sprang at the knights seemingly from the ground, and Rowena knew they'd come from the caverns, the entrances nearly covered by grass and peat. The ring of weapons echoed through the hills. The knights formed a rough circle with Camille in the center, and her searching eyes weren't looking for more enemies but obviously checking to make sure Rowena was all right.

Well, she didn't need any knights to protect her.

Rowena ripped up some grass and balled it in her fist. Then she dropped in a few leaves of clinging ivy, the heartiest, most stubborn plant she knew. When she'd made a rough sphere of the lot, she pressed a few snake scales in for fast movement. This didn't need to be as precise as a dragonfly. She needed speed.

Rowena threaded her life force into the ball, infusing it. Then she smashed it into the ground by her knees, feeling the jolt pass through the earth and to the grass at the edge of the fight.

Pushed by the spell, the grass combined with the force of ivy and snake rocketed toward several cloaked figures, winding about their legs and pulling them down. Their hoods fell back, and Rowena gasped at the sight of their golden, scaly heads.

"Dragon and human characteristics," she whispered, remembering what Camille had said. "What in the bloody blazes is going on?"

The creatures were soon cut down by the knights; the Kells followed, outnumbered. A cry from the other side of the fight drew Rowena's attention. Another group of cloaked creatures had emerged and overwhelmed two knights who'd become separated by the rest. But instead of killing them, the creatures gathered them up and ran.

If whoever was meshing dragons and humans needed more human parts, the knights were in for a terrible time. Rowena managed a jot of pity.

The other knights gave chase, taking Camille with them. They balked at a dark entrance to the caverns below, but they rallied at once, a few lighting lanterns and then all plunging into darkness. Rowena grinned and lowered her hood as she followed. This was more like it.

She hurried through the dark entrance, not able to keep in a sigh as the comforting stone surrounded her. When the lights stopped ahead, she paused. The knights had reached a large cavern, the ceiling dotted with holes that let the daylight stream in. Tunnels led off in all directions.

"Which way?" one of the knights called.

They split up, searching the ground and calling back the tracks they found. Camille kept peering at the tunnel they'd come from, and Rowena wished there was a way she could signal. If Camille didn't stop looking this way, the knights would know someone was here, but her natural concern seemed to override her good sense.

The knights couldn't seem to tell which way the enemy had gone. The mud was too churned. Rowena waited until they all seemed distracted, then crept forward, hoping Camille could see her. She waved.

Camille took a step toward her before squinting as if having trouble seeing. Rowena waved again. Camille stopped, her eyes widening, and Rowena sighed in relief. Then Camille discreetly pointed to one of the tunnels, her eyebrows raised.

Rowena looked that way but saw nothing. She shook her head. Camille frowned and pointed again but signaling what? Rowena thought about her wave. Did Camille think she was signaling the right path? Shaking her head again, Rowena put both hands up.

And noticed several knights looking right at her.

"You," one shouted. "Come out of there!"

She couldn't outrun them. She might be able to fight them all, but if she was caught or killed, that wouldn't do Ember or Camille any good. Smothering a curse, Rowena licked her lips and crept forward.

"Oh, dearie me, good knights," she said, pitching her voice higher. "Thank goodness I've found some…strong warriors to help me. I am so lost."

They glanced at one another, but several put their weapons away. "Who are you?"

"Me? I'm…" She swallowed. "I am…a milkmaid. I was, um, milking my cows when these…creatures set upon me." She put her hands to her cheeks and tried to look terrified. "I got lost in these caves, so lost, and I'm…please, help."

Camille's lips were pressed tightly together, and she was nearly vibrating, probably with repressed laughter. Rowena fought not to glare and ground her teeth.

The knights continued to stare, though some seemed sympathetic to her imaginary plight. She remembered Camille's stumble, put her hand to her head, moaned as if the life was leaving her, and crumpled to the floor.

They hurried to surround her, calling for water, rubbing her hands to wake her and cradling her head. It was all she could do not to snap at them and bite the hands that smoothed water over her brow and cheeks. She heard one wonder why a milkmaid was carrying two packs and a bag slung around her torso. She'd have more explaining to do when she "woke up."

For now, she got to relax as they carried her to the center of the cavern. It was the least they could do for bringing her to this humiliating predicament.

Sydney told herself that there were lots of reasons for keeping secrets. It wasn't like lying, which was inexcusable. No, secrets like Ember's heritage were for the keeper's own good. Once the knights had gotten to know Ember, they could understand what she was. But Sydney couldn't just drop something like that on their shoulders and expect them to hold their feelings inside. Who knew what might get said?

And that was doubly important with this group of recruits. They were young. The officers who'd been with them had been killed or kidnapped. They were grieving. They couldn't absorb great slabs of new information all at once.

And she had a job to do.

She thought of the captives and wondered why they were taken. Hostages, surely. She glanced around the meager, hastily erected campsite. The knights could hold their own captives here, if they ever took any. Then there could be a prisoner exchange. That was no doubt what the enemy wanted, and it made her breathe easier; that was war she could understand, and she was so ready for that.

But it wouldn't be easy. This situation still wasn't regular combat, not with lizard people in the mix. Or dragons. She shook her head at herself again. She should have let the knights know there was magic involved and *possibly* a dragon, but she'd known they'd laugh at her like they'd laughed at Ember. She would have shouted them down, but an outburst would have cost her respect.

And, a little voice whispered, if she said it aloud, that meant dragons were possibly real, and the world did not have room for magical creatures anymore. Her life didn't have room for anything so beyond the pale.

Like a not-wholly-human lover? Ember's heritage had meant a great deal when they'd first met, cropping up whenever the situation turned even slightly romantic. Somewhere along the way, that had ceased to matter, but now…

Sydney cursed herself and rose. Now that the knights were settled, she had a difficult conversation to deal with. Ember had been wandering the edge of camp as if afraid to be part of it. She'd come in now and again to help where she was needed, but she looked like someone who'd accidently kicked her granny. Her head was down, face wrinkled in sadness, and tears stood in her eyes.

"Stop being a piece of shit, Major," Sydney muttered to herself. She cleared her throat. "Ember, a word, please?"

Ember followed her as she limped to the side of camp. Ember's expression turned wary, and Sydney hated that, too. It was as if she'd taken the eager, excited, carefree woman she'd met and ground her on a millstone.

"I'm sorry," Sydney said. "You see, these recruits don't know anything about what's going on, and they're grieving, and I didn't want to drop too much on them at once. You understand?"

Ember only frowned.

"It's not forever," Sydney said, feeling herself start to sweat. "If there are…dragons, well, they'll find out for themselves, and I bet they'll feel awfully silly for laughing." She tried to chuckle and knew it stunk of desperation. "They'll fall over themselves apologizing to you. And well, after we defeat, um…"

"The dragon," Ember replied flatly.

"Well, yes, after that, well, you and I can…pick up where we left off." She tried a brighter smile. "And then it's up to us, well, you, or… Um, it's none of their business who you are unless you want to tell them, which you don't have to."

Ember stared for a long moment. "I thought you didn't lie."

Sydney backed up, feeling as if she'd been kicked in the chest. She wanted to cry a hundred objections, plead her innocence, or get angry at even the hint of an accusation, but the pain in Ember's eyes wouldn't allow it. Before she could say anything, Ember walked away.

Out of her life? Sydney watched, not knowing what to do if Ember should cross the camp's boundary and keep going. Run after her? Leave the knights? She gasped at the feeling of being torn in two, but Ember stopped at the other edge of camp and helped one of the knights start a fire.

Sydney breathed out slowly and tried to put all these personal problems from her mind. She had a job to do, and daylight was running out.

She put together a tracking group. Her wound hurt less as time went on, and she managed to walk without limping too badly. She might not find where the prisoners were being held tonight, but they needed a trail to follow. She was beyond pleased when Ember decided to join them, but she took a position up front with the trackers. Sydney tried to force herself not to worry, to keep an eye on the column as they marched, but her gaze kept coming back to that lithe figure, her hair a red pop of color in this drab wilderness.

Who wouldn't want her? She had beauty, skill, endless curiosity, and boundless enthusiasm. Some of the knights had flirted with her already. And they wouldn't care if their major had a lover as long as she wasn't canoodling when she was supposed to be working. Many had known Camille was her lover, and though it was embarrassing when they thought she was having sex in her tent, she wasn't embarrassed by Camille herself.

Oh, shit. She was embarrassed by Ember. When they were alone, it didn't matter, but among others, there'd be questions and rumors and looks. Teasing she could handle, but some would think Ember was magical, and not in the way Sydney knew she was. They'd see a romantic relationship as sleeping with the enemy, especially if they knew Ember's connection to the Hawk.

Not long ago, Sydney would have thought the same if one of the other knights had been in her predicament.

And that made her so...angry.

She surprised herself, but yes, she was angry at herself for feeling this way and at her environment for fostering these feelings. It wasn't Ember's fault that magic had created her; she was a fantastic *person*, and nothing else should have mattered. And here Sydney was, robbing herself of that fantastic person, robbing them both of comfort they desperately needed, all for an organization run by some asshole she was dashed well planning to overthrow.

The knights would have to change in order to accept Sydney's new ideas, to accept people like Ember. And if they wouldn't, Sydney would go elsewhere, start a new order. And she needed to start working on that acceptance right now. She'd march up to Ember and kiss her.

Or maybe not. She frowned and after a breath, told herself not to be a complete fool. She couldn't stop this expedition to declare her love. The captives were depending on her, and the recruits would think her insane.

Wait. Love? She couldn't be in love with someone she barely knew.

Could she?

A call from one of the trackers shook her out of her reverie. She hurried forward and saw them pointing to something on the ground.

"It's a steep hole," Juzail said. The bandage around his head was just beginning to soak through with blood from his ear, but he'd said it didn't affect his eyes, so she'd let him come along.

Private Diasi's legs poked out of the hole, and as Sydney watched, she came wriggling out, dragging a lantern behind her. She stood as tall as she could, not quite reaching Sydney's chin, and tried to brush the dirt off her tabard but smeared it instead. "Goes down into a big cavern, Major," she said. "Tracks everywhere and multiple tunnels."

Sydney nodded slowly. "That's how they've been appearing and disappearing," she said. "Can you tell which are the most recent tracks?"

"Not from up here, Major."

"Here is another way down," Ember said quietly as she kneeled by a tumble of boulders. Her voice wavered between cool and hurt as if trying on different reactions.

Sydney tried to give her a kind, hopeful smile. She couldn't share her epiphany yet, but she would. Soon. "Lead the way."

❖

Ember stood in the cavern and thought of home, wishing for a moment that she'd never left. Everything outside the mountain was too complicated, and Rowena had been right. There wasn't enough to eat, and people were consistently strange.

And feelings got hurt.

Sydney hadn't turned on her physically, but Ember almost wished she had. That would have been easier to deal with. And Sydney's explanation of why she hadn't let Ember explain about herself or the dragon just made things worse. They were excuses, not reasons, not real ones that made any sense. If Sydney had said she'd been afraid and embarrassed, Ember could have forgiven her, but to say that not speaking was better? It was like pretending, like lying. Ember was what she was, and there was a dragon involved in this fight. Anything else wasn't the truth.

Rowena had been right about trusting people; it never led anywhere good.

Ember sighed as she looked around the cavern at the tracks. Many people had moved through here recently, too many for her to tell who was whom. Diasi and Juzail might have better luck. She liked them, but she told herself not to like them too much. She would continue to help the knights, to help Sydney, because she'd said she would, and her curiosity was dampened but not forgotten. She wanted to see how this would all turn out. She wanted to see the dragon.

"Find anything?" Diasi had a smudge of dirt on her pale, narrow nose, and her straw-colored hair was dusted with gray from the cavern walls.

"Nothing certain."

Diasi nodded and continued searching. Ember stayed by her side. "Where did you learn to fight so well?" Diasi asked. "The army?"

"No, I..." Ember hesitated. Both Rowena and Sydney had said she needed to be careful when mentioning her origins, and now she feared telling the truth, but she didn't want to lie. "I've just had a lot of practice."

Diasi glanced over from the corner of her eye. "Sorry, didn't mean to pry."

But prying was good; all questions were good. If Diasi asked some, Ember could ask some; more things to learn. Excitement began to build again. If she could get the knights to talk to her, they could become friends, and then they wouldn't care that she was made instead of born, and she—

Ember stopped as she spied a track leading from this large cavern into the largest tunnel. Huge, with a deeper impression at the front than the back, and three birdlike toes. The dragon had been here.

Sydney might not want to admit it, but here was proof. She'd acted as if she didn't want the knights to know, but she'd also said she wanted them to find out for themselves.

Ember swallowed. So, she wasn't supposed to tell, but Diasi wasn't looking in the right place. "What's that?" Ember said as she pointed to the track. She grinned at finding a medium between not telling and not letting the knights walk ignorantly into a dragon's lair.

"I have no idea." Diasi held her torch high and approached the enormous track. "I thought one might be a drag mark, but with three in front and one pointing the other way, it looks like a big...chicken foot, doesn't it?"

Ember laughed as she imagined it, and Diasi joined her. "We'd never have to hunt again if we catch it," Ember said.

"Not with those eggs."

Juzail moved to join them and marveled at the print, and they were three friends sharing a laugh about something that might possibly kill them. Ember supposed that was better than crying. She kept waiting for one of them to say "dragon," but they just went back and forth about what it could be and making jokes about giant chickens until finally, Juzail frowned.

"Isn't quite bird," he said. "Looks a little like…lizard, like the ones that ran all over the buildings in Thornstone where I grew up, but they're only this big." He held up his hand, thumb and forefinger a few inches apart.

Ember continued to wait, willing them to put the pieces together.

They looked at her at the same time, and she almost cheered at the realization in their faces.

"You said something about a dragon," Juzail said slowly.

"But that's nonsense," Diasi said with a laugh that wasn't real. "I mean, we all laughed."

"Maybe we shouldn't have." He stared at the print, then at Ember. "I hope you don't mind me saying that even with this print, I hope you're wrong."

"I don't mind," she said. "Hopes are fine, but the truth is more important." When she looked pointedly at the print again, they both nodded, and Ember felt a sense of victory even as she hoped she was wrong, too.

The hope was a small one. She really wanted to see a dragon.

CHAPTER FIFTEEN

Camille was afraid she'd have to stab her thigh to keep from laughing. Rowena the Hawk was playing Hilga the milkmaid, whose best qualities seemed to be speaking haltingly and fainting a lot. And glaring.

"Stop that," Camille said quietly. They were sitting together in the center of the cavern while the knights searched the nearby tunnels, looking for the kidnappers' tracks. "Hilga's got no reason to be angry at me."

"It was all I could think of."

"You did well."

"Then why are you laughing?" Rowena asked between clenched teeth.

"I'm trying not to, but it's hilarious."

Rowena poked her in the side. "What should I do if they ask me why a milkmaid has two packs which are stocked for traveling and a bag of reagents and spell components?"

"Tears always work. Or you can faint again." Camille bit her lip to keep from sniggering.

Rowena turned a slow, murderous look on her again.

"Here," Camille said, reaching for the packs. If Rowena lost her temper and the knights found out she was *not* a milkmaid, there might be more than recriminations, especially if the knights thought Rowena had anything to do with Kells, lizard creatures, or abductions. She slid one of the packs closer and hid the other behind it. Rowena kept the bag slung around herself. "Now, I put one on when we leave as if I'd had it this entire time, and we hope for the best."

"Fantastic." She rested her chin in her hand. "Bloody knights are taking their time about things."

"It's too bad you can't…" She drew a circle in the air, hoping Rowena got the gist. She didn't want to say anything about spellcasting.

"Too bad I can't do a lot of things," Rowena muttered.

Camille's eyes took on a sympathetic cast. "How's your arm?"

"Well enough. The bleeding's stopped completely."

"Let me know if—" She stopped speaking as one of the knights finally came over.

Bennia, the sergeant who'd first helped Camille on the rocks. She had short, dark, spiky hair, a crooked smile, and the kind of cocksure manner Camille would have gone for if she wasn't embroiled in a dragon conspiracy.

And if she didn't already have a fascinating woman sitting beside her.

"We can't be sure of the way, so we're picking one and going for it," Bennia said. "Better than sitting here doing nothing. And I'm afraid we don't have enough people to escort you to the safety of your village." She put a reassuring hand on Rowena's shoulder.

Camille cleared her throat and grabbed Bennia's hand before Rowena could bite her. "Thanks so much for all your help, Sergeant. We don't want to inconvenience you any further. Hilga and I can make our way to the village. Together, we're certain to avoid danger."

Bennia kneeled. "No, no, Camille. I couldn't send a librarian and a milkmaid outside in this wilderness without an escort. I'd never forgive myself."

Rowena growled, and Camille nudged her, making her jump.

Bennia nodded to her. "See? Poor Hilga trembles at the very idea. You must come with us but stay at the rear of the company."

"No." Camille laughed shakily. "I'm sorry. That…fills me with fear, too. It fills, um, both of us, right, Hilga?"

"Yep," Rowena said between clenched teeth. "Fear."

"What we should do is climb out of these caverns and find a hiding spot on the moors. We won't move again until you come and find us." She crossed her fingers and held them over her heart like a child making a promise.

Bennia looked back and forth between them. "And what will you do if those creatures discover you?" She rested her hands on their knees. "I'm not trying to frighten you, only to make you consider the possibilities."

"They won't find us," Rowena said quietly, and her voice had a dangerous edge.

Camille put an arm around her and turned Rowena's head into her shoulder. "That's right, Hilga. We'll be so petrified with fear, we won't make a peep, and no one will know we're there."

Bennia sighed and looked toward her waiting troops. From how they'd acted, none wanted any civilians to be hurt, but they didn't want civilians among them, either. It was just one more distraction they didn't need in a fight. "All right." She insisted on seeing them up to the surface and approving their hiding place at the base of a rocky tor. Then she kissed each of their hands and bid them farewell with many promises to return as quickly as she could.

"Fucking assholes," Rowena cried when the knights were gone. "Bloody, condescending, smarmy, uptight, buggery wankers." She breathed hard as if she'd been underwater. Camille supposed she had been holding her breath in a way or at least holding in a string of heinous swears.

"Use your location spell," Camille said, trying to bring her back to business. "Maybe we can find the captives ourselves."

"What for?" Rowena paced up and down, staring. "If we wanted to find them, we should have stayed with the wanking knights."

"Not with you ready to kill them," Camille said, fighting to keep her patience. "And they don't know where they're going, and we still have a chance to help."

With a few more swears, Rowena kneeled and began to dig in her bag.

Camille grabbed her by the front of the cloak and pulled her close. "Don't get me wrong. I was about ready to stab that fawning sergeant myself."

Rowena froze and then kissed her, knocking her back slightly. Camille deepened the kiss and held them together. Rowena could be a pain, but when the situation was dire, she acted for the good of the many whether she liked those involved or not. And Camille was proud of her for not killing anyone and for playing a helpless milkmaid. Whatever she did, foolish or not, she did it with passion.

When she pulled back, Rowena was grinning like a fool. "I know why I kissed you, but what was your kiss for?"

"Lots of things, Hilga."

Rowena narrowed her eyes and leered. "Turned on by the milkmaid, were we?"

Camille barked a laugh. "Only because it was you."

"Hmm. I didn't know farmhands were your thing."

"They're not."

"I suppose I'll have to invest in a costume."

"Would you get to work, please?" Camille chuckled as Rowena got out what she needed for the spell. Camille let her thoughts linger on costumes for a moment before she shook her head. Now was not the time to contemplate that particular future. Or any future. She'd never been one to look too far ahead, especially with lovers. She'd thought of them as temporary, Sydney included, just hot sex until they tired of each other, then they'd go their separate ways. Just because her time with Sydney had been more interesting than usual didn't mean Camille had ever thought of them as being in any kind of long-term relationship.

When she'd first been attracted to Rowena, she'd thought the same thing. If the attraction was mutual, they'd have some fun. Then when this adventure was done, they'd part ways.

But now, watching this fascinating woman who could go from angry to playful in a blink, who was crabby, intelligent, mercurial, charming, vulnerable, and beautiful at the same time, Camille let herself think casually of the future, of a relationship that could last more than a few weeks. She'd been tongue-tied by Sydney's beauty, but that hadn't happened with Rowena. As lovely as she was, she'd always been easy to talk to. And that suddenly meant a great deal more than she'd ever thought it would.

Rowena's location spell showed her the knights they'd just left, or so she assumed. They felt the closest, but she detected others, too. She and Camille would just have to pick one and head that direction. She couldn't say who they were or what they were doing, but she wanted every piece of this puzzle she could get.

Even if that meant helping some captive knights, the bastards.

As they hurried toward the next signal, Rowena tried to tell herself that maybe she'd get lucky, and Ember would be with one of these knightly squads. If that proved so, she hoped Ember hadn't revealed her heritage. She would be safer with a group of warriors if they thought she was human, but if they knew the truth, they'd no doubt turn into a group of morons who'd kill her for no reason.

Stupid bloody knights. She should just let them rot.

But Camille was right to know that she'd bloody well help. Whatever was being done to them couldn't be good and was probably incredibly painful and evil. She had to stop the evil part, at least.

The signal led them to a small group of knights embroiled in a fight with more lizard-skinned warriors. Rowena pulled Camille into hiding. "We can't let them see us."

"Aren't we going to help them?" Camille asked.

Rowena shook her head, worry replacing anger and not just for what the knights would do. "There are more knights than enemies, and...does it look like they're not trying very hard?"

Camille peered at the fight as Rowena did. The cloaked creatures feinted and pulled away as if leading the knights. Or distracting them.

"Like the last fight," Camille muttered. "If they're just a distraction—"

A group of more lizard-skinned fighters rushed from a hole in the ground. "There," Rowena said, pointing as the new group subdued two knights and lifted them. "We can follow them while the knights are distracted." She ran after the captives, Camille at her side. They ducked through an opening into the caverns again, and when the sunlight from behind faded, the hurried footsteps of the kidnappers slowed but didn't stop, and they seemed to vanish into the gloom.

"We need a light," Camille whispered.

"No, they'll see." Rowena took a few vials from her pack and mixed some finely ground cat's eye stone with oil and a pinch of luminescent fungus. She infused it with life force and smeared it over her eyelids.

A jolt of pain went through her eyes, but when she opened them again, the sides of the tunnel stood out in sharp relief, and she could see Camille peering fearfully into the dark. "Here, close your eyes," Rowena said.

Camille gasped when Rowena anointed her lids and put a hand to her forehead. "What the fu—" She gasped again when she opened her eyes and looked around. "That's amazing."

"Come on." Rowena hurried after the kidnappers; they hadn't gotten far. It seemed they could see somewhat in the dark, too.

"How long does this last?" Camille whispered.

"Maybe an hour. I hate using body augmentation magic. Those who augment their bodies too often have to keep doing it more and more just to function normally, and our eyes will be sore after it wears off."

They walked so far into the dark that Rowena feared the spell would run out, but at last, light shone from ahead. The kidnappers brought their victims into a huge cavern whose ceiling was open to the sky. The middle of the floor sunk into a pit, as if when the ceiling had caved in, it turned the cavern into a sinkhole.

A ledge ran around the pit, and tunnels branched off the sides of the cavern, including one that glowed with artificial light. The lizard-skinned creatures dumped their captives into the pit, and cries of pain, surprise, and protest sounded from below.

They'd found the jail.

Rowena scanned the rest of the room and tried to see down the neighboring tunnels. The lizard-skinned creatures stood close to the pit, talking quietly or peering at the captives below. She tried to count the enemies so they could tell the knights how many there were, but a familiar scent caught her attention.

Sage, rosemary, and other herbs. She thought the lighted tunnel might lead to a kitchen, but she also caught the rancid smell of brimstone and an unpleasant tang like tanning hides. All put her in mind of her workshop, her reagents.

Someone was doing magic.

After a look at Camille, Rowena gestured toward the lighted tunnel. Camille nodded, and they edged around the cavern, staying in the shadows on the opposite side of the pit from the guards. They crept among stalagmites and finally reached the lighted tunnel, which led immediately into a short-ceiling, room-like cavern. Rowena used a mirror to peek inside but saw no one. She glanced at the lizard-skinned creatures to make sure no one was paying attention, then hurried inside.

Two large tables dominated the room, and the sight of reagents and tools scattered across their surfaces reminded Rowena so much of home that her heart wrenched. Camille stepped around her and peeked into a different room that led off this one. When she gasped, Rowena hurried to her side.

Corpses. On the floor, in jars, stacked in the corners like firewood.

So many words went through her mind. Cemetery, mausoleum, morgue, but this was none of those things. It was a workshop.

And the things in the jars weren't dead.

Winged lizard creatures like the kind that had attacked the village floated in viscous liquid and twitched in their sleep like puppies. Other jars held the lizard-skinned creatures who also seemed not quite alive. As her heart sank, she spotted other human and dragon hybrids. Tables at the back held half-dissected mutations that had probably never walked or breathed, with too many limbs or too few or something bizarre like wings where their eyes should be.

"What is this?" Camille asked breathlessly. She put a hand to her mouth as if she might be sick.

Rowena shook her head. The corpses on the floor and in the corner were human, but their skin was dry, their bodies shriveled as if all the moisture had been wrung from them, but why?

It almost didn't matter. She wanted to burn this whole abominable place to the ground.

She made herself breathe. Answers first.

Rowena looked again to the jars and noticed that each held a smaller jar on top. She couldn't believe her eyes as she stepped closer. The little jars each contained a human heart that pulsed with blue light. "What are they doing?"

If Camille answered, Rowena didn't hear. She went back to the corpses and rolled one to see a gash across the chest where the heart had been removed. Hearts: the organ that held the most life force. "They've taken the hearts, harvested the life force, and stripped the bodies of moisture." She pointed to the jars. "And they're using those to give these...things life." Camille was staring at her with horror in her eyes. Rowena found herself putting facts together almost woodenly. "Just one human would provide enough to power a host of new creatures for a short while."

She recalled giving her own life force to Ember, making a new heart beat. She'd felt such joy when their eyes had met for the first time.

But this witch was stealing that same life force, turning a gift into…

"Perversion," she spat, rage taking over from surprise and awe. "They've taken creation magic and twisted it into something evil." And this was where the knights and their ilk thought all magic would lead, but they were wrong. Every witch she'd ever known would fight against this.

The knights didn't matter anymore; Sydney didn't matter. Nothing mattered but putting a stop to this. Rowena marched to the corpses and began laying them out, drawing a circle around three at a time.

"What are you doing?" Camille asked.

"Making husks. It won't be pretty, and they won't last long, but they can get a few licks in before the life force I give them is depleted."

Camille looked at the door. "Are you sure? What if—"

"I have to stop this, Camille." She took a deep breath, everything in her crying out to send Camille away, to claim she could do this on her own, that she didn't need anyone to help her defend her craft.

No, she couldn't go back to that. "Will you help me?"

Camille smiled and went to the door. "I'll keep lookout."

Sydney stared at the dragon print and *wished* it belonged to a giant chicken. Then she could at least act surprised. Instead, she had to stand there with heat in her cheeks and Ember's stare on her neck.

She told herself to remember her resolution from earlier. She wasn't going to deny Ember anymore, not even if she felt stupid or ostracized. It wasn't right.

"*You* were right," she said, staring into Ember's eyes. "I didn't want to see it, but you were right about this monster." She pointed at the print. "You were right, and I should have let you speak."

Ember's eyes softened a little, and she smiled for the first time since their argument. The rest of the squad was looking back and forth between them with questioning expressions.

"Diasi, Juzail?" Sydney said. "Is this the newest trail?"

The trackers nodded, and Diasi pointed out some smaller prints that led into one of the tunnels. "Near as we can tell, Major." She cleared her throat. "And there are no, um, monster tracks entering or leaving."

Sydney frowned and glanced around the cavern. "How'd it get in here?"

"Well..." Diasi glanced at Juzail.

He stepped up beside her. "There aren't any more large prints coming in or going out, Major. Even with all the activity, we should see more. But there's just this one, and another that's slightly obscured. It's as if this monster appeared here, then disappeared without really moving."

"Like the spell that brought us here." Sydney glanced up. This cavern was tall. Maybe if the Kells had a witch, they brought in a dragon when they needed it and when the terrain could accommodate it.

What did that say about the dragon? Was it happy with this arrangement?

Unless the dragon was also the witch, and it was moving itself.

No, that was too preposterous. She was too tired for such questions.

She motioned for the trackers to continue down the chosen tunnel. Whatever was going on with the dragon—and she dashed well hated admitting that there even might be one—they weren't going to find out by standing there. Several knights lit lanterns, and they moved as quickly as they could, following the most recent line of tracks. The lack of wind and sun began to make Sydney's shoulders twitch, and she had to fight the feeling that the rock surrounding her would suddenly collapse and entomb them.

She'd focus on rescuing the captives and save thoughts of the dragon and the tons of stone and every other upsetting thing until she couldn't ignore them any longer.

Or until the cave collapsed.

Under the weight of a dragon.

Sydney sighed and tried counting the moments instead, but minutes seemed to crawl by. Climbing over piles of rubble and ducking under low-hanging shelves of rock sent fatigue through her muscles; maybe she could tell how far they'd come by how sore she was. A hundred miles? A thousand? Why couldn't the dashed dragon and its cronies make their homes outside where she could breathe?

At last, a cry came from down the tunnel.

"Company, halt," Sydney said. She tried to make the call soft enough that it wouldn't reach beyond the column, but sound echoed weirdly down here. She stepped to the front, past where Ember and the trackers gathered.

A cry came again, followed by the sound of ringing metal. Someone was fighting ahead, and unless their enemies were fighting amongst themselves, this battle had to include an ally.

"Forward," she cried, leading the charge with Ember beside her. She let anticipation for battle and dread from her surroundings fill her, using those emotions to ignite her heartfire. The bluish-white flames sat in the middle of her palm like a tiny sun, the tendrils licking her fingers as she ran. She had more than enough anger and fear to keep the flame burning as she burst into a larger cavern whose top was open to the sky.

Corpses. Lurching. Fighting. Reaching for the living.

Her mind catapulted her back to her fight with the witch of Elion and his shambling horde.

The stumbling corpse horrors froze her, creating enough stomach-knotting terror to quench her flame as if it had never been. They had the same peeling skin as those from that long-ago battle, the same dead eyes and lank hair that had fallen out in clumps. Their bony fingers reached for lizard creatures now instead of her, but a walking corpse was a walking corpse, and her heart lodged in her throat.

One of them turned toward her, and by the gaping remains of its tabard, she knew it. A knight. The face was too desiccated for her to tell exactly who it was, but that didn't matter. Someone had killed her comrades and turned them into the foulest horrors that ever walked.

Chapter Sixteen

Sydney had to move, couldn't let these shambling corpses tear her and her company apart, no matter who they might have been in life. She ground her teeth, pulled on her horror and fear, and her heartfire burst to life again, engulfing her hand. With a roar, she threw herself into the fight, swinging at both the lizard creatures and the corpse horrors. Her knights followed her example, but by their terrified cries, she knew they were as unsettled as she was.

"Stop, stop," Ember yelled, but Sydney didn't know who she was talking to or why.

Others were calling, too, voices coming from the pit that dominated the center of the room. Other people were trapped here, too, no doubt destined to become corpses like these, but she wouldn't permit it. She'd save them all.

Another of the shambling horrors went down before her, but she had to keep hacking to prevent it getting up again. She slammed its chest with heartfire, and it ignited and tumbled away to burn quietly in a corner. Sydney cast about for another enemy, and a form appeared out of the smoke. It wore a dress not well suited to fighting and had its hands in the air, the face framed by a mass of curls; dark eyes stared in concern.

"Cam...Camille?" Sydney faltered, certain this was a trick, then certain that Camille had fallen to the same foul creature who'd created these shambling horrors. She leaped forward with a cry, reaching, hoping it wasn't true, and when Camille's eyes shone with recognition, Sydney could have wept.

"I thought…I thought you were…" She couldn't say it, just so happy Camille was alive, that Sydney hadn't led her to her death.

"I'm fine," Camille shouted over the battle. "Stop destroying the husks."

"The…" Sydney glanced behind her. Her squad had almost finished with the lizard creatures and the shambling horrors, though some were calling to the dead as if trying to get their attention. They'd recognized fellow knights and couldn't seem to believe their eyes.

The horrors weren't attacking them.

Sydney's stomach shrank. Were they still alive? "By the flame. Column, attention," Sydney cried as the last of the lizard creatures succumbed.

The knights backed toward her. The corpses had stopped shambling and stood dumbly. Diasi was mumbling, "What in the world, what in the fucking world, Major?"

"Just stop, everyone, stop." Sydney looked to Camille. "Are they…what are they?"

Camille had her hands out in a placating manner. "I'll explain everything."

"Are they alive?" one of the knights shrieked. "That's Gemma. Is she alive? Gemma!"

Camille moved closer. "No, they're not alive. They were killed by…" She gestured at the lizard creatures.

"Then why are they…walking?" Sydney tried to get her thoughts to stop spinning. Only one kind of person could make a corpse do anything. She looked for Ember and spotted her across the room, her arm around the shoulders of a pale skinned, dark haired woman in a silver bodice and black dress with ragged sleeves and hem. Even from across the room, Sydney knew her eyes were green. In the crystal ball, they'd almost shone.

"Hawk," she said, feeling the word rattle through her rage. "You did this." She pointed her sword at the horrors.

Camille took another step. "It's all right, Sydney. She was helping. We were trying to rescue the other knights." She gestured to the pit. "One last fight for…" She pointed to the corpses. "Maybe they would have wanted that?"

"To be a mindless puppet?" Sydney asked. "Dancing to the tune of a witch?"

"They were already mindless," the Hawk said. "Wouldn't you use any weapon at your disposal to achieve victory?"

Sydney's heartfire flared again, and she stepped forward. "People are not weapons."

"Everyone, take a deep breath," Camille said loudly. "We are all on the same side, and your comrades in the pit still need our help."

Sydney signaled to her knights, and they began scrounging materials to help the knights to the surface. Other people were mixed in with them, villagers or other captives. All were confused, full of questions Sydney couldn't answer because she couldn't take her eyes off the corpses. Her heartfire still burned, and when everyone was safe, the Hawk met Sydney's eyes and lifted a hand.

Fire burned there as well. "If we're going to do this, let's bloody well do it," the Hawk said.

Ember said something in the Hawk's ear. Camille sighed loudly and moved to stand between them again. "Seriously?" Camille said. "The only way we can settle things is by lighting each other on fire? Aren't we smarter than that?"

"She *is* a witch," one of the knights muttered. The rest of them moved to stand at Sydney's back or ushered the villagers to the wall.

Juzail stepped to Sydney's side. "Did she really make the corpses walk, Major?"

Sydney could feel the knights behind her like a coiled spring. Camille wasn't giving way, keeping between the knights and the Hawk, and Sydney could tell by the stubborn look in her eyes that she wouldn't be moving. Ember had her hand on her blade, but she frowned as if torn, gaze flicking from Sydney to the knights. She didn't want to fight.

The Hawk stepped forward, closing her hand around her flame and dousing it.

"I meant no disrespect," she said evenly. "Camille and I couldn't defeat the guards on our own, and we couldn't leave your comrades and the villagers behind." She licked her lips. "If it were you, and someone could use your body, your skills, to fight evil one more time after you were gone, wouldn't you want that?"

Sydney took in her words as well as a few deep breaths. She tried to put herself in the place of the corpses who stood back against the wall, almost out of sight.

"The little life I gave them will fade soon," the Hawk said. "And they can rest, having done their duty."

Muttering still echoed behind Sydney. She took another breath and shoved past memories, trying to lock them within a door in her mind. Now wasn't the time, and witch or no, the Hawk had helped them. And helped Camille, it seemed. She couldn't repay that with a sword. She stepped to Camille's side before facing her company. "Stand down."

"But, Major," Juzail said, "she's a witch."

"Doesn't matter," Sydney said. "We'll lay those brethren to rest with the others. They died in the service of good, which is all any of us can ask for. And we were lucky the witch was here to keep anyone else from joining them in death before we arrived."

Sydney took another breath, sensing she needed a push more to keep this situation from exploding. "This is the Hawk, the woman who has been helping us, the one who cast the spell that got us here." When the muttering increased about how they were not where they were supposed to be, Sydney held up a hand. "Her spell was disrupted by Sir Robert, who employed some kind of..."

"Witchstone," Camille supplied.

Sydney nodded to her. She'd obviously been busy. "He used a stone to mangle the spell. It's because of him that we were scattered. He'd planned to use the Hawk for her magic, disrupt the spell, then have me kill the Hawk for being a witch."

Gasps and arguments filled the room. Sydney held up her hands again and gestured to Camille. "Both of us were witness to it."

Camille nodded.

"Where is Sir Robert?" one of the rescued knights said. "He should be here to answer these charges."

"He was captured," Juzail said.

"He was never here." The rescued knights spoke amongst themselves and with the villagers, all certain that Sir Robert and a handful of high-ranking knights must have been held somewhere else because they'd never passed through the pit.

"We'll find him," Sydney said. "And I will confront him." She caught the Hawk muttering something about how Sir Robert was probably part of this lizard creature debacle. With a glare, Sydney said quietly, "People can only absorb so much information at once, Hawk, so shut it."

The Hawk rolled her eyes, but this time Camille had a word in her ear, and her hand on the Hawk's arm seemed very familiar. Sydney turned away, not able to process jealousy at the moment, if she had any jealousy at all. She rubbed her forehead and felt warm fingers take her free hand. She looked up, expecting Camille but smiling to find Ember.

"Thank you," Ember said softly. "For what you said."

Sydney nodded, smiling. She gave Ember's hand a squeeze. "Form up," she called to the knights. "Let's get back to camp."

She looked to Camille and the Hawk to see if they would come, but a rushing sound drowned out all conversation. Sydney glanced around, looking for rushing water, but the sound was too rhythmic, and it filled the space around them, bouncing off the walls.

The light dimmed, but night never came on that quickly. Sydney looked up, shielded her eyes from the little light still trickling down and saw the source of the sound, many pairs of flapping wings.

"Scatter," she cried, running toward the wall as more lizard creatures landed among them, but these were more animal than human. Taller than her, they had the same golden scales as those she'd already fought, but wings sprouted from their shoulders behind their arms, and their faces bore little trace of humanity, almost as if someone had taken the head of a lizard and sewed it to a human's neck. They raked with talons on their fingers and snapped with tooth-filled snouts. She couldn't argue that these were lizards of any kind. They were dragon monsters.

Sydney blocked the claws of one, and the strength of it nearly ripped the sword from her grasp. Several of her comrades fell, some squashed to the floor as the monsters landed on them. The foul things fought with abandon like wild animals, without tactics.

They could be beaten.

Sydney worked her way to another group of knights, calling for them to form up in areas where they couldn't be attacked from above. Before she could pull one in line, he went down from a ball of fire that smacked against his chest, catching his tabard alight. Sydney dropped beside him and rolled him to quash the flames. She glanced up, ready to kill the Hawk. Even if this was an accident, the witch would die for it.

One of the monsters had a bag tied around its waist, and it reached in with a clawed hand and pulled something forth. Her jaw dropped as it threw another flaming ball into another group of knights. Sydney blinked, not believing her eyes.

These monsters were stronger than those before. They could claw and bite. They could fly.

And at least one of them was casting spells.

❖

Ember was so relieved when she didn't have to fight Sydney that she threw herself into this new battle with relish. She stood in front of Rowena, slashing at flesh and dodging the attacks of these new opponents, glad to see they were faster and stronger than anything she'd fought so far. She could finally test her skills to the fullest.

She'd always known she was stronger and faster than Rowena. She could see better in the dark, too, but she hadn't known she was better at all of these things than most humans. Her speed had once unnerved Rowena, so Ember had always felt the need to pull back. Now, she let everything out, only slowing when she hit one of these strange dragon people so quickly, it nearly wrenched the sword from her grasp.

Still, it was *so* thrilling, she couldn't help a grin.

And it helped that everyone she cared about was all right. Rowena stayed behind her, casting into the mass of dragon people. Ember could feel her determination through their connection. When she'd felt a rush of emotions in the tunnels, she'd put it down to her circumstances, but it had grown the closer she'd come to Rowena.

Now, everything was right with the world.

Except for the dragon people.

Or maybe they were helping. It was a good fight.

Sydney was holding her own while standing against the wall. Even Camille proved useful. When one of the knights fell, she bent double and hustled onto the battlefield to drag them to relative safety.

Ember's grin faltered when the enemy began throwing fire. That wasn't good. "They have a witch," she cried to Rowena.

"I see. Can you get to them?"

Ember stabbed through the scaly breast of one opponent, and as it fell, she used the gap to peer through the rest. The dragon witch had a bag tied around its waist. The rest wore nothing, so she wouldn't lose the witch in the crowd. "Yes."

"Here."

Ember grabbed the object Rowena pressed into her hand. She recognized it as a yew stick spotted with cold iron, good for blocking spells, though it wouldn't prevent their casting. She held it in her off hand like a dagger.

"Ready?" Rowena asked.

"Yes."

"Go." A column of smoke sprung from the ground as Rowena cast a spell.

Ember dove around it, using it to screen her rush. The dragon witch turned her way and flung a small blob of fire. Ember swung the yew stick and knocked the blob out of the air, the magical fire fluttering and dying as the yew and iron negated it. The dragon witch stumbled back and brought up its claws. Both hands flared with a blue-white flame.

Heartfire.

Ember blocked the strike, all the more delighted that the dragon witch could cast both creative and destructive magic, though it seemed weaker than Rowena and Sydney. As if responding to a signal, some of the other dragon people brought heartfire to life as well. They might be weaker than some of the knights, but that didn't mean the others couldn't be overwhelmed.

Ember slashed faster, not trying to connect as solidly, going for as many cuts as she could land in as little time. The dragon witch faltered, Ember ripped the bag from its waist, and it stumbled back, getting lost in the fray.

Across the cavern, Sydney called for retreat as another knight fell before the onslaught. The closest knights bunched together, lifting their injured as they moved toward Sydney's position. Ember began to work her way to Rowena, hoping to shepherd her in the same direction. Rowena would definitely need to spend more time with Sydney if they were going to become used to one another. They both might have maddening qualities, but Ember wasn't ready to let either of them out of her life, especially since Sydney had apologized and stood up for witches.

Ember's grin was back. As long as too many of the knights didn't die, the future would remain bright.

A tremendous roar echoed through the cavern, bringing several people to their knees as the hideous noise reverberated upon stone.

Rocks and pieces of earth began to rain down, and a tremendous shadow blocked the sun.

The real dragon. At last.

The enemies pressed their attack. It became difficult to keep track of Rowena and Sydney, fight, keep hold of the bag, and watch for the dragon she'd been waiting for. Some of the knights fled down the nearest tunnels along with the villagers, retreating in small groups. Rowena had come closer to Sydney, but a cluster of enemies still blocked Ember's path.

"Rowena!" Ember leaped straight up and flung the witch's bag. She saw Rowena clutch it before a set of claws grasped Ember's shoulder as she landed. Ember twisted, shaking off her attacker and slicing them across the belly as she spun. The debris fell faster, though the shadow didn't seem any closer. Maybe the dragon was happy burying them while staying out of harm's way.

Ahead, Camille was helping a wounded knight into another tunnel, but the boulder tumbling from above would squash her flat.

Rowena would be sad.

Ember bashed her opponent in the face and turned. She ran, pulling on all her speed, and the cavern became a blur. She smacked into Camille and the knight and sent all three of them flying into the tunnel so quickly, their feet left the ground. She turned in midair and tried to cushion their landing but only managed to shield a bit of them. The impact with the wall rattled her teeth.

It was all very fascinating and required further experimentation.

Some other time.

Camille and the knight let out cries that cut short when they hit the ground, and Ember heard the air leaving their lungs in a rush. She sat up and looked back to see the boulder sitting where Camille had been, blocking the exit. She ran to it and stood on tiptoe, peering over the top, watching the debris continue to fall as Sydney, Rowena, and the knights with them made it to safety before a rain of stones filled the entrance to the tunnel and blocked her view.

Camille was coughing, a good sign. The knight wheezed and moaned. Not so good. Ember could barely see them, which meant Camille and the knight probably couldn't see at all. Ember kneeled beside them, touching each on the shoulder.

"Are you all right?" she asked. "I mean, obviously you're not completely all right because you were attacked by dragon people, and then I tackled you into this cavern, but I really mean, do either of you feel as if you're going to die soon?"

When neither answered, she bit her lip. "If you can't talk, touch my hand to let me know you're dying, and I'll try to think of something. I never paid much attention to Rowena's lessons on anatomy and medicine because I didn't care. I never get sick, and I don't get hurt that often, and when I have been hurt, Rowena's always fixed me."

"I'm...fine," Camille said between gasps.

"Okay." That didn't make Ember as happy as the thought of Rowena and Sydney being fine, but she'd told herself she had to save Camille for Rowena's sake, so she supposed she had to be at peace with Camille's good condition. If Camille decided to try to win Sydney back, though, she'd rethink that. "And you?" She gave the knight a gentle squeeze, but he only moaned again. "I think he's not fine."

Camille's big eyes roamed the gloom before she reached out as if trying to feel her way to the knight. "Here." Ember took her hand and put it on the knight's shoulder.

"You can see?" Camille asked.

"A little."

Camille felt along the knight's body. "He had a head wound before, but he was conscious. It seems like he's passed out, or maybe he's barely aware." She sighed. "I only know a little about healing from books, so I'm at a loss." She put a hand to her forehead. "And I left my stupid pack in that horrid workshop."

Ember watched her think. She felt a little thrill at being able to see someone who couldn't see her. Camille couldn't complain about her staring if she couldn't see it. She was very pretty with her mass of curls, curvy body, and big cheeks. Ember's ire grew a little, but she pushed it down. "The way is blocked, but I saw Sydney and Rowena make it out as well as many of the knights."

"Good, that's good." Camille closed her eyes as if she needed even more dark to think. "Well, it seems like all these tunnels are interconnected, so I say we find a way to the surface and look for the others up there where we can both see."

"Agreed." Ember looked to the knight. She could probably carry him, though with him being taller, it would be awkward, and Camille would need her to guide them. "Can you get him under an arm?"

Camille nodded and stood, wincing as if she was injured. Ember wanted to ask what was wrong but didn't. Curious. Was her hesitation because of Rowena's words about respecting privacy or something different? She didn't really care about Camille's privacy, didn't care if Camille liked her or not. Her hesitation had to be something else.

Fear. Not of Camille or of her relationship with Sydney, but that Camille's injury would make Ember happy somehow. Curiouser. Even though the connection told her that Rowena and Camille had grown closer, supplanting Sydney, Ember's resentful leanings toward Camille remained.

She sighed again. Rowena was right. Feelings were often stupid.

❖

Camille's left side burned like fire. She'd read about broken ribs and supposed she could have one, but she could still move. Probably just deeply bruised. Being tackled into a wall by a homunculus certainly hadn't helped. And it was too dark to see, yet Ember seemed to be doing fine. And they had to aid a semi-conscious knight who also hadn't been helped by that same tackle. And on top of all that, her eyes ached as Rowena warned they would when the augmentation magic wore off. Camille couldn't help feeling as if the lack of even one of these problems would make her life so much easier.

The knight shuffled along, still groaning, with his arms slung over Camille's and Ember's shoulders. Camille couldn't help a bit of groaning herself every time she put weight on her left leg, and jolts of pain ran up and down her side. Ember wasn't even breathing hard, and though Rowena said Ember had a tendency to be overly chatty, she hadn't made a peep since they'd started walking.

"You all right over there?" Camille said, desperate for something other than wheezing to fill the dark silence.

"Fine."

Camille rolled her eyes. Maybe the tendency to become tighter than a clamshell was a trait Rowena had passed to her. "Rowena's told me quite a bit about you."

Silence for a moment, then, "She did?"

"How you like to spar with the husks, how you're very curious." She mentally prodded her to take the hint, but no such luck. "I noticed you came in with Sydney. Did you get sent to her like I got sent to Rowena?"

"Yes." She stretched the word out as if filling in a gap before blurting, "I kissed her. She kissed me, I mean. Well, we kissed, and I want to do it again." The words had a note of challenge that nearly made Camille laugh. Did she think Camille would stop her?

Would she do something to make sure that didn't happen?

Camille swallowed. "Oh, good."

"Good? Aren't you...mad?"

"Well, since I've been kissing Rowena, and she's been kissing me, no, I don't see how I can be mad." Though anger would be easier to deal with than guilt. Unwarranted guilt, it seemed. Still, she had to wonder what Ember would do if she said yes, she was mad.

No, she didn't want to find out, not after remembering Ember's skill in a fight and the force with which she could hurl herself at someone else.

"I thought you might have," Ember said quickly, and now she sounded happier. "There's a large rock in your path. Scoot this way."

Camille followed instructions, happy they were talking if only to be warned of further obstacles. "I care about Sydney, of course, but I'm not usually one for...long-term love affairs. Though, I really want to get to know Rowena better," she added quickly.

"Sydney wants someone to love her. I can tell."

"Ah. Good." Another small wave of guilt passed through Camille. She'd sort of had the same sense about Sydney but knew she couldn't provide that love. Ah well, it wasn't as if she'd made promises. They'd both had their eyes open.

She hoped.

"I'm sure you'll be good together," Camille said.

"How?" Ember asked. "Is that a sense you have? Can you always tell just by hearing about a relationship? Are you ever wrong?"

Camille nearly staggered under the barrage of questions. "Um... that's just a platitude, sorry."

"Rowena says platitudes are a buggery waste of time."

Camille snorted a laugh. "Sounds like her. It's what people say when they don't know what else to say. It means something like, I hope it'll turn out okay."

Ember repeated this softly. "Why don't you say that, then?"

After a sigh, Camille said, "I hope it'll turn out okay." She sensed one had to carefully pick their battles with Ember.

"I hope you'll turn out okay, too. Rowena will be fun for you to get to know when we aren't being attacked by things that want to kill us. She has layers."

"Don't I know it."

"You do? That'll help. I love Rowena."

Camille smiled, about to stay silent, but the dark lent her courage. "I think I could, too."

Ember made a happy little squeal. "I hope that'll turn out okay."

"Shh," Camille said through a laugh. "There's bound to be more than knights in these tunnels, and we don't know how keen dragon hearing is."

"You know about the dragon, too?" Ember said quietly.

"*The* dragon?" Camille said, her heart beating faster. She tried to turn her head to look Ember in the eye, but she still couldn't see a cursed thing, and the knight groaned with the movement. "You've seen an actual dragon? I just guessed because the creatures who've attacked us seemed to have human and dragon characteristics."

"A Kell told Sydney and me that a dragon is in charge of them, and I saw its shadow when it knocked that cave in on us. It was huge. And I've seen big footprints."

Camille archived this information and tried to make orderly rows of it in her mind. "The Kells working with a dragon."

"He called it Nightmare. Said it and the Kells were asleep, and everyone they encountered was just a dream and didn't matter." Her voice took on a tinge of sadness. "But even if we are dreams, we still matter. They attacked a village, and I saw a little girl, and she was…"

Camille's eyes stung anew as they teared up from the pain in Ember's voice. "How horrible, Ember. I'm so sorry." She could only imagine what had been done, but with what she'd read about Kells, it couldn't be good.

"Thank you. I'm…sorry I had mean thoughts about you."

"Ha. You won't be the last, I'm sure."

Ember huffed. "Are other people having mean thoughts about you? Do you know who they are? Did you do something to them, or are they making assumptions like I was? I didn't enjoy it. It made me feel quite nasty. So, maybe I can talk to these people, or you can, and then they won't have to feel nasty or have mean thoughts, and that can all be okay, too."

"It...I..." Camille chuckled as her head swam again. "I was speaking hypothetically."

"Aha. I can do that, too, if you want."

She launched into theories about Kells and dragons, some of which made sense—that the dragon wanted to kill humans out of revenge for the rest of its kin—and some that were too farfetched—the dragon had fallen in love with the Kells and would do anything to help them.

"Did you tell any of this to Sydney?" Camille said when Ember finally took a breath.

"She doesn't want to talk about dragons," Ember said with a sigh. "She thought the idea was stupid and embarrassing when we met some knights, then she came around when the soldiers saw a dragon footprint, but I think she's still skeptical. She's probably telling herself that the giant shadow that knocked the cavern down was a really big bird or something."

Camille scoffed. "Rowena tried to deny it, too, saying all the dragons are dead. As if once a thing is commonly accepted, that makes it the truth forever. But those of us who read a lot know that there are always more discoveries to be made, and that theories require testing before they can be labeled truth." She nodded, feeling smug.

"I like that. I want to read the books and find out all the things." She sighed. "Even if Sydney doesn't believe them first."

"Well, there's two things we have in common," Camille said, her affection growing. "We both like to uncover the truth, and we both have our sights set on very stubborn women."

CHAPTER SEVENTEEN

Rowena was getting tired of bullying the wounded knights into letting her help them. Ever since her sight augmentation spell had worn off, her eyes had throbbed with pain, and the knights' stubbornness compounded that annoyance into a right bloody headache. Plus, the bite wound on her arm ached anew at all the casting she'd been doing.

It all added up to one simmering pit of anger in her belly that wouldn't go away easily.

"Yes, I'm a witch," she said to a knight who flinched away from her. Many of those she or Sydney had already helped were limping down the tunnel, and only a few left needed a hand getting to their feet. "Yes, I might use magic to help you, but lucky for you, most healing magic is temporary, so it'll get you out of here, then you can get back to nonmagical suffering, all shiny and pure."

This one reluctantly relaxed like some of the others, and she wanted to laugh in his face if he actually believed that magic wearing off was preferable to magic actually healing him.

The lot of them were a waste of life force.

For the hundredth time, she asked herself why she was even doing it. Would they do the same for her? Doubtful. Together, she and the knights had a better chance of defeating any enemies, but the knights no doubt thought they didn't need a witch's help. Bloody ingrates.

She sighed, knowing it was more than just safety that prompted her. She'd wanted to find Ember. Mission accomplished, except now, she'd lost Ember again. At least she knew Ember was alive. Their connection had gotten weaker as they'd ventured farther apart, but it was still there.

Ember wasn't the only reason she was helping the knights. It was because Camille would have helped them. Oh, she'd understand if Rowena wanted to leave them behind, but she'd never do such a thing. She'd bite her lip, deliver a scathing recrimination or two, and pitch in. And it would have shamed Rowena not to do the same. Besides Ember, no one had ever inspired her before.

Even to do something for someone so bloody asinine.

"Are you all right?" Sydney asked, and Rowena knew she'd been muttering under her breath.

"Fine." She finished bandaging the knight's leg and smearing the outside with a bit of clay. When infused with life force, it would act as a stabilizer, a temporary muscle to use instead of the injured one. Maybe when it gave out and the knight dropped like a wet sack, he wouldn't be so quick to flinch from magic. "This one's done."

Sydney pulled the knight to his feet and sent him lumbering after the others. The uninjured few stood at intervals down the tunnel, helping the shufflers move faster before catching up. Their row of lanterns looked like a sparkling bridge in the dark.

"The way to the cavern is blocked," Sydney said. "I tried to find a way through, but every time we shifted some stones, others tumbled down." She stared at the rock just a few feet above their heads as if it might collapse, too. "I hope everyone found a way out. I hope…they got out."

Rowena didn't have to ask who they were. "Ember is alive. She'll head for the surface. We'll have a better chance of finding them there." She included Camille without even thinking about it. Her being dead was an impossibility.

Sydney picked up a lantern and took up the rear of the column at Rowena's side. "Thank you for your help." Sydney swallowed as if the words hurt her throat, and Rowena wanted to punch her. But maybe she was learning, too.

"Welcome," Rowena muttered, and she knew it had a snide edge to it, but she got the buggery words out.

"Did you see them? Did they get clear?"

Rowena didn't mention her connection with Ember, not wanting to share that unless she had to. But she'd also caught a glimpse of her across the tunnel, her and Camille both, though she had to guess what had happened when Ember went leaping. "They dove into a tunnel after Ember threw me this." She held up the enemy spell bag.

Sydney shuddered as if Rowena held a bag of human heads. "I saw you bandaging as well as casting magic. Did you learn anatomy from raising dead bodies?"

Rowena rolled her eyes. Oh yes, she would have to bring that up again. "Yes," she said flatly, daring Sydney to say more. Camille would just have to forgive it if Sydney got a bloody nose.

When Rowena had seen the joyful look Sydney had given Camille on their reunion, she'd felt a flash of jealousy. But Camille had never gone to stand at Sydney's side; she'd stayed in front of Rowena, protecting her. She stared at Sydney now and lifted an eyebrow.

Sydney sighed, her mouth drawn tight before she moved up the line. Another knight fell back a bit and walked at Rowena's side. He hadn't needed healing magic, but she'd wrapped his bitten left wrist, and he had the remains of a dirty bandage wrapped around his head with a large bloodstain over one ear.

"Um, thanks for this," he said, lifting his wrist. The words sounded easier, less like pulling teeth than the other knights, but he was the one who'd stood at Sydney's side when it seemed as if the knights would attack her.

Maybe they were all learning.

He cleared his throat. "I know we're not supposed to…"

Supposed to speak with witches? Rowena fought the urge to snap at him to spit it out.

"Well," he said, "doesn't matter. Thank you. That's all I wanted to say. You're not like I expected, and I realize that's my fault and not yours, but I thought I should—"

"I get it," she said, wanting to stop him before he was teary eyed. Soppy words about how he'd been wrong about witches was almost worse than flinches and grudging thanks. It would just make it sadder when he eventually turned on her.

"All that stuff that the major said about Sir Robert, is it true?"

Rowena blinked, not expecting that. "You really want to know?"

"Yes."

"Might destroy your hero."

He seemed thoughtful before nodding. "I can't remember a time when I didn't want to be a knight." He gave her a quick glance. "And it wasn't about getting rid of magic. It was the honor, the camaraderie, protecting those who couldn't protect themselves. That's what I wanted. So, yeah, I want the truth no matter the cost."

She studied his face but found no deception. She'd have to ask Camille to rate him later. "What's your name?"

"Juzail."

She pretended to think while she stuck a hand in the pocket of her dress and grabbed a bit of brimstone. No matter what he said, if the truth made him violent, she was going to be ready.

"Well, Juzail, the major spoke the truth. I communicated with both her and the master researcher before your journey. I knew they needed my help, and I knew Sir Robert planned to ambush me during the spell. He was trying to trick me, use me, kill me. Call it whatever you like, but you can't call it honorable."

He swallowed so hard she could see it. It seemed as if he might speak, but he stared straight ahead and clenched his fists. She let him pull slightly ahead and readied herself.

"Are witches always honorable?" he muttered, his jaw tight.

"How many witches do you know?"

He didn't answer, but he did glance at her.

"Based on your hesitation, I reckon it's just me, and you only really know *of* me. You'll have to make up your own mind and believe your own eyes." If Camille or Ember had been there to watch her back, she would have stalked ahead, but she couldn't show her back to him here, surrounded by so many potential enemies. She couldn't even count Sydney as a true ally.

But instead of spitting venom, Juzail's shoulders relaxed slightly, and his angry look was replaced by a hangdog expression. It wasn't contrition or acceptance, but it wasn't anger, either. That was fine. If he needed to mourn his hero, she'd give him room. She didn't say anything else, and after a moment, he sped up and got lost in the column.

With a sigh of relief, Rowena slipped the brimstone back in her pocket.

❖

When the column of weary, wounded knights stopped for a rest, Sydney wandered down the line, asking each one how they felt and if they needed anything. Most seemed peppier than when they started, and she wondered just how long the Hawk's magic would last.

Probably not as long as the effect she had on the knights. Most seemed less wary of her; the few looks cast her way seemed more curious than anything. Juzail especially seemed thoughtful, and Sydney recalled that he'd spoken with the Hawk more than the others.

After she'd checked on the entire column, she settled next to the Hawk and stretched her legs out on the floor. "What did you and Juzail talk about?"

"Just the things you said back in the cavern about Sir Robert. I confirmed they were the truth, but I don't know if he believed me."

Sydney leaned her head back and cursed Sir Robert again. "My word should have been enough for him."

The Hawk snorted.

Sydney resisted the urge to lash out, but someone who reanimated the dead had no room to judge anyone for anything.

"Thank you for saying what you did," the Hawk said.

Sydney shrugged, still wary. "I had to deescalate that situation as well as tell the truth." She couldn't resist a dig. "The corpses certainly didn't help."

The Hawk sighed as if the whole world was a cradle of stupidity. "Yes, yes, let's have that conversation again, by all means."

"No, I'm too tired to argue." Sydney sighed, too. "Sorry. It's just...creepy."

"So, change the subject. I noticed you and Ember seemed rather close."

Sydney's wariness tipped over into a strange sort of fear, the kind normally reserved for meeting a lover's parents. "Um."

"Were you stuck together from the beginning of this little adventure like Camille and I were?"

So, she and Camille *had* been together a while. No wonder they'd seemed close, as close as Sydney and Ember must have seemed. "Yes, and we...bonded." She took a sip from her canteen and hoped the lantern was dim enough to hide the color burning in her cheeks.

"The kind of bonding where someone throws her head back in ecstasy?"

Sydney spit the water across the tunnel. The knights looked back between her and the Hawk. She gave them a calming wave. "That's...I...what dashed business is it of yours?"

"You know what she is?"

Sydney's insides couldn't seem to decide between embarrassment and anger. She took a deep breath to keep from sputtering again. "Yes. It…doesn't matter to me." Not quite a lie, but she still flinched. It *didn't* matter to her, but she hadn't been able to let the other knights find out.

The Hawk was staring with eyes hard as jade, and Sydney wondered if she had a spell to read minds. "I'm the closest thing she has to a mother," the Hawk said.

"And?"

"So, tell me your intentions."

Sydney barked a laugh and quickly stifled it. The Hawk hadn't cracked a smile. "You haven't told me about your time with Camille."

"You didn't make Camille in your workshop."

True. "Ember is a…loyal, steadfast companion." Where had all her charm gone? Why did this awful woman make her so nervous?

The Hawk said nothing. She didn't even blink.

Sydney took another sip of water. "And she's lovely."

"Thank you. I tried." Still no smile.

Sydney glared. "She's kindhearted, which I wonder if *you* can take responsibility for. She's…" She sighed and let her mind go back over her time with Ember, letting the feelings carry her if she couldn't summon any confidence. "She doesn't like killing, and she cried for a dead child. She…held me." With a cough, she came back to herself.

The Hawk only tilted her head, unmoved, it seemed. "She's also naïve. It wouldn't be difficult to break her heart."

Sydney's own heart sank, and she felt like a heel. "I know."

"Did you hurt her?"

Sydney met her eyes and wondered if she had a different spell ready now, one that might kill rather than invade one's mind. "Yes, but I'm trying to make it better. I've already started." She took a deep breath. "If you want to punish me, I deserve it."

The Hawk snorted, and her face finally relaxed as she leaned her head back and closed her eyes. "You'll have to flagellate yourself. I don't have the time or the energy."

"Fine. Good talk." Sydney stood, ready to see if anyone needed her help again. She much preferred physical problems to emotional ones.

"Don't hurt her again."

The words had a tone of warning. Everything in Sydney wanted to respond nastily, but no good would come of it. If she wanted to be close to Ember, she had to make nice with the people Ember cared about. And the Hawk seemed to love her creation. That boded well for Camille, though Sydney didn't envy her.

She found the rest of the column to be as exhausted as she was. Outside, it had to be getting late. As much as Sydney wanted to continue, wanted to find a way out, find Ember and Camille, she knew they all needed rest. She told the column to bed down as best they could, noticing that the Hawk kept to herself at the rear rather than joining the clumps of sleepers or those on watch. With the cave-in, it wasn't likely that anyone could come at them from behind, but Sydney had watchers back there anyway, just in case something large—like a dragon—tunneled through the collapsed rock to get at them.

Those on guard duty at the rear of the column stayed well back from the Hawk, leaving her as the first line of defense should something attack from that direction. Sydney tried to take no pleasure in the thought that she'd be attacked first.

She failed at that.

When the black tunnel began to take on subtle shades of gray, it took Camille a moment to notice. She blinked, thinking her imagination might be filling in the darkness, but when Ember warned her of a large stone she could already see, she nearly whooped with joy.

"There must be light somewhere ahead."

"Finally," Ember said. "Do you think it's daylight or—"

They turned a corner and found their answer. A shaft of sunlight shone into the tunnel far ahead like a beacon. They hobbled faster, the knight dangling between them. He moaned at the movement, but Camille took that as a good sign. It showed he was alive. And he was trying to stumble along without much success. Camille's shoulders were beginning to ache, adding to the headache caused by Rowena's earlier spell. Her side was still throbbing, too. Ember hadn't whined at all, so Camille tried to keep her complaints to a minimum. She looked forward to talking with someone who could share her pain.

Someone she wouldn't mind asking for a massage.

A vision of Rowena wearing an abbreviated milkmaid costume flashed into her mind, and she suppressed a giggle. That wouldn't be a good idea; Rowena was sexy enough in her own clothes.

When they reached the hole that led to the surface, Ember leaped the few feet upward and caught a lip of stone. Camille balked under the knight's weight and had to lean against the wall to help support him.

Ember's head reappeared a moment later. "There's no one about, but it is getting dark. Should we stay in the tunnel or sleep out here?"

Camille bit her lip and let the knight sag to the ground. In the dim light, he seemed very young, not yet twenty; too young to be suffering like this. She wished she knew his name.

"Camille?" Ember asked.

"Yes. Right. Decisions." She put a hand to her head and tried to think. Her mind was muddy, thoughts easily distracted. She needed rest. The young knight probably did, too. "I guess it's safer in here, even though we stand the chance of missing the others."

Ember dropped down into the hole again and nodded. "And I've seen enemies both above and below." She sat beside the wounded knight, and they huddled in the fading daylight.

"You can sleep," Ember said. "I'll keep watch."

Camille's eyes jerked open, and she started with guilt. As soon as she'd sat on the knight's other side, her eyes had slipped closed. She hadn't even noticed. "Thanks." She had a dim thought that she'd once had trouble sleeping while surrounded by protectors and under the shelter of a cart. Now she was dropping away easily in a rocky tunnel alive with enemies with a homunculus and a knight who was barely old enough to shave.

Oh well. She was too tired to be picky.

The halt gave Rowena time to dig in the enemy spell bag. The reagents were rudimentary, most used in simple, offensive spells. The bag didn't even contain any chalk needed to draw a circle for something complex, and there wasn't any clay for healing or ingredients for augmentation spells.

And it was very badly organized.

She wondered if the dragon-like beasts were really alive as Ember was or if they were a step more complex than husks, animated matter made to obey a single task. They seemed cleverer than that, though, perhaps fitting into some nebulous area that included a bit of independent thought but not free will?

She shuddered. That would make them far creepier than any husk, though she doubted Sydney and her sanctimonious knights would see it that way.

Rowena looked toward where Sydney was chatting with the knights. She had to admit that Sydney had come a long way from the moron Rowena had first spoken to in a crystal ball. She seemed to have accepted Ember, even though she knew Ember wasn't really human. And she seemed genuinely sorry for hurting Ember's feelings, though Rowena still wanted to give her a bit of fireball for hurting Ember in the first place.

Ember probably wouldn't appreciate that.

Neither would Camille.

Rowena sighed, feeling as if she was pulled in many directions now, one of the reasons she hadn't left her mountain in years. She couldn't afford to dwell on those thoughts, not when she had to work with Sydney, and not when she needed to distract herself from the fact that they'd soon be outside again.

"Got everything you need for the night?" Sydney asked from a short distance away. The wariness in her stance was laughable. It was all Rowena could do not to yell, "Boo."

The knights would probably stab her a million times.

"I could use a nice large bed if you've got one handy."

"Sorry." With a ghost of a smile, Sydney stepped a little closer. "I've got a spare blanket." She held it forth.

Rowena took it and put it by her side. When Sydney turned to go, Rowena cleared her throat. She wouldn't be dropping off to sleep any time soon, so she thought she might as well get as much information about their predicament as she could.

She did not want Sydney to stay because she was lonely. Or frightened. That was nonsense.

"I noticed some humans guarding the captives back at the pit before you came in," Rowena said as Sydney turned back toward her. "Kells?"

Sydney nodded. "We fought a few outside, too. They burned a village." She flinched as if reliving that sight.

Rowena didn't even want to imagine it. "Bastards."

Sydney gave her an amused look. "Do you think they're the ones providing the magic?"

"Could be. I don't know a lot about them." She frowned, something about this entire situation not sitting right with her, logically speaking.

Besides the obvious dragon angle.

"We've only seen a handful of Kells so far," Sydney said. "If that's the entire invasion force, Arnvild is going to be fine." She sighed, though, taking the humor and confidence out of the words.

"That's what's bothering me. Where are the rest?" Rowena had a vision of an army of Kells sneaking around the knights, the supposed advance force who was supposed to stop, or at least thin them, at the border. "If they know these tunnels—"

"They could be past us already." Sydney wiped a hand down her face. "Oh, please, no." Even in the dim light, she looked paler.

"Don't panic just yet. The ones we've fought could be an advance group." She gave a quick rundown of what she'd seen in the workshop, watching Sydney go from pale to slight green. "Everything I've seen smacks of an experiment. Get the knights out here, split them up, attack them and me with all these different creatures—supported by the Kells—and see what works best." Her stomach turned over, and she bet she looked a little verdant herself. "With the added bonus that your experiments kill some knights *and* a witch." She shuddered. And those experiments were down in these tunnels hunting them.

But the only place they could run was outdoors, with the wind and sky that went on and on forever.

With her head aching and the cavern seeming to spin, she lashed out. "And kill some who are both knights *and* witches."

Sydney's head whipped toward her. "Heartfire is not magic."

"Bugger that."

Sydney bristled, then took a deep breath. Rowena did the same, though she dearly wanted a fight. No, not here, not now. That was what Camille would say.

"What does all this theorizing mean to us right now?" Sydney asked. "When we're limping through these caves?"

Rowena had to shrug. "We need to get out of here and find your knights." She sighed. "Though I wouldn't mind staying underground after I find out that Ember and Camille are all right."

Sydney nodded. "After we find them, staying in the tunnels isn't a bad idea, except for the fact that we don't know our way around. At least up top, we can see where we're going, even if we can still be ambushed."

And even when the sun and the open air could threaten to crush them. She doubted Sydney would agree with that, though. "Maybe we got lucky back in that sinkhole cavern, and the cave-in destroyed that workshop."

"If that's the only one," Sydney said with a snort.

Rowena's stomach shrank further. "I hadn't even thought of that."

Sydney gave her a smug look, and Rowena wanted to punch her. "Glad to see I'm not the only one who's overlooked some possibilities."

Wanted to punch her harder now, but she resisted, making herself think of Camille. "There are spells to locate reagents in the wild. Maybe I can use one to find other workshops." At Sydney's flinch, Rowena grinned. "Yes, a spell. I can use a *magic spell* because I am a *witch* helping the Knights of the Flame." She leaned toward her. "*Magic spells* not that different from—"

"Shut up."

Rowena chuckled. "Let me know when you're ready." She let a few moments pass. "For the spell. Or when you're ready to learn more about your own magic."

❖

Sydney felt as if her brain were on fire. The thought that all the deaths the knights had suffered was merely a distraction for a Kell invasion force infuriated her. The idea of even more Kells following the few she'd encountered terrified her. The possibility of more workshops making abominations sickened her.

And the insistence that heartfire was magic made her want to shove the Hawk down a dark hole.

By her smirk, the Hawk knew exactly what she was thinking.

"It's destructive magic," the Hawk said. "Magic based on emotions."

"Please, stop talking."

"I have to give you credit. I'm not very good at it because my emotions are usually all over the place."

Sydney rubbed the bridge of her nose and knew she wasn't going to will her way out of this conversation. She could leave, head up the column and do something, anything, else, but she really hoped they could talk more about their current situation rather than magic or spells.

But reason insisted that their current situation was up to its eyebrows in magic.

"Anyone can learn heartfire," she said, trying and only partially succeeding at not talking through her teeth. "Not everyone can be a witch."

"Sure, they can." Rowena's voice held a note of false joviality that made Sydney want to shove her even harder. "People who can master their emotions can cast destructive magic; those who are better at marshaling their thoughts and controlling their breathing can summon their life force and cast creation magic." She leaned close. "And both are witches."

Part of that made sense, even though her superiors had always told her that witches kept magic for their own use, that only someone born with the potential to be a witch could become one, but everyone could cast heartfire. It was a level playing field.

But that wasn't precisely true. Some knights were hopeless at it. She imagined them being able to breathe the right way and control their thoughts and cast…magic instead. She couldn't bring herself to use creative and destructive. As far as she was concerned—as far as all knights should have been concerned—heartfire wasn't *destructive*. It was *defensive*. There was a difference.

"You could learn more, you know," the Hawk said.

Sydney rolled her eyes. "Oh, how lovely that you think I have mental discipline."

"Oh, I don't." When Sydney glared, the Hawk smiled, no doubt trying for disarming but looking like a viper. "I meant, you can learn other destructive spells besides channeling flame."

Sydney pulled back, aghast. "I can't…I'm not…"

The Hawk rolled her eyes.

Sydney fought not to gag. It was unbelievable, utterly impossible. She was not a witch. She could not learn *spells*. She was a knight;

knights could use heartfire. They were not wielding magic. They were *not* witches. And she wouldn't entertain the thought of knowing spells.

A flash of the battle surfaced in her memory. Many of the knights seemed weaker than the horde of monsters and Kells plaguing them. And Sydney could no longer argue that there *wasn't* some other, larger enemy she hadn't yet seen. The thing that brought down the cavern on top of them had been rather...dragon-shaped.

She had a duty to defend the people of Arnvild, her fellow knights, Camille, Ember, and—if it came to it—the Hawk. If someone offered her a new style of martial combat, she'd learn it, wouldn't she? She'd seek to master any new weapon that would help. Why not this?

Her very soul rebelled. Too many certainties had crumbled lately. Her worldview had been challenged so many times in the past weeks. She didn't know how much more she could take.

Then she thought of her friends, her family, all the people that she loved. Ember, whom she knew she could love if given the chance.

Sydney sighed. She worshiped the truth; she desired it in all things. And here was a chance to learn whether heartfire was magic or not, whether using it made her a witch. If she could learn other... spells...she would have her answer.

"Show me," she mumbled.

The Hawk leaned closer. "Beg pardon?"

"You are so lucky there isn't a big hole around." Sydney took a deep breath. "Please, if you would be so kind."

To her credit, the Hawk dropped the smirk quickly. "Settle in. This might be difficult."

"You've no idea," Sydney muttered.

CHAPTER EIGHTEEN

Camille awoke with a snort. When she'd closed her eyes, the sun coming into their tunnel from a hole above had been fading. Now, it seemed as dim, but she could tell it was growing brighter by the moment.

Ember leaned into her line of sight. "You're awake. Good. I was afraid you were going to sleep more when you already slept all night, but now it's dawn."

Camille blinked slowly, trying to parse the words. As she sat up, she lamented the lack of coffee and her quiet apartment. And the fact that she'd slept on stone. Her neck and back ached, though, surprisingly, her side felt better. Maybe her rib hadn't been broken after all.

That did nothing to help the rest of her, though.

Ember chattered on, but Camille's brain refused to listen. Instead, she looked at their wounded knight. His color seemed a little better, but it was hard to tell in the dim light. He was breathing deeply and evenly, but when she tried to rouse him, his eyelids only fluttered.

"How are we going to get him out?" she asked after a yawn.

Ember shrugged. "Easy." She hauled the knight upright, letting his limp body lean on her shoulder.

"Gently." Camille moved to help, and as soon as she'd taken some of the knight's weight, Ember let go so the knight leaned on Camille. "Hey!"

"Just one second." Ember jumped up, hauled herself out of the hole, then lay down on the edge. She reached down just as Camille began to sag and grabbed one of the knight's arms. While he let out a groan, she pulled him from the hole as if he weighed nothing, and they disappeared out of sight.

Camille's heart thudded even as she marveled at Ember's strength. As seconds went by, and Ember didn't reappear, Camille licked her dry lips. Surely, Ember wasn't going to leave her there.

Camille straightened, trying to ignore her fear. She wasn't helpless. She crouched, then jumped, missed the rock Ember had caught, and came down in a stumble. Her cheeks burned, but she wouldn't let one failed attempt stop her. She tried again and caught the lip, her elation rising.

Until she tried to pull up, and her body stubbornly refused. She grunted, thinking she couldn't weigh that much, but her arms felt dead. She dangled, swinging gently, and her fingers were already getting tired.

A shadow blocked the light, someone seized her wrists, and she flew from the tunnel to lie in the grass. Ember crouched beside her, grinning. "Were you tired of waiting? I was trying to make the knight comfortable."

Camille breathed hard as if she'd done all the pulling. She fought the urge to grouse. "Thanks."

To her credit, Ember didn't mention Camille's lack of muscle. She helped her up, and Camille stared at the rolling hills and rocky spurs surrounding them. The knight lay nearby, still breathing if not otherwise moving.

"Where should we go?" Ember asked. In the daylight, Camille realized how cute she was. Slim and muscular, she wore leather, had light brown skin, bright green eyes, and a mop of short, unkempt red hair. A row of earrings dangled from her right ear, and a pale scar stretched across her face, but it did nothing to mar her pixie-like features.

Camille looked away so she wouldn't be caught staring, but when she glanced back, Ember was studying her. Ember smiled again, was probably bursting with questions, if Rowena was to be believed, but she held them in.

"I have no idea," Camille admitted. She took another look at the nothingness of the moors. A haze had built up to the east, and the horizon had become lost in the glow of the rising sun. She couldn't see Rowena's mountain, but the gentle hills hid most of the north and west. As she tried to think through fog, she missed her coffee again.

"Look."

Camille turned to find a troop of people skirting one of the rocky tors. The meager light glinted off metal, and Camille recognized a pack of knights. They seemed to spot each other at the same time; one lifted a hand just as Camille did.

A recognizable someone. Bennia, the knight from the troop that Camille and Rowena had originally joined with.

And who thought she was a lost idiot and Rowena was a milkmaid. Great.

"We looked everywhere for you," Bennia called as she got closer. She smiled, then frowned as if torn between worry and anger. "You weren't supposed to leave your hiding place."

Yes, they had promised that, but she and Rowena had only wanted to get away. She didn't think it would do any good to admit that now.

"We ran from an attack," she said quickly. "And we found some friends, then got separated again."

Bennia reached them, her expression skeptical, but when she saw the downed knight, she hurried to his side.

"He was hit in the head," Camille said. "I've done what I can for him, but…"

Another of the knights kneeled and examined him. Bennia stood and bowed to Ember. "Sergeant Bennia Aziz, at your service."

Ember grinned and bowed back. "I'm Ember. I wouldn't say I'm at your service, but I like to help when I can."

Bennia seemed charmed, grinning in return before she turned a questioning look on Camille. "What happened to the milkmaid?"

"She's one of the people I got separated from. Ember is a friend of Major Sydney Blakely, and I think the milkmaid wound up with her." She gave Bennia an abbreviated version of events, leaving out the magic, the corpses, and the accusations against Sir Robert. She'd feel better mentioning that with Rowena and Sydney at her back.

Bennia seemed grim as she nodded. "We'll find them." She turned to her troop. "Spread out. Keep in sight and earshot and look for tunnels."

"If you call for the other knights, you might find the dragon people," Ember said.

"Dragon?" Bennia lifted an eyebrow.

Camille had described the wings and claws but hadn't used that word. She sighed. She was very tired of knightly condescension about the possibility of dragons. "Yes, Sergeant. Dragon people. People with dragon wings and dragon claws and dragon teeth. They were akin to dragons. Dragonkin. If we meet them again, you should ask them all about it."

Bennia stepped back, blinking before scattering her knights. Three of them lifted the injured man and carried him along as they searched. When Bennia turned back to Camille, she said, "You two stay close," before joining the rest, who seemed as if they'd search while they walked.

Camille took Ember's arm, and they walked along a bit separate from the others. If they didn't go along, Bennia would only want to know why, and they had a better chance of finding Sydney and Rowena with more eyes.

Ember laughed and gave Camille a squeeze. "I'm so glad you said dragon so many times. I like the word dragonkin rather than dragon people. But who is this milkmaid?"

Camille sputtered a laugh and related the whole story. Ember threw her head back and guffawed, garnering some reproachful looks from the knights, but she didn't stop for a minute or two and wiped her streaming eyes.

"I was reluctant to like you, but now I'm glad that I decided to," Ember said.

Camille frowned but nodded. "Thanks?" At least she was honest. And whatever her reasons for not wanting to like Camille, she appeared to be over it. That was good. If she and Rowena stayed together for any length of time, Camille wouldn't feel like an unwanted stepmother. "I'd like us to be friends and not just because of Rowena."

Ember's smile was heartbreakingly beautiful. "It is nice to have friends."

As the day wore on, their band of knights discovered stragglers in the various tunnels, knights who'd been with Sydney and others who'd been wandering around, looking for anyone. They all banded together, the injured carried or helped along. Camille peered eagerly at each newcomer, but none were Sydney or Rowena. She kept telling herself they were fine; Ember had seen them reach safety. They had to be all right.

If the dragonkin hadn't found them again.

A scream came from the right, and one of the knights fell back as a dragonkin rushed at them from a tunnel, its claws moving like scythes. The knight fell back as others raced to join him, but cries erupted from all around as more dragonkin rushed into the light.

Ember's arm shot out, moving Camille behind her as she turned in a circle with her sword drawn. She guided them toward a larger group of knights, and when one dragonkin came too close, she slashed it across the back, nearly severing one of its wings. It staggered sideways with a howl like a saw over rusty metal.

Camille clapped her hands over her ears and tried to keep calm while staying out of Ember's way. She tried to keep watch, but Ember turned and whirled so fast, she was like a tornado, and she saw any danger before it reached them.

Bennia was calling for the knights to rally, and clumps of them moved toward one another. Camille and Ember reached one, and Camille didn't need to be told to find the middle of the circle and stand with the wounded. One of the knights stumbled back, screaming as a set of claws raked through his shoulder. Camille caught him and lowered him to the ground. She cried out at the sight of so much blood and yanked his tabard free of his belt, using it to staunch the wound. He shrieked again and met her eyes, his filled with agony as he clutched at her.

"It's okay, it's okay, it's okay," she muttered over and over, breathless. It wasn't okay at all, far from it. She glanced around for something to help but saw only other wounded people and the boots of those still on their feet. "I need...I just need..."

A miracle. She wasn't a healer; she had only rudimentary knowledge, and this was much more serious than the fight at the village. There she'd wound bandages over small wounds and washed others with alcohol. She'd kept things clean and suggested stitches, but this...

The knight slumped in her arms, his eyes turning glassy.

"No, no." Camille pressed harder on his wound, but the tabard was already soaked. Blood oozed out over her hands, into her lap. "No, someone help!"

But they were busy fighting, and she stared at them helplessly, wishing the enemy would disappear. When no miracle occurred, she laid the knight down gently, and the noise from the fight seemed to drift away, taking feeling with it and chilling her to the bone.

Do something.

Yes, what she needed was a task. Something to do. The injured knight she'd helped in the tunnel seemed perilously close to someone's feet. She dragged him toward the center. Another knight was sitting on the ground, clutching her face. Camille looked for a discarded pack, took a canteen hanging from the side, and forced the knight's head up to wash it. The knight had a claw mark along her cheek and hairline, but her eye was still there. Lucky. Camille yanked out some cloth without looking to see what it was, balled it up, and helped the knight press it to the wound. Good, that was good.

She moved a few more wounded people, focusing on their faces and not on the feelings held by a tremulous dam inside her. The sounds of the combat seemed to fade. Each moment poked another hole in that barrier, and she knew it couldn't hold.

Ember appeared, her mouth opening and closing as she looked up and down Camille's body. She frowned, concern writ plainly on her features, but Camille couldn't hear her.

She tried to speak.

Her personal dam shattered.

She threw her arms around Ember and wept into her neck until sounds began to ease back.

Ember's arms were strong around her. "Are you hurt?" Ember asked softly.

"No…it was…it…"

"Shh. I know. I felt the same once and have no doubt I will again. You can cry all you want, my friend."

Camille wanted to get lost in the sympathy in her voice, but she forced herself to stand on her own and take a few deep breaths. "Are you hurt?" she managed. Her throat hurt as if she'd been swallowing rocks, and her grief and horror still tumbled inside her, making her nauseated.

"No," Ember said. Around them, the knights were tending each other with more skill than Camille had ever shown. "Don't panic."

Camille nearly laughed. The fight seemed to be over. What was there to panic about now? She hoped Bennia was all right, hoped all the rest were all right, all but the one who'd died in her arms.

Ember's grip around her shoulders turned to steel. "There he is. Try not to be scared, okay? Don't let him know what we know. That's what Rowena would say."

Camille frowned and turned, ready to ask what Ember was talking about, but she spotted Sir Robert at the same time.

Sitting off to the side of the knightly gathering, Camille listened in surprised silence as the knights praised Sir Robert for swooping in with a handful of officers and saving the day from the dragonkin. And some of the knights who'd just fought had been with Sydney; they'd heard her denounce him, but they rejoiced along with everyone else, no doubt happy to think it all had been a mistake.

Ember sat by Camille's side. "What do we do?" she asked from the side of her mouth, a move that seemed very obvious.

Camille shook her head. In her mind's eye, she kept seeing the knight who'd had his shoulder ripped out, and her shock blunted any surprise or indignation. Blood had soaked her skirt and turned tacky on her hands, and she didn't know if she'd ever be clean of it.

No, no; she made herself think of something else.

Sir Robert caught her eye and smiled, an oily, satisfied smile.

He knew something about her, maybe how she'd revealed his treachery to Rowena, maybe how Sydney planned a coup.

And he didn't care.

She shut her eyes and made herself look at the other knights, trying to see what else she could do. Besides the one with the torn shoulder, it looked as if two others had died, and the knights were already burying them as best they could in the limestone and shallow earth. Others had cobbled together stretchers and had the wounded well in hand.

"Are you all right?" Ember asked.

Camille's chest felt tight, and she wondered if this panicky, trapped feeling was the same as Rowena experienced whenever she ventured outdoors. "I don't know what to do."

"Wait," Ember said quietly. "That's all we can do." She squeezed Camille's arm. "I'm with you. I'm your friend. I hope everything turns out okay."

Camille breathed a laugh that wanted to become a sob, but she beat it down. "Me, too. I'm glad you're here, friend."

She and Ember moved away from the wounded and dead. Camille had hoped they could simply walk away from the busy knights, but several stood as perimeter guards, and they warned everyone to stay close. Leaving would cause a definite stir, and Camille wasn't ready to answer questions or try to force her way free. Instead, she had to listen to Sir Robert tell the tale about how he and a few officers had been captured but managed to make a heroic escape.

With barely a scratch.

Camille sneered, desperate to denounce him, but most of the knights wouldn't believe her, might even take her for an enemy. They might not kill her, but she had no doubt they would restrain her, probably with many apologies and explanations about how it was for her own safety. Then Sir Robert could arrange an "attempted escape" which would leave her and Ember dead.

When the wounded were ready, the knights began to march, shepherding Camille and Ember along. Bennia found them and rejoiced that they remained alive. She walked near their backs as if guarding them. She wouldn't let them leave easily, if only from her sense of honor.

Shit. Shit. Shit.

"Maybe we can slip away," Ember whispered. "If we work our way toward the fringe of the group."

Camille nodded, but her stomach dropped when Sir Robert fell back through the ranks to walk beside them.

He gave Ember a curious look before speaking to Camille. "Dashed sorry you've been drawn into this, librarian. Stick close to us, and you'll be safe enough." His smile turned her stomach, but she kept her tongue.

"Because you've teamed up with a dragon?" Ember asked quietly.

Camille burst into a coughing fit, surprised beyond curses.

Sir Robert's eyes widened, then he chuckled. "My dear lady, what an imagination you have. Who ever heard of such a thing?" He leaned close, confident smile still in place. "But I know who you are, my scarred friend, and who your friends are." He glanced at Camille. "None of you will stop us from eliminating the witches."

"Even those working for you?" Camille said when her coughing was done. If they weren't going to keep quiet... "I saw the workshop and the dragonkin using magic."

His grin only widened. "Again, such imagination."

"We could tell everyone," Ember said.

Camille held her breath, not sure that daring him like that was a good idea.

He shrugged. "Feel free. It won't change anything. In fact, *everything* you do is completely beneath my notice." He marched toward the head of the column again.

Ember half drew her sword, staring at his unprotected back. Camille put a hand on her arm, stopping her. "We can't start a fight with all the knights."

Ember frowned but nodded and sheathed her blade.

"Right now, we need to get away and find our friends, so be on the lookout for the opportunity." He seemed rattled, if the hasty exit was any indication. On the one hand, it satisfied her to think he might be nervous, but on the other, he'd watch them closer if he really thought them a threat.

Ember had never been a fan of waiting, but marching along with Sir Robert—who they all knew was bad—until he attacked them made her skin crawl and her shoulders tighten to the point that she had to fight not to hunch.

If she bolted or fought back, she didn't think they could stop her, not now when she knew how much faster and stronger she was. The problem was Camille.

Ember fought the urge to sigh. Just how many times on this adventure would her problem be Camille? Except now it wasn't that she disliked Camille or wished her harm. No, if something bad happened to her, Rowena would be sad, and Sydney would be sad, and Ember would even be sad. Camille seemed to care about people she didn't know, which seemed like the mark of a good person, and she'd wept over the dead, which Ember could understand.

And she didn't want Sydney anymore, which was the best. That was selfish, but it still felt even better than Camille wanting Rowena, which was nice.

Finding someone who liked Rowena had been Ember's plan from the beginning, though she'd get no credit. In fact, admitting that she'd switched the witchstone because she wanted Camille and Rowena to get together would probably get her yelled at, and then Rowena would be all awkward and snappish, and Camille might leave, and Sydney might want to follow her to see if she was okay, then they'd both be mad at Rowena, and everything would fall apart like an old husk after a bad fall.

So, best to keep quiet about her plans and make sure Camille didn't die.

No attacking the knights, then.

But maybe she could still get away.

She'd once read that it was the duty of captives to escape. She wasn't sure who that duty was *to*, exactly, but she liked the idea because it was better than waiting. Camille might not be as fast as her, but Ember could grab her and run. It might not slow her down too much.

Camille might still get hurt.

Escape alone, then?

Would Camille be all right by herself? If the knights intended to kill them, they should have attacked already. Bennia seemed to like Camille, and some of the others did, too. Camille could claim to be innocent of any escape plan, just as she'd been in the story where Rowena had been a milkmaid.

Hilarious. She nearly laughed again.

"Where in the seven bells are we even going?" Camille muttered.

Ember winced. Camille didn't talk from the side of her mouth like she was supposed to in captive situations. "Looking for the other knights?"

Camille blinked. "You look really obvious when you talk like that. Just speak quietly."

"The stories all say—"

"We're not wandering around peeking into holes," Camille said, clearly not wanting to know the correct way to converse surreptitiously. "I think Sir Robert has a destination in mind."

After a glance around, Ember thought so, too. "We might not have much time, then. If we're going to get away…"

Camille frowned hard. "How?"

"I'm fast. I can see in the dark." She nodded ahead to where one of the moorland's many tunnels opened to the surface.

Camille's eyes widened before she nodded. "I'll create a distraction."

Ember fought the urge to take a step away in surprise. Part of her had been certain that Camille would argue or want to go with her or be angry that Ember was leaving her alone. Ember's estimation grew. Volunteering to stay so Ember could get away was something Rowena would do, though she'd probably light someone on fire in order to accomplish it. "What are you going to do?" she asked, excitement warming her belly. The tunnel was now close enough to reach.

"How do you feel about a fake fight?"

"A—"

"Just act surprised. I won't hurt you. And please, don't hit back."

"Hit?" Her mind whirled. "I'm not good at act—"

Camille threw her arm back and swung in a loose, dramatic fashion for Ember's shoulder. Ember fought the urge to dodge, seeing a great many opportunities to do so. She had time to promise herself she'd later tell Camille not to do this during a real fight.

When the blow landed on her shoulder, Ember staggered and bent, trying to make it seem as if the loud, obvious hit got her face, too. "Ouch."

Camille cried and screamed and babbled in such a high-pitched voice that dogs would be howling for miles around. Such an explosion of emotion was fascinating, but Ember couldn't stop and watch. She backed away, hands up as Camille stumbled backward, too, still pointing and gibbering, and the eyes of the knights followed her.

Fighting a grin, Ember turned and leaped nimbly into the tunnel mouth.

Chapter Nineteen

Sydney knew she was going too fast, nearly stalking through the tunnel. The wound on her thigh, which hadn't troubled her since yesterday, was starting to throb anew, and the company huffed as they tried to keep up with her. She wasn't doing them any favors, especially the wounded.

But she'd woken up as angry as she'd gone to sleep.

She slowed and grabbed a fist-sized stone from the ground. Instead of striding so quickly, she turned it over and over in her hand, seeking to bleed away some of her tension.

But it only brought back memories.

The night before, the Hawk had tried to teach her how to create force instead of fire. It took less emotion, the Hawk claimed, and unless someone knew to look for the distinctive shimmer it created, no one would see it coming.

And it could do more than burn. The Hawk had demonstrated after reiterating that destructive magic wasn't her forte. She'd still managed to scoot a pebble across the ground just by putting her hand near it. Then she'd smirked.

The look combined with the litany that heartfire was indeed magic had set Sydney's chest to boiling. She'd called heartfire immediately when she focused her emotions.

The Hawk had given the fire a bored glance. "Like that," she'd said, "only completely different."

Sydney had tried again and again, but only fire had come until she'd finally stalked away angrily and had fallen asleep. She wanted to be happy about the outcome. Her failure to conjure force might mean the Hawk was wrong. Sydney's power wasn't magical, and heartfire had nothing to do with these destructive powers the Hawk kept mentioning. Sydney had never cast a spell in her life.

Except the Hawk could conjure heartfire, too. Not as much as Sydney, and it took her longer to bring her emotions under control enough to focus, but she could do it.

And it wasn't a trick.

Sydney *had* been using magic.

Now, she squeezed the stone hard, anger and disbelief and a strange sort of grief building inside her.

The stone crumbled. Sydney halted, staring at the dust and pebbles that cascaded from her fist. Her heart pounded, and her mouth went dry. It…must not have been a stone, must have been something fragile, like an egg.

But she'd squeezed it hard, and it hadn't broken until…

"Nicely done," the Hawk said.

Sydney jumped and stared. "When did you get to the front of the column?"

The Hawk strode past, then turned to the side as if to watch everyone. She had one hand in a pocket of her dress, but her posture seemed anything but casual. "I wanted to keep an eye on you since you seemed upset. With the amount of power you can conjure—"

"Shut it." Sydney stalked farther ahead, giving the knights watching them a placating smile. "Everything's all right. I just need to have a few words with our friendly witch." She outpaced the column quickly, listening with half an ear as one of the sergeants ordered that the column hang back a bit.

The Hawk was still smirking, though she looked over her shoulder far more than she'd done when at the column's rear.

"Relax. They're not going to hurt you," Sydney said.

"I'd be more worried about you hurting someone else." She glanced at Sydney's dirty hand. "You didn't just move that stone. You shattered it."

"Nice to know you were spying on me."

"I was ready to stop you if need be."

Sydney glared, her anger fanning again. "Stop me from what? Throwing my knights around?"

"Yes," the Hawk said, her voice low and serious. She sighed. "Or worse. I've been thinking about it ever since last night. Your heartfire keeps to your body. You can't hurt anyone else unless you touch them, but a force spell can affect everything around you."

"It was not a spell," Sydney said through her teeth.

"Luckily, all destructive magic happens in short bursts." She tilted her head. "Though you can keep your heartfire going for quite a while. I thought it best to be prepared in case you start casting force the same way."

"I. Am not. Casting." She felt the coil of power within her too late. Trying to channel it into heartfire didn't work, as if her power was a river that had discovered a new path and would flood it no matter what she wanted. The air between her and the Hawk turned hazy, and Sydney reached, desperate to grab her before she was flung into the wall.

The Hawk held a hand up, palm out, and her sleeve slipped down to her elbow, revealing something wrapped around her forearm. The force rippled around her as if ignoring her. When it slammed into the wall, the tunnel shuddered, then went still.

The knights were staring. Sydney was, too, appalled beyond belief.

"Everything's fine, nothing to worry about," the Hawk called. "I just cast a quick spell to...keep us safe."

Some of them muttered, but they seemed curious or mystified rather than angry. The Hawk took Sydney's arm and marched her down the tunnel.

Sydney went along, too many emotions tumbling through her to name. "What? I... You lied."

The Hawk snorted a laugh. "To save your ass." She held up her arm again. "This is an anti-spell strap. It has effect-cancelling components like yew, cold iron, and leather from a spotted cow, all dyed under a new moon and infused with my life force." She turned her hand this way and that as if admiring the thick black strap. "I think I'll keep it on when I'm not casting, especially since Ember has my yew stick."

Sydney's mouth worked as she tried to digest all that. Magic talk sickened her anyway, and now she had to hear about magic-blocking apparatuses that were necessary because of *her*? "I'm sorry. I didn't mean..."

"My own fault. I shouldn't have gone with force, but it's supposed to be the easiest destructive magic to learn." She shrugged. "You're going to have to get a bloody grip on yourself."

Sydney's anger kindled again, and she forced herself to breathe through it. "I didn't ask for this."

"You bloody well did."

Yes, she had asked the Hawk to teach her, hadn't she? "That's not what I meant. I didn't ask for power." Also, not true. She'd trained to use heartfire, had reveled in it. "I didn't want to be so fucking powerful."

"Lower your voice, please." The Hawk cast another glance over her shoulder. "I don't relish getting rushed by your team if you can't control your buggery big power."

"They wouldn't…they won't…" But she'd been one of the people who'd taught them to mistrust magic, to hunt it down. They wouldn't readily accept that they'd all been using it, that now Sydney knew even more ways to do so. "By the flame, what have I done?"

The Hawk snorted again, but her expression seemed slightly sympathetic. "Don't go all broody. What you've done is learned another skill to fight the enemy with. What does any of the rest matter?"

"By the rest, do you mean my order? My calling? The thing I've dedicated my life to?" She felt as if she might start vomiting and never stop.

"Camille said you were planning on rebelling anyway," the Hawk whispered. "Using magic is something you're going to have to address. You can't go back to being ignorant."

That was true, and oh, how she wished it wasn't.

"Now," the Hawk said with a no-nonsense tone, "you have to learn how to control it. Let's do some breathing exercises."

Sydney remembered many of the same exercises from her knightly training, and that made her even sicker. Who'd introduced heartfire to the Knights of the Flame? Had they known it was magic all along? She couldn't lay it at Sir Robert's feet since the knights had been using heartfire for generations. But someone in the past had to have gotten the knowledge from somewhere.

Sydney put the thought aside and breathed along with the Hawk, trying to forget who she was and where they were. One truth was paramount at the moment; she didn't want to hurt any of her comrades.

She was breathing and watching the shadows of the lanterns play on the rock around them, forcing herself to be calm. But someone stepped into the shadows ahead, and she nearly jumped out of her boots. Her sword was halfway out of the sheath before she recognized Ember.

The Hawk said something, but Sydney bounded past her. With one worry put to rest, happiness came tumbling out, dispelling her negative emotions as if they'd never been.

But the adrenaline had been left, and now it was easing, too, leaving her raw. She threw her arms around Ember and held her close. "I'm sorry," she muttered into Ember's strong shoulder. "I'm sorry I wouldn't let you tell them who you are, and I'm sorry about denying the dragon, and I'm so sorry for getting separated from you."

"It's all right, Sydney. Shh, now, it's all right."

Sydney wasn't yet in tears, but she might crumble at any moment, and she didn't want the knights to see. She leaned back, taking deep breaths and trying to bring herself under control. The loving smile on Ember's face nearly undid her, though.

"I forgive you," Ember said. "All the other stuff can wait."

Sydney took another deep breath, nearly undone again. She looked past Ember, desperate for something else to say that wouldn't turn her into a soppy mess. "Where's Camille?"

The Hawk stepped in for her own hug, muttering something about greeting a creator before a snogging partner, but Ember spoke before Sydney could complain.

"Camille is above with a group of knights." She glanced back at where the column had gotten closer, many of them with a happy wave for Ember. She returned the gesture than leaned in between Sydney and the Hawk. "Sir Robert is with them."

For the first time since starting this adventure, Rowena wished she was outdoors instead of in these damn tunnels. At least she'd have more room to pace. After Ember had quietly told them about Sir Robert, Sydney had blurted it out much louder, and now the knights were either excited or trepidatious, and the excited ones were making Rowena nervous. They wanted to believe their leader was a good man, and no doubt they'd fight to prove it. Also, once they saw him again, they'd probably blurt out Sydney's accusations, and things would come to a head, leaving the knights on one side and her, Ember, Camille, and Sydney on the other.

But once they found him, Sir Robert would hold Camille in front of him like a shield.

And Sydney was standing there thinking. Rowena had expected a bit of anger, a few bursts of force. She kept herself between Sydney and Ember, ready to lift the strap again.

"Where is Sir Robert?" Sydney finally asked.

Ember told them of the route she'd taken. They weren't that far from one another, even taking into account Ember's speed. Sydney went silent again.

"We have to go now. Camille is his hostage," Rowena said.

A few of the knights grumbled. Rowena put her unbound hand into her pocket, ready with her brimstone if she needed it.

Sydney held up a hand, and everyone went silent. "The knights with him are hostages, too, if he's the man I know he is." She turned to the knights. "Have I ever lied to any of you?"

A chorus of nos answered her, the loudest coming from Juzail at the front of their rank.

"Do you trust me?"

Juzail and all of the younger knights answered yes. Some of the others seemed unsure. "We want to," one said. "You're a good leader, Major, and you've always looked out for us on missions, but…"

"I know," Sydney said, her face drawn tight as if she was clenching her jaw. "I've always looked up to him, too, but every word I've told you is the truth, and I will hear his answer to my claims."

Now all the knights nodded, happy to confess their suspicions to Sir Robert like idiots instead of attacking when they saw him, taking him prisoner, then getting the truth out of him.

Though from what Ember said, they'd probably have to go through *some* knights in the process. Rowena sighed. Maybe they could take those knights prisoner, too? For a moment, she wished she'd never gotten involved in all this. Then she could have kept on hating the knights and not worrying about keeping them from getting hurt.

When she looked at those she'd healed, those who'd thanked her, spoken to her, seemed to be learning how to think for themselves, she knew she couldn't go back. Even after that farm boy had struck her, she hadn't killed him, hadn't gone back and annihilated his family, his town. If he came to her now and pleaded for an unselfish cause, she'd probably help then, too. She wouldn't turn her back, didn't plan on turning it now, but she'd do what she could for those who deserved helping.

And there were more lives at stake here than those of the knights.

"He seemed to have a destination in mind," Ember said, shaking Rowena from her reverie. "If attacking is bad and talking might get bad, why don't we find out where he's going and what he wants to do? If he's planning on something evil, and we stop it, that's a good thing, right?"

Everyone stared, but Ember didn't wilt, smiling boldly under the scrutiny. Rowena was so proud she could have burst. The knights looked to one another, but none seemed able to find an objection. If Sir Robert was on his way to evil deeds, Sydney would be proven right, and they could all put a stop to it. If he wasn't, he'd be exonerated, and Sydney would no doubt resign from the knights or throw herself on her sword or something equally stupid.

"We already talked about the possibility of another workshop," Rowena said. "I can perform the spell to locate reagents, and Ember can tell us if it's in the same direction Sir Robert is heading." She kept her voice pitched low. Since the thought of doing spells nearly made Sydney wet her pants, Rowena didn't want to see what reaction the rest of them had. "We'll destroy whatever we find either way."

"Yes," Sydney said as she rubbed her chin and stared at nothing. "A good deed no matter how you look at it." For the first time in a while, she seemed hopeful rather than angry, depressed, or moronic. "I like it, but…" She glanced at where the knights were leaning forward as if trying to hear better.

Rowena rolled her eyes so hard it hurt. "I'll cast my odious, horrible spell out of sight of your knights, don't worry."

"Thank you," Sydney said.

"Wouldn't want to take their large-spell virginity."

"*Thank* you."

"They've seen me cast already," Rowena said as she walked toward a bend in the tunnel. "Surely, no one would be surprised at this point."

"*Thank you.*"

By the time Rowena turned the corner, she was grinning.

❖

Camille's hopes soared with every knight or villager her escort found, but none were Sydney or Rowena, and her heart was tired of sinking. After the fight in the cavern, everyone had scattered, and most of the knights were just now making their way aboveground. Camille wished she'd seen Sydney and Rowena make it to safety as Ember had; she couldn't help doubting the fact that it had ever happened.

And Ember wasn't there to say it again.

After she'd fled, there had been silence for a moment, then the questions started. Camille had to keep reminding herself that the knights didn't see her as a captive, even if Sir Robert's stony stare implied otherwise. She'd tearfully said to Bennia that Ember had been musing about their troubles and the origins of the creatures they'd fought. Camille had spoken about her love of magical creatures and had again called the newest enemies dragonkin.

The knights who'd already heard that word glanced at one another as if to see which of them might agree with such nonsense. Sir Robert's officers scoffed. His face didn't change.

"I started wondering aloud if these creatures or the ones we've fought before really did have anything to do with dragons," Camille had said between sniffles. "She called me a blind fool and said such complacency was why a dragon could have shown itself after all this time, and no one would believe it existed. She said she was going to prove it." She blew loudly into a borrowed handkerchief, trying not to laugh at words that she couldn't imagine Ember saying. "I...I'm ashamed of what I did, hitting her and calling her names, but I've been so scared, and I'm worried about Hilga and Sydney and everyone, and I couldn't take someone naming me a fool." She let the real emotions of the past week flow over her, calling on them to help her dissolve into tears. Bennia held her and suggested they give no more thought to Ember. As long as she wasn't plotting against them, it was better not to have a madwoman in their ranks.

The other knights had agreed but looked to Sir Robert. He licked his lips slowly as if buying time before he spoke. Camille wondered what he was feeling. If the Kells and the dragonkin were allies, he had to know of the dragon itself. She wondered if he was angry about the knights thinking the beast nothing but a bit of nonsense. According to Ember, the Kell had spoken of the dragon with reverence, had called it Nightmare, a fellow dreamer. Camille had never read of them acknowledging anyone outside their own people as actually existing.

Dragons had been known to inspire feverish loyalty in their underlings. It was too bad they used those underlings for thieving and murdering so they might increase their hoards.

Or defend their broods.

By the seven bells, she hoped that wasn't happening now.

Sir Robert had finally managed to say, "Keep marching."

Camille walked on her own with Bennia just behind her. When they found another group wandering up from the tunnels, Bennia had gasped and began to rush toward them but stopped herself. "Oh, thank the flame she's all right."

Camille stood on tiptoe to look, but none of these proved to be Sydney or Rowena either. "Who?"

"Recruit Diasi." Bennia cleared her throat. "She's a tracker, will make a fine knight. I was…worried."

Camille gave her some side-eye. She'd been worried about all the knights, but none had warranted such a reaction before. "I see."

Bennia's skin was just lighter than Camille's, but there was still a definite tinge in her cheeks. "I'm a sergeant. She's a recruit."

"I didn't say anything."

"It's against regulations."

"All right."

"Fraternizing could get us both thrown out of the knights."

Camille fought a grin. "Okay."

Bennia sighed, and the conviction had gone out of her words well before the last sentence. When Diasi turned toward them as if searching, her face lit up under a coating of dust, and she took a few hesitant steps. Bennia leaned forward as if pulled by invisible force.

Camille smiled, happy someone got to find their lost love. She gave Bennia a little push. "Rules are made to be broken." When Bennia didn't move, she added, "And everyone else is hugging right now, too."

Bennia rushed forward, and Diasi met her halfway. No one else was swinging anyone around in welcome, but no one looked at them too harshly either. When they were done greeting each other, they stared longingly into each other's eyes. Camille joined them hurriedly. She didn't want Bennia or her lover to get thrown out of the knights just yet, not when she needed allies.

She silently promised she'd help them make up for lost time later on.

If any of them lived.

"Urgh," she said as she reached them.

Diasi looked to her questioningly. "I'm sorry?"

"I was going to say, I'm glad to meet a friend of Bennia's," she said, and Bennia gave her a slightly frightened look before pulling out of the embrace.

"Right, yes. Thank you," Bennia said hurriedly, straightening her tabard. "I'm glad you're all right, Recruit. This is Camille, the master researcher from the library in Kingston."

"Yes, thank you, Sergeant. Hello, Camille. I'm Diasi." She gave a half salute before she seemed to remember Camille wasn't a knight, then reached out as if to hug her before dropping one arm and patting Camille awkwardly on the shoulder.

Camille had to roll her lips to keep from laughing. "You two are going to have to become a lot better at acting like nothing's happening if you're going to start sneaking around."

Bennia stuttered, and Diasi went pink, but Camille waved their feeble protests away. "Nice to meet you. Were you with Major Sydney Blakely during the fight in the cavern?"

Diasi nodded. "But we didn't escape together." She looked over the rest of the knights and gasped as Sir Robert ordered them to march again since the new wounded had been tended.

"He's…" She pointed. "We're still following him? What about all the things the major said?"

"What things?" Bennia asked, frowning.

Camille took both their arms and kept them slightly apart from the others as they walked. She let Diasi tell the story, knowing it carried more weight from her. Bennia's mouth stayed open for the entire tale.

"We have to ask him about it, ask the others," Bennia said, her dark brows turned down. "If it's true, we can't let him lead us any longer."

Camille bit her lip. "If you attack him, the loyal knights will fight you."

"They'd never—"

At the head of the column, Sir Robert hopped atop a small boulder and raised his hands. "My brave, loyal knights, we have reached our destination." He pointed to a large cave in the side of a nearby tor. "Down there is where my fellow officers and I were held, but when we escaped, we could not search the adjoining tunnels for other captives as these foul creatures pursued us. Now, we make certain that no other comrades suffer as we did."

The knights began to ready themselves for battle. One of the officers set up a temporary camp for those too wounded to fight. Camille didn't know whether to rejoice or lament. In the caverns, she had a better chance of slipping away to find Sydney. Or get lost. But she knew Sir Robert couldn't be leading them toward anything good.

"If we offer to guard the wounded, we can stay up here," Diasi said, her face pale.

Bennia shook her head. "I won't abandon those under my command. We'll just have to see what he has in store. If he's leading us for some nefarious purpose, we'll have reason to take him prisoner."

Camille didn't think it would be that easy. Part of her still wanted to denounce him right then, create enough confusion to at least slow the knights down, but she couldn't force herself to move.

The thought created a little bubble of panic. It wasn't indecision. She actually couldn't move.

Her breath came quicker. Bennia and Diasi were still talking; the knights were ready to move out. They separated into orderly ranks, and Camille spied Sir Robert watching her, confident smile returned. He rubbed his thumb across a small, dark object in his left hand and grinned as he turned away.

"Camille, you should stay up here," Bennia said. "Even if—"

Camille lurched forward, walking hurriedly, following the knights. She tried to make herself stop, screamed inside her own head, but she couldn't form words, only teetered slightly but didn't lose her balance. She fell in between two knights she didn't know and marched through the black cavern maw.

CHAPTER TWENTY

Camille could only move her eyes on her own. Without any input from her brain, her body marched through the gloom of the tunnels. The knights on either side of her carried lanterns, but they didn't speak to her. She couldn't tell if anyone spoke to her at all; she couldn't turn her head because of something Sir Robert had done to her.

Her thoughts and emotions kept churning. She thought of a thousand plans but couldn't execute any of them. At every pause, every juncture, she'd think, "As soon as I get free..." but then they were moving again, and she had to readjust. She would regain control at some point, and she intended to be ready.

At last they came to a large-roofed, oval-shaped cavern. They'd been heading downward for most of their journey, and though Camille couldn't tilt her head far enough back to get a good look, she sensed space in the cool air, and by the light of a great many braziers, the cavern walls went past where she could see.

Her body turned without her permission, and she would have gasped had she been able. Tables and large jars dotted the floor as they had in the other workroom, but there were so many more here. The knights faltered, mumbling and staring. Their words sounded awed, then angry as they came closer to the jars and saw their hateful inhabitants. Dragonkin, the large, part human, part dragon creatures they'd last fought floated inside, flexing their clawed hands and feet, wings, and scaly bodies.

Sir Robert had stopped in the middle of all the equipment, waving the knights to crowd closer. Camille struggled and screamed again in her mind, trying to warn them off. She should have confronted Sir Robert a thousand times already, should have denounced him or fought him or done anything just to keep them from this place.

"Spread out," Sir Robert said in a commanding voice. "I know this place appalls you, but we must check each vessel for human captives."

Camille stayed where she was, but the knights scattered around her. She tried to glare at Sir Robert but didn't know if she managed anything. He smiled, and it seemed to have a tinge of pity.

When he walked toward her, she struggled anew in her mind, but her body still wouldn't obey her. He stood with his hands behind his back and looked around proudly. "You know, I didn't think this part would work," he said softly. "I kept waiting for you to say something, but you let me lead them all the way here. I've never had captives just *walk* into my workshop before."

In her mind, Camille called down every curse on him. She'd seen something in his hand when she'd lost control of her body but couldn't see it now. If he brought it out again, maybe one of the knights would notice and ask and release her.

He scratched his black beard. "Of course, I was ready for any little thing you could say, but except for that one outburst when the homunculus got away, you didn't do anything." He chuckled. "Oh well, what did I expect? You're only a librarian; you have no power."

She tried to fight through her shame. If he let her loose, she'd show him power. She might not have a sword or magic, but she could kick him in the balls as well as anyone. He moved aside, and she saw the knights rubbing condensation off the large jars and peering into them. Some rubbed their hands or smelled them as if they'd encountered more than water. Camille would have railed at them to stop touching things they weren't familiar with, but they'd all been infected by the same curiosity-borne disease.

Soon, they all staggered, mouths open in shock before they passed out on the floor.

A yell came from behind her, but she couldn't turn her head to see what caused it. Still, she rejoiced. A few knights were still on their feet, and they would help the others, and—

Fear froze her innards as she heard a clatter and the sound of claws on stone. Sir Robert watched calmly over her shoulder, and Camille fought the urge to shut her eyes as a dragonkin passed into view. It dragged a knight by the arm. More passed through the tables and jars, gathering the other knights, too.

Sir Robert sighed happily, and she tried to swallow her horror, wondered if she could even be sick with the state she was in.

"Now," he said, turning to her. "You will tell me about the Hawk's informant network, who you used to contact her, and where they might be found. You're also going to tell me who you shared your suspicions with about me or the Kells or whatever else passed through your small, idiotic mind."

She'd never wanted to give someone an obscene gesture so much in all her life.

Rowena led the way toward the reagents she'd detected. She'd never found so many in one spot before, so it had to be a workshop or some kind of storeroom. She walked as quickly as she could, glad to have Ember with her. She didn't have to keep looking over her shoulder now that she had someone guarding her back.

Though she had to keep watch on her side since Sydney marched there. Her jaw was tense, her brow wrinkled as she stared forward. She cast the occasional glance Rowena's way, too, and Rowena wondered if she was thinking of starting some pissing contest about who was leading this expedition. Not that Rowena actually cared. As far as she was concerned, they were just going in the same direction, but if Sydney started shit with her again, Rowena would have to give as good as she received.

That was just the way things were.

Ember seemed happy they were together; she'd been all smiles even with the danger, and their connection hummed with satisfaction. She'd claimed she was worried about Camille, but it was clear to Rowena whose company she preferred.

Rowena had to perform her spell again at two branching tunnels, but finally, flickering light filtered down the path in front of them, the glow of flame instead of sunlight. Sydney held up a hand to halt her column of knights, then moved back to join them. Rowena sidled that way, too. It was best if she knew what dumb things they might do.

"Put out the lanterns," Sydney said quietly. The knights hurried to obey, and they were all plunged into gloom. "Everyone who can't fight will wait here and keep watch for anyone coming from the other direction."

To their credit, the knights obeyed silently except for a few rustles and thumps as they settled. Sydney gave them a few moments as she drew her sword and moved up with Rowena.

"Leading the charge?" Rowena whispered.

Sydney's eyes glittered in the low light. "Think you should?"

Rowena fought her own sarcasm. "I'm going to be somewhere near the middle. I'll need time to assess before I cast."

Ember glanced between them, clearly torn. Before Rowena's pride could make assurances that she didn't need help, Sydney nodded to Rowena. "Stay with her. I don't want anyone near me in case…"

Ember frowned, and Rowena leaned close. "She's learned force magic, and she can't quite control it."

Sydney straightened her shoulders. "When we're fighting, I won't want to."

Ember gave her a quick hug while Rowena frowned and said, "That's a good idea."

"I'll keep the dragonkin away from you," Ember said as she took Rowena's hand. "So, you'll be able to cast as much as you want." She grabbed Sydney's hand, too. "And you'll be able to fight the dragonkin on your own, so you'll be fine. Everyone will be fine."

Rowena frowned just as Sydney did, both of them saying, "Dragonkin?" at the same time.

Ember grinned widely. "You're already more alike, speaking at the same time. Dragonkin is what Camille called the dragon people, the creatures that are the size of a human but with dragon heads and wings and claws because—"

"We've got it," Rowena said, knowing Ember would feel her affection.

Sydney didn't even smile, simply moving away. Rowena sighed, supposing she should feel a little sorry for Sydney. She didn't want to hurt her comrades, and with her force power, she could hurl them across the room or smash them to bits. After all this was over, Rowena would just have to teach her again and hope it did some good.

The column of knights followed Sydney from the tunnel, all of them with weapons drawn. Rowena joined their ranks about five knights in, Ember at her side. She compartmentalized her thoughts so she could remember which reagents and components she had and where they were in her bag. She flicked through the spells she might need. The knights practically ran down the tunnel, the party too large and armored for stealth.

After a deep breath, Rowena burst into a torchlit cavern and immediately peeled off to the side so she could have a clear view.

A group of dragonkin blinked up at the new arrivals. Their scaly arms were full of unconscious knights, either being carried or dragged.

Sydney's knights had frozen, staring at Sir Robert where he stood near a table at the large cavern's center. Camille stood in front of him, staring at nothing as if hypnotized.

"Oh, for fuck's sake," Sir Robert cried. "Couldn't you have gotten here either a little sooner or a bit later? This is very awkward." He sighed and rubbed his chin. "Oh well, can't be helped. I don't suppose you'd search these jars for captives, would you?"

"Sir Robert Scarborough," Sydney cried. "Your dark deeds end now." The tunnel they'd emerged from led onto a wide ledge that rose eight feet or so off the main floor. Sydney clambered down the slope, ruining the effect of her speech slightly, but her knights followed her anyway.

Rowena began to circle, trying to stay in shadow and count the enemies. Camille still didn't move, and Rowena's stomach shrank. What had that bastard done to her?

Sir Robert backed up across the workshop, moving to keep several tables between him and the approaching knights, leaving Camille frozen where she was. The dragonkin dropped their captives and moved closer to Sir Robert. "Even in dire straits, you do make a pretty speech," he said. "And it's nice to finally have you all in one place. Kudos to those of you who've survived the experiments so far. It's been a very successful test." He held up his hands. "Even if the two most powerful witches left in Arnvild didn't kill each other as planned."

Rowena frowned, almost stopping. On the floor, Sydney had pulled closer to her own knights, forming ranks against the dragonkin, but she frowned, too, maybe worried about harming her fellow knights or wondering who this second witch was.

"It's you, dummy," Rowena whispered, suddenly seeing Sir Robert's plan. He'd wanted the witchstone to pull a witch and a witch-hunting knight together so they'd end each other for him. But he hadn't planned on Ember or Camille or the fact that they would convince two stubborn people to work together.

Convinced them with cuddles and kisses and the promise of more to come. It was the strangest love spell she'd ever heard of.

"Surrender," Sydney cried. "You can still be taken prisoner, can stand trial and tell your story—"

"Blah, blah," Sir Robert said. "Do you want to give the command to attack, or shall I?"

"This place is large," Ember whispered. "He could summon the dragon."

Rowena hadn't thought of that, but what did it matter now? Sir Robert glanced toward them as if he'd heard, and Rowena knew there was no hiding from him.

He smiled. "What a fantastic idea. It's only fitting that you meet Nightmare since you're all about to die."

Rowena cursed as she hopped down to the floor. He'd have to draw a summoning circle, so maybe she had time—

Sir Robert removed something from under his shirt and dropped it on a nearby table. "It's harder to cast in this form anyway." A wall of force pulsed from him, rattling the nearby jars and scooting the tables away. The host of dragonkin didn't turn, but Sydney's knights backed up. Camille toppled where she stood between Sir Robert and the dragonkin. His form blurred and pulsed again before it stretched and grew, changing like taffy as he grew larger and scalier, his color shifting to burnished gold.

Rowena knew her mouth was open, but she couldn't close it. An extra two limbs sprouted from the blob, solidifying into wings, while his neck grew, and his head turned sleeker, ending in a muzzle filled with sharp teeth. His ears stretched back along his oblong head, horns arcing over them and pointing back toward his ridge-covered neck. His legs twisted, the knees cracking backward like a dog's as he sat back, digging talons as long as Rowena's arm into the rock of the cavern. When he towered over them by forty feet or more, he spread his arms and wings as if giving them a good look at his armored skin; even the wings were covered in scales the size of armored plates.

The muzzle twisted in something like a smile, and the turquoise eyes with their reptilian slits glinted in the light. He was shining and golden and beautiful. "How's this?" He blinked at Rowena and leaned forward to peer at her.

Rowena shook off her awe and noticed two things besides the majesty of Sir Robert the dragon. Both Ember and Camille were gone.

❖

Ember wanted to cheer. Finally, the dragon showed up. She hadn't expected it to *be* Sir Robert, but she wasn't disappointed, either.

As soon as she'd stepped into the room, she'd sensed something significant was happening. The heroes and the villain had finally met. One of them was being held hostage. When Sir Robert had begun to glimmer and stretch, she'd hoped for something very exciting, but she'd also known something else would happen.

Everyone was going to stop and stare.

So, she acted. The knights and Rowena were watching Sir Robert; she couldn't see anywhere in his amorphous mass to strike. The dragonkin were watching the knights, but she didn't want to use this opportunity to take just one out. That left one critical task.

Remove the hostage.

Camille had fallen over. She still wasn't moving, but Ember had already spotted her breathing. Ember bent low as she ran, and when she reached Camille, she grabbed her close and rolled under the tables, over and over, getting as far away from the dragonkin as possible before she risked a peek from behind a row of jars near the wall. Sir Robert had finished being a sparkly blob and was now a magnificent golden dragon. His clothing lay in shredded piles near him as if it had simply exploded under the power of his transformation and had been hidden by his...blobbiness. Even his chain mail had become tiny metal shards. She saw his sword lying some feet away from him as well as a few other objects that had flown away rather than exploded.

He extended his wings and asked, "How's this?" Then he peered at the place she'd been standing. Uh-oh.

Ember ducked back behind the jars and looked at Camille. Her eyes were open, moving as if frantic, but her body was as stiff as a board. Ember didn't ask if she could speak; she would have been yelling by now if she could.

"Blink if you can hear me."

Camille blinked once.

"Good." Ember risked another peek. The dragonkin and the knights had come together in a rush. Dragon Sir Robert had plucked something from a nearby pile of rubble and squashed it in his large, clawed hands. A shard of light shot toward Rowena, who took cover behind a table.

Ember's mouth dropped open. He was a knight and a dragon *and* a witch. It was the most marvelous thing she'd ever seen.

She shook her head. She could not get caught up in that right now. She looked back to Camille. "One blink for yes, twice for no. Did Sir Robert do something to you?"

One blink.

"Did you see what it was?"

Two.

"Hmm." He had to have cast a spell, but the knights hated magic, which meant he shouldn't be casting it, but she'd save that thought for later. It had to be something he could cast without anyone noticing, so nothing with a chalk circle.

The knights and the dragonkin were a clash of steel. Sir Robert stayed in one place as he threw spells at Rowena. He probably didn't want to destroy this place, which was a point in the heroes' favor. But now they were going to have to find a way to stab a dragon, which was a point in his. Camille was supposed to be very smart; she could no doubt help them fight a dragon, but first, Ember had to figure out what had been done to her.

She pushed away the sounds of combat and thought as hard as she could. Sir Robert wouldn't have used a burst of magic; that would have been seen. Something he'd put on Camille?

Ember investigated as quickly as she could, ignoring Camille's wide eyes. It would have been somewhere he could have sneaked something on her that she wouldn't notice immediately. It wouldn't be under her clothes or on her hands. Ember searched Camille's neck and back but found nothing. She probably wouldn't have let Sir Robert touch her anyway.

Something external, then. She thought faster as the sound of combat behind her grew. Rowena didn't control people. The husks controlled themselves after she gave them a bit of life force.

But not until they were programmed.

Ember looked to Dragon Sir Robert's discarded possessions again. Until husks could perform tasks on their own, they had to be steered, and that required an idol, a little representation of the husks that a witch used to drive them.

Sir Robert had managed to hook one to a living person.

And it had to be among his things.

"Just wait," Ember said to Camille's glaring form. "I'm going to help you, and I hope it'll turn out okay." She left Camille there and ran, trying to stay out of Dragon Sir Robert's sight. She glanced over the ground, but so many things had fallen onto the floor. Rowena used a person shaped hunk of stone for husk idols, so maybe Ember could find something like that?

Dragon Sir Robert's tail flicked slightly, and she looked toward his head, but his eyes were fixed on Rowena. Good, that was good. She had another stray thought. Instead of helping Camille, maybe she could slay the dragon on her own.

Interesting. Exhilarating. She could run up his back to get at his head, but then what? His eyes? Even if she jammed her sword to the hilt, she'd only blind him, and she didn't think he'd just let her put out one of his eyes.

A bit of table flew her way. She ducked. The knights had spread out a bit, knocking tables out of their path, and the dragonkin were using pieces of wood as weapons when they didn't use their claws.

Ember shook her head. Back to Dragon Sir Robert's stuff. He'd taken something off before going shimmery blobby, so maybe that was it? She ran around him, trying to stay out of sight, but he almost reached the cavern wall. She leaped over the end of his flicking tail and saw a glimmer of shininess from one of the nearby tables.

If she rushed to get it, he'd see her.

She kind of wanted him to.

She sprinted for the table, calling on every bit of her speed. When she grabbed the glimmering object, she kept running; the force of her rush pulled the table after her a few inches, but it exploded to splinters as Dragon Sir Robert's scaly fist smashed down where she'd been. Surprise nearly made her stop and turn.

He was almost as fast as she was.

She kept going, streaking toward where she'd last seen Rowena. A sizzling noise behind her made her turn again. Rowena leaped out from behind an overturned table, got between Ember and Dragon Sir Robert, and raised a hand in the air.

Ember turned as something flashed into Rowena, sending her tumbling backward. Ember grabbed Rowena and scooped her up to hide them both behind an overturned table.

Rowena clutched her arm, cursing. She was wearing an anti-spell strap, but it was smoking gently. "Bastard's spells pack a punch," Rowena said with a snarl. "I can't block many of them this way."

"I have the idol controlling Camille," Ember said. Without looking, she bent low and carried Rowena behind a row of jars. "We have to keep moving."

"That's not an idol," Rowena said. "Let me go. I can still run."

Ember did as she was told and looked at the object in her hands. It was a silver chain and medallion, not the idol she'd hoped for. Sir Robert must have just wanted to keep the chain from exploding into tiny links. Ember cast it aside.

"He's got her with an idol, huh?" Rowena dug in her bag while peeking around the jars. "He probably has her tied to it with a strand of her hair or something." She squished a few things together. "Here, put this in her mouth. It should sever her from any parts of her that…aren't part of her any longer."

Ember took it with a sigh. Now she had to run all the way back around the cavern without getting squished or melted. She really wanted to fight the dragon, but she supposed she could evade it for a little longer.

❖

Camille blinked, wishing she could see what was going on. Her anger and despair had grown by the minute as she'd fallen, been carried, been searched, and been abandoned. The moments seemed to stretch on like hours, and all she could see was one of the dragonkin floating in its jar, the fluid gently sloshing as the cavern shook with the sounds of battle.

She blinked, and Ember appeared above her as if by magic. Camille would have yelped in surprise if she could.

"This probably isn't going to taste very nice."

Camille felt her jaw moving, and then something dropped into her mouth. She tasted grass or some other kind of plants and the tang of iron. She tried to cough or spit it out but couldn't. The iron settled on her tongue as the other stuff seemed to melt, and she squeezed her eyes shut and felt her face draw up as she grimaced.

She could move her face.

As soon as the thought hit, her body came back to her. She sat up, coughing and spitting out tiny leaves and a piece of metal. "What was that?"

Ember put a finger to her lips, but she was still grinning. "Feel better?"

Camille shook off a pall of lethargy and peeked around the jar as Ember did.

A dragon stood in the workshop.

A fucking dragon.

"I knew it," she whispered.

"Me, too," Ember said. "It's Sir Robert. He went shimmery and blobby and turned into a dragon."

Camille wished she could have seen that. It almost would have been worth the terror and impotent fury she'd felt on the way down here.

A glittery thing shot through the air from the dragon and hit one of the tables, leaving a scorch mark. From behind another table, Rowena stood and hurled a ball of fire. The dragon swatted it away into the cavern wall.

Camille grabbed Ember's arm as electric fear shot through her. "He's a dragon and a witch."

"I know!"

She sounded way too excited for the gruesome situation.

"How do we fight him?"

"Right. Dragons." She'd read all about them, had been somewhat of an expert even as a child, before she'd found rare texts that had been written when they were actually around, old, crumbling texts that had been copied from even older, crumblier texts, both of which only researchers got to see. She meshed it with her knowledge of other large creatures.

"The bigger something is, the slower it usually moves."

"Not true this time," Ember said.

Camille threw that train of thought out the window, then. The dragon sat upright, and its belly seemed as armored as the rest of it. No help there. She looked to the head. "Dragon eyesight is supposed to be fairly weak."

Ember nodded as if filing that away.

"What about the magic he used to hide this form?" Camille asked.

"You'll have to ask Rowena."

Camille bit her lip. She wanted to go to Rowena, wanted to see if she could help, but... "How do I get over there?"

Ember hadn't lost her grin. "I'll distract the dragon. You run."

"Wait." Camille's heart sped to double time, but Ember was already running. She picked up something from the floor and chucked it at the dragon's wing. "Shit." Camille wouldn't waste the effort. She ran faster than she'd ever run, angling around the knights and seeking to work her way toward Rowena while keeping an eye on the dragon. She skirted the knights where they were fighting, but it wasn't until one of the dragonkin sprang at her that she realized she had more to watch out for than the very big dragon.

Chapter Twenty-one

Sydney glimpsed Camille darting past just as one of the dragonkin broke from the fight. She knew what was going to happen as if she could see the future, and when the monster leaped toward Camille, Sydney came hard after it. She opened herself to heartfire, and it blazed around her hand, but a shimmery force burst out of her as well, catching the dragonkin and launching it over Camille's head to crash into the wall.

She wanted to curse, but she was out of breath. That wasn't the first time such a thing had happened during this fight. Luckily, none of her allies had been caught by the force spell yet.

Spell. She was casting spells.

"Are you all right?" she called to Camille. Whatever had frozen her at the beginning of the battle seemed to have passed.

She nodded. "I have to get to Rowena. We need to work together."

Sydney nodded. "Right. You two figure out the dragon."

"No, we all need to work together."

Sydney was already turning back to the fight and didn't stop. She looked past the press of knights and monsters and eyed the fucking dragon.

"Sydney," Camille yelled. "Don't touch the jars with your bare hands. Tell the others."

Sydney barely listened. Sir Robert was a dragon. She could barely wrap her mind around it.

A dragon had been leading the Knights of the Flame for nearly thirty years.

A magic-casting dragon. It betrayed her on so many levels.

She skirted the battle and ran for the dragon, screaming as she went. Heartfire flickered in her vision, the flames surrounding her. A shimmery wall preceded her, but when it touched the dragon, he only looked down.

The snakelike neck bent, and the snout with all its teeth pointed right at her. "Ah, Major. Still alive, I see."

Sydney slashed his nose, but the blade grazed harmlessly across as if she was trying to cut a building. She swung her heartfire-shrouded arm, but he merely lifted his chin. Overbalanced, she almost fell but righted herself at the last minute. Her ire and rage began to fade under a cloud of utter hopelessness.

"It's a pity we could never see eye to eye, Major," the dragon said. "My kind does so appreciate loyalty. And I did love how determined you were to eradicate every witch in Arnvild."

Sydney snarled. "I believed in you, trusted you."

"Our ability to inspire dedication is one of the reasons humanity tried to eradicate us." Flames seemed to burn in his eyes. "But now, with the witches nearly gone, the time has come for us to rise once more." His face moved closer, his hot breath like a gale. "I didn't know when I started the Order of Flame as Sir Simon Shockley that it would take such a short time." He shrugged, making his wings flutter. "But after I started the Witch Wars, people were happy to turn on those with power."

His toothy grin was back. "I had planned for your death another way, but this will be as satisfying as that."

One of the clawed hands swung for her almost lazily, and she dove out of the way. The dragon stopped short of hitting one of the jars, pulling his hand up quickly.

He didn't want to lose this workshop.

Sydney eyed the jar and heard Camille's parting words. She didn't know why she shouldn't touch the jars with her bare hands, but Camille said nothing about her booted feet. She braced against a table, put her feet on the jar, and pushed. It rocked slightly before toppling.

"No!" The dragon lunged, catching the jar though the top fell off, and some of the liquid sloshed over the dragon's hands. He hissed as if it burned him and shook his clawed fingers as if to rid them of the liquid. Sydney didn't quite understand why, but she rejoiced at having something to use.

❖

Rowena cursed when Sir Robert the dragon swatted her fireball away as if it were a fly. She flipped through spells but couldn't think of anything she could do quickly that might penetrate the dragon's armor or limit his casting abilities. She supposed she should be grateful he wasn't rampaging around the cavern, but he seemed to want to protect his workshop.

She'd heard the rumble of his voice and knew he was talking to Sydney but only caught a few words above the fight, like the fact that he'd been hunting witches over several human lifetimes. She wondered if she should get closer, but she was having a hard enough time staying ahead of Sir Robert's spells from a distance.

Camille ran past the knights and stopped, craning her neck as if searching. Rowena ran closer in a crouch, waving to get Camille's attention. As soon as Camille joined her, Rowena kept them both low as she found a different hiding spot behind some jars.

To her surprise, Camille pulled her back from them. "Don't touch them with bare skin."

"Why?"

She described the unconscious knights as doing so before they'd fallen. Rowena got close to a jar, ignoring Camille's protest, and sniffed.

She smelled valerian root and a few other things she couldn't identify. Valerian was a sleep aid. No doubt Sir Robert had made some concoction, then infused it with his life force to make it magical.

Rowena grinned. Finally, something she could counter.

"Come on," she said to Camille.

"Where? We have to talk about the dragon."

"Talk and run." Even thinking about the dragon couldn't dull her elation. She hurried toward the nearest downed knight and used his tabard to wash his hands off before she laid the hand bearing her anti-magic strap across his forehead. She pushed a tiny bit of life force through, and he came awake with a snap.

"Wha—" he started.

Rowena pulled him upright, silencing him. "Fight now. Talk later." She turned his head so he could see his fellow knights engaged in combat. Without another word, he staggered to his feet, went still when he saw the dragon, then continued to join the fight.

"There's one." Camille led the way to the next closest knight.

Rowena kissed her cheek. "I'm so glad you catch on quick."

Camille beamed. "I don't remember any particular dragon weaknesses."

"No soft spot?"

"Not even for cake or anything."

The words were said without humor, but Rowena snorted anyway. Not only did Camille catch on quick, her sense of humor never left her, an aspect of her personality Rowena could come to love.

No, scratch that. She knew she loved Camille. Whether the feeling would fade after their adventure was over or not, she didn't know, but she'd never met anyone besides Ember who could put up with her bullshit, a yeti, giant spiders, trapped tunnels, horrid monsters, and a fucking dragon and not only stick by Rowena's side but make jokes about cake.

"I...think I love you."

Camille's eyes went wide. Rowena cursed herself for adding the word think. She knew it. Why couldn't she say it? Why was she always so bloody—

"I love you, too."

Rowena let her breath out in a rush, gasping it back when Camille kissed her.

"We can talk and run, but we can't kiss and run or kiss and talk," Camille said. "So, we'll have to save the rest for when we have more time." She began to lead the way again. "And a milkmaid costume."

Rowena laughed, dragon and all. "So, no weaknesses." She peeked at the dragon as they worked. To her delight, Sydney was making things as difficult for Sir Robert as she could, running around trying to make a mess of the workshop while Sir Robert attempted to stop her. Rowena noted the way the dragon snarled when he touched one of his jars, the way he sought to wipe his claws on the ground or on tables. So, he wasn't immune to his own sleep potion, but it would probably take a lot to knock him out.

Though he did seem slower.

She filled Camille in on what she saw.

"I don't think we can wait for that to work," Camille said, nodding over Rowena's shoulder.

When she looked again, Sir Robert left Sydney and grabbed a knight to throw across the room. The knight hit the wall with a sickening thud and lay still. Sydney let loose a rage-filled cry and rushed Sir Robert again.

"Bugger," Rowena said. As expected, Sydney's attacks did nothing but get her in range. When Sir Robert turned to accost her, Ember tackled her out of the way, and Rowena breathed a sigh of relief until Sir Robert reached to snap at them with his great teeth.

A shimmery wall burst from Sydney. It shoved Ember away along the floor, but it also slammed into Sir Robert's head hard enough to avert his jaws. Rowena hoped it rattled some teeth loose.

"We can't fight him like that," Camille said. "Can you force him to be human again?"

"Did he happen to talk about how he'd done that?"

Camille shook her head.

"He said he's been alive a long time," Rowena said. "He'd have to pretend to be different people."

"None of the books I read said anything about dragons being able to naturally change their shape."

They sent two more knights off to join the battle. At this rate, the dragonkin would be overwhelmed quickly. Sydney and Ember were both up again, Sydney trying to knock down jars and Ember herding the knights back from the dragon as best she could, though he still managed to get a few. If they could scatter among the jars…

"Rowena, pay attention."

She shook her head and returned to the task at hand, trying to think of what to do. "No spell can do that, none that I've heard of anyway. It would take a massive output of power every time, and he bloody well couldn't do it without a spell circle."

"Are you sure? If he's ancient—"

"I don't care how ancient he is. You may get more knowledge as you get older, but you can't get more powerful. The only way to change one's shape at will would require…a magical bloody artifact."

"Like the witchstone?" Camille asked. "If he has one artifact, he might have more."

"And dragons are a bunch of buggery collectors if there ever were any."

"What did he do when he transformed?" Camille asked, but she looked away as if talking to herself, another aspect of her that Rowena loved. "Before the actual transformation? Before I fell?" She put a hand to her chest and lifted. "He took something off."

Rowena thought back, too, but she didn't have to go as far back as the actual transformation, just to a glittering pendant in Ember's hand, one she threw away. "Oh, for fuck's sake."

❖

Ember had gotten sidetracked. There was just so much going on. She'd been about to help Sydney against the dragon, then she'd seen an unconscious knight about to get squashed by the dragon's tail, so she'd darted in and moved him. Then she'd seen another knight about to be killed by a dragonkin, so she'd helped that one, then another had come staggering by, so she'd kept him from being eviscerated, and so on.

And no one seemed to really notice her, which was both thrilling and annoying.

By the time she'd looked back to the dragon, Sydney was about to get squished, so Ember had tackled her out of the way.

And then the dragon had been going to eat them.

She was going to be eaten.

Was it wrong to be curious?

Then a blast of force had come out of Sydney, and Ember had felt as if she'd been shoved by a giant hand, and Dragon Sir Robert's face had wobbled, and he drew back. Ember shot to her feet and ran to lift Sydney. She stared as if shocked by Ember's strength before she turned back toward the dragon, who regarded them more warily than before.

"Protect the knights," Sydney shouted, then she was off trying to knock over one of the jars.

Dragon Sir Robert lifted one corner of his snout in a good approximation of a sneer before he reached over the dragonkin for the knights.

Ember called on all her speed and darted for him. She leaped onto his hand and ran up his arm. As expected, he drew back in surprise, his arm lifting. She jumped to his shoulder before he could fling her off, her feet skidding on his scaly hide. She tried to cut him, but her blade wouldn't penetrate, and when he shook his long neck, she fell down his back.

Tucking her limbs in and keeping her blade to the side, she twisted to roll in a series of somersaults down his back and tail. When she hit the floor, she tried to run, but his tail had knocked over some of the jars, and the floor was covered in goop and half-grown dragonkin. She skidded, but so did Dragon Sir Robert when he turned to face her.

He cried out at the sight of his jars. A crash came from the right, Sydney continuing her rampage.

"Filthy human bastards," Dragon Sir Robert cried. He scooped at a large, foul-smelling pile of brimstone near the back of the cavern and held it in front of his mouth.

Ember knew this. He was going to hurl a ball of fire. "Sydney, watch out!"

Sydney looked up. Dragon Sir Robert blew across the brimstone like Rowena did, but where she threw, he exhaled faster and longer, and a jet of fire streamed from the brimstone and blanketed the jars where Sydney dived for cover.

Ember's heart sank into her stomach. "No." Sydney had to stay alive. She'd never considered anything else. Sydney with her golden hair and fabulous stories and generous heart couldn't die. People Ember knew and loved didn't die. She'd never considered her own end, let alone theirs. She didn't want Sydney to die. Didn't want Rowena or Camille or the knights or anyone else to die.

She hadn't wanted those villagers to be dead, especially the child who should have been running and playing and not lying in a field without breathing because some bugger assholes didn't believe she was real.

Ember's anger was a hotter flame than Dragon Sir Robert's.

She did a standing leap onto a nearby table, clearing a great swath of floor. She kicked off her goop-covered boots, tore off her socks, then jumped for Dragon Sir Robert again. Her bare feet gave her better purchase as she ran up his back. The fire had ceased. His long neck turned, and he regarded her.

She punched him in his dragon face as hard as she could.

He staggered, shaking his head again and dislodging her. She angled for another table and shattered it when she hit, jarring something in her shoulder. Her fist, still curled around the grip of her blade, ached, too. Both had a deep, pulsing burn as if she'd been scorched, but she hadn't. This was the same pain as when she'd stepped off a cliff to see what would happen.

She'd broken something inside.

Trying to ignore the ache, she left her hand curled around her blade, hoping she could ignore that pain enough to fight. No, that was too hard. She switched the sword's grip to her uninjured hand and arm and tried to let the other hang, but as she clambered out of the table's remains, the arm screamed with so much discomfort, she had to hug it close to her chest. Rowena could fix her.

Her anger and frustration lifted slightly. Rowena could fix Sydney, too.

Ember looked for her. Dragon Sir Robert was blinking as if she'd really hurt him, and she was beyond happy. When he straightened, he spat a red wad of phlegm, and she saw a tooth in the middle.

"Yes," she cried. She was taking that tooth home; she didn't care what Rowena had to say about it. And she spotted movement from where Sydney had taken cover. She ran closer, trying again not to feel her arm. Sydney stood from behind a soot-covered jar. Her tabard was scorched, and her face and hands were far redder than they should be, but she seemed all right.

It was shaping up to be a good day after all.

When Sydney gave her a shaky smile, Ember made a decision. If they both lived, if they were both not too injured, and if Sydney was amenable, they were totally having sex.

And falling in love.

Or maybe they were already there.

Either way, Sydney needed to know about it.

"Don't die," Ember yelled. "I love that you're alive, and I want to have sex with you and cuddle you and sleep together, and I don't care who knows."

Sydney's face seemed to morph when lots of emotions passed across it. Then she laughed, and it was the sweetest sound. "I love you, too, and all the other stuff. Don't die, either."

Ember beamed, then tried to put a serious expression back on as she faced down Dragon Sir Robert, ready to punch every part of him she could reach.

CHAPTER TWENTY-TWO

Camille wondered just how many times she'd be floored by disbelief that day. Searching for a magical necklace Ember and Rowena had thrown away took the prize so far.

"Why the fuck would she throw it away?" she grumbled as she shifted through scraps of table and bits of spell components. At least when the dragon had destroyed several tables in this corner of the room, there hadn't been anyone nearby. She didn't know if she could have handled sifting through blood and body parts.

Though she was angry enough to do almost anything.

The roar of fire had made her look up briefly, and her heart thumped painfully as Sydney dove to avoid a blast of flame. She looked for Rowena, but she was also on the floor, searching, seemingly ignoring the fight.

And it was *so* wrong that Camille felt happy Sydney was the one in danger and not Rowena. The wrongness didn't stop the feeling, though. She feared for Sydney, but the thought of Rowena in peril left an ache that felt like a wound.

By the seven bells, she was in love.

She growled. "All the fucking women I've been with and I have to fall in love while fighting a dragon." Why couldn't it have been Cristine in references? Janie from the post office? Leila, who'd frequented Hetty's bookstore? Someone whose life was nice and sedate and dragon-free?

"Shut up, Camille," she said to herself. "She's a wonderful woman, and you're lucky to have her."

"Are you looking or just muttering to yourself?" Rowena called.

Maybe lucky wasn't the right word. "I'm doing the best I can. Why did Ember throw it away?"

Rowena grumbled something. The fight between the knights and the dragonkin was dying down, but the residual clatter still made it hard to hear anything else. Camille continued to turn over shattered planks of wood and bits of whatnot, searching for the glint of metal. As she crawled past an overturned table, a hand shot from the dark and grabbed her ankle.

Camille gasped but held in a shriek. She began to jerk away, then paused, thinking it might be an injured knight, but just as she registered the golden skin, the claws bit into her, and she cried out at five little points of pain.

"Let go!" The rational part of her brain tried to think tactics, but the primitive part was happy to kick with her free foot. She tried to twist and pull away, but the grip was like steel, and she had a sudden vision of her foot parting from her body as the pain grew.

A boot slammed down on the reptilian arm. It was Rowena, stomping for all she was worth. The grip released, and Camille dragged herself backward. Holes in her flesh dribbled blood, leaving a trail on the floor. The clawed hand swung for Rowena, and the top half of a dragonkin eased into the light.

It bled from nose and mouth, its expression dim, even thoughtless. Still, it swung its sharp claws as if seeking any target. Camille pitied it; it seemed no more than a husk, but life glimmered in its half-lidded eyes. Sadness nearly overwhelmed her as well as hatred for Sir Robert for giving these things such stunted life, programmed only to hurt and maim and kill until the spark of life fled.

Rowena picked up a piece of detritus and swung at the creature. Camille hobbled to join her, bashing the dragonkin's skull in and putting it out of its misery. The expression on its face didn't change as it made the transition from life to death; only the eyes shifted from glassy to dull.

Camille looked away, eyes stinging with tears.

"Are you all right?" Rowena asked softly.

"No." She began to wipe her eyes, then spotted a gleam of metal from where she'd been sitting. She limped to it and picked up a silver medallion dangling from a long chain. "Let's go get that motherfucker."

❖

Sydney's anger was still alive, but she didn't know how much more her body could take. It wasn't just the damage; she'd never tapped into her...magic so often before. Her chest ached as if she'd run for miles, and her head throbbed with every heartbeat.

She supposed she was dashed lucky her body wasn't worse. The gout of fire would have finished her if she hadn't found a gooey, half-formed dragonkin corpse to roll over herself. A table was on fire behind her, and several of the jars had been scorched or knocked over. Sydney's limbs felt leaden, and she wondered if whatever toxin Camille had warned her about was affecting her. The dragon seemed slower as it recovered from Ember's punch.

That had been the sexiest thing Sydney had ever seen. When Ember declared her feelings and intentions, all Sydney could do was return her love. By the flame, she hoped they all lived.

But what were they going to do against a dragon?

Punch him again, obviously.

Sydney moved toward Ember. Every inch of her ached, but she couldn't have stopped herself if she'd tried. Ember stood awkwardly, right arm bent against her chest, probably broken or dislocated.

The dragon straightened and narrowed his eyes. "I will kill you all."

"Going to be harder with one less tooth," Sydney shouted.

Ember roared with laughter and moved to meet Sydney. They no doubt painted quite a sorry picture, wounded and singed as they were. Would Sir Robert try to squash them? Bite? Cast another spell? It depended on whether or not he still cared about saving the rest of this workshop.

The fire had spread. If they drew this out, everything would be consumed, dragon and all. Even the knights, even the Hawk and Camille.

And Ember.

"If I'm going to die, I'm glad it's with you," Sydney said.

The look Ember gave her was full of love.

Sir Robert didn't seem to care about love. His clawed hand lashed forward, forcing Sydney to dive out of the way. Even wounded as she was, Ember was still fast. She sidestepped Sir Robert's giant hand, rocked back on a foot, and kicked him. He grunted and snarled but came at her with his other hand. Sydney pushed up and leaped. Her force power built, coiled within her emotion, but she kept it in until the last moment, until she actually touched him, then she let it out in a focused rush.

Scales splintered, and his golden skin peeled back under the strength of her force. She fell away as Sir Robert screeched, blood pouring from his hand. He jerked it to his chest, and Sydney hoped she'd broken a few bones.

Ember pulled her up and grinned like a maniac. "Now we can both punch him."

Sydney returned her smile but doubted her words. She didn't know if she had too many of those bursts left. The dragon was scowling, but he wasn't striking again, no doubt considering how he could best do so without being hurt.

Maybe this was the first time anyone had ever hurt him. At least in a long time.

"Wait," someone behind them said as Ember took a step. The Hawk pushed a necklace into Ember's hands. "We need to put this on him."

Sydney's brain seemed to stutter. "You want to give the dragon jewelry?"

"He took it off before he transformed," Camille said. "It's probably how he changed so quickly."

Sydney barked a disbelieving laugh. "Which part of him do you think that's going around?"

"Anywhere on his head should do," the Hawk said with a snarl. "Now, are we going to work together or keep flapping our gums in front of the buggery dragon?"

He was watching them, and as if guided by her words, he seemed to notice the necklace. He snarled and backed up a step.

Maybe it would work.

"We split up," Camille said quickly and softly. "I'll knock over one of the jars to get his attention."

"I'll throw fire at the back of his head," the Hawk said.

Sydney nodded. "While I come in from the front and hit him in the belly with force."

Ember clutched the necklace. "Then when he's low enough, I'll leap onto his head and put the necklace over one of his horns. Or maybe an ear. Whichever. I'll decide in the moment."

That was more information than they needed, but they had a plan. "Go," Sydney said.

❖

Rowena hoped everything would go as planned but knew it wouldn't. As Camille ran toward the jars, however, the dragon turned his back on her, picked up one of the empty, tipped over jars, and flung it at Ember.

She dodged, but she was getting slower. They all were. And she clearly couldn't use her right arm anymore. With a roar, he charged her, leading with his unwounded hand.

Rowena had prepared a few spells, the reagents ready in her pockets. She picked out a wad of snake scales, earth, and wood, and slapped it on a broken table. She shoved, infusing the wad with her life force, and the table flew from the floor and smacked the dragon in the shoulder.

He grunted but appeared unharmed. It did get his attention, and she gave him an obscene gesture. With a snarl, he picked up the table and threw it back.

"Shit." She dove for cover, but she wasn't as fast as Ember, and the table clipped her hip, spinning her around and to the side. She landed badly, wrenching her back. With a groan, she pulled herself up, her hopes falling.

"Hey, asshole," Camille yelled from across the room. She held a flaming brand, and when the dragon turned, she ran from jar to jar, igniting them. Whatever it was coating the outside seemed to be extremely flammable.

Thank goodness.

The dragon screeched and started for her, but Sydney darted into his path. Hazy waves of force radiated from her as she punched the dragon in the belly.

He whooshed like a bellows and went double, mouth and eyes wide open as if surprised. The sound of Ember's bare feet slapping past made Rowena turn in time to see her leap atop a table and then the dragon's neck. She grabbed one of his spines with her left hand and pushed off, angling for his head, her form nearly a blur.

The dragon stood and whirled, shaking his neck. Ember grabbed another spine, not yet at his head, and he would throw her soon.

"No, you don't." Rowena pushed through the pain and sent another bit of junk into one of the dragon's feet, making him stagger. She threw whatever she could lift, anything to keep him distracted and off balance. Sydney attacked from his other side, and Rowena heard a many-throated roar come from the front of the cavern. Camille had rallied the knights, and they waved their arms and called out to distract the dragon or flung things at him to keep him dancing.

Ember inched along, clinging with her unwounded arm until she finally reached his head.

Sydney circled around the back, and waves of force cascaded around her again as she delivered a hit to the dragon's spine, stiffening him long enough for Ember to loop the medallion around one of his horns just as she slid off and fell to the ground.

He blurred, fading, wavering and shrinking until he was no more than a wounded, naked man wearing only a necklace, shuddering amidst a pile of wreckage and goo.

The knights swarmed him, binding his hands behind his back.

"Just kill him," Rowena yelled, but they didn't listen.

They carried him from the cavern along with Sydney, who'd collapsed, and Ember, who could barely walk. Camille limped to Rowena and tried to help her, but Rowena could hardly move. She didn't even complain when a pair of knights lifted her and carried her away.

Dragon Sir Robert was a dragon no longer, and everyone was still alive. All in all, Ember thought it was a pretty good day; even if she was broken, Sydney was unconscious, Rowena was hurt, and Camille was hurt *and* bossy.

Ember supposed it was the good kind of bossy. The knights seemed as if they needed someone to tell them what to do. Even Sergeant Bennia obeyed as Camille directed them to tend the wounded who'd been rescued and set up camp. The knights were all together again. Well, those who were alive and not at the camp Sydney had set up, but they'd be all right for the time being. Camille would no doubt send someone to get them as soon as she knew where they were.

And Ember had managed to grab her dragon tooth before the knights helped her out. She cuddled it to her chest, letting it infuse her with happiness. And for the moment, it was enough to sit in the sun next to where Sydney was sleeping and let one of the knights set her arm.

"This will hurt," he said. His eyes seemed nervous.

"That's okay. I won't hit back," she said. He didn't seem comforted, so she tried to smile. "All the people I love are alive, so it won't hurt as bad as if that wasn't true."

Again, he only seemed confused, but he pulled on her arm, complaining loudly when it didn't "act like any arm I've dealt with." He did what he could, and Rowena would do the rest later.

Rowena rested nearby, lying on her belly while Camille massaged her back under a healer's direction. Camille had a bandage around her ankle and another around her arm, beneath a patch of singed sleeve. She smiled at Ember, and Ember knew Rowena couldn't be that bad if Camille was smiling.

Sir Robert wasn't smiling. He had a blanket wrapped around him and was bound hand and foot and mouth. One of the knights said something about taking him to Kingston to stand trial.

A trial for a dragon. She wanted to see that.

Chapter Twenty-three

E ven though Camille knew it wasn't far, it seemed like a long walk back to the village at the base of Rowena's mountain. It was the closest settlement, and the knights needed to rest and tend their wounded. Camille had to admit that she and Rowena needed some rest, too, never mind Ember and Sydney.

The villagers were reluctant to welcome them at first. They'd heard about the knights' anti-witch sentiments, and the villagers were very pro-witch. The knights seemed mystified by the reaction, by the idea that the villagers might not let them enter, but when Rowena said the knights would behave themselves under the new leadership of Supreme Commander Sir Sydney—as soon as she woke up—everyone seemed happier.

Sir Robert's senior staff didn't argue with her promotion. They'd thought their leader had some top-secret mission to rid the world of witches. They'd never known he was a dragon, and they should have guessed something odd was happening. They were getting off easy just having someone promoted over their heads.

At least for the moment.

Rowena was granted a bed in the way station, and Camille joined her in her room without hesitation, certain she'd be welcomed, and she was. The tub and hot water she'd asked for were already in place. Rowena stared at them in surprise.

"How did you manage that?"

"A sense of purpose and a tone of authority." She lifted an eyebrow before she started undoing her dress.

Rowena swallowed visibly, watching every movement of her hands with rapt fascination. It stirred Camille deeply, making her feel even more naked, more desirable.

"I thought you might need some help bathing," she said, noting the huskiness in her own voice and loving that just Rowena's gaze could make her feel such need.

"I…yes…" Rowena tried to undo her own garments, but a pained look crossed her face.

Camille moved behind her, chuckling when Rowena tried to keep staring. "Let me." She took her time, careful of Rowena's injured back and hip but delighting in every shudder and gasp. She soon lowered Rowena into the large tub before joining her, kneeling before her. She winced at the slight pain in her injured foot.

"Let's see if I can make you feel better." Camille kissed her, delighting in the fact that Rowena returned her kiss with more passion than Camille expected from an injured person.

"You already have," Rowena said when they broke apart. She pulled Camille close, and the heat from the skin-to-skin contact seemed hotter than the water. "Stay with me?"

Camille knew she wasn't talking about just right then. The possibility of forever would have scared her before, but now it seemed right, natural. She kissed every inch of Rowena she could reach. "I will," she whispered as she traced Rowena's ear with her tongue. "Be my milkmaid?"

Rowena laughed, and even that sound was laced with desire. "I will."

Sydney woke and stared for a moment at the roof over her head. She blinked, trying to place it before she finally sat up and jumped at the sight of Ember sitting cross-legged on the end of her bed, watching.

She beamed, lighting her brown face and wrinkling the scar that ran across it. "You've been asleep for two days, and everyone is alive and okay, except for some of the knights, who were wounded, but they're all together now in the village by my home mountain, and Robert isn't a dragon or a sir anymore. He's locked up in a cellar."

Sydney blinked again, trying to process. "Oh?"

"Yes, and you're bandaged up, and the healers from your order washed and changed you. I didn't do it because I thought you'd want to remember the first time we were naked together."

That conjured up images that finally drove the sleep from Sydney's mind. She sat up, remembering hitting the dragon one last time before it felt as if someone hit her hard enough to turn her brain off.

"Rowena says you overtaxed your magic, though she said she didn't know if I should call it magic since you might still be bloody touchy about the whole thing."

Sydney held up a hand, smiling. "So, everything's okay?"

Ember cocked her head. "Is that all you heard? Do you want me to start over?"

"No, I've got it, thanks. How is your arm?"

Ember moved the limb around. She wasn't even wearing a sling. "Rowena fixed me. She always does."

Glad of that, Sydney held out an arm, and Ember crawled up the bed to curl up in her embrace. Sydney kissed her head. "Thank you for taking care of me and the whole…no nudity thing."

"You're welcome. You're in charge of the knights now."

Sydney wondered how that had happened while she was unconscious, but she let it go for the moment, grateful for the soft bed and the fading sunlight in the window and the amazing woman in her arms.

"Are you hungry?" Ember asked.

Sydney thought about it, but as Ember tilted her face so their lips were tantalizingly close together, Sydney couldn't think of food. She wanted to use some line like, "I'm only hungry for you." Her paramours of the past had expected something like that, something to add to the story of a charming knight, but she didn't want to be a story to Ember.

Even if Ember really appreciated a good story.

"No," Sydney said. "I want to show you how much I love you."

Ember kissed her, starting slow but working quickly to eagerly passionate. Sydney let her lead the way where she would have taken control before. She never thought it would feel so good to surrender.

When morning came, she'd never been so happy to wake up with a woman, either. They lay in a sprawling tangle, and when Ember shifted, Sydney realized what had woken her. "After all the exercise we got last night, I thought you'd sleep longer," Sydney murmured.

Ember kissed her nose. "I always wake up at dawn. You can keep sleeping."

"No, I've slept enough." And where she hadn't been hungry before, she was ravenous now. After they'd eaten and Sydney had greeted her knights, she knew what she had to do.

Robert, no longer sir, sat in a dark cellar, manacled and gagged and guarded night and day. He had only a blanket wrapped around him for clothing, and his guards explained that they hadn't wanted to let him loose long enough to dress.

She regarded him coldly, searching for the feelings of awe and loyalty she'd always had for him, but they'd been carried away on dragon wings.

"They're going to try you and hang you," she said.

He snorted. She wondered if any of his dragon resiliency remained in this form, if when the noose tightened around his neck, he'd just swing there, glaring.

"I loved you like a second father."

He cocked his head. She felt a dip of fear as she stepped forward and loosed his gag, but he could do nothing with his voice alone.

"I'm not at all sorry to have disappointed you," he said.

She wanted to slug him but held it back. "Why didn't you just stay in hiding since you could pass for human?"

"If roaches took over the kingdom, would you happily live as one?"

Her fist tightened again. "Are you trying to get me to kill you?"

He sniffed. "As if you could. And Kingston won't kill me either, not the noose or the headsman's ax or anything else you dream up."

She felt a jot of satisfaction as she bent closer. "Magic will."

Now he snarled and seemed as if he might start up, but she also noticed the sweat begin to form on his face as if he knew she spoke the truth. "Go ahead. Let me join my kin, my broods, all the dragons that passed before me, murdered by your ignorant race."

Sydney felt a bit of sympathy, but not after Camille's dragon lecture at breakfast, which included the dragons' entire known history. "Humanity rose up against your kind because they tried to annihilate humanity. The other magical creatures just seemed to die out."

"Pushed out by the human tide." His face flushed, and his mustache seemed to bristle. "You breed like rabbits and eat everything in sight. You would have killed us had we not fought you."

Sydney shook her head. She didn't know who was right, him or history, and it was too long in the past to worry about now. She imagined him, one of the last of his kind if not *the* last, nursing his revenge for hundreds of years, trying to kill humanity again and again and failing. Had he been trying to make another brood with those monsters? He'd called them experiments, but maybe he'd just been waiting for the perfect batch before he gave them real life.

She managed some pity again but didn't know what to do with it. If she let him go, he'd try again. Try forever if he was as immortal as the legends claimed.

"You're the past," she said. "Mine and the world's." Anger and frustration built in her again, but she only replaced his gag so he could mutter curses as she fled.

Ember waited at the top of the stairs with the Hawk and Camille. They all turned to stare as Ember said, "Some of the knights went to clear out the mountain so it can be a home again, but don't worry about them. I'm sure they'll be fine."

Sydney's heart seized; she wasn't worried about the knights. "Are...are you going to stay? I've got so much to do in Kingston. I can't—"

Ember took her hand and squeezed. "Don't be scared. I'm coming with you. You were scared, right? I thought I was reading your face right, but—"

"I was, I was. It's okay." Sydney laughed weakly. "Thank you."

"Are you really going to put a dragon on trial?" the Hawk asked.

Sydney sighed. "I don't know. I guess. He broke the law, but it feels like putting a horse on trial or something, even though he broke the law *as* a man."

The Hawk tsked. "Policing the world; nothing good can come of it."

Sydney glared at her. "Listen, you—"

Ember kissed her just as Camille kissed the Hawk. Sydney stuttered in surprise and heard the Hawk do the same.

"Every time you argue," Camille said. "From now on." She pointed at the Hawk. "And don't you dare say you'll have to argue more."

The Hawk's mouth shut with a snap.

Sydney had to laugh. She supposed they'd have to figure a lot of things out, not just how to put a dragon on trial. If they were going to execute him, they'd need magic, and Sydney would have to help bring it back. She sighed as the prospect still gave her a shudder. They had a lot of work to undo.

About the Author

Barbara Ann Wright writes fantasy and science fiction novels and short stories when not ranting on her blog. *The Pyramid Waltz* was one of Tor.com's Reviewer's Choice books of 2012, was a *Foreword Review* BOTYA Finalist, a Goldie finalist, and made *Book Riot*'s 100 Must-Read Sci-Fi Fantasy Novels By Female Authors. It also won the 2013 Rainbow Award for Best Lesbian Fantasy. She's won five other Rainbow Awards and has been a Lambda Award finalist.

Books Available from Bold Strokes Books

A Moment in Time by Lisa Moreau. A longstanding family feud separates two women who unexpectedly fall in love at an antique clock shop in a small Louisiana town. (978-1-63555-419-9)

Aspen in Moonlight by Kelly Wacker. When art historian Melissa Warren meets Sula Johansen, director of a local bear conservancy, she discovers that love can come in unexpected and unusual forms. (978-1-63555-470-0)

Back to September by Melissa Brayden. Small bookshop owner Hannah Shepard and famous romance novelist Parker Bristow maneuver the landscape of their two very different worlds to find out if love can win out in the end. (978-1-63555-576-9)

Changing Course by Brey Willows. When the woman of your dreams falls from the sky, you'd better be ready to catch her. (978-1-63555-335-2)

Cost of Honor by Radclyffe. First Daughter Blair Powell and Homeland Security Director Cameron Roberts face adversity when their enemies stop at nothing to prevent President Andrew Powell's reelection. (978-1-63555-582-0)

Fearless by Tina Michele. Determined to overcome her debilitating fear through exposure therapy, Laura Carter all but fails before she's even begun until dolphin trainer Jillian Marshall dedicates herself to helping Laura defeat the nightmares of her past. (978-1-63555-495-3)

Not Dead Enough by J.M. Redmann. A woman who may or may not be dead drags Micky Knight into a messy con game. (978-1-63555-543-1)

Not Since You by Fiona Riley. When Charlotte boards her honeymoon cruise single and comes face-to-face with Lexi, the high school love she left behind, she questions every decision she has ever made. (978-1-63555-474-8)

Not Your Average Love Spell by Barbara Ann Wright. Four women struggle with who to love and who to hate while fighting to rid a kingdom of an evil invading force. (978-1-63555-327-7)

Tennessee Whiskey by Donna K. Ford. Dane Foster wants to put her life on pause and ask for a redo, a chance for something that matters. Emma Reynolds is that chance. (978-1-63555-556-1)

30 Dates in 30 Days by Elle Spencer. A busy lawyer tries to find love the fast way—thirty dates in thirty days. (978-1-63555-498-4)

Finding Sky by Cass Sellars. Skylar Addison's search for a career intersects with her new boss's search for butterflies, but Skylar can't forgive Jess's intrusion into her life. (978-1-63555-521-9)

Hammers, Strings, and Beautiful Things by Morgan Lee Miller. While on tour with the biggest pop star in the world, rising musician Blair Bennett falls in love for the first time while coping with loss and depression. (978-1-63555-538-7)

Heart of a Killer by Yolanda Wallace. Contract killer Santana Masters's only interest is her next assignment—until a chance meeting with a beautiful stranger tempts her to change her ways. (978-1-63555-547-9)

Leading the Witness by Carsen Taite. When defense attorney Catherine Landauer reluctantly becomes the key witness in prosecutor Starr Rio's latest criminal trial, their hearts, careers, and lives may be at risk. (978-1-63555-512-7)

No Experience Required by Kimberly Cooper Griffin. Izzy Treadway has resigned herself to a life without romance because of her bipolar illness but wonders what she's gotten herself into when she agrees to write a book about love. (978-1-63555-561-5)

One Walk in Winter by Georgia Beers. Olivia Santini and Hayley Boyd Markham might be rivals at work, but they discover that lonely hearts often find company in the most unexpected of places. (978-1-63555-541-7)

The Inn at Netherfield Green by Aurora Rey. Advertising executive Lauren Montgomery and gin distiller Camden Crawley don't agree on anything except saving the Rose & Crown, the old English pub that's brought them together. (978-1-63555-445-8)

Top of Her Game by M. Ullrich. When it comes to life on the field and matters of the heart, losing isn't an option for pro athletes Kenzie Shaw and Sutton Flores. (978-1-63555-500-4)

Vanished by Eden Darry. A storm is coming, and Ellery and Loveday must find the chosen one or humanity won't survive it. (978-1-63555-437-3)

All She Wants by Larkin Rose. Marci Jones and Tessa Dalton get more than they bargained for when their plans for a one-night stand turn into an opportunity for love. (978-1-63555-476-2)

Beautiful Accidents by Erin Zak. Stevie Adams and Bernadette Thompson discover that sometimes the best things in life happen purely by accident. (978-1-63555-497-7)

Before Now by Joy Argento. Can Delany and Jade overcome the betrayal that spans the centuries to reignite a love that can't be broken? (978-1-63555-525-7)

Breathe by Cari Hunter. Paramedic Jemima Pardon's chronic bad luck seems to be improving when she meets police officer Rosie Jones. But they face a battle to survive before they can find love. (978-1-63555-523-3)

Double-Crossed by Ali Vali. Hired thief and killer Reed Gable finds something in her scope that will change her life forever when she gets a contract to end casino accountant Brinley Myers's life. (978-1-63555-302-4)

False Horizons by CJ Birch. Jordan and Ash struggle with different views on the alien agenda and must find their way back to each other before they're swallowed up by a centuries-old war. (978-1-63555-519-6)

Legacy by Charlotte Greene. When five women hike to a remote cabin deep inside a national park, unsettling events suggest that they should have stayed home. (978-1-63555-490-8)

Royal Street Reveillon by Greg Herren. Someone is killing the stars of a reality show, and it's up to Scotty Bradley and the boys to find out who. (978-1-63555-545-5)

Somewhere Along the Way by Kathleen Knowles. When Maxine Cooper moves to San Francisco during the summer of 1981, she learns that wherever you run, you cannot escape yourself. (978-1-63555-383-3)

Blood of the Pack by Jenny Frame. When Alpha of the Scottish pack Kenrick Wulver visits the Wolfgangs, she falls for Zaria Lupa, a wolf on the run. (978-1-63555-431-1)

Cause of Death by Sheri Lewis Wohl. Medical student Vi Akiak and K9 Search and Rescue officer Kate Renard must work together to find a killer before they end up the next targets. In the race for survival, they discover that love may be the biggest risk of all. (978-1-63555-441-0)

Chasing Sunset by Missouri Vaun. Hijinks and mishaps ensue as Iris and Finn set off on a road trip adventure, chasing the sunset, and falling in love along the way. (978-1-63555-454-0)

Double Down by MB Austin. When an unlikely friendship with Spanish pop star Erlea turns deeper, Celeste, in-house physician for the hotel hosting Erlea's show, has a choice to make—run or double down on love. (978-1-63555-423-6)

Party of Three by Sandy Lowe. Three friends are in for a wild night at billionaire heiress Eleanor McGregor's twenty-fifth birthday party. Love, lust, and doing the right thing, even when it hurts, turn the evening into one that will change their lives forever. (978-1-63555-246-1)

Sit. Stay. Love. by Karis Walsh. City girl Alana Brendt and country vet Tegan Evans both know they don't belong together. Only problem is, they're falling in love. (978-1-63555-439-7)

Where the Lies Hide by Renee Roman. As P.I. Camdyn Stark gets closer to solving the case, will her dark secrets and the lies she's buried jeopardize her future with the quietly beautiful Sarah Peters? (978-1-63555-371-0)

Beautiful Dreamer by Melissa Brayden. With love on the line, can Devyn Winters find it in her heart to stay in the small town of Dreamer's Bay, the one place she swore she'd never remain? (978-1-63555-305-5)

Create a Life to Love by Erin Zak. When sixteen-year-old Beth shows up at her birth mother's door, three lives will change forever. (978-1-63555-425-0)

Deadeye by Meredith Doench. Stranded while hunting the serial predator Deadeye, Special Agent Luce Hansen fights for survival while her lover, forensic pathologist Harper Bennett, hunts for clues to Hansen's disappearance along the killer's trail. (978-1-63555-253-9)

Death Takes a Bow by David S. Pederson. Alan Keys takes part in a local stage production, but when the leading man is murdered, his partner Detective Heath Barrington is thrust into the limelight to find the killer. (978-1-63555-472-4)

Endangered by Michelle Larkin. Shapeshifters Officer Aspen Wolfe and Dr. Tora Madigan fight their growing attraction as they work together to destroy a secret government agency that exterminates their kind. (978-1-63555-377-2)

Incognito by VK Powell. The only thing Evan Spears is focused on is capturing a fleeing murder suspect until wild card Frankie Strong is added to her team and causes chaos on and off the job. (978-1-63555-389-5)

Insult to Injury by Gun Brooke. After losing everything, Gail Owen withdraws to her old farmhouse and finds a destitute young woman, Romi Shepherd, living in a secret room. (978-1-63555-323-9)

Just One Moment by Dena Blake. If you were given the chance to have the love of your life back, could you ignore everything that went wrong and start over again? (978-1-63555-387-1)

Scene of the Crime by MJ Williamz. Cullen Matthews finds herself caught between the woman she thinks she loves but can no longer trust and a beautiful detective she can't stop thinking about who will stop at nothing to find the truth. (978-1-63555-405-2)

CPSIA information can be obtained
at www.ICGtesting.com
Printed in the USA
LVHW021751041119
636282LV00002B/224